Unholy Blood

JEFF THOMSON

Unholy Blood
ISBN: 978-0-6456581-2-5
First published 2018
Second Edition 2022

facebook.com/UnholyBloodBook

Cover Photo: Cliff Dorian
Cover Model: Victoria Ferrara
Typesetting & publishing by Rack and Rune Publishing
https://rackandrune.com

RACK & RUNE
publishing

Contents

Prologue

The club throbbed with the pulse of the band that pumped out their music on stage. Lights flashed in time to the insistent beat. Fists were raised and shaken, and amongst the heaving crowd, bodies leapt into the air, dreads and cyberbraids flying. Teeth were bared in joyous abandon as the band drove the mob into frenzy. The heat was stifling, and sweat poured from the writhing figures that stomped thunderously on the floor, matching the band's metronomic 160 beats per minute. Sweet smelling smoke wafted through the room, enhancing the effects of the lights, which flickered and pulsed without pause. Here and there were small pockets of shadow, intermittently exposed by flares of brilliance.

On stage, *Maschinekult* came to the end of the song. With a final crash of industrial sound, they stopped abruptly. Ears rang in the comparative silence, and then rapturous applause roared through the club. The crowd howled and screamed for more.

Elektra, the lead vocalist, swept the crowd with her eyes. Her contacts were red, with slitted cats-eye pupils. Her dreads were black and red, and she wore a black catsuit that fitted her curves like a wetsuit. She smiled as her guitarist came over to her side. Amidst the deafening calls for an encore, they conferred as to what song they would finish with. As he stepped back, he nodded to her, grinned, and then turned to the keyboardist, mouthing a song title. She nodded in return, and looked to her laptop, and started the backing sequence. As the first heavy subsonic notes began, the audience screamed in anticipation of one of their favourite songs.

Erik, the drummer, grinned and wiped his face with a towel. He knew that he had twelve bars before he came in. He scanned the crowd for the Spanish babe he'd glimpsed before. After a moment of frustrated searching, he finally saw her. Whoa! She was a goddess! Long black hair descended in waves to her waist; her waist that was so slim, before flaring out into an awesome set of hips. He imagined a perfect set of legs beneath her Gothic dress. His eyes travelled upwards taking in her impressive rack. *She must at least be a D,* he thought. A black vinyl corset encircled her waist, and pushed her cleavage out before his admiring gaze. Then he saw her face. It was angelic, but held the fire that he was used to in hot-blooded Spanish chicks. Her eyes flashed as they met his, and she gave him a wicked grin, showing prominent canines in a dazzling white smile that invited him. *Oh, yeah,* he thought, *bring it to me, baby!*

He looked over to the left side of the stage. Peach, his drum tech, roadie, and procurer of babes and illicit substances leaned there staring out at the crowd. Erik attracted his attention, and then gave Peach their secret sign that let him know that Erik wanted him to fetch the girl backstage. The roadie checked her out, raising his eyebrows and whistling in admiration, and then gave the drummer a wink of respect concerning his choice. He gave him a thumbs–up, and left to reach her before the show ended.

Twirling his sticks, Erik locked eyes with her, and threw one of them straight towards her. This was a test he gave them all to see how keen they were to meet him. As the stick spun through the ever–changing lights, he saw with a sense of disappointment that a surge in the crowd meant that she wouldn't be able to catch it, as she was suddenly surrounded by an eager horde of hungry girls, all clamouring to be the one to get the prize for herself. They were all regulars at the band's gigs, and they knew that this was how he chose his nightly companion.

Suddenly, as the spinning drumstick came closer to the mass of screaming girls, his Spanish honey did the impossible. She leapt into the air, arm stretched out. To his astonished eyes, she seemed to jump at least six feet, and appeared to be suspended there for a moment. She calmly caught the stick, and looked like she floated down to the floor. The other girls gave her a look of hatred, knowing that they'd missed out, but at a glare from those electric eyes, they all turned away from her, unwilling to challenge her victory. She gave him another of those sexy smiles that left him breathless.

He was so shocked by her amazing display of agility that he missed coming in at the right time in the song. *Shit!* He thought, *Elektra's gonna have my balls!* As he started playing, the singer turned, glaring. She fumbled the first verse, and the band played awkwardly on. Finally, as they reached the first chorus, they kicked as they should, but Erik knew that he was in deep trouble. Elektra was a hard task-master, and was unforgiving about such mistakes. As the song eventually finished, he flailed about, drumming like a fiend, hoping that the big ending would somehow redeem himself in Elektra's eyes. She was yelling over the onslaught, telling the crowd that they were amazing, we love you, etc. But as the last note crashed out, she locked eyes with him, and he knew that she was going to chew him out. As the cheers and howls of appreciation threatened to take the roof off, they came to the front of the stage, and linking arms, they bowed to the frenzied mob.

Elektra was next to him, and when they bowed forwards, she turned to him and asked: "What the *fuck* was that about?"

"Sorry, boss," he replied sheepishly, "I was distracted."

As they stood upright, he pointed down to where Peach had arrived at the girl's side. He yelled in her ear, and she nodded, giving the sweating ensemble onstage another wicked grin, as she flourished the drumstick.

"Yow!" The keyboardist, a cyberpunk; a pierced and tattooed girl, showed her admiration. Her foot-high fluoro green cyberhawk bobbed as she took in the girl's amazing curves, and she grinned in appreciation. She addressed the singer, saying: "Holy shit, 'lektra, that's one fine babe 'ol' Erik here spotted. If I'd seen her, I probably would'a lost it too!"

The guitarist and bassist cracked up, knowing her tastes, and appreciating her taking the piss out of the drummer. They knew that she was also trying to soften Elektra's anger. The singer looked out over the sea of faces and thrusting fists. She saw the girl with Peach, and agreed that she was a real looker. "You're lucky this time," she said to Erik, raising an admonishing finger, "But do it again…" the unfinished threat hung on the air.

He grinned at her, knowing that Suzi, the keyboardist had saved his manhood from a shredding. "No way, boss," he said, "I'll be good."

They turned to leave the stage, Elektra giving him a mock stern gaze. He bowed to her, hands together. Suzi gave him a stinging smack on the butt, and left with the other two, laughing uproariously. Erik mentally wiped his brow. *Whew! That was close.* He was the eighth drummer to play with the band, and he knew that Elektra had fired his predecessors for much less. *And over a babe too. But what a babe!* As he thought of her, he turned to see Peach escorting his lovely towards the backstage area. He hurried to get there to meet her.

At the bar, and around the room, stood four individuals. Their leader leaned against the bar languidly, his eyes hooded like a hunting cat's. Those eyes followed the form of the girl as Peach lead her backstage. He was tall and lithe, dressed all in black; stretch jeans, silk shirt, and full-length leather coat. His feet were shod in black shoes that shone with polish. Long whitish – blond hair was tied in a ponytail that hung to his waist. Impeccably manicured nails, long and pointed, flashed in the room lights that came up now that the band was finished. The crowd started to disperse, and one of the blonde man's companions shot him a look of enquiry, as he watched the girl intently.

Should we take her? Came the thought in his mind. He sought out his comrade, who was standing at stage right. He was close to her, it would be easy...No, and he had been given strict instructions about not exposing themselves in public. He shook his head in negation.

Not here, he sent. *There are too many witnesses. Outside...*He straightened up, and gave his group a signal to leave with the crowd. They slowly walked in his direction.

As you wish, master, sent the one near the stage. He took one last look at the girl, who suddenly turned, and looked them all in the eye.

So, sent the blonde man, *your senses are not dulled after all.* His eyes were like glass, an electric pale blue that seemed to be made of ice. He smiled sarcastically, steepling his fingers before himself.

The girl's own eyes flashed in anger. She locked her gaze with his own stare. For a moment, all five were held in a stasis that was broken when Peach, who had gone on, realised that she had stopped, and came back to her. She smiled at him, and then turned to follow again. As she was led through the door, she turned and blew a kiss to her watchers, disappearing as it closed behind her.

Backstage, the usual crowd of punters, liggers, groupies and hangers–on thronged around the band, who were talking, signing photos, and relaxing after the gig. The only dull spot of the entire night had been Erik's little mistake, and now that Elektra had seemingly forgiven him, he enjoyed the adoration of the crowd along with the rest of the band.

All eyes turned to the door as Peach entered, followed by the girl. Erik smiled and headed over to them. Just as he reached her, Suzi stepped forward and introduced herself.

"Hi! I'm Suzi. Did you like the gig?" she was definitely interested in the girl. Her eyes were taking in her dusky beauty, drinking in her curves and lovely face. The girl smiled in return, flattered by the keyboardist's attention. She was studying Suzi's piercings and tattoos.

Her voice came, liquid as honey, sounding much deeper than they expected it to. She seemed to be about eighteen years old, but that voice held in its tones the years of a much older woman. "I liked it very much," she said, "Especially those Beethoven variations that you played in the third song."

Suzi laughed. "Hey! Someone who's cultured as well as hot!" She turned to indicate the rest of the band. "No-one else has noticed that." She shook her head in mock seriousness. "They're all barbarians." She noticed Erik waiting for his chance to butt in. She put her arm around his shoulders. "Especially this one," she said with a grin.

He shrugged out of Suzi's embrace and reached forward and took the girl's hand. To his shock, it was cold. As he shook it, he gazed into her electric eyes, and saw mirth dancing there.

"Pleased to meet you," she said.

As he released her frigid hand, the door opened, and a huge man entered, wearing a long grey coat. He was beaming through a thick blond beard, which matched the long hair that fell to his waist. "Erik!" he bellowed, coming forward with a small box. He reached the drummer and gave him a bone-crushing hug. "I have present for you!" he brought the box up, and gave it to Erik. Finally, he saw the girl, and smiled widely. "Who is this vision of loveliness?"

Erik coughed in embarrassment. "This is..." Then he realized that he didn't even know her name.

"I am Romana," she said, her eyes twinkling at his discomfort.

"I am Sergei," said the man, "But call me Bear."

"Hello, Bear." She turned to Erik. "And you are Erik. Are you not going to open it?"

"Open it?" he echoed.

"Your present," she said.

"Oh, yeah!" He looked at the box, and saw that it was a wooden case with a clasp on the front. He opened it, and raised the lid to look inside. He smiled, and reached into it, to bring out a pistol.

"A Very pistol, my friend," said Sergei. "An English one from Second World War. There are even flares to go with him."

"Thanks man," said Erik. "She's a beauty."

A look of puzzlement crossed Romana's angelic face. "This is a strange present."

"Erik collects weapons," said Sergei, "And I have certain contacts."

"World War One and Two," said Erik, feeling like a bit of a geek. He hoped that she didn't think he was just a little boy with his toys.

"Yeah," put in Suzi, "Erik's gotta whole bunch'a guns hanging on the wall at his place." She laughed. "He cleans 'em all the time, and I bet he plays with 'em at night too!"

They laughed as Erik blushed, embarrassed. "They're a part of history," he said, abashed.

"You like weapons, Erik?" asked Romana. "Have you ever killed someone?" The laughter died as they saw a strange look come upon the girl's face. "Have you felt the life flow out of them? Or watched as that life fled? Did you ever have a friend die in your arms?" Her face was now melancholy, and in the depths of her eyes was a sadness that seemed burned into her soul.

"I just like to have a part of history in my hands," said Erik into the uncomfortable silence that had fallen. The others in the room had sensed the unusual vibe, and were watching them in puzzlement.

"I need a drink," said Peach, and he strolled over to the bar, taking up a bottle of Jack Daniels and swigging from it with relish. As this commonplace thing occurred, the strange feeling in the room evaporated, and everything returned to normal; the others continued where they had left off, and soon they had forgotten the little interruption.

Suzi was staring at Romana strangely. Her attitude change had taken her by surprise. The keyboardist had obviously been keen on the girl, but the weird event had struck her as very odd.

"Did it hurt?"

Suzi jumped, startled out of her thoughts. She realized that Romana had asked her a question. "Hurt?" she said, puzzled.

Romana smiled, saying; "The things in your face, and the – tattoos."

"Oh yeah," laughed Suzi, "They did, but ya gotta suffer to be fabulous!" She was relieved to see the girl's smile again. She had been shaken by Romana's strange question, and now she was somehow afraid of her. She excused herself and went over to Peach, and grabbed the bottle from him, taking a deep gulp.

Erik was relieved that Suzi had left their little group. It wasn't the first time that he'd had to compete for a girl with her. He and Sergei exchanged a glance, a knowing conspirational look, which said: *You win.* The Russian put his huge arm around the drummer. "You should see his collection," he said, "Is many good pieces in him."

The girl grinned in return. Sergei was surprised to see her prominent canines. *It makes her look a little dangerous,* he thought. *Still, my Erik likes danger.*

"I would love to see it," she said. Her eyes danced with mirth.

Was that also interest there for him? Erik thought. He was absolutely hot for her. "Okay," he said, "Let's go." He shook Sergei's hand and they turned to leave.

"Erik!" They stopped as Elektra came over to them. She looked the girl over, obviously impressed with Erik's catch of the night. "Don't forget rehearsal. We need to tighten a few things up." She smiled at the girl. "Don't wear him out, darling, he's got work to do tomorrow."

Romana slipped her arm around the drummer's waist. Her body was hard underneath her dress. And cold too, like her hands. Erik shivered at her touch, but said nothing, grinning inanely at his singer.

"I won't hurt him," said Romana, "Well, not *too* much."

Elektra laughed. "I like this one, Erik," she said. "She might give you a run for your money."

Erik laughed. "See you tomorrow, boss." He shook Sergei's huge hand again, and the Russian winked at him. "Thanks again, dude."

Sergei nodded non-chalantly. "Not a problem, my friend. Now is your turn to find me present, yes?"

Erik gave him a thumbs – up. "I know just the thing. A Nine Inch Nails bootleg. I'll bring it tomorrow." He grabbed an old WWII flight jacket near the door. Emblazoned across its back was the Flying Tigers patch. It was one of the most favourite items in his collection. He and Romana left the room, to a chorus of catcalls and whistles.

As they walked down the corridor to the rear door, he noticed that she walked soundlessly, like a hunting animal. Her stride was long, like a man's, and she checked their surroundings ceaselessly. He remembered her cold body and hands, and asked her: "Are you cold?"

She turned her smile on him again. "No, It is just that you are still hot from playing." She reached over and hugged him tightly. "You should be able to warm me up." She smiled wickedly.

Oh yeah, he thought, *I'll heat up that cold skin.* His arm encircled her waist, and he joyed in the feeling of her body swaying next to him. They reached the back door, and he opened it, and they stepped through into a grungy alleyway that ran along the rear of the club. The street was littered with debris, and paper blew about in the wind. Several wrecked cars sat forlornly, their wheels long gone, and their glass windows long since smashed. Along the graffiti laden walls, dumpsters overflowed with trash, and rats could be seen scuttling furtively in the garbage that was strewn about.

The four figures that had been in the club were standing in the alley, spaced out as though they were covering all avenues of escape. They were. Their leader came forwards as Romana and Erik stopped. He smiled at them, and his voice was honeyed as he said: "Romana. It has been too long." His accent marked him as English; it was very exact in its pronunciation. Erik thought he sounded like one of those upper class Brits who think they are a cut above everyone.

The girl's face showed her dislike of him. "Gerald." Her eyes quickly scanned the others, and noted their positions. "What do you want?"

Gerald feigned a hurt expression. "I am shocked. Surely you know I want you?"

Erik felt anger rising in him. Who was this freak? Romana was his for the night, and from her own expression, she didn't want anything to do with this guy. "Hey, buddy..." He stopped as Romana's fingers closed around his arm like a vice. She shook her head as he glanced at her.

Gerald's smile became mocking. "Ah, another hero." His eyes burned with an unnatural light. Erik wondered if he was on something. He didn't consider him to be a threat; he was skinny and looked as if he could be snapped in half. Erik was almost twice his weight, and most of that was muscle, thanks to his gym workouts.

"Has she told you how many heroes she has had?" Gerald sneered. "It must be at least a score by now."

Ignoring Romana, Erik said: "Why don't you fuck off, Blondie?" Placing the case on the ground, he readied himself for a fight.

Gerald came closer. "*What did you say?*" he hissed. His eyes pierced Erik, seeming to look into his soul. He looked as though he was ready to lash out, and Erik braced himself. Romana stepped between them.

"Gerald." In her own eyes was a wild light. She seemed filled with an elemental force. Erik could feel the tension between her and the weirdo.

As he looked at their faces, he was shocked to see that they both had an animalistic stare. Their teeth were bared, and they appeared ready to leap and rip each other's throats like beasts. The others came closer, and Erik had the impression that they were somehow like a pack of wolves, scenting their prey. *Four against one, hey?* he thought. *Well, you're first, prick.* He clenched his fists, ready to rumble.

Just as it looked that a fight was inevitable, the stage door opened behind them, and the crowd that had been backstage poured out into the night. Blondie and his friends stopped, exasperation on their feral faces. With all of these witnesses, they could do nothing. The alley filled with people, all laughing and talking, in high spirits after the gig. The band sauntered out, crowded by their fans. Elektra looked over at them, sensing the tension. She led the band to them, having seen plenty of fights before, and the crowd followed.

Suzi came over to them. "Hey, stud. You're wastin' time, baby!" She looked Blondie over. The rest of the mob halted around their little group.

"Is there a problem?" asked Elektra. Around her, the crowd suddenly sensed the change of atmosphere. Peach produced a flick knife from nowhere, and proceeded to toss it into the air, a look of casualness on his face. Others grinned, and cracked knuckles and made fists. No-one messed with *their* favourite band.

Faced with this opposition, Gerald and his cronies looked outnumbered. The truth was, they could destroy all of these fools, but he knew himself that he had been forbidden to bring such destruction into the public eye. They must remain hidden from those that they preyed upon, that was their unbreakable law.

Gerald's smile of anticipation fell. His eyes slitted, and he waved his lackeys off. "Until later," he said, and then turned and stalked away. The others joined him, and they strode quickly down the alley and out of sight.

"Well," said Elektra, "Lucky we came along." She gave Erik a grin.

"Nah, I could have taken 'em." The drummer returned her grin. "Especially the blonde fag." He picked up the case.

The singer rolled her eyes at his bravado. "Sure, You're too good. Come on, Suzi." With a wave, she strolled over to her car. The crowd, seeing that there was no action coming, broke up.

"Hey, Ro', who was that? He's hot!" Suzi had watched Gerald leave, and had obviously been interested in the pallid blonde.

"No," replied Romana, "He is as cold as ice."

Suzi pouted theatrically. "That's two I've missed tonight." She winked at them, and then went over to Elektra's car.

Along the dirty street were parked several cars, all owned by the band. Two trucks were there also, which they used to carry their gear from one gig to the next. The throng slowly made their way to their own vehicles, in the manner that people do when they aren't in any hurry.

Looking out of place in this squalor was a Porsche convertible. Its brilliant red duco glowed in the dim light. Seated in the driver's seat was a big man, covered in tattoos, wearing a leather vest festooned with band patches. He had long dyed black hair that reached his waist. As they approached, he stepped out of the Porsche, and came to take Erik's hand in a firm handshake. "Everything okay, man?"

"Yeah, just some dickheads. No problem." Erik shook off the memory of those wicked faces.

"Hey, bud, who's this?" The giant checked out the girl at Erik's side.

"Jess, this is Romana. Romana, this hulk is my friend Jess. He likes to sit in my car."

Jess laughed. "If I didn't, she wouldn't be here long."

Romana nodded and smiled at him, and then slid into the car as Erik opened the door for her. He put his present in the back seat. Jess gave Erik a wink as the drummer got in. "Seeya, man."

Erik waved in farewell, and then started up the car. Putting it in gear, he revved the engine, and then turned and roared down the alley.

As they sped into the night, his mind was full of the image of the unnatural way that Gerald and his friends had moved. He was still struck by the feeling that they were like some predatory group. He'd seen plenty of gangs, but they didn't seem the same. They were more like feral animals, hunting and out for blood. As he turned onto the freeway, he asked Romana: "Who was that freak? An ex?"

Romana laughed, displaying her prominent canines. "Gerald? I would not have him in a million years!" Her eyes twinkled with merriment. Their hair blew back in the wind, as they rushed down the empty road.

She reached over, and ran her hand up his leg, her nails scraping along the denim, creating five tracks of pleasure that burned their way up his thighs. He felt a stirring in his loins as she hitched closer, and shuddered with delight as she kissed his neck. Her lips were cold, and once again he wondered how she could be so icy. He turned to glance at her as she slid one hand inside his jacket. Her fingers were like ice, but her eyes burned with a passion that he knew was reflected by his own.

With a thud, something landed on the back of the Porsche. Shocked, he looked around, and saw one of Gerald's followers. In quick succession, the other two fell out of the night sky, and dropped onto the speeding car. Another impact on the bonnet drew his amazed attention. Gerald stood there, impossibly keeping his balance as they hurtled onwards. With a sneer, he knelt, reached down over the windscreen, and ripped on the handbrake.

Spinning wildly, the car careened across the lanes. Erik struggled with the wheel, attempting to control the spin. Gerald's face, hatred written all over it, was inches from his own. The pale blonde's eyes held a sarcastic look, as he watched Erik's great efforts to bring the whirling Porsche under his command. He watched dispassionately, as though Erik's fate was unimportant. Suddenly, he wrenched the wheel from the drummer's hands, spun it hard, and with a flick of his taloned nails, slashed Erik's seatbelt away.

The car screeched and rolled, throwing Erik out, to hit the road and tumble like a rag doll. As the car rolled over and over past him, he finally came to a stop, lying in the middle of the road. The Porsche also came to rest, upside down, its wheels rotating aimlessly.

Erik struggled to sit up. His jacket's right sleeve was torn to the armpit, and hung down to his knees. He bore many cuts on his face and hands, and his head was gashed open, from which blood ran down profusely. He shook his head, and attempted to stand. After falling several times, he finally managed to get to his feet.

"Romana!" He stumbled and staggered towards the wreckage, horrified that the girl had been killed. His head pounded, and his ears were filled with a hissing sound, and he heard nothing beyond a dull rumble, as though everything were wrapped in cotton wool.

As he looked up, his unbelieving eyes were met with a nightmarish scene. The four goons that had somehow attacked them in the car were standing in a circle. They now had the unmistakable look of feral beasts; crouched for the attack, hands curled into claws, and eyes burning with the desire to kill. Silhouetted against the lights of the freeway, they made a macabre scene.

In the centre of this circle of death stood Romana. Her own orbs flashed with hatred, and were filled with the same blood–lust that was on the faces of her pursuers. She displayed her teeth in a grimace of defiance, and Erik was appalled at how much like a deadly animal she had become herself. Her hands too, were clawed and ready to rend and tear. Her hair whipped about in the wind, the mane of a wild thing.

Suddenly, one of the figures leapt forwards, his arms stretched out to rip into her. With a lithe sidestep, she whirled and dodged his attack. As he spun and came again, something happened that Erik knew was impossible. She thrust her hand forward in a move too swift for his eyes to see. Her fingers, outstretched, tore through her opponent's chest, and she ripped out his heart, which she flung away. He shrieked, and turned to a fine dust, which scattered in the wind.

What the fuck! Erik shook his head in disbelief. *No way! I'm seeing things.* He stumbled towards the figures, thinking that he'd been concussed, and couldn't have seen what he thought he'd seen.

Another one of the four, now three, snarled inhumanly, and came to the attack. Romana and he exchanged several heavy blows with their hands, and their sharp claws drew blood. With savage slashes, they each inflicted deep cuts on the other's face, from where dark blood flowed immediately. As Erik watched, amazed, the livid wounds closed up, healing themselves, until there wasn't any evidence that such injuries had marked the combatant's skins.

This time, Erik knew with certainty that what he saw was real. Romana slapped her enemy's hands away, and grasped his head in both hands. With a sickening wrench, she twisted it to one side, and his neck snapped with a crack that the drummer heard clearly. She tugged violently, and her enemy's head came off, and she held it in her hands. The corpse joined its companion in dusty dissolution. The head disintegrated, following the body into nothingness. Romana then assumed a defensive stance, and waited for her remaining two foes.

"Christ!" exploded Erik. What had he got involved in? As he watched, aghast, the two men started to circle the girl. He knew that this time, they'd make sure that they stayed out of reach of her deadly hands, and while one held her attention, the other would make the kill. He had to help her.

As he stumbled towards them, he tripped over something and fell heavily. He rose to his knees, and saw that he'd fallen over the case, which had been thrown from the car. The case! The flare–gun! With desperate fingers, he scrabbled at the clasp, snatching rapid glances at the stalking forms. He finally opened it, and tore the Very pistol from the plush lining. His shaking hands attempted to pick up a flare, but he dropped it several times. As he frantically tried to load his weapon, the pair closed in on the girl. With an inarticulate roar of rage, he miraculously snatched up a flare, snapped it into the gun, and stood. He drew a bead on one of the freaks. "Hey!" he yelled at the top of his lungs.

The thing turned, its deadly teeth bared in a terrible gape. With an impossible blur of speed, it hurtled towards him, fangs yearning to sink themselves in his flesh. Its eyes burned into him, as he pressed the trigger. The pistol coughed, and its white – hot missile sped toward its target. Full in the chest it took him, and he exploded into incandescence, as though he were magnesium. An unearthly shriek shattered the night as he turned into a living torch. In seconds, he'd joined his comrades.

Shivering with shock, Erik stooped, and grabbed another flare, which he loaded into the pistol. With hands shaking, he levelled it at Gerald, who'd witnessed his lackey's destruction. Taking a final glance at Romana, who stood ready for his attack, he snarled at both of them, and then his coat swirled as he leapt into the air, to fly into the shadows of the night air.

The drummer's eyes widened as Gerald flew away. He lowered the flare-gun, staring up into the black sky above. He started as he realized Romana was by his side. He turned, bringing the pistol to bear on her.

She opened her arms in a gesture of friendliness. Her face was unreadable, but Erik could still see that she was on-edge, like a predatory beast. A slight smile was on her lips. But all he could think of was how terrifying she'd looked, and how she'd destroyed her foes.

"*Stay away from me!*" he yelled. He breathed in gasps, the adrenaline pumping through his body. His heart crashed in his chest, and he was covered in sweat. He blinked as some of the blood on his forehead got in his eye.

She looked at his trembling form, great pity in her inhuman eyes. Her voice came, honeyed and soothing: "I will not hurt you."

He laughed, a shrill bark, in which insanity dwelt. "Are you fuckin' crazy! What were those things?" He shivered violently, and the gun wavered in his hands. "What are *you*? No human could have such strength!"

Her eyes held the same unnatural light that had burned in her enemy's eyes. She smiled, and said: "I am not human. Nor were they." She paused, to let that statement sink into his throbbing brain. "We are vampires." She watched for his reaction, her attention on the gun. She knew that if he fired, she would be incinerated.

"*What!* You gotta be shittin' me!" He stepped back a few paces. "Are we in some sort of movie?" The Very pistol's barrel loomed in her sight, a dark cavern that held death. He pointed it at her face. "So, you were going to... to..."

"Drink your blood?" Romana shook her head. "No. I have already drunk. I want something else from you." Her eyes flared with passion once again.

"*Get back!*" Erik stepped back, until he backed up to the overturned Porsche. He bumped against it, and realised that he had nowhere to go. "I warn you – I'll shoot!" He trembled in shock, and the gun dipped.

With lightning speed, Romana leapt forward, too fast for him to see, let alone react. She ripped the flare-gun from his shaking hand and tossed it far away. Defenceless now, he closed his eyes, thinking that any second her fangs would find his throat. When nothing happened, he slowly opened his eyes, to see her still standing before him.

The girl smiled at him; not the wicked flash of fangs that he'd seen before, but a genuine smile that lit up her face. She spoke in gentle tones: "I will not hurt you, Erik. Can you trust me now that you are unarmed, and I have not attacked you?"

He stared in disbelief. She *could* have killed him easily. He wiped the blood from his forehead. Suddenly, he swayed, feeling the loss of blood, and the shock of everything that had happened. Instantly, she was there, and he felt her strong, cold arms supporting him as he slumped.

Romana lowered him to the road, her chill hands stroking his head. He gasped: "So I'm not to be dinner tonight?"

She laughed. "No. Well... Maybe dessert." She helped him rise. "Let us get to your home, and I will look at your wounds."

"You're a nurse too?"

"I have been many things. I have treated many wounds in over six hundred years." She held him upright. "Can you stand?"

"I think so." He swayed as she released him. He looked mournfully at his dangling sleeve. *"Sonovabitch!* My fuckin' jacket! That bastard ruined my jacket!"

"Better your sleeve ripped, than your throat." She went over to the Porsche.

"Shit," said Erik, "My goddamn car's a wreck." He made a fist. "That prick's gonna pay!"

The girl shook her head. "Pray that you never see him again. He is very dangerous, and would make short work of you."

Romana reached down under the upended car. With a flip of her hand that looked effortless, she righted the Porsche, and came over and lifted Erik like a child, carried him to the car and placed him in the passenger seat.

With another flash of movement, she was gone and back again, bringing the case and the Very pistol. She put them in the back seat, and slid into the driver's seat. She experimented with the gears, running them through the changes, and then she started the car. It ran a little roughly, but she knew that it could be driven.

"Can you drive, too?" Erik was sitting low in the seat, and she could see his bemused look.

"Yes," she replied, "I learnt to drive in one of the very first cars, a Mercedes in 1912. Shall we go? You will have to direct me."

Sure, he thought, *why not? Bring a vampire home. Still, she hasn't killed me.* He coughed nervously. *Yet.* "Okay, follow this road to the end, and then turn left."

Romana put her cold hand over his own. "I promise that I will not harm you. Please believe me. I am tired of being on my own, and I really like you." She put the car into gear, and they slowly headed off down the road.

Behind them, high above the street, squatting atop a streetlight, was a shadowy figure that watched. As the Porsche picked up speed, it leapt into the air, and its long coat flapped in the wind as it flew after them, following its prey.

Jeff Thomson

1

Romana

E rik woke slowly, his head throbbing. He groaned, and then sucked in a deep breath. The sun blazed outside, and a long ray of it came through the open doors that led to the balcony. The heat of the day was stifling. The drummer's body was lathered in sweat, and the sheets were wet against him. He sat up, groggy, and rubbed his eyes, slitted against the brightness that poured into the room.

He coughed, and peered around. He remembered…Romana! Wow! She was amazing. He recalled how she had fought off Gerald and his lackeys, and then she'd driven him home. Leaving the wrecked Porsche in the garage below, she'd carried him upstairs like a baby. She'd tended his wounds with a professional air, as if she'd done such things many times before. Of course, he remembered, she'd told him she had.

And then…she'd taken him. The sex had been mind-blowing. Erik's mind was suddenly filled with the images of the night before. How they'd writhed in passion on his bed, her face, filled with lust, her eyes flashing as she rode him, tossing her hair with wild abandon. He remembered him covering her body with his own, the hardness of it, like she was made of stone. Her form was as perfect as a marble statue, every line and curve stood out in sharp relief in the light. As they made love, he could feel the heat of his body warm her own. Her kisses began as cold as ice, but they still fired his passion. Finally, she burned with a heat that filled her body and his own with fire.

Now…where was she? Had she left him? Didn't vampires avoid the daylight, and sleep in coffins? The sun destroyed them, didn't it? He searched the room, finding her dress on the floor, mingled with his own clothes.

"No," came her mellow voice. She laughed. "The sun does not destroy us." She appeared from the kitchen on the left, carrying a plate that steamed with cooked food. She came to the bed, and set it down on his lap. She was wearing only one of his t-shirts, an Orgy band shirt. She smiled one of those dazzling smiles, and sat on the side of the bed. "Breakfast?"

He'd been staring at her legs, as she'd come towards him. Now he looked at the food in front of him, and then looked up, into those electric blue eyes. "Uh," he began, "I haven't eaten breakfast since I was eighteen."

She made a mock stern face. "Well, today you do." She leaned in for a kiss. Her lips were cold again. She could see that he was surprised that she could withstand the sun. The many common depictions of her kind, both in print and on film were false. As he began to eat, she explained: "Despite what many authors have written about us, we can live in the sun, and be active in the day, but we are weak." As he started to eat, she continued: "But we mostly sleep, sometimes in coffins. I prefer a nice big bed." She watched him eat, enjoying the look of satisfaction on his face. "Good?"

"Mmmm," he mumbled, his mouth full. "'Cell'nt." He swallowed. "You're a fine cook." He drank down the glass of orange juice, and then wiped his mouth with the back of his hand. "What now?"

"You have rehearsal today. Did you forget?" She took the tray, and sashayed out into the kitchen, where he heard her open the dishwasher, and place the dirty dishes inside. He watched her as she came into the room again, and stood over him.

"Hey, you knew what I was thinking." He looked up into her beautiful face.

"Yes, it is a part of our power; the reading of minds." She sat by him again. "Do not let it trouble you." She took his hand.

Suddenly, he exploded with laughter. "Shit, you knew I wanted you..."

She smiled. "Yes. And I wanted you." She leaned over, and stroked his face gently. "I want a companion, Erik, and I liked you the moment I saw you."

"Does that mean you want to make me like you?" He looked pensive.

"No. I will not force that on you. It will be your own choice to make."

"But can you have a - *mortal* - as a companion?"

"Yes. If they wish to be with one of us, it is allowed."

She looked as though she were remembering things of long ago. He wondered how many companions she'd had. How old was she? Didn't she say something about...?

"Six hundred years." She nodded. "Yes, I have existed for that long a time. I was born in 1405."

"Born?" Erik echoed. "I thought that vampires were - *created* - or something, they had to drink from a vampire?" His face showed his puzzlement. "They can't have children." He saw the look on her face. "Can they?"

"Yes, they can. Only it is not allowed. They are permitted to mate, but offspring are forbidden. There is an ancient vampire, who was once a Chinese herbalist when he was mortal, who provides the Clans with a herb that the females take, which allows them to enjoy sexual pleasure, but ensures that they cannot reproduce."

"Why?"

"Because they found that when two vampires created a child, that child was filled with the powers of both of the parents, and they were very powerful, so much so that almost on every occasion, they would turn on the parents, and destroy them." Her face became grim. "The Clans realised that such children were a threat to their very survival, and for a time, they tried to control them, but the offspring were too strong. A great conflict began, with the children being hunted down and destroyed."

Erik listened intently. He'd never heard of such things. To think that there had been such creatures more powerful than what he'd witnessed last night! He shuddered.

Romana continued: "After all of the children had been wiped out, the Clans held an enclave to decide what to do. They passed an unbreakable law that made the creation of such abominations forbidden. The herbalist had been made into one of them, and they all agreed that the herb would be used from that time on. That was in 1056."

"Then how did you come to be born?"

A faint smile appeared on her face. "In 1350, the Black Death was raging through Europe. Thousands had fallen, so many that none could tell whose house belonged to whom. Father abandoned son, mother left daughter. Even the closest of familial relationships meant nothing in the face of the plague. Many thought that they could escape by being ascetics, becoming almost like hermits, locked up in their houses. They would see no-one, and existed on the most frugal food, and water. Others became hedonistic, indulging themselves with rich foods and wines, and partaking in orgies. They thought that they would not be touched. Still others took a path that was between the other two: they did not starve and purge themselves, neither did they carouse and feast. They ate simply but well, and lived as well as they could, under the circumstances. However, they all could not escape. Many died."

He nodded. He'd heard some of this at school, but wished he'd paid more attention to history.

"Into this hell on earth came my father, a Spanish lord from Castile. He'd been visiting some relations, when he was struck down with the plague. When his servants discovered he was sick, he was left on the road to die, as thousands more had been. He lay there all day, in agony, wanting to die, surrounded by the rotting corpses of the dead. That night, as he laid trembling and sweating in his extremity, his feverish brain registered a dim form standing beside him. He looked up into the burning eyes of a vampire. It was a male, clad in the richest finery, which looked down upon my father with compassion. *Do you wish to live?* The sepulchral tones throbbed in his ears. He thought of his family, his wife and daughter, he wanted to see them again; he did not want to die like this. His wife was one of the most beautiful women in Spain. And his daughter was the light of his life. To lose them would be unthinkable.

Yes, he croaked. The figure smiled, then with a flash of movement, took him up, and its terrible fangs pierced his throat. Gasping, he felt his lifeblood draining from him, until he was nearly spent. The vampire lowered him to the ground, and then asked again: *Do you wish to live?* Unable to speak, my father nodded weakly. The vampire knelt at his side, and tore its own wrist with its deadly teeth. As the black blood oozed forth and dripped down from the frightful wound, it said: *Drink from me, and join me for eternity.*

My father grasped the vampire's bleeding wrist, and began to drink. Instantly, he could feel the surge of energy flowing into his veins. His heart began to beat in a wild rhythm, in counterpoint to the drumming of the vampire's own heart, and he sucked at the wound like a calf drinking from its mother. The vampire's face took on a painful expression, which alternated with fleeting signs of pleasure.

Finally, my father fell back, and his body went into spasms, as the dark blood of the vampire invaded his throbbing veins. He gasped for breath, thrashing on the ground. Suddenly, his struggles ceased, and he felt all of the pain of the plague leave his body. He sat up, hearing all sorts of sounds that he had never heard in his life before. He could hear his blood coursing through his body: even the tiniest sound could be perceived. He listened, amazed.

The vampire smiled at him, saying: "Welcome, brother."

He came to his feet, staring at his benefactor. "I am alive!" he said in astonishment.

"Much more than just alive," said the vampire. "You are immortal" He bowed. "I am Gabriel."

"Diego," replied my father. He now could see the other as if it were daylight. He looked around, wonderingly at how the night had now become so bright. He could see all that had been dark to his eyes. Suddenly, he was aware of a vast emptiness inside him, and felt pangs griping his stomach. "I am hungry."

The other smiled. "Not hungry. Thirsty. That thirst will never leave you. It must be satisfied." His glassy eyes bore into Diego. "Come," he said, "I will show you how to hunt." He floated into the air, looking down upon my father.

"How can I fly?"

"Just imagine that you can fly."

My father concentrated. He imagined himself floating into the air. To his astonishment, he did! He rose to float beside Gabriel, and the other smiled at his amazement, showing the deadly fangs.

"Come," said Gabriel, and he flew along, following the road. My father came after him, relishing the feeling of flying, his new vampire eyes taking in everything; his heightened senses thrilling to all of the sensations that now filled his being.

"There," said Gabriel. He pointed downwards. Below them was a wagon, surrounded by a group of men, weapons in hand. It was clear that they were attacking the wagon, and the people who travelled within. The pair stooped like hunting birds of prey, and came to earth, startling the men with the swiftness of their assault.

Gabriel took several of the men, and my father, his brain and body filled with the Dark Thirst, grabbed a fellow, and before he knew it, had sunk his own fangs into his throat. Everything else fell away; only the sensations of drinking his victim's blood were his entire world. He could hear nothing else; felt nothing else but the flow of the blood that would now be his only sustenance from this night forth.

As he dropped the corpse, he looked about, and saw that Gabriel had taken care of the other attackers. With a swift movement, Gabriel came and took my father's arm, and they leapt into the night sky, flying rapidly away from my father's first kill."

Erik listened, entranced. The story was incredible. If he'd not seen Romana kill Gerald's lackeys last night, he wouldn't have believed it. But he knew otherwise. She spoke the truth. "That's how your father became a vampire," he said. "But your mother?"

She smiled. "My mother? In 1400, Diego and Gabriel had been companions, my father having been taught all of the knowledge which Gabriel possessed. He held fast to Gabriel's law; that they should only destroy those who were evil. Thus, they slew many wrongdoers. They travelled throughout Europe, living well, for they had amassed a great fortune, and owned a villa in Spain.

One night, as my father hunted, he heard with his preternatural hearing a woman screaming, and he went to investigate. In a wood, he discovered that a small group in a wagon had been attacked by a group of robbers. Two of the men were raping a woman; it was she who screamed, fighting them with her nails and teeth. My father descended upon them like an angel of death. He took up one of the men, and did not even drink from him, but snapped his neck like a twig. His companion, hearing the terrible sound, leapt up from the woman, and ripped out a small dagger. He had not seen his comrade's death, and thought that my father was only a fool who had involved himself in something he should have left alone. The man's eyes showed his contempt; my father was still accustomed to wearing finery, and this robber thought that such a dandy would be easy to kill.

Imagine the bully's surprise as my father slapped the dagger away, and grabbed him like a terrier takes a rat in its jaws. He drank his blood, and then threw the corpse away disdainfully. He then turned his eyes on the other robbers. They wailed and fled in terror, scattering in all directions, until they had vanished into the darkness of the trees.

My father then came to see how the woman had fared. He could see that she was only a girl, perhaps sixteen. She stared at him in amazement. She was a Gypsy, clad in the dresses and wearing the jewellery and bangles that they wore. She had a great mane of midnight-black hair, which was in disarray. Her eyes that peeked out of her hair were an electric blue, flashing in the moonlight. Her skin was an olive hue, and her teeth were a brilliant white. Her body beneath the torn dress was voluptuous, her curves appealing to his eye. She panted in short gasps; her breasts rose and fell with the exertion.

My father knelt down, she tried to scramble away, but he reached out in a flash of movement, and took her wrist in his strong hand. Her eyes widened; she thought that he was going to drink her blood. He hushed her, stroking her hair. She calmed down somewhat, but still stared at him in terror. He lifted her to her feet. She staggered, and he could see that she had been badly hurt by her assaulters. Blood stained the front of her dress; she had been stabbed by the man whose blood my father had drunk. Suddenly, worn out by both the blood loss and in shock, she fainted. My father took her in his arms, and looked about. He went over to the wagon, to see if there were any others who lived.

Slumped in the driver's seat was a man, he was dead, his throat cut. Sprawled on the ground were six others. All were dead. They had been a small family of Gypsies. Their belongings were strewn about the forest floor. He knew that the robbers would return to take it. He smiled to himself, and then looked down at the beautiful creature in his arms. Her life was draining away, running down his arms, to drip down onto the forest floor. He knew that she would not last long; she had lost too much blood. If he left her here, she would certainly die. Coming to a decision, he rose into the air, and flew towards the villa where he and Gabriel resided."

Romana stopped talking, and looked at a clock on the wall. "Should you not get ready for rehearsal?"

Erik checked the time. "I only need to shower, it won't take long." He got up, and padded towards the bathroom. "Keep going."

The girl followed him into the bathroom. As he ran the shower, she continued her story: "When they reached the villa, they landed on the balcony, and Gabriel appeared. He had seen all that my father had done, through the link that they shared in their minds. He came forward, and looked at the girl. He stared deeply into Diego's eyes. He knew what he intended to do."

Erik stepped into the shower, luxuriating in the hot water that cascaded down his body. Romana's voice came to him clearly.

"Gabriel addressed him: "If you do this, you must take her as your companion." Diego nodded. "I cannot let her die. She is exquisite. I must have her." Gabriel sighed. "I knew that one day, you would find such a one as her. So be it. Come." He turned and walked into the villa, and Diego followed him to one of the bedrooms. Here he laid the ailing girl on the bed. Instantly, the blood flowed out and stained the covers. Her eyes fluttered open. Her face was pale, and sweaty. She looked at them, and she trembled as she realised that Gabriel was a vampire like Diego. "Do not be afraid," said Gabriel. "We will do you no harm. But if we leave you as you are, you will die." The girl shuddered, and her breathing slowed. My father came to her side. "Do you want to live?" She looked up at him. "*You mean to live like you...*" Her voice was small and whispery. "Yes," said Gabriel. She turned her head away from them. "*Let me die...*"

The two vampires exchanged a glance. If she wanted to die, they should honour her wish. *No!* Thought Diego, *such a beautiful girl should not die!*

"If that is your wish," said Gabriel.

"If you die," said Diego, "You will not avenge your family." He had thought hard, trying to find a reason that the girl would want to live for.

She turned to face them. *"Avenge?"* she husked. A fire was lit in her eyes.

Diego came and put his hand on her head, stroking her gorgeous mane. "Yes. If you become as we are, you can destroy those who killed your family." He watched her face intently, trying to judge what the girl would decide. "I will care for you. Join us forever."

Her glazed eyes strayed between them. They appeared as statues to her dulled senses; hard and cold. And yet…they could help her to avenge her family. She suddenly found that she did not want to die, and her hand came trembling to take Diego's hand. *"I accept,"* she said weakly. *"What must I do?"*

Without replying, Gabriel came to her, and tore his wrist open. Holding it over the girl's wan face, as the black blood dripped down, he said: "Drink and live forever."

She took the offered wrist, and began to drink. She pulled greedily at the blood, which now flooded her with unnatural energy. The girl could feel it pulsing inside her, as her heart thundered, and she heard it throbbing in her veins.

Diego watched, entranced, as she drank. Gabriel's face contorted as he felt the ecstasy of their union. Pain and pleasure were written upon his visage. Suddenly, the girl fell back, to writhe upon the bloodied and sweat-soaked bed. She thrashed as the vampire blood coursed through her, invading every atom of her body."

Erik stepped out of the shower, and grabbed a towel off the rail on the wall. He looked at his reflection in the mirror, feeling the bruises on his face. The small cuts that he'd received from the crash stung. He threw his head forward and back, as though he was headbanging at a show. His long dreads flailed, water flying everywhere. She laughed merrily at this display. As he dried himself off, Romana continued: "The girl's struggles ceased, and she sat up, amazement on her beautiful face. Diego knew what she was experiencing; she was listening intently to all of the sounds she had never heard before, and her eyes saw as sharply as any predator of the night. The weakness and pain had vanished from her torn body, and she felt her wounds closing up of their own accord. She rose from the bed, and stood before them.

Diego's breath was taken away. If she had been beautiful before as a mere mortal, now she was a goddess. She came to him, and kissed him deeply. She knew how he felt about her, and she now realised that she felt the same about him. He crushed her in his arms. "What is your name?" he asked.

"Sophia," she said. She stepped out of his arms. Going to Gabriel, she kissed him, but in a sisterly way. "Thank you," she said.

Gabriel bowed. "It is Diego you must thank. It is he who found you, and brought you here."

As he said this, she remembered the forest, and the terrible thing that had been done there. She smiled, showing her deadly fangs. "Now," she said.

They all walked to the balcony, and Gabriel and Diego rose into the air. She looked at them for a moment, and then floated up to join them. They turned and flew into the night, heading for the scene of the attack."

Erik walked into the bedroom, put on a pair of boxers, and slipped into his jeans. He pulled on a Nine Inch Nails t-shirt; Trent Reznor's face glowered at Romana. He sat on the bed, and put on a pair of socks, and grabbed up his boots from the floor, tying the laces quickly. He looked up at her. "If you're coming to rehearsal, you'd better wear something." He got up, and went to an old dresser. Opening the third drawer, he pulled out a pair of black jeans. "These should fit." He came back, and gave them to her. She slithered into them. He gazed appreciatively at her. "Now you're a rock chick."

She smiled, and picked up her shoes. Slipping them on, she pirouetted. "Nice?"

"Mmmm…Very."

She came to him and put her arms around his neck. "Do you want to hear the rest?"

He looked up at the clock. "I'm running out of time…"

"Tonight then," she replied. "We must not let you get in trouble again."

He laughed. "Yeah, Elektra's pretty hard to work for."

"She is a very good performer. Perhaps she is worth it."

He rolled his eyes. "Yeah, I guess so. Let's go." Walking towards the stairwell, he picked up some keys from a ring on the wall. They went down the stairs and into the garage. He looked mournfully at his car.

She came and put her arm around his waist. "I will pay for it."

"You? What would a vampire need money for?"

She smiled. "I have amassed a great fortune over the many years of my existence. It would be only fair that I pay to have her repaired, since it is because we met that she was damaged. If you had not met me, last night would not have happened."

Erik thought back, remembering. He remembered Gerald and his vampire crew, the confrontation in the alley behind the club, and the attack on the freeway, and the Porsche being wrecked. But he also recalled Romana's great courage, and her defeat of the gang, and how he sent Gerald packing. Then he remembered how they had made love. "If I hadn't met you, last night would've been boring."

She laughed. "Boring! I do not doubt for a moment that you would have had another of your girls share your bed." Her look was mischievous. "But they are only mere mortals."

He grinned. "I guess I'll never have another one of them again." He made a mock sad face.

"If you do, I will rip out her throat." Her eyes twinkled with laughter. She turned and indicated another car that sat in the garage. "Will we take this one?"

All silver and chrome, a Corvette Stingray sat there, looking like it was breaking the speed record even when standing still. "No," replied Erik, "I've got to get the motor fixed in her." He walked over to the far wall, and lifted up a tarpaulin. "What about this?"

Beneath the tarp was a Harley, all custom painted, shining in the floodlights.

She came over to him. "A motorbike. I love motorbikes."

He wheeled the bike over to the roller door, Romana following. As he pushed the button that opened the door, he asked: "What if your friend Gerald shows up?"

"He would not dare attempt anything in broad daylight. It is a law of the Clans that they must not reveal themselves to humans."

The door rolled up and stopped. They got on the bike.

"In any case," she said, "He is weak due to the sun. He will return to the Clan and report his failure. They will want to send others back with him, because he cannot destroy me alone."

He nodded, and as her arms went around him, he passed her a set of mirror shades. He reached inside his jacket, and pulled out another pair, and put them on. He looked over his shoulder at her, and smiled at how she looked with them on. He kicked the Harley into life, and then he revved the engine. He pushed the button again to close the door, and as it came down they roared out into the daylight, and down the road towards the club.

Across the road, in the deep shadows of a building, a figure stepped out into the sun. Gerald watched them until they vanished from sight. Then, he turned and walked swiftly away.

2

Erik

The Harley sped along. Erik and Romana's hair was streaming in the wind. Erik had a huge grin on his face; he enjoyed the feeling of rushing along into the breeze. Romana's arms were tight around him; he could feel the hardness and great strength that she possessed. She was smiling too. *It was almost like flying*, she thought.

They came to the alley and turned into it. They roared up to the club. A large roller door at the dock was open, and they rode inside. The bike came to a stop, and they got off. Standing up on the loading platform was Jess. He was wearing the same clothes as Romana had seen him in on the previous night. Perhaps he'd slept in them.

"Hey, man," he said, jerking a thumb to indicate the club, "Ya better get in there. They've been waitin' for ya."

They climbed the steps and proceeded inside. As they walked along the corridor, they could hear music coming from inside the club ahead of them. Erik grimaced, knowing that he was late. Elektra was a stickler for rehearsal times, and he'd been chewed out before. As they came into the main room, the music stopped, and the band members regarded them. Peach stood by the mixer, and he shook his head.

Elektra came to the edge of the stage. "Well, if it isn't the *late* Mister Davis." She stood with hands on her hips, and her eyes blazed with anger. The others stood and watched, waiting to see what the outcome would be.

"Ah…" Erik began sheepishly.

Elektra silenced him by raising her hand. "I don't want to know. Get up here and do your job."

He nodded and climbed the steps up onto the stage. Romana followed him, and they stood before the band. Suzi let out a laugh when she saw his injuries, but stifled it when Elektra turned and glared at her.

"What's this?" she asked Erik.

He was gloomy. Surely this time he'd be sacked. "I like it rough."

This time the whole band laughed, and even Elektra smiled despite herself.

"No," said Romana, coming forwards. "Gerald and his friends attacked us, Erik was injured."

The drummer looked at her amazed. Surely she wasn't going to tell them what really happened?

Elektra's mood changed instantly, as though a switch had been thrown. She came over to Erik, and looked closely at his lacerated and bruised face. She was solicitous in her concern. "You should have called. Are you all right? Does it hurt?"

He grinned, and then winced at the pain. "Nah. Well, not much. I'm okay, boss."

The singer's face became serious. "What happened?"

Erik wondered what he should say. They couldn't tell them the truth.

Romana spoke: "They followed us to Erik's place. They jumped us as we got out of his car." She put her arm around the drummer. "But they did not expect him to be so fierce in a fight." She smiled as he looked at her, his face clearly showing that he was wondering what she would say next.

"Is that right?" asked Suzi. "Did ya beat 'em up, Erik?"

"Nah," he said. "I took two of 'em, but Romana here saw the others off. She knows Kung Fu or somethin'"

The girl smiled. "I know some of it."

"I don't like this," said Elektra. "What do they have against you,

Romana? Who is this Gerald?"

"He is someone who hates me. I am sorry that Erik was involved."

"If that bastard shows up again, I'll gut him like a fish," said Peach.

"I don't want him bothering us. What gives him the right to assault you?" Elektra obviously thought that Romana was trouble. Romana could see that she didn't want anything to cause the band any drama.

Romana's eyes were fierce. "Do not worry. He will not bother you again. I will deal with him myself."

The singer's blood chilled at the girl's voice. Romana radiated such hatred it was palpable. They all felt the intense anger that filled her. An uncomfortable silence fell, with them all staring at the girl.

Erik broke it: "Well, what are we runnin' through?"

Elektra shook her head. "You're not playing anything, hero. Go home and rest."

"No way. I came to rehearse." He looked contrite. "I'm sorry I was late, boss. But that don't mean I can't play. It looks worse than it is." He walked up to the kit, and sat down. He picked up his sticks and twirled them. "Well?"

Elektra smiled at him. "Okay." She nodded to Suzi, who grinned and looked to her laptop. She started the backing. Deep bass tones throbbed out, followed by discordant drilling sounds. Four hi-hat strikes came in, and then the band kicked in. The singer strutted over to the mic, and began singing.

Romana walked over to the side of the stage, and sat on a drum case. She watched and listened as the band ran through the song.

An hour later, they stopped for a break. They'd played seven songs, pausing only to dissect different parts that had to be cleaned up. As the guitarist and bassist wiped down their instruments, Elektra came over to Erik as he got up and stretched. She gestured to him, and they walked over to the bar. They sat down on some stools. He looked back at the stage, and saw Romana and Suzi deep in conversation. The girl was fascinated by the cyberpunk's keyboard, and Suzi was gladly showing her how she got her sounds. Occasionally, some tone would ring out, as the keyboardist demonstrated something to her.

"Erik."

He turned around. Elektra's face was serious. *Uh oh*, he thought, *here it comes.*

"Is this girl going to cause us trouble?" She folded her arms across her chest.

"Nah, boss."

"I don't want anything to disrupt the band, Erik. We're doing great. You know that I'm talking to several labels for a distro. If she brings us any hassle…"

He shook his head, and spread his hands in a placating gesture. "She won't." His eyes held a pleading look. "Please, I know that she won't cause any drama."

Elektra indicated his face. "She's already done that."

"That wasn't her fault. She didn't know they were there. You can't blame her for me gettin' beat up."

"If you hadn't been with her, you wouldn't have got involved." She looked over at the stage at the girl, and then turned back to Erik. "Who is she anyway? You don't even know anything about her."

He thought for a moment. "I feel like I'm falling for her…She's not like any of the other chicks who follow us. She's not even like *any* chick I've had before."

Elektra laughed. "Excuse me," she said. "But the way I've seen you go through girls –"

"It's not like that," he interrupted. He shook his head. "I don't know why, but I feel deeply for her. I can't explain."

The singer looked at him closely. "You're telling the truth. Usually, you just use them, and then discard them just as quickly." She looked at the girl up on the stage again. "She must be hot stuff."

Erik looked down at his feet. "It's not the sex, boss. There's more to it than that." He was sheepish.

Elektra hadn't seen him like this before. He was usually confident to the point of arrogance. Now, he was like a little boy who'd been caught with his hand in the cookie jar.

The guitarist and bassist were walking over to them, followed by Peach. They could see that the pair were having a serious conversation, so they stopped just out of earshot. Elektra waved them on, and they came over.

"Do you want something to eat?" asked Nick.

They told him what they wanted, and watched as the three of them left the club.

The singer mulled over what Erik had told her. Did he really feel for this girl? Elektra wondered. Erik the love-'em-and-leave-'em falling in love? Did he even know what love was? She stood up, and pointed her finger at him. "Whatever you think you feel is none of my business. But if you allow this girl to cause us any problems…"

"I know," he said, "I'm out of a job."

"Just so we understand each other," she said, "If any more shit happens around you that is her fault, I'm cutting you loose. I can't afford to let anything to fuck this band up, and I won't let anyone spoil it for all of us." She folded her arms. "Do you get me?"

He nodded. "Yeah, I understand."

"Good. I want you to find out everything about her, and this Gerald guy. I don't want him hassling us again. Is he some sort of criminal?"

"I don't know. She didn't say."

"Well, *find out*. He could be dangerous, maybe even have a record for something." Her face was stern. "Now, I need the bathroom. Go talk to her." She turned and walked off.

Phew, he thought, *so I've still got a gig.* He got up and went over to the stage. He climbed up the stairs and went to stand with them. Romana and Suzi had been playing with the keyboard. He could see that Suzi was now standing back, watching as the girl fiddled with dials, bringing up different voices. Romana found a harpsichord sound, and gave a gasp of delight. She played an arpeggio, and then her fingers flew over the keys, moving so fast that the two onlookers could barely see them move. She was in an almost trance-like state, and as her flashing digits blurred with the speed of their passage over the keys, Erik glanced at Suzi. The cyberpunk stood there with her mouth open, astonished. It was plain to him that she'd never seen anyone play as fast as Romana. Suddenly, he realised that Romana was blowing her cover. Surely Suzi already suspected that there was something strange about her, but with this little demonstration…He had to do something.

"Hey!" He stepped up to Romana's side, and grabbed her arm. "That's great!"

The girl stopped playing. Her glazed eyes turned to him, and for a moment, something vicious was held in their depths. Then, she realised who he was, and flashed him one of her breath-taking smiles "Erik! This is wonderful. So many amazing sounds!"

"Fuuuuck!" Suzi burst out. "You sure can play, babe!" Her face showed her amazement at Romana's dexterity on the keyboard. "How can you rip it like that?"

Romana realised that she'd done something that would add to Suzi's suspicions, suspicions that should be allayed, unless they reveal her true nature. "Paganini," she said. "I have played it since I was a child. It is second nature to me. I have always played it very fast."

Erik could see that her explanation didn't wash with Suzi. The keyboardist was staring at the girl strangely. He knew that Suzi knew there was something weird about Romana.

"What was that?" They looked down, to see Elektra looking up at them.

"Uh," Erik began.

"Suzi was showing me her wonderful keyboard," said Romana.

"I don't mean that. How can you play so fast?" Elektra came up the steps at the side of the stage, and came over to them. She looked at Suzi, who was still looking dazed at Romana's display. "What's going on here?"

Oh, nothing, Erik thought, *just that Romana's a vampire, and has super-fast reflexes.* He stood mutely, his gaze taking in the other three.

"It is nothing," the girl said. "I have played such pieces since I was very young. When you play something for so long, you can easily play it fast."

Elektra and Suzi looked unconvinced. Erik knew that they thought there was something unusual about Romana, and now she'd done something to further their suspicions.

"Aaah, that's right," said Erik. "There's lots of drummers who can play a roll with one hand, and can play double-kicks at ridiculous speeds. You can bet that they played that stuff over and over."

The singer and keyboardist looked uncertain. What Romana had done seem impossible. A machine could only achieve the speed that she had played at.

Elektra was just about to ask another question when Nick, Jon, and Peach arrived with the food. With a look that told Erik that she wanted to ask Romana more, Elektra led the way down to the tables.

An uncomfortable silence fell as they ate. Nick and Jon exchanged a glance, and Erik knew that they suspected that something strange had happened when they were out. For the moment they said nothing, but he knew that by the way they watched Romana and Elektra, they assumed that the girl had done something to get the singer riled up. They had played with her for several years, and knew her moods. Usually when they had a break, she kept up a running flow of talk, talking about different songs, and what had to be rehearsed and dissected for improvement. Music was the only thing that mattered to her, and the fact that she was silent could only mean that she was angry about something.

Erik knew better. He could see that she was not only silent, but she was thinking deeply about the events of both the night before, and also the incredible display that they'd just seen Romana perform on the keyboard. The drummer was in deep thought himself. He could understand Elektra's reservations about having Romana around, and because Gerald seemed to be an unknown factor, and a possible danger to the band, he felt that she was thinking about getting rid of him anyway. But he also knew that she was trying to justify such an action, because she'd told him herself that he was the best drummer that had ever worked with the band, and she didn't want to lose him.

So, she was in the grip of a dilemma. On the one hand, she had him, and wanted him to stay; on the other, there was Romana and her strangeness, and the threat of Gerald and his unknown background and whether he could cause more trouble. *Shit.*

Peach was sitting and taking it all in. As the roadie, sound tech, and Erik's drum tech, he'd been involved with the band since the beginning. He also was very aware of Elektra's moods, and Erik could see that he was only waiting for the singer to say something. He finished his taco, and got up and walked towards the door, going outside for a smoke. He gave Erik a look as he left, and the drummer realised Peach was not going to support him if Elektra decided to get rid of him.

They all cast sidelong glances at the girl. She hadn't ordered any food, which was just another weird example of how different she was. *Sure,* Erik thought, *tell them she doesn't eat; she'll just wait for nightfall, and drain someone's blood. Shit.*

Romana got up, and headed towards the toilets. All of them watched her until she entered and the door closed.

"So," said Nick, "What did we miss?" The guitarist finished his can of Coke, tossed it in a bin, and leaned back in his chair, waiting.

Elektra glanced at him. "Nothing," she said curtly.

Jon and Nick looked at the singer, and then at Suzi. Nick raised an eyebrow questioningly.

Suzi was still amazed by Romana's playing. She knew that it was impossible to play such stuff at the speed the girl had played it. *It wasn't natural,* she thought. She met their eyes and shook her head, and shrugged.

"Okay," said Jon, "What's going on?"

Elektra turned to give the bassist a withering glance. *"Nothing, I said."* Her voice was tight with the anger that she was trying to control.

Jon sat back. He realised that Elektra was just about to explode. "Okay. C'mon, Nick." He got up, and made his way towards the stage. Nick sat up, and after a brief glance at the singer, sighed and followed him. As they began to pack up their gear, Suzi got up as well, and joined them. They all broke down their equipment in silence, from time to time casting a glance over at Erik and Elektra.

Romana came out of the toilets, and came over to them, sitting down next to the drummer. She made as if to speak, but lapsed into silence.

"Well," said Erik hesitantly, "I'll go and break down my kit." He got up and went over to the stage. He opened his cases, and started to take the cymbals off.

"Romana."

Elektra came and sat next to the girl. Romana could see that the singer was wary of her. She knew why. The events of the previous night, and the way she'd played, were on Elektra's mind. Not only that, Romana had listened to their conversation as she was looking at Suzi's keyboards. Her vampire hearing had allowed her to eavesdrop on the pair. She was aware of everything that they had said. She had gone to the toilet to allow them to talk about her, and had listened to that brief exchange too.

"I like you," said Elektra. She smiled at the girl.

"But –" Romana added.

The singer nodded. "But," she echoed, "I don't want anything to wreck this band. I've worked hard to get us where we are, and I'm on the verge of signing a deal with a label. Obviously you can see that nothing else matters to me than my music." She paused, thinking, and then carried on. "Can you say with all honesty that you or your friend Gerald won't cause us any grief?"

"I cannot speak for him, but I will tell you that I will not bring any harm to Erik or your band." Her eyes pierced the singer through, and Elektra shuddered. "The matter between Gerald and I will be settled. I will deal with him without involving you."

Elektra considered the girl. Was she telling the truth?

"I know that you doubt me. Please, let me assure you of my good intentions." She turned her gaze to the stage, where Peach and Erik were lugging the drummer's cases to the truck that waited in the loading dock. Elektra followed her eyes. Could it be possible that she was in love with Erik after only one night?

"Ah, I think you've got to know something about our Erik," Elektra said. She had a wry grin on her face.

Romana held up her hand. "I know what you will say. He is not the type of man to give my heart to."

"I'm sorry, darling, it's just...that's the way he is, he just *uses* women. I don't want to see you get hurt."

Romana seemed to be looking at something far off. Perhaps she was remembering another man who had been like Erik. She turned to Elektra. "I am lonely, Elektra. I have been alone for a long time. I am tired of being alone. I know that Erik really feels something for me. I know that sounds strange to you, but I felt an instant connection when our eyes met. He told me that he feels the same way. I believe him."

The singer looked at the girl intently. Erik had told her the same thing. Could it be possible?

Up on the stage, Erik and Peach had lugged the last cases, and the drummer kept looking over at the two women as they were talking. Every time he returned for another case, he glanced in their direction. *What could they be talking about,* he thought. *Does Elektra want her to piss off?* He made a show of checking the stage for anything that had been left behind, but still watched them covertly.

Suddenly, he heard laughter, and he looked up, to see them both coming towards him, laughing all the while. He stood frowning down at them.

"Are you finished?" asked Elektra. She had a huge grin on her face. Romana at her side flashed her teeth in a brilliant smile.

What the fuck? He looked from one to the other, seeing the mirth on their grinning faces. *One minute she's about to throw Romana out, the next...Women!"* He smiled lamely. "Uh, yeah, boss. Everything's packed up. Everything okay?"

The two women shared a conspirational glance. "Of course," said Elektra.

"Why would it not be?" asked the girl. Her eyes were wicked.

Erik stared at them, a puzzled expression written on his face. *Who could understand women?* "No reason. It's cool." He climbed down the stairs and joined them in front of the stage. Romana put her arm around him and kissed him playfully. Peach came back, and stood waiting. The rest of the band came in behind him, and gathered around them.

"I guess we'll take my kit home," said Erik. He searched Elektra's face for some indication of what she was thinking. She still had an enigmatic smile on her face. How had things turned around so quickly? Did she now accept Romana's word that there would be no more trouble? He decided he would question the girl when they arrived at his place.

"Enjoy the week," said the singer. She picked up her bag, and the group broke up. Jon and Nick shared a glance. Jon shrugged, and the guitarist smiled wryly. Erik was still in the band. Suzi and Elektra were walking ahead, talking about some keyboard part in one of the songs. Everything was back to normal. They walked down the corridor, the atmosphere relaxed.

At the dock, Jess waited for them. He and Peach got into the truck, and the tech leaned out of the door, saying: "See you at your place." He slammed the door closed.

Erik nodded, and went over to sit on his bike. Romana got on behind him. At the roller door, Elektra and Suzi paused, and the singer gave them all a wave. Then they turned and went out to her car. Jon and Nick left the dock as Peach started up the truck. Erik shook his head in bemusement, still thinking about Elektra, and her abrupt change of heart.

Romana's arms went about his waist. "Do not worry, my love. I have assured Elektra that there will be no more trouble."

The drummer looked over his shoulder at the girl. She beamed at him, flashing one of those stunning smiles. He turned in the seat to face her. "I don't get it. Why did she change her mind? I was sure she wanted you gone." He saw her smile fade. "She told me it was either you or the band. If you caused any more shit, she was going to dump me too. What happened to change that?"

The smile slowly returned to her beautiful face. "I cannot tell you."

"Why not?"

She leaned forward and kissed him deeply. As she drew back, she said: "It is a girl thing." She made a mock serious face. "I must have some secrets."

He shook his head again. "Okay." He turned in the seat, and then he kicked the Harley to life. They rolled across the concrete towards the roller door, and he manoeuvred the bike up close to the wall. He reached out, and pushed the switch to close the door. As it came down, he revved the bike, and they rode out of the dock with a roar.

3

Gerald

The truck pulled up at Erik's place. Jess opened his door and jumped down. The Harley came down the street, and roared up to the roller door. Erik pulled out a remote, and activated the door. It rolled up, and they rode inside. The truck rumbled into the garage, and Jess opened the back door. As the truck stopped, he climbed up inside. Erik stopped the bike, and he and Romana got off.

The drummer went to the back of the truck and climbed into it, helping Jess to move the cases to the door. As they did this, Peach walked around and stood at the truck's door. Erik and Jess passed the cases down to him, and he put them along one wall. Romana carried some cases over to him. He raised an eyebrow as he saw her lug the heavy traps case as though it were light. He shook his head in bewilderment. He knew that the case was heavy; it usually took two of them to lift and carry. Romana met his puzzled gaze, smiled, and went back to get another case. Soon they were finished lugging, and Jess and Erik came over to them.

"Thanks, guys," said Erik. "Want a drink?"

"Okay," said Jess.

"Yeah," added Peach.

They all walked over to the stairs. With Erik leading, they started up them. Jess stopped, and stared at the wrecked Porsche. Erik sensed the halt and turned around.

"Shit, man," said Jess, "Those pricks sure trashed ya ride."

Erik and Romana exchanged a glance.

"Uh, yeah," said the drummer, "She's pretty wrecked."

Peach walked over to the car. He inspected the damage minutely. "What did they use? Sledgehammers?"

Erik thought for a moment. "Baseball bats."

"Fuuck!" said Jess. "Those guys are crazy!"

"I'm sorry. Erik," said Peach, "She's a write-off."

"No," said Romana, "I will pay to have the damage fixed."

Jess whistled. "That's a lotta fixin'. Can ya pay for it?"

"Yes, I can. Do not worry, I have the necessary money."

Erik smiled at this, and then turned and continued up the stairs, and the others followed him.

They walked into the huge lounging area, one wall of which was decorated with Erik's weapons collection. As Romana looked at the assorted rifles, pistols, and other paraphernalia, Erik went into the kitchen, and returned with a bottle of Jack Daniels and three glasses. Peach and Jess fell into a lounge, and Erik opened the bottle, and poured their drinks. He sat in a reclining chair, and took a long pull at his drink. He put the bottle on a coffee table that was in front of the lounge.

Jess looked over at the girl. "Ain't you havin' any?"

Romana turned. "No. I never drink...alcohol." She came over and sat next to Erik on another lounge chair. The furniture was all mismatched, different chairs, and three diverse lounges. All were a bit shabby looking, but comfortable. Another wall was lined with band posters, and against the far wall was a drum kit, next to an old quadraphonic stereo. A long cabinet held hundreds of records, and on its top was a cd player, with another large collection of discs. A table in the corner had a computer sitting on it that looked as though it had been made from half a dozen different machines.

For a while they sat and drank in silence. Erik knew that both Peach and Jess were filled with questions: What had happened when he and Romana were attacked? Who was this strange girl? What did she and this Gerald guy have between them? What did she and Elektra talk about? He and Romana waited for the pair to query them, but they didn't speak. Finally, Erik broke the silence, saying; "Well, that was a pretty good rehearsal, considering."

Peach looked over at the drummer. "I guess so." He drained his glass. "C'mon, Jess." He got up from the lounge.

Jess followed suit. He put his glass on the coffee table. "Thanks for the drink, bud."

"Anytime." Erik got up to see them off.

"Goodnight, Romana," said Jess.

"Goodnight."

Peach just nodded to the pair of them, and then walked towards the stairs, Jess and Erik trailing. Romana sat in the chair and watched them leave. Clearly they would question Erik, and she would give them space. She could hear what they asked him anyway.

As the three descended the stairs, Peach turned and addressed Erik: "I hope you know what you're doing." He pointed upstairs.

Erik knew what he meant. *Romana.* "Yeah, me too. Elektra seemed to finally agree to let her stay."

"I dunno," said Jess, "She's nice, 'an all, but what about this Gerald dude, and his freaky friends?" The big man looked at Peach. *Back me up, man.*

"What did she and Elektra talk about?" Peach stood, his arms crossed.

"I don't know," answered the drummer, "But she would've told Romana to piss off, if she thought that there'd be more trouble."

Peach unfolded his arms. He pointed a finger at Erik. "You better hope there's no more shit. I know Elektra better than you do. She's only waiting for something else to happen. You owe her, Erik. She gave you a good gig, and you know that she's bled for this band. Don't fuck it up."

"I won't. D'you think I want that?" The drummer walked over to the switch for the roller door. He activated it, and the door rolled up. "Trust me. Trust Romana. She promised me that everything will be cool."

Peach came over to him. "It had better be. I won't back you up this time, Erik. Elektra's given you more than a fair chance."

Erik smiled. "I know. Don't think I don't appreciate it."

Peach nodded. "Okay. Friday night then." He opened the truck door, and climbed up inside.

"See ya later, man." Jess walked around to the other door, and joined Peach. "Shit." He leaned out of the window. "Sergei said he'd drop around tonight sometime. Somethin' about a Nine Inch Nails thing you were gonna give him. Sorry I forgot."

"Thanks." Erik waited as Peach started the truck, and reversed out of the garage, turned, and drove off, the horn blaring twice. Jess waved, and they were gone, the engine sound diminishing in the distance. He stared out at the twilight, the sun having gone down before. He pushed the switch, and as the door came down, walked over to the stairs, and climbed them back up to the lounge and Romana.

And Gerald. The dandy was standing in the open doorway to the balcony. Romana stood in a defensive stance, her eyes fixed on the blonde vampire. He looked over at Erik as he came up the stairs.

"Good evening, hero." He smiled sarcastically, and came into the room. His savage eyes flared and filled with blood, as he smelled Erik's scent. His smile widened, to show his deadly fangs.

Romana hissed, a vicious sound. She advanced, to stand between them. Her own eyes were filled with a predator's hunger. She seemed on the verge of exploding into violent action. *"Stay back!"* she spat.

The two vampires faced each other, their eyes locked. The tension in the room was palpable. Erik had stopped when he'd seen Gerald. He knew that to move could mean his death, and perhaps Romana's too. He stood stock still, his heart pounding inside his ribs like a frantic animal. He realised that both Gerald and Romana were aware of the throbbing organ. As he thought this, Gerald sneered.

"Oh, I am not here for your blood tonight, mortal. I am but a messenger." His gaze never left Romana, watching for any sudden move.

"Messenger?" echoed the drummer. He licked his dry lips.

"Yes. I have something to tell you, Romana."

Romana laughed once, a cynical bark. "I am not interested in anything that you have to say."

Gerald smirked. "Not even if it is about Abdullah?"

The girl started, shocked. "What?"

"Aaah, I thought that would get your attention." Gerald stepped towards her. "I am to tell you that we have your mentor. You must come with me, or he will die." He watched her for any reaction.

The girl wore a stunned look on her face. She appeared to have been kicked in the stomach. As Gerald came over and stood right in front of her, she looked deeply into his vampire eyes. "Abdullah?" she whispered.

"Yes." His gaze went to Erik.

Romana's hands flashed upwards. Gerald moved backwards in a movement too fast for the drummer to see. In an instant, he was across the room. Romana stood with both hands clawed, talons ready to rend and tear.

"*Do not touch him,*" she rasped. The killing look had returned to her eyes.

Gerald allowed an indifferent smile to cross his face. "I told you, I am not interested in your pet." He walked over to the far lounge, and lowered himself into it, watching her carefully all the while. He sat leisurely, crossed his legs, and folded his arms. "Will you listen to my words? They come from the Clans."

The girl watched his every move intently. When she could see that he didn't pose an immediate threat to Erik, she slowly lowered her hands.

Gerald was examining his nails. He watched her as she too sat down. Erik remained standing; he didn't trust Gerald, and he knew that the foppish vampire could reach him with one blur of supernatural speed. He hoped that they would talk, and ignore him. *Where did I put that flare gun?*

Gerald wagged his finger at him. "Now, now. None of that. I told you I am here to speak to the lovely Romana." He placed his hands on his chest with his fingers splayed in a persuasive gesture. "I swear to you I have no interest in you, mortal." He smiled, showing his lethal fangs. "At least for tonight."

"Give me your message," Romana said impatiently.

He inclined his head in acquiescence. "The Clan leaders have sent me to tell you that we have Abdullah."

"You have already told me that lie." Her lovely face was flushed with anger.

Gerald shook his head. "It is no lie. You were there when the oasis was attacked, were you not?"

"Yes. But the Clans had nothing to do with it. There was a group of soldiers, they came in helicopters, and Abdullah told me to flee. He faced them, and destroyed several of them, but they used some sort of darts on him, like the African hunters, and he fell. They trussed him in a net, and took him aboard one of their machines. I would have tried to save him, but the men with the guns were very wary, and I would only have joined him in captivity." Her eyes were misty with tears as she related her tale, and Gerald could see that she was seeing that day vividly.

Erik listened intently. Surely this was the other part of her story that she was going to tell him? Who was this Abdullah?

Reading his thoughts, she said: "Abdullah was like a father to me. Before the Clans took my parents and slew them, they gave me to him to raise and protect. A dead baby was substituted for me, and the Clans were duped into thinking that I had perished." The memories flew in front of her eyes; the long, long years of her life, and the images of the only one that she knew that cared for her; the Arab who lived in the Qattara Depression with her in a secret oasis. He was there for her when she started to feel the Dark Thirst, the calling of her vampire blood. He showed her how to hunt, and explained to her how different she was from the mortals that filled the waking world.

"Do you remember anything of the way these men were dressed? Any insignia that they bore?" Gerald stroked his chin, his eyes on Romana.

She thought deeply. Her memory of that day intensified in her mind. She saw again how the helicopters had arrived, bringing thunder to the lonely oasis. *White, all of their machines were white.*

"Yes," prompted Gerald. "And?"

"The helicopters were white, and the men wore white too." Her gaze was fixed on the past.

Erik stood rooted to the spot, as Romana remembered that day. He kept a wary eye on Gerald, but the vampire didn't even look at him. Obviously, if he wanted to take the drummer, there was nothing that Erik could do about it.

"Did you not see any markings at all?" Gerald smirked.

"There was something…" Romana shook her head. "I cannot remember."

Gerald sighed. "On each of the uniforms and the helicopters was the sign of a lit torch, surrounded by a wreath of holly leaves."

The girl's face was blank.

"You have not seen such markings before?" The smile widened on his face, and Erik watched as Gerald's fangs appeared. In a condescending tone, he explained, speaking as though he were addressing a small, dull child: "It is the insignia of the Duvall Biogenic Laboratory. Philippe Duvall, a Frenchman who has a debilitating spinal condition, runs it. You do not know of him?"

"No. Should I?" Now she crossed her arms, impatiently. Her eyes grew angry.

The blonde vampire laughed. He leaned forward in his seat. "Yes, you should. It was he that experimented with all manner of means to rid himself of his illness. It is progressively becoming worse. In the end, it is fatal." His voice took on a conspirational tone. "He has even experimented with the Dark Blood."

A shocked look appeared on Romana's face. She unfolded her arms, and her mouth opened as she saw his meaning. "Abdullah?"

Gerald nodded. "And others before him. Duvall thinks that our blood will cure him; more than that, it will make him immortal." He watched her closely. He knew that his words would have a profound effect on her. Gerald knew that Romana felt deeply for Abdullah, and it was this connection that would bring her to the Clans, as he had promised them.

"How long has he been doing this?" The girl was horrified. *A mortal who drained the blood of vampires, and experimented with them as though they were animals.* Her thoughts churned in revulsion.

"Fifty years," said Gerald. "His laboratory is in Switzerland, and for all of that time, he has hunted us, taken us prisoner, and used us for his terrible works." He recalled the past; how the Clans had become aware of this mortal who searched for a way to become like them. "You would not know of him, because you were apart from us, reposing in blissful ignorance of the world outside your little refuge."

Erik could see that Gerald's words were firing Romana's fury. He interrupted before the girl could leap into violent motion: "How did he find out about vampire blood?"

Gerald's eyes swung to the drummer. Again the sneer wrote itself across the foppish visage. "He found one of us badly injured. When he became aware of the nature of his find, he recalled the tales that have been told about us; how we cannot be affected by disease, and that we are immortal.

He set out to find a way to transfuse himself with our blood, so that he would be rid of his condition. His first trial failed, and his subject died."

"So he searched for more of us, and used us to destruction." Romana's voice was hushed, as though she spoke to herself. She thought of Abdullah in the hands of this fiend.

"Indeed. His lust for knowledge is endless, and his thirst to find a cure using our blood has become an obsession with him, to the detriment of our people." Gerald addressed Romana: "The Clans met, and it was determined that we must do something about this mortal. We spoke also about you, the Abomination. Two things were decided: The Clans would not tolerate his interference. We would find a way to stop him."

"And the other thing?" Romana asked coldly. She knew the answer.

Gerald smiled. "In the past, it was the Clans intention to destroy you."

Now Romana returned his smile. "They have failed. They will always fail. Because I was Born, not Made, I am the most powerful vampire on earth. None of you can defeat me."

"Perhaps." Gerald rose, and Romana came quickly to her feet. She and Erik readied themselves for an attack. He looked at them, humour twinkling in his preternatural eyes. He slowly backed towards the door that led to the balcony, his smile fixed on his face. He watched Romana intently, knowing the danger she presented to him. It was no idle boast that she made; he knew the truth of her words. In all of the centuries that the Clans had sought to destroy her, they had indeed failed. "What if I told you that there is a change in the Clan's thinking?" He stopped, standing in the doorway. He leaned nonchalantly against the doorjamb, his arms folded, and he crossed one leg behind the other indolently.

Romana watched him warily. She tried to sense any subterfuge, but she couldn't feel any deception in his mind. His thoughts were open; She read them, and saw that they matched his words. "What change?" She sent her perception outside to see if there were any other vampires waiting to take her by surprise. There were none. She was impressed; despite her loathing for him, Gerald had come alone, and his words were as the Clans had told him.

"We have made contact with this Duvall. We know that in all the years of his experiments, he has failed to cure himself with our blood. He has tried both males and females; it has been useless. We told him that he needed blood from the most powerful vampire in the world. There is only one."

Erik and Romana looked at each other. The drummer knew that Gerald meant Romana herself.

"A deal was struck," Gerald continued; "The Clans would provide Duvall with some of your blood. In return, Abdullah would be released to you. You would be imprisoned, but not destroyed. In this way, we would be rid of both his interference, and you would be in our custody."

Now it was Romana's turn to sneer. "So I am to be imprisoned, not destroyed?" She laughed derisively. "I cannot believe that. I have been hunted for hundreds of years. What could have changed the Clans decision about me?"

Gerald came upright. His manner was suddenly grim. "Duvall has changed it. His disgusting experiments must be stopped."

"He is only a mortal. Why have you not killed him?"

The blonde vampire looked contrite. "We have tried." His voice now held none of his brash humour. "He is guarded by such impenetrable security, that we cannot get near him. He has machines that surround him with deadly energies. We cannot approach him. His men are armed with weapons that spell obliteration for us; they burn us with fire. Many have been slain, and others taken captive, to be used for his vile works."

"How do we know that he won't just kill her anyway, once he gets his hands on her?" Erik stole a glance at Romana; she was deep in thought. Surely she couldn't believe what Gerald was saying?

"I did not ask your opinion, *mortal*," Gerald hissed. "Be silent. This does not concern you." His blood red eyes flashed a warning: *Stay out of this!*

"He speaks the truth as he knows it, Erik." Romana turned her beautiful face to him. "He trusts this Duvall, and he trusts what the Clans have told him. I cannot sense any lie in his words." She looked over at Gerald. "Give me a day to think over your offer."

Gerald inclined his head in acceptance. "Very well. One day, no longer. You must understand the seriousness of this. This Duvall is the only mortal to be a danger to us in all of our existence. We must remove this threat."

"And what of me? I have been hunted for my difference; the very fact that I exist at all is a breaking of your most unbreakable law. I am the last of my kind, and the Clans have never tolerated my existence."

A faint smile appeared on the blonde vampire's face. There was no scorn in it; it was an open and warm smile. "Not all of us think as the Clans do." He bowed, and then turned, and with a flash of movement, he disappeared into the night.

Romana stared out into the darkness, her mind turning over the blonde vampire's words. Was the offer genuine? She once again recalled all of the long years that she'd been hunted by the Clans. Were they really going to end that hunt? The only place on earth that she'd felt safe was the oasis. It had been a refuge and a secret hideaway, until the men had come with their machines, and had stolen Abdullah away. Many times before, Abdullah had shown her the wide world, educating her about the many ways to hunt and survive the attacks of the vampires who wished to destroy her. They'd often been pursued, but none of those who were against her had located the oasis.

"You don't believe him, do you?"

Romana came out of her introspection. Erik walked over to her. He took her by the shoulders, looking deeply into her eyes. He was relieved to see that her rage of before had faded, now that Gerald had gone. She smiled pensively at him.

"I do not know. As I said, there was no sense of subterfuge in his mind. What he told me he believed to be the truth."

"But what if the Clans didn't *tell* him the truth? What if they didn't let him in on what they planned, because they knew that you'd read the trick in his mind, and turn their offer down?"

Her face was still thoughtful. "That has occurred to me. It would make sense; if they did intend to trap or try to slay me, they could not let him know of it, because I would learn of it by reading his thoughts." She put her arms around him. "Hold me." He embraced her.

Erik felt the unnatural hardness of her body against his own. *I don't want her to go,* he thought. Would she decide to accept Gerald's proposal? From what he'd seen and experienced first-hand, the dandy wasn't to be trusted; he was ruthless and without mercy. "Romana…"

"I know what you want to say," she said softly. She pulled away from him, to look him in the eye. "I know your thoughts, Erik. I understand your misgivings about this, but please let me decide for myself. You do not know what it is like to be hunted for centuries, hounded by those who would destroy you. I am tired of running and hiding, always eventually being discovered, and having to run again. If they will honour this bargain, then I will go to the Clans, and offer my blood to this Duvall."

The drummer made to speak, but she placed her hand over his mouth, shaking her head.

The bell for the door downstairs rang. Erik started in surprise. They released each other. Romana smiled. "It is all right. It is the Bear."

Sergei! Shit! Erik started to walk over to the stairway. "I'll tell him to go," he said.

"No," she replied, "He is your friend, and I must go and drink. I need to be alone, to think this over." She smiled. "Do not worry, I will come back."

He came back over to her. "You promise?"

The girl nodded. "Yes. I promise." She suddenly grabbed him, and kissed him deeply. She crushed him in her powerful arms. When they broke away from each other, Erik gasped for breath. The bell sounded again. "Go and let your friend in."

He turned and walked over to the stairway. At the top, he stopped, and swung around. Romana was standing in the doorway where Gerald had been. She smiled at him, and blew him a kiss. Then, with a movement too quick for his mortal eyes to see, she vanished from view. He went down the stairs, his mind filled with misgiving.

He opened the door. His big Russian friend filled the doorway, a bottle in his hand. Sergei came in, and hugged him. "Erik, my friend! I hope I do not interrupt you and the lovely Romana!" He stepped back, and the smile left his face as he saw the concern on the drummer's visage. "What is it?" He placed his huge hand on Erik's shoulder. "Something is wrong?"

Erik wondered what to say. He couldn't tell Sergei the real reason for his mood. "Gerald showed up again."

"Ha! Elektra told me what happened. I do not like that one. He is trouble."

"Yeah. Don't worry, she told him to piss off." He grinned. "Come on up. I got somethin' special for you." He climbed the stairs, and Sergei shrugged and followed.

They entered the lounge area, and sat down. Sergei held up the bottle. "Some vodka?"

Erik nodded absentmindedly, his thoughts still on Romana. What would she decide? Could she trust the word of the Clans, who'd pursued her for hundreds of years?

Sergei looked at his friend closely. He knew that Erik was troubled. He got up, and went into the kitchen, and returned with two glasses. He opened the bottle, and filled them. He went over to Erik, and handed him a glass. The drummer accepted it, and the Russian sat down again, waiting for Erik to speak.

The silence dragged on. They both sat, occasionally taking sips of the vodka. Finally, Erik broke the silence. "Sergei…"

The huge man held up his hand. "Whatever you want, I can do. What troubles you, Erik?" He could see that Erik was reluctant to talk about his problem. He looked around the room. "Where is Romana?"

The drummer hesitated. What could he tell Sergei? He knew that the Russian was very astute, and because he'd known Erik for years, was attuned to his moods. He took a deep breath. "She went with Gerald. They had to talk about something."

Sergei raised an eyebrow. "She went with him? Elektra said she hated him." He leaned forwards in the chair. "She could be in trouble." He looked at the drummer closely. Something was wrong. Sergei could sense that there was something strange here; the girl wouldn't just go willingly with a man she detested. He sat back in his chair, studying his friend. He put his empty glass down on the coffee table. He looked Erik in the eye. "You lie. Why? I am your friend, Erik."

Shit. What can I tell him? Erik licked his lips. He stared at Sergei for a long time without speaking.

The Russian got up, and walked over to him. He sat down on the lounge next to the drummer. He put his hand on Erik's shoulder. "Tell me."

Erik finished his drink, and placed his glass on the table. He glanced at Sergei. "It's okay. I can deal with it." He got up, and walked over to the cabinet. He picked up a cd, and came back to the lounge. He handed the cd to Sergei. "Nine Inch Nails, live at KROQ." He sat down, and picked up the bottle, refilling their drinks. He gave the Russian a glass. He leaned back in the lounge, and sipped his vodka.

"Thank you. Is good present." He got up, drained his glass, put it on the table, and put the cd in his coat.

"Are you going?" Erik put down his glass and stood up.

"Da. If my friend will not tell what is wrong, I will leave him to think." He started to walk towards the stairway.

Erik hurried over to him, stopped him, and took his arm. "Don't go. I'm sorry. I'll tell you." He was thinking of what story he could tell his friend, when he saw Sergei's eyes widen. He turned, and in the doorway to the balcony he saw the tall figure of a woman. She sauntered into the room. She had a mane of flaming red hair, the greenest eyes he'd ever seen, and the body of a goddess. She was dressed in black jeans, a crimson blouse, and wore a black coat. She looked them over, and when she smiled, they saw her fangs.

"You must be Erik." She came closer, her hips swaying suggestively. "I am Valeria." Her voice was husky, and held them spellbound.

They stood in shock, Erik still holding Sergei's arm. They watched, fascinated by her.

Sergei whispered, *"Vampyre!"*

Erik looked at him in amazement. Had his friend seen such creatures before?

Valeria laughed. "What do you think? He *is* Russian." She smiled, again showing her deadly teeth. "Tell him, Sergei, or should I call you 'Bear?'"

The Russian swallowed nervously. He stared at her, and sweat began to bead on his face. He looked at Erik, and said: "Da. A vampyre I have seen before." He glanced at Valeria, and her expression told him to continue. "It was when I serve in Afghanistan. We were on patrol, and had stopped to camp. That night, our sentry disappear. We look, but could not find him anywhere. The next night, the same thing happen. We thought that maybe the Afghans had taken them prisoner, or killed them." He thought for a moment, remembering. "So," he continued, "We set a trap. One of our men was used as bait. We pretend to sleep, but wait to surprise the enemy." He looked over at Valeria, and Erik saw the fear in his eyes. "At night, *something* crept in. It attack our man, and as they struggled, the rest of us jump up to take it. We shone torches, and we see...we see..." He stopped, his mouth dry.

Erik gripped his arm. "It's all right, Sergei."

"*No!*" The big man wrenched himself out of the drummers grasp. His breath came in gasps, and his eyes were wide with terror. "The... *thing* we saw in the torchlight, it was not human! Eyes of blood...fangs...it turned to us, and it *laughed!* We fired, but it stood there, our bullets tearing into it, and it ignore them! It had killed Dimitri, and now it rushed at us." He stopped, and he closed his eyes tightly, and tears welled out, and ran unheeded down his face.

Erik put his arm around him. He tried to calm him, and was amazed at how the huge man trembled in fear. "What happened?" he asked softly.

Sergei's eyes sprang open. "It attack us. It was among us, like a storm. It killed many of us. The *screams...*" He took a shuddering breath. "The fire. Our Captain, he pick up a burning piece of wood, and thrust it into the thing's face."

Erik knew what he was going to say. He'd seen it himself. The vampires were destroyed by fire. Perhaps it was the only way to destroy them.

"It screamed," said Sergei, "like an animal. It burned, and nothing was left, but ash. We were amazed. Half of our patrol was gone. We pick up our gear and ran. We reported it, but were laughed at, and told not to speak of such things again. Later, I find out that such attacks had occurred before, and our officers did not want the men to panic. We were told that if we told anyone, we would end up in a gulag."

Valeria said: "An interesting little adventure." She came towards them. She addressed Erik: "You were going to tell him something?"

"What do you want?" Erik asked, ignoring her question.

The vampire came closer, and sat on the table, crossing her long legs. She picked up one of the glasses and sniffed it. She put it down, and her eyes bored into him. "Gerald sent me to ensure that you behave yourself while little Romana is off hunting." Her glance flicked to the Russian. "Do not worry, tovarisch. I have already hunted tonight. I will not harm you."

Sergei spoke: "So this Gerald is one of you?"

"Yes. And so is Romana." Valeria laughed again. "I think you have a story to tell, Erik." She indicated the lounge, inviting them to sit down. They exchanged a glance, and went warily towards her. They sat down, their eyes never leaving her. "Well?" she said.

Erik began.

4

Romana and Gerald

Romana flew through the night. The wind whistled in her ears, and her long hair streamed out behind her. She looked down upon the city, its lights twinkling like stars. It never ceased to amaze her how those lights pulsed like the throbbing blood of some vast and fabulous beast; the streets with the moving traffic that flowed like the life giving blood that kept the city alive. Blood was also what she sought. She sent her perception ahead of her, to find a victim to provide her with what she needed to exist.

As she flew along, she suddenly sensed two people below her. They struggled, locked in mortal combat. She swooped lower, coming in over an alleyway, where the two combatants fought. A man and a woman were at the end of the alleyway; he strove to stab her with a knife, and she was desperately trying to ward herself. Her arm was slashed and bloody from their struggle, and her clothes were painted with her blood.

Romana landed behind the man, her gaze taking in the pair. The woman saw her, and her eyes widened as Romana bared her fangs, her blood – filled eyes burning with the bloodlust that could only be slaked by a living victim. The woman gasped, and went limp. The man, thinking that the struggle had gone out of her, struck her with the back of his free hand, and the woman fell to the dirty street, her terrified gaze fixed on Romana's approaching form.

In a blur of speed, the vampire was upon the man, taking him in her powerful arms. In moments, her deadly teeth had ripped into his throat, and his blood pumped into her hungry mouth, as she took the Dark Drink. The man dropped the knife, which clattered to the road. The woman, staring at the horrific spectacle of Romana drinking from her victim, started at the sound. She looked at the knife, and then leaped forwards, swept the blade up, and held it protectively before herself in trembling hands.

Romana was in the throes of ecstasy that every vampire experiences when they drink. The man's heart pumped his blood into her; her own heart beat in counterpoint as his life flowed into her. In moments, she had drained the man, and she dropped the corpse, turning her attention to the woman.

The woman stared into her eyes. They were still filled with blood. She dropped the knife, and backed away, scrabbling on all fours like a terrified animal. Her frightened stare never left Romana. She came up against the wall of the alleyway with a shock, her head banging against the bricks. She panted, desperately seeking a way of escape, her eyes darted around the alleyway, but no way out came to her urgent gaze.

Romana slowly approached her. She held her hands out before her in what she hoped was a gesture that could calm the terrified woman. Now that she looked closely, she could see that the woman was actually a girl, perhaps only sixteen. She had long blonde hair, which was matted and dull. Her clothes were only a very short skirt; one that allowed Romana to see the girl's panties, and a black t-shirt, covered by a red leather jacket. Her shoes had come off in the fight, and lay on the street. They were high heels, but were worn and grimy. In fact, all of her clothing had the same battered look.

Suddenly the sensation of being watched impinged upon Romana's awareness. She spun around, to see Gerald sauntering down the alleyway towards them.

The girl found her voice, screaming: "Help me!"

Gerald came closer, and as he came up to them, smiled. The girl saw his fangs, and realised that instead of a rescuer, this new arrival was just like the creature that had killed her attacker. She moaned in terror, obviously thinking that they would both drink her blood. She lay there trembling.

Gerald glanced at Romana as he passed her, going over to the girl. He held out his hand to her; she looked at it, her eyes wide with horror. He reached down and roughly jerked her up off the road. Gerald took the girl by the back of the neck, and walked towards Romana. He stopped in front of her, holding out his captive. The girl dangled in his grasp, her feet off the ground. She kicked her legs, struggling for freedom, whimpering like a frightened animal. She tried desperately to remove his hands, pulling at them with all of her strength, but it was to no avail. She started to sob hysterically. She dropped her hands to her sides, and her legs ceased their wild kicking. She stopped struggling, realising the awful truth: she was no match for the vampire's unnatural strength.

"Why do you feel for these *cattle*?" Gerald asked scornfully. "They only exist to provide us with nourishment." His smile was mocking.

"Let her go, Gerald." Romana's face was fixed with determination.

He leaned his head to one side. "No," he said.

"She is innocent. Let her go."

"*Innocent!* Ha! Did it ever occur to you to wonder *why* she was being attacked?" He laughed. "Read her mind, you will see."

Romana looked at the girl. She hung helplessly in his grasp, sobbing. She sent her perception into her mind. She saw the girl with men, many men. Bodies writhed in different positions on a filthy bed. The girl did what she had to do to survive. She hated them all. She hated herself. She only did it so that she could pay for the poison that she injected into herself. Romana saw the man that she'd killed. He *owned* the girl, and procured the men for her. He'd attacked her because the girl hadn't given him his...cut? Cut, yes, that was the word that she saw in her mind. He wasn't going to kill her; he only wanted to scare her; after all, she made money for him, and he only sliced her up a bit to put fear into her.

"You see," said Gerald scornfully, "she is only a whore."

"Even so," said Romana, "she does not deserve death just for doing such things. She was only trying to protect herself from him."

Gerald sneered. "They all deserve death. Weak, pitiful things that they are, they are nothing compared to us. Their lives are over in the blink of an eye, while we last forever."

"Their lives are full for them. You cannot measure their brief existence against our own immortal life."

"You are wrong," he continued, "our powers are far beyond their own pathetic limitations. We are as gods compared to them." His eyes suddenly showed terrible intent.

"No," gasped Romana.

With a contemptuous flick of his wrist, Gerald snapped the girl's neck like a twig. Her sobs were cut off abruptly. He flung the corpse to the road at Romana's feet. It lay face upwards, the sightless eyes staring into the night sky, surprise held within their depths. Romana looked at the pitiful shape, sprawled in the dirt. She felt anger rising within her; anger at such a needless act of brutality that Gerald had just committed. She looked up, hatred written all over her beautiful face, her eyes blazing with fury.

Gerald stood smirking, his arms folded casually. He met her burning gaze calmly.

"Why did you do that?" she rasped.

The vampire shrugged. "I do not know. I do not thirst, for I have already drunk tonight." He watched her carefully, knowing her strength was far beyond his own powers. "Perhaps I wished to make a point."

"You did not have to kill her!" Romana cried.

"But we kill all the time," he said reasonably.

Romana stared at him, her rage boiling over. "Not like that! It was without reason."

Gerald shook his head. "My, you do suffer for them. Do not forget what you are, Romana, a killer."

"I know what I am," she replied, her voice thick with anger. "I do not murder the innocent."

"Ah yes," Gerald said mockingly, "'Slay only the evildoer.' One of Abdullah's most unbreakable commandments."

She started to back away from him. "Leave me alone." She braced herself to take off into the night.

He smiled. "Are you going back to see your pet?"

She flared up again. "Leave Erik alone!" she hissed. She clenched her fists, and her nails bit into her palms, to draw black blood, that dripped steaming upon the road. She stalked back towards him, and she raised her hands, talons ready to rip and tear. She bared her fangs, and snarled.

Now you are dangerous, Gerald thought. "He is safe," he said, warily eyeing her, "both he and his big Russian friend." He unfolded his arms, ready to flee. "I sent Valeria to –"

"*Valeria!* That *bitch!*" exploded Romana. "If she hurts them, I will kill you all!"

Gerald held up his hands in a placatory gesture. "They will not be harmed. She is only there to ensure that they do not go anywhere, or tell anyone of your…condition."

"But she is unpredictable. How can you promise me that they are safe?"

"I give you my word."

Romana laughed. "You have taught me not to trust you. How can I believe you, after all that you have done to me and those who I have loved? You have pursued me relentlessly, always leading the groups of hunters that follow the bidding of the Clans."

He smiled wanly. "That is true," he admitted. "I serve the Clans. I am responsible for the destruction of the Abominations; I hunted them down and wiped their kind from the face of the earth." He looked deeply into her eyes. "Except for one."

Romana lowered her hands. "And that one has always eluded you."

"Indeed. But how long can she do so?"

"As long as you continue to hunt me."

Gerald shook his head. "Now you want to go to your mortal pet." He spat on the ground. "It makes me sick, the way that you want to be with these creatures."

"Erik truly loves me, he accepts me for what I am. He wants to stay by my side."

"But he would not be by your side forever."

"He understands that, and yet he still loves me."

"Oh yes?" he answered, a tone of inquiry in his voice. "How long can that love last, when he finally realises that he will grow old and die, while you continue to live on, unchanged, beautiful as you are now?" His eyes bored into her. "Even though it says it in their bible, the lion would not lie down with the lamb; it would kill it and feast on its flesh with relish. How then can you expect to be with this mortal; he being like the lamb,

and you a predator like the lion, hunting down your prey in the darkness of the night?" He stepped forward, and his tones became beseeching. "No, lovely Romana, the only fit companion for you is one of your own kind."

Her eyes flared. "My *own* kind? There are none. All have been destroyed, thanks to you and your hunters."

"Please excuse me. Maybe there are no Born vampires, but you could be with one of us, a Made vampire. Such a one could be your companion for all of eternity."

She laughed again, bitterly. "Where would you find such a one? I am an outcast, an *Abomination*, according to the Clans, and they are very strict in their laws. Any who fail to meet their rigorous conditions are slain."

"You do not understand. There are members of the Clans who desperately wish that they had your powers. Some of us even admire you, and think of you as a beautiful and powerful creature. Such a vampire would gladly become your companion, suffering imprisonment for the chance to be with you forever." He paused, thinking. "Listen to me, Romana, the Clans have sent me to tell you that they have decided to cease this futile conflict. They want you to come with me. They have offered you the chance to live."

"How? Why would they change their edict to have me killed?"

"Because their very existence is in danger."

She raised an eyebrow. "Danger?"

He nodded. "I told you of Duvall, and of his sickening experiments."

"Yes. Is he such a threat?"

His face was grim. "Yes. In all of the ages that we have existed, no other mortal has presented such danger to us. He takes us and uses us without any fear of reprisal, and his protection is absolute." He came closer, slowly approaching her, until only a small space separated them.

She considered him warily. Was he attempting to trap her? Many times before, he'd tried to trick her, and she had become very guarded.

"It is no trick," he said, reading her thoughts.

"Surely I disgust the other vampires? They have hunted me down the long years; the Clans have always tried to destroy me. Can you honestly tell me that they have changed their decision, and will leave me alive, but their prisoner?"

"I speak the truth. If you still doubt me, read my thoughts."

She wondered if he would allow her to truly read his innermost thoughts. She doubted it; he would never open himself up to her totally.

"Take my thoughts," he said, reading her own. "I have nothing to hide from you." A shrewd look came to his face. "Or are you afraid of what you might find?" His voice held a note of humour.

"I am not afraid of you," she said. She considered his offer. Sending her perception into his mind held no appeal for her; he revolted her. "Tell me again how this companion could be found. Surely not even one of you would wish to be with me."

"You are wrong." He held his hands over his heart. "I would."

Romana stared at him, aghast. What was he saying? He would give himself into captivity for her sake?

"Yes," he said softly, "I love you, dear Romana."

She was appalled. "You cannot be serious! How can you say that, when you have been my most implacable enemy, hunting me always, trying to kill me? How could you be the Clan's staunchest servant, carrying out their evil commands, and have feelings for me, your quarry?" She looked at him with loathing, her mouth twisted with distaste. "It is a lie."

A pained expression came to his face. "It is no lie." When she made to retort, he held up his hand, silencing her. "Please listen to me. It is true that I do the Clan's bidding. I have destroyed all of your kind, and am indeed the hunter who has pursued you. But centuries ago, after we had slain the other Abominations, we had no idea that you still lived. The two who had created you were cunning, replacing you with a dead baby, while you were spirited away by Abdullah. For many years, the Clans were ignorant of your existence; until one night, we discovered you, quite by accident, in Cairo. I was sent to destroy you, and I would have carried out that task, but when I saw you, I felt something that I had never felt before; it was the sensation of longing that the mortals call love."

She listened, shocked at his admission. How could it be possible that he loved her?

"I know that you find it hard to believe, but I assure you that I speak the truth."

"No, it is not possible. How could you profess to love me, when all you have ever done is try to kill me, and have killed anyone who was ever close to me?"

"When I saw you, I knew that I would protect you always, slay anyone who tried to hurt you. I would suffer imprisonment for all eternity, to be by your side. I would always be your protector."

Romana gasped as though she had been struck a physical blow.

He closed his eyes, and held his arms to his sides, hands open, in an unguarded posture. "If you do not believe me, slay me now. I am defenceless. I will not try to stop you."

She stared at him, astonished. What he stated was impossible. Wasn't it? She could leap forwards, and kill him before he had the chance to defend himself. But a doubt was in her mind. She thought for a moment. "You said that you would always be my protector. The very fact that you led the hunters against me gives the lie to your statement."

He opened his eyes and smiled. "Does it?" He stroked his chin. "Let me see. There was that time in Paris. We pursued you. I am sure you remember that."

She cast her mind back over the years. Once again she saw the night that Gerald spoke of. They had closed in on her, chasing her over the rooftops of Paris, cutting her off from all avenues of escape. She had fled into the graveyard, hemmed in by the hunters. Romana had desperately sought a way out, but it was futile; Gerald had planned this hunt too carefully, there was no chance to escape this time. There had been thirteen of them. Four or five she could face, but not that many. She had found herself in the centre of a ring of death; the fangs of her relentless pursuers closing in like the jaws of a trap.

She had seen Gerald on the outside of that ring. She hated him with a passion that knew no bounds. *If only I can reach him and destroy him,* she had thought furiously, *my own death would at least count for something. I can avenge my kind, even if it means my own destruction.* She had steeled herself for a leap forwards into that deadly mob. Suddenly, the hunters had broken their ring and attacked, coming at her recklessly. Romana had been astonished; normally, they would attack singly, searching for an opening. They had got in each other's way, and in moments, three were down, torn and dead from her savage defence. As they had milled about in confusion, she had seen the impossible; a break in the wall of bodies that surrounded her. She had raced into the gap, slashing about herself madly. She had broken through, and had leaped into the night sky. She had fled, hearing Gerald's voice fading behind her as she plunged through the Parisian air: "You fools! You let her escape!" She had laughed like a madwoman, revelling in her incredible escape from certain death.

"Yes, an incredible escape," said Gerald, his voice bringing her out of her reverie. "How could you have possibly got away?"

"Luck," she said.

"No. There is no such thing. Take my thoughts. You will see how it really happened."

Romana searched his face for any sign of deception. There was none. He stood waiting for her to do as he'd asked. She warily sent her perception into his mind, and the memory of that far – off day came to her. Once again, she saw the frenetic chase over the rooftops, but this time, she saw it from Gerald's perspective. She saw the ring of hunters close about her fleeing shape as it fled into the graveyard. Then, they circled her snarling form, waiting for the kill. Gerald ordered them forwards, and the vampires came to the attack. She watched in amazement, as Gerald suddenly pushed the hunters himself within reach of her deadly talons and fangs. She killed them swiftly, and while the attention of the others was on her, she saw Gerald slay two of his own hunters, and make the gap himself. Her rush to escape was made possible by him! She watched, amazed, as the drama played itself out. She watched herself break through the demoralised vampires, and take to the air, laughing shrilly.

She returned to the present with a jarring shock. He spoke the truth! It was *he* who had helped her to escape, killing his own hunters to allow her to break free. She stared at him in mute astonishment.

"Do you see? I told you the truth. All of the times that you barely escaped, it was *I* who helped you. In Tokyo, Berlin, Hong Kong…I could go on…"

"How can you do this? You have killed your own hunters, rather than let me be taken or slain. You have broken the most immutable law, to kill your own kind. No vampire may slay another, excepting only the Abominations."

He looked down, and his voice came to her softly: "I have done all of these things, I have risked destruction at the hands of the Clans, who I serve. I have broken all of our laws, for your sake. I would do anything to be at your side." He looked up, and she was amazed to see tears, tears of blood welling in his eyes. One ran down his face, and he reached into his coat, and took out a silken handkerchief. He wiped the blood from his eyes and face, and then put the handkerchief back in his coat. "So you see, lovely Romana, I speak the truth. If you will but come with me, give this Duvall your blood, I promise that you will not be harmed, and I will stay at your side forever. I will love you until the end of time."

Romana was unconvinced of his sincerity. Somewhere deep within her, a voice was shouting *"No!"* Could it be a trap? Could the Clans have sent him to her, and not told him that they indeed intended her destruction? But his mind held no other information but that which he professed to be the truth. Could she believe him? She considered his words, and then said: "I will go with you." He smiled, but she held up her hand. "Yes, I will come, but only for Abdullah's sake." She watched the smile run away from his face. "I will do as the Clans ask, but only on my terms: I will give this Duvall my blood. Abdullah must be set free, and I will not allow myself to be made a prisoner."

"I do not think that will be acceptable," he said, frowning. "Perhaps you can reach a compromise with the Clan leaders?" He stared at her hopefully, and she could see the pain in his eyes. Her words had cut him deeply.

"Perhaps. I do not think so."

He sighed. "Well, let us dispose of this first." He looked down at the corpse of the girl at his feet. His eyes flared, and he sent fire into it. It burned swiftly, brightly, until nothing was left but ash. He turned to her and raised an eyebrow.

She looked at the man's body. She sent the fire, and it too blazed fiercely. In moments, it had been consumed, and the ashes of the man and the girl swirled in a breeze that had sprung up. Within a minute, they had blown away, leaving nothing to show that two mortals had met their end.

They took to the air, mounting swiftly into the night sky. As they flew back towards Erik's place, Romana's thoughts were filled with the expectation of seeing Abdullah again. She'd had no idea that he still lived. She owed everything to him; he'd shown her how to deal with the Dark Thirst, how to hunt and be cautious, so that she wouldn't be discovered and hunted down. They had lived in their own little world in the oasis, far from other vampires, and had been content with each other's company. Much more than just a companion, Abdullah had been a great teacher; her mentor, without his guidance, she would have been lost. She smiled, her joy filling her at the thought of once again having him at her side. *Erik*, she thought pensively, *I hope you understand the position I find myself in.*

At her side, Gerald sensed her thoughts, and flew along silently. He knew that Romana wanted to be with this mortal, but the pull of her desire to be with Abdullah was far stronger. He would bide his time. *She will be mine*, he thought, and then forced his mind elsewhere.

They reached the apartment, and landed on the balcony. Entering the doorway into the lounge room, they saw Erik and Sergei sitting on the lounge, warily watching Valeria, who was inspecting Erik's weapon collection. As they entered the room, Erik saw her, and came to his feet. He was about to address Romana, but when he saw the troubled look on her face, he subsided. At his side, the Russian sat shivering, sweat beading his face. He stared at the other two vampires, and licked his lips nervously.

Valeria turned. "Ah, Romana," she said silkily, "How pleasant to see you again." She smiled, showing her fangs.

"I doubt that very much," said Romana. She walked over to the two mortals. She hugged Erik, and sat down on the arm of the lounge.

Valeria sighed theatrically. "You wound me, dear Romana. Here am I, making sure that your two friends are safe and sound, and you do not even greet me civilly." She made a mock serious face.

Romana put her hand on Sergei's shoulder, and he trembled under the hardness of her fingers. His eyes were wide; one vampire scared him, but three positively terrified him. He expected to be killed at any moment. "Do not be afraid," Romana said soothingly, "No one will hurt you." He looked up at her, terror written all over his face.

Valeria laughed scornfully. "I told them that, but they would not believe me. *Stupid* cattle! They –"

"Valeria," Gerald said, his stern tones cutting her off, "Leave us."

She turned to him, her face unreadable. She slowly walked over and stood before him, and said in a babyish voice: "But I do not want to leave." She pouted like a little child.

A very dangerous little child, Erik thought. What would happen if they fought? Would he and Sergei be in even more danger? Valeria had not molested them, but her very presence was a threat, and the drummer knew that if they attempted to do anything, she would kill them without any qualms. Now that Romana and Gerald had returned, would she take Gerald's orders? And would he himself be a threat to them?

"I do not care what you want," Gerald said, his voice icy.

The redhead bristled at his tones. Her eyes narrowed in anger. She seemed about to leap into violent action, and Erik saw Gerald tense, readying himself. Valeria subsided, and the blonde dandy watched her carefully. She smiled disarmingly, and came back towards the lounge. "But we were having *so* much fun," she said lightly. "I was admiring all the little toys that Romana's pet has collected." She smiled at them, but her eyes were cold. Romana rose from the arm of the lounge, intending to stand between her and Sergei, who goggled at the two of them.

Suddenly, Valeria attacked in a blur of speed. She struck Romana aside, and wrenched Sergei to his feet, her steely arm went around his throat. Romana came to her feet, and went to throw herself at the redhead, but when she saw the Russian's plight, she stopped herself. *"Release him!"* she cried.

Gerald came storming over. *"Valeria!"* His eyes filled with blood.

Valeria looked at them scornfully. Her own eyes were crimson with bloodlust. She stroked Sergei's neck, her wicked talons making a scratching sound as she drew them along his vulnerable flesh. He whimpered like a trapped animal. The four of them stood frozen in a deadly standoff. Gerald and Romana hesitated; for fear that she would kill Sergei out of spite. She stared, gleefully defying them.

"Let him go, you bitch."

She started at the sound of Erik's voice. She looked, and he stood pointing a pistol at her. She laughed derisively. "Fool! Do you think your little gun and its puny bullets scare me?"

Erik looked her in the eye. "Not bullets, no...but a *flare*...well, ask Gerald here how one of his friends left us the other night." He cocked the hammer back.

Gerald regarded the drummer with new respect. Erik had moved quickly and carefully when all attention was on Sergei and his captor. *He is brave,* he thought, *for a mortal.* He addressed Valeria: "It is true, Valeria. The gun he holds is a Very pistol, a flare gun. You know what happens when one of us is exposed to flame..."

Valeria's face contorted in anger. "You would not *dare*!"

Erik stared her down. "Try me."

Her eyes blazed. Then a cunning look came to them. "I do not think you will do it," she said contemptuously. "You would kill your friend along with me."

"I'd rather him die like that than to have you drain his blood." His gaze shifted to Sergei, and he said: "What d'you say, Bear? Should I shoot this fuckin' bitch?"

The Russian was terrified, but Erik saw him regain some of his courage. "D-da! Shoot her! Do not…let her…kill me!"

"You are bluffing, mortal. I know how much your kind values their pitiful existence, and those of their *friends*." She sneered at the drummer. "You will not do it." Valeria stared at Erik disdainfully, her lip curled in contempt.

Erik met Sergei's wildly staring gaze. "I'm sorry, man." He started to put pressure on the trigger, and Sergei gulped and closed his eyes in anticipation of the fiery death about to engulf him.

Valeria gave the drummer a look of grudging admiration. It appeared that he would fire. "One moment," she said.

Erik paused. "Well?"

The redhead smiled wickedly. "You have forgotten something." With her free hand, she indicated Gerald. "You will certainly kill me with your little gun, but Gerald would take you before you could reload it."

Erik nodded. "True." Then he smiled. "But – "

"But what?" echoed Valeria.

"You've forgotten something too."

"And what is that?" said Valeria impatiently.

"Romana."

Romana stepped forwards, her gaze fixed on the redhead. Her hands spread open, talons ready, and she bared her fangs.

"Wait!" Gerald cried. "No one need die here tonight." He held his hands up in a beseeching gesture.

Ignoring him, Erik went on: "Gerald could kill me. But I'm sure

Romana would take him in turn." He matched Valeria's scornful expression with one of determination. "D'you want to see what happens?" His finger tightened on the trigger.

"*Stop!*" Valeria hissed. Her eyes flashed with fury. She snarled like an animal, and then she flung Sergei to the floor. In a flicker of movement, Romana had taken the Russian up, and she moved him away from his tormentor. She lowered the shaking man to the floor, and then stalked back towards Erik and Valeria.

The hatred that now filled Valeria shocked Erik to the core. Her anger of before appeared like mere irritation compared to the storm of rage that now emanated from every atom of her being. She seemed about to throw herself on him and tear him limb from limb, but the unwavering barrel of the Very pistol kept her in check. Still, her furious eyes bored into him, and he knew that if he relaxed for an instant, she would attack fiercely.

"Now," he said, "I think you'd better leave." His arm was growing tired; the weight of the gun was dragging his hand down, and it was all he could do to keep it aimed.

Gerald addressed the redhead. "Valeria." When she didn't answer, he raised his voice: "*Valeria!*"

She turned her savage face to him. For a moment, her gaze was unfocussed; her fury had taken away all of the reason that she possessed. She stared at him blankly, as though she wondered who it was that dared to speak to her in such tones. Then, slowly, Gerald saw her recognize him, and she remembered his authority. She backed away from the drummer, and came to Gerald's side. Her eyes never left Erik, or the pistol that held her in its sights.

"Very well," said Gerald, "We will leave. Remember what I have told you, Romana. I will return tomorrow for your answer." He backed towards the door, not trusting the drummer not to fire. Valeria at his side kept pace with him. *There will be another time*, he sent to her.

She glanced at him for a moment. *When that time comes*, she sent, *he is mine*. An almost imperceptible nod was Gerald's reply, and she smiled with satisfaction, knowing that he agreed to let her kill the foolish mortal who had dared to defy her.

They stood in the door; the sky behind them had turned a dull red, heralding the dawn. Valeria glowered at the three in the room, and then, with a movement impossible for Erik and Sergei to follow, they were gone.

Erik lowered his shaking hand. "*Shit,*" he said, a tremor in his voice, "That was lucky." He wiped the sweat from his brow.

"Lucky?" said Romana. "What do you mean?"

Erik opened the gun, showing her the loading chamber. It was empty.

"I didn't have time to find a flare to load the fuckin' thing." He looked sheepish. "Sorry."

Sergei looked up from where Romana had laid him. "*Bozhe Moi!*" he exploded. He staggered to his feet and stumbled over to the drummer, and took him in a hug that was deserving of his nickname. "Erik! You are fucking brave man!" Tears of relief ran down his reddened face into his beard. "You fool that bitch from hell!" He released the drummer, and his fearful gaze went to Romana. "I – I…"

"Do not worry, Sergei," she said softly. "I am not offended. Please believe me when I say that I will not allow you or Erik to be harmed."

The Russian regarded her with bewilderment. *How could she be different than those terrible creatures?* His mind whirled in confusion.

"Do not be mistaken," she said. "I *am* like them, a vampire; a creature that must have the blood of mortals; your kind, to survive." She reached out cautiously, and placed her hand on his shoulder. "But I will not harm those I care for. Erik is my love, and he is your friend. I will not hurt either of you."

Sergei looked at her, bewilderment written on his face. "But I do not understand –" He glanced at Erik, and then forced himself to look her right in the eyes. "How can this be?"

"It is part of the code that my mentor lived by. He taught me to live by it as well. To him, we were privileged to have the powers that we possess, and to show mercy on the innocent and to protect our friends was his most important rule."

Erik added: "And we're still alive, thanks mostly to Romana."

She smiled disarmingly. "And your little trick with the gun."

Sergei laughed. "Da! You are clever man, Erik, to think of that." His brow furrowed, as he considered Romana's words. She seemed to be telling them the truth. For a moment, his face showed the turmoil in his mind, but then, he reached a decision. He took Romana's hand, and shook it firmly. "If you speak truly, then I am your friend."

"Thank you, Bear." At the mention of his nickname, all tension in him melted away. Romana was surprised when he took her in his arms. She returned his hug, and when they parted, he grinned.

"You are still fine woman," he said. "If Erik will trust you, then is good enough for me."

Erik shook his head in bemusement. Only moments ago, Sergei had been terrified; now he accepted Romana, even though he knew what she was.

"Ah…" Sergei began.

"What's up?" Erik asked.

The Russian looked embarrassed. "I wonder if…" He trailed off, uncomfortable.

Romana put her arm around the drummer's waist. "He does not know how to ask you –"

Sergei rushed on, his words tumbling out: "I do not want to go home. Those…things – Can I sleep here somewhere? Please, Erik?"

"Sure, man. I'll get you a blanket." Erik went into the bedroom. He came back with a blanket, and laid it on the lounge. "Good night."

"I think you mean 'Good morning ,'" said Romana.

The early morning light was stealing in across the floor. Erik walked over to the door, and closed it, and the room became dark.

"Sleep well, Bear," Romana said. "No one will disturb you."

Sergei bowed to her, and then lay down on the lounge. He pulled the blanket over himself, and in moments, was sleeping soundly.

Erik and Romana regarded his peaceful face for a while, and then they walked into the bedroom. The door closed, and the only sound was Sergei's deep slow breathing.

5

Erik and Sergei

Romana burned like a torch. She blazed, wreathed in flames, her beautiful form incinerating in the deadly fire that consumed her. As Erik watched, horrified, she turned her gaze to him, and her eyes pierced his soul. He tried to scream, but nothing came; he felt that he was smothering; his breathing was being choked off. He attempted to go to her, but his legs refused to move. He was rooted to the spot, standing like a statue made of stone. He stretched out his arms, straining to touch her, but she was just out of his reach. He watched her burn; anguish contorting his face as tears flowed unheeded.

"This is your fault."

The voice came from behind him. He tried to turn around, but he couldn't move an inch. Sardonic laughter exploded into the air. Suddenly, Gerald stood in front of him. The blonde vampire sneered at him, mocking his immobility. "You want to save her?" He grinned wickedly, his fangs bared. Instantly, his demeanour changed. His face was suffused with anger; the drummer could feel it pouring from him in palpable waves of hatred. "You did this - *you*!" Gerald's teeth ripped at his throat, and he felt his blood flowing out of his body, and into the vampire's hot mouth. He stared at the still burning Romana over Gerald's shoulder, his heart thundering in his chest as his life fled.

Impossibly, the girl spoke from out of the inferno that she had become: "I love you." The flames rose higher, and he couldn't make out her face or form. With a final burst of awful heat, the fire suddenly died out, and nothing was left of Romana but a small pile of ash.

A scream of agony finally left his tortured throat. He sat up, crying out her name. He realised that he was in his bed. He shivered with the memory of the nightmare; sweat poured off him, and he rubbed his eyes vigorously, trying to blot out the terrible images. *"Fuck!"* His heart hammered, and his lungs worked like a bellows. He suddenly laughed in relief. He fell back, and then he looked at Romana's side of the bed, expecting to see her beautiful face.

It was empty.

He leapt to his feet, going to the bathroom. She wasn't there. He went into the kitchen, which was empty too. He ran into the lounge room, but only the sleeping form of Sergei met his anxious gaze. The Russian woke, sensing Erik's presence. He looked at the drummers face, and knew instantly what was wrong. "So, she is gone."

Erik shook his head in disbelief. "No, no, no, no, no!" He balled his fists, and he scanned the room, searching for someone to vent his frustrated anger upon.

The Bear sat up. "Easy," he said quietly. "You know where she goes. To this place in Switzerland, to save her friend."

Erik gritted his teeth in anger. "She told me she wouldn't go! Why did she lie?" He smacked his fist into his palm.

"This Abdullah, he means much to her." Sergei rose to his feet, and came and placed his meaty hand on the drummer's shoulder. "She looks on him as a father." He glanced down, and then hurriedly looked up and met Erik's eyes. "Maybe you get dressed, my friend."

Erik suddenly realised that he was naked. He blushed. "Sorry, man!" He quickly walked towards the bathroom.

"Is okay," the Bear said. "You have shower, and get dressed, I will find this laboratory."

Erik tossed him a look of thanks over his shoulder. Sergei went over to the computer that sat on the table. He sat down, and fired up the modem and turned on the PC. As it booted, he tried to remember the name of the place in Switzerland. *What was that name? It was French...* He absently looked at the monitor as he wracked his brain. Finally, the computer came up to the desktop, and he laughed to see that there was a picture of he and Erik there. They had their arms around each other's shoulders. Erik had a bottle of Jack in his free hand, and they both were grinning like idiots. He recalled where the picture had been taken. *Ah, yes. That was good night!* He grabbed the mouse and clicked on the Firefox logo, and waited for the Internet access. Once he was online, he went to the Google search page. He put biogenics in the search bar, and got six million, four hundred and twenty five results.

He made a wry face. He narrowed the search by adding Switzerland. That came down to fifty. *Good.* He scrolled down the page of results, until he came to Duvall Biogenics. *Aha! Yes, Duvall, that was the name.* He clicked on the page.

In the bathroom, Erik stood under a cold shower. He was still angry, but he was trying to understand Romana's reasons for leaving without telling him. He knew Sergei was right. She had told him herself that she owed Abdullah her life, and he knew that she felt obligated to do anything to save him. *But goin' with that fuckin' Gerald!* He thumped the wall of the cubicle with his fist. *That bastard's trouble. If he hurts her...*He shook his head. *Dickhead! She could take on five of him.* He turned off the shower, and stepped out, grabbed a towel, and began to dry himself off. He pulled on a pair of black jeans, a Rammstein t-shirt, put on his socks and boots, and walked out into the lounge room.

Sergei spun around in the chair. "I find him. Duvall Biogenic Laboratory. Is in the Swiss Alps." He pointed at the display.

Erik came and looked at the screen. The logo that Gerald had told

Romana about was there: the burning torch and holly leaves. He read parts of the information, but his mind was whirling with thoughts of what he could do. "Yeah, that's it alright. Now what?"

"Now, I think we need transport." The Russian grinned.

"*We?*" Erik said.

"Da. I am your friend, Erik. This Romana, you love her. She save us both, and keep those others from killing us. She keep her word." He stood, and placed his hand on the drummer's shoulder. "I come with you to Switzerland."

"Aren't you scared?" Erik remembered how Sergei had reacted to the vampires.

"Petrified." He laughed, but then his face became serious. "I know the danger. But I not let you go alone." He held out his hand. Erik took it, and felt his friend's strong grasp. They stood there for a moment, grinning as they shook hands. "Now, I call some friends." Sergei went over to the lounge room table, and picked up his phone. He dialled a number, and spoke rapidly in Russian.

Erik sat down at the computer, and read through the page. *Switzerland. Never been there. Chocolate, Nazi banks. Snow. Cool.* As the Bear's voice murmured in the background, he looked intently at the map that displayed the location of the laboratory. *How are we gonna get there?*

Sergei finished his call, and rang off. He came over. "Is good. I have jet take us to Switzerland, and helicopter take us up to the mountains."

Erik whistled in appreciation. "You don't fuck around." His brow furrowed. "How can we protect ourselves from Gerald and his pals?"

Sergei's face showed deep concentration. "Hmmm." Suddenly, his eyes lit up. "Tracers." He nodded to himself. "Da. Our vampires do not like fire, eh? Tracer bullets, and flares, we make sure we have them." He winked. "I have friends who can supply this."

Erik smiled. "Friends, eh?"

"Da, from when I serve in Russian Special Forces. Black market. I can get anything." He placed his finger along one side of his nose. "Is where I get the fine pieces you add to your collection."

"I hope you didn't have anyone killed so I could get them."

The Bear shook his head. "No, no. Never killed." He paused, and then he grinned. "Scare, maybe."

Erik laughed. "Well, that's okay. Who are we gonna get these weapons from?"

"There is group who sell weapons that I know. They send jet for us. Four of their team will go with us to Switzerland."

Erik frowned. "Do they know what the situation is?"

"No. I tell them only we have to rescue Romana and Abdullah."

Erik stood up. "I dunno, Bear. Won't they think it's a bit strange? Shouldn't you tell them about the vampires? Won't they wonder why you need tracers for every round?"

"I pay good money. They don't ask questions." He spread his hands. "Anyway, who would *believe* such creatures exist?"

"*You* do. You've seen them before." He became thoughtful. "I don't like it, Sergei. We can't hire these guys, and expect them to face Gerald and the others without knowing the risk." He paused. "Shit. They mightn't even go if they know what we're up against."

Sergei gave him a grim look. "Da. They are not stupid. Maybe I tell the leader, but not others, make him promise to keep secret."

The drummer could see by Sergei's expression that he didn't have much faith in that suggestion. "Would he do that?"

"Maybe."

"Have you told him about your experience in Afghanistan? Did he know about your vampire encounter?"

The Russian shook his head. "No. It was forbidden to speak of it." He shrugged his huge shoulders. "Maybe he hear of it, but think it lie."

"Did you ever ask him if he saw one?"

"Ha! No." Sergei walked over to the lounge, and sat down heavily. Erik came and joined him, putting his feet up on the table. The Russian leaned forwards, and picked up his glass of the night before, and the bottle of Stolichnaya. There was a little vodka left in it. He poured it into his glass, and drained it. He made a face. "Ecch.Warm." He put the glass and bottle down. "Erik?"

"Hmmm?" the drummer was turning over their situation in his mind.

"What if I bring Gyorgi here? We explain to him, you and I?"

"Do you think that would work? He mightn't like keeping his guys in the dark."

"Is possible. He may agree to keep secret. I call him." He pulled his phone out of his pocket, and dialled a number. He counted the rings: four, five, six. *Pick it up!* Nine, Ten. He was about to ring off, when someone answered, their voice heavy with sleep. "Ah, Naomi! Is Sergei here, can I speak to Gyorgi?" He waited while Naomi mumbled something, and then held his hand over the phone. "She get him," he said to Erik. They sat and waited for what seemed a long time. Finally, Gyorgi's raw voice came from the phone. "Gyorgi, I have question for you. Would you come to Erik's place to talk –" The Russian stopped. He listened, nodding. "Da, da. Okay. Where do we meet you? Da, I know it. Two hours? We see you then." The phone went dead. Sergei put it back in his coat. "He won't come here," he said. "He told me where to meet him."

"Pretty cautious." Erik got up. "Want some breakfast?"

"Da. Thank you. His business is dangerous, Erik. He must be careful."

"But he knows you. Doesn't he trust you?"

The Russian gave him a wry grin. "Trust? Gyorgi trusts no one."

The drummer smiled wryly, and turned and walked into the kitchen.

The Bear rose, and walked over to the weapons arrayed on the wall. His gaze roved over them while he thought of all the dealings that he'd had with Gyorgi. Most of the weapons had come from him, through the many contacts that he had. *Now, we have different job for you, my friend.* Sergei stroked his beard, wondering how they could explain the situation. The sounds of Erik cooking came from the kitchen, along with the mouth – watering aroma of fried eggs and bacon. The Russian's stomach grumbled. He patted it. *Patience, I will feed you.* He thought about the vampires; how he'd been so scared of them, especially that red – headed bitch. Now he was deliberately going to put himself in their way. He owed it to Erik, and Romana too. She *had* saved his life, even though she was one of them. Her love for his friend Erik was strong. *But this Abdullah, his hold on her is stronger.* He frowned. *What if she stays with him? My Erik will be crushed.* He turned at the sound of Erik's footsteps.

The drummer was carrying two plates, heaped with eggs, bacon, and slices of toast. He put them down on the lounge room table. "Dig in." He sat down, and followed his own advice.

Sergei joined him, wolfing down his food.

"Good?" Erik asked.

"Da. You save my life."

The drummer laughed. "I hope that's the only time I have to."

The Russian's face became serious. "Da."

They shared a look of foreboding. Then they turned their attention to their food, and ate in silence.

In two hours, they were sitting on a seat in a shopping mall. People wandered by; kids with skateboards, dressed garishly. Punks, emo kids, and metalheads. Parents led their young charges along, and here and there were a few old – timers, the men wearing socks and sandals, and colourful shirts. The old women wore dresses, mostly featuring patterns of flowers. Erik shook his head. "If I end up lookin' like that, shoot me."

Sergei laughed. "You are too cool, my friend. Nothing but black for you."

"What's wrong with black? You can wear anything with it." He stopped as he saw the Russian's eyes sharpen. Turning, he saw a tall, blonde man approaching them. He was well dressed in a green sharkskin suit, and wore a red Pierre Cardin shirt. On his feet were shiny black shoes of the finest quality. Here's a guy who likes the finer things in life, Erik thought. Behind him, two hard faced men in dark suits trailed along, their eyes constantly scanning the crowd. They wore earpieces.

The man stopped in front of them. He smiled, and Erik saw that he had many gold teeth. His eyes were an icy pale blue. "Sergei." His voice was raw, like he lived on cigarettes and whisky. Maybe he did. His two companions stood behind him, heads turning like the turrets of a battleship scanning for the enemy.

Sergei rose. "Gyorgi, this is Erik."

Gyorgi looked the drummer over. "You play music?"

"That's right. Drums."

"Yes, you look the part. Sergei tells me that you want to talk about our little venture." Those blue eyes bored into him. "Why?"

Erik wondered what to say. How could he tell this guy that they were going to save two vampires from a bunch of other vampires?

The Bear spoke: "Is important you understand the situation."

"Situation?" Gyorgi echoed. "What situation?" He folded his arms. "Explain."

"There's something you need to know…Ahh, about –" Erik stopped as Sergei gripped his arm.

The Russian looked about, and lowered his voice. "When you were soldier, did you hear of strange things that happen at night? Men missing? Attacks on camps?"

Gyorgi's eyes focussed on Sergei. "What do you mean?"

The Bear licked his lips. "*Vampyre*," he whispered.

Gyorgi grinned, displaying his wealth of gold teeth. He snorted derisively. He laughed once, a short bark of mirth. But then he saw the serious look on Sergei's face. He glanced at Erik, and saw that look mirrored there. His brow furrowed. "Surely you jest."

"No," said Sergei. "Is true. I myself have seen them."

Gyorgi looked at them like they were something that he'd just stepped in. "Are you *serious*? You want me to take you and your drummer friend here to Switzerland to see some *vampires*?" He laughed heartily, shaking with amusement until tears came. He wiped his eyes, flashing his gold teeth in a wide smile.

Suddenly, the atmosphere around the little group changed. The two minders scanned the area, sensing the subtle difference. Gyorgi spun around, and he too searched the people around them for an unknown threat. Erik rose to his feet, but Sergei gulped, and sat down and cringed on the seat. A mane of gorgeous red hair that was coming towards them attracted their attention, as it loomed over the crowd. Erik looked down at the Bear. They both knew whom that hair belonged to. The crowd parted, and they saw her.

Valeria strode up to them, beautiful and deadly. Her sensuous form swayed suggestively as she walked, the undulations of her body fascinating the two guards, and Gyorgi stared at her as though she was the most beautiful woman on earth. She was wearing a long green dress that matched her eyes and fitted her voluptuous figure like a second skin. It shone, and caught the light like some sort of metal. It was slit up the side, and her white thighs flashed as she walked. The low cut of the dress drew their eyes to her full breasts. She was stunning to look at. She smiled at them, and Gyorgi and his companions saw her vicious teeth. Gyorgi frowned in puzzlement, and the two minders stepped forwards, intending to stop her advance. She poked one of them in the chest with a finger, and he folded up like he was a puppet whose strings had been cut. The other minder stopped, and looked down at his comrade. Without taking his eyes off Valeria, he knelt down, and helped the stunned man rise. They staggered over to a bed of flowers that had a brick surround, and sat down on the edge. The injured man breathed heavily, and coughed as his friend held him upright. He bent forwards, and put his head between his legs. People in the crowd who'd seen the incident walked past, not wanting to get involved.

The redhead came and stood in front of Gyorgi, who stared at her, hypnotised. She waved at Erik and Sergei, and then turned to Gyorgi, pouting. "You do not believe that we exist," she said. "I am upset." Her green eyes flashed. "Would you like a demonstration of my powers?" She bared her fangs at him. Her lips were like blood on snow in her pale face.

The arms merchant gazed at her, his eyes going wide. He took in the palest skin that he'd ever seen; the predatory eyes that locked him in their unblinking stare, the wicked fangs, and he felt the abnormal strength that radiated from this unnatural creature. Then he looked over at his minders, and shook his head. "No. I think you've already shown me what you can do." He began to sweat. He realised that Erik and Sergei had spoken the truth; here was a vampire, alive – no – *undead*, in front of his amazed eyes.

"I am disappointed," she said in mock hurt tones. She shrugged, and then came over and sat next to Sergei, who moved as far along the seat as he could. The vampire crossed her long legs, and leaned back languidly. "Are you not pleased to see me?" she asked Erik.

The drummer watched her carefully. Surely she wouldn't attempt to do anything in the daylight, and with so many people around? Romana had told him that one of the Clans strictest laws was that the vampires could not show themselves.

She laughed huskily. "Do not worry," she said smiling. "I will not do anything." Her gaze went to Gyorgi. "I only came to show your friend here what he would have to deal with, if he went to Switzerland with you." She played with her hair, twisting the long red locks in her pale fingers. "Gerald would not be happy to see you. He told me to ensure that you do not come to interrupt him."

"I'm only interested in Romana, I don't care about the others," said Erik.

"Aah, but that is the point, hmmm? Romana agreed to come, and she must honour her word." She saw his expression change; the hurt look that came to his face. She smiled knowingly. "I see. You are upset because she did not tell you that she was leaving you." She rose in a single fluid motion. "Poor mortal. You are not the first that she has left behind." She came close to him; her face was inches from his own, and those green eyes looked into his soul. Valeria seemed to smell him, taking in a lungful of his scent. "You are attractive," she said. "You would make a fine companion. I can see why she loves you."

"Love?" Gyorgi echoed. "Is that possible? Can a human being feel anything for...for – "

"A creature like me?" Valeria stared at the arms merchant over Erik's shoulder. Her green eyes filled with blood. In a flash of movement, she had Gyorgi in her arms. As he stared into her pale face, shocked by the rapidity of her move, she leaned forwards, and kissed him deeply. He felt the coldness of her mouth, and her probing tongue was icy. Her body was as hard as any statue, and her breasts and hips pressed against him. Despite his horror of her unnatural flesh, he found himself becoming aroused. She was cold, but the ardour with which she kissed him was as hot as fire. An answering fire burned in his loins.

The two minders leaped to their feet, but Erik waved them back. They stood, uncertain what to do. The one who had been poked in the chest reached inside his coat, but his comrade stopped him.

A mother with a young boy and girl was passing. The boy stared, and the girl giggled to see them kissing. The mother hushed her, gave the couple a scathing look, and hurried her children along, disgusted by such a public display.

Valeria released Gyorgi, who gasped for air. As she drew back, the others saw two drops of blood on his lips; she had bitten him. She smiled at him. "Am I not beautiful?"

He took out a handkerchief, and dabbed at his lip. "As Death," he said. He winced.

The redhead laughed. "I will take that as a complement." She stepped up to him, and he flinched. She held up her hands. "I will not hurt you. I can fix that."

Gyorgi stared at her. "How?"

Valeria cocked her head to one side. "Let me show you."

He looked at her warily. Surely she wouldn't kill him in broad daylight? "Very well," he said cautiously.

She grabbed him under the chin, bit her own tongue, and licked his lip. It was done so quickly that he had no time to react, and his minders also were taken off – guard. This time, the one with his hand in his coat came forward, and stepped up to the vampire. She regarded him with disdain. Erik and Sergei watched closely; would the minder be so stupid as to try something? No. He backed off, staring at Valeria with a surly look on his face. But he realised that he was no match for her.

"I am sorry that I hurt you," Valeria said, "But we are easily aroused, and you are so – tasty." She grinned wickedly.

Gyorgi's tongue tingled. Her blood burned in his mouth, and on his lip. He felt it gingerly, and was shocked to find that not only had the bleeding stopped, but also there was no sign of any wound at all. He stared at her. "How?" he said again.

She flipped her hand casually. "It is our blood. We have very fast healing properties in it." Her green eyes gazed into him. "With enough of it, you would become like me – immortal."

"Is that how you became a vampire?"

"Yes. We call it Making." She indicated Erik. "Erik's lover is a Born vampire, not Made. She was created by two of us who disobeyed one of our strictest laws."

"Vampires can be *born*?" he said in disbelief.

Valeria nodded. "But not any more. Once they were, but they were hunted down and destroyed. Now, only Romana is left."

"And they want her blood for some freak who's been experimenting on them," added Erik.

"Professor Duvall would not like to hear you speak of him that way," Valeria said.

"I don't give a fuck what he thinks. I want to see Romana."

Valeria turned and glared at the drummer. "Remember who you are talking to, *mortal*," she hissed. "I am here to ensure that you do not try to go to her. Gerald told me to keep you away; he did not say if you should be alive or dead." Her eyes filled with blood. "I would prefer you dead." She stepped away from them rapidly, and then turned. "I will be watching," she said, and disappeared into the crowd.

"What a magnificent creature," said Gyorgi.

6

Gyorgi

Erik and Sergei sat in the back of the Mercedes. Gyorgi and his two heavies had taken them from the mall, and driven them to a warehouse down on the docks. He'd got out of the car, told them to stay put, and gone inside. That was an hour ago. The two goons stood on either side of the car, scanning the area for potential threats.

"Well, this is *fun*," said Erik sarcastically. He leaned forwards, and peered out of the window. Seeing nothing but the same old buildings that he'd seen since they got there, he fell back into the seat, drumming his hands on his thighs. He sighed.

The Bear smiled. "Are you bored?" He used a toothpick to clean his nails.

Erik threw up his hands. "This Gyorgi brings us here in a rush, says we mustn't waste any time, and then we sit around for ages," he said impatiently. "What the fuck is he doing in there?"

As though his words were a signal, the side door that Gyorgi had entered by opened, and he appeared in it. He walked over to the car, and the guard on his side opened the door. He put his head in, and regarded them. He smiled when he saw the irritated look on Erik's face.

"You don't like to wait, do you, eh? Well, everything is ready now, you can come in." He stepped back and swept back his arm in a gesture of invitation. His golden teeth flashed as he grinned again.

The pair got out of the car, Erik stretching like a cat. He didn't like to sit for so long, not unless he was sitting on his drum stool. He took another look around, and coughed, as he smelt the stench of the docks. There was garbage everywhere, and the buildings had stains that looked as if they'd been pissed on for a thousand years. It sure smelt like it.

"Shit, what *stinks*?" he held his hand over his mouth and nose.

Gyorgi looked at him with amusement. "You do not like the heady aroma of fish?" He turned and led the way, chuckling to himself.

Erik glared at his back, and then he and Sergei followed him. They entered the warehouse, and the door closed.

Inside was a hive of activity. Men worked at a conveyer belt, packing guns into crates, and then sending them down the line, where they were loaded onto pallets. As they walked through the busy area, Erik saw trucks waiting for the pallets in a loading bay at the rear of the warehouse. Forklifts were loading the trucks, filling them with the instruments of destruction. Others worked at computers, filling orders, and communicating with buyers online. Several men walked about the floor, checking amounts and dispatch orders on clipboards. The drummer shook his head amazedly at the organized chaos. The thrum of machinery and the sound of the forklifts as they tore around the floor were deafening. It was hot, despite the large fans in the roof, which turned rapidly. They walked past the conveyer belt, and ascended stairs that led to an office high above the factory floor.

Once inside, the door closed, and the noise of below was cut off. They felt the temperature drop instantly. An air conditioner mounted in the window hummed softly to itself. The office was sumptuously furnished with antique furniture. A large desk dominated the room; behind it was a high-backed leather chair. A long leather lounge filled one wall, and a small coffee table sat in front of it. On the floor was a Turkish rug, blazing with colour. Hung around the walls were pictures of weapons, blueprints, and exploded views of pistols and machine guns. The two minders took up positions on either side of the door. Gyorgi walked over to an ornate cabinet that stood along the opposite wall. He opened it, and produced a bottle of Stolichnaya. He picked up some glasses that were on the top of the cabinet, and came over to Erik and Sergei. He motioned for them to sit. They sat down on the lounge as he opened the bottle, and poured for each of them. He handed them a glass each, and then took the bottle and sat behind the desk. He raised his glass. "Success."

They returned the toast. The Bear sat back and enjoyed his drink, but Erik leaned forwards, asking: "Are you sure you understand what we're going up against?"

Gyorgi regarded the drummer. "Of course," he said. "Nosferatu. The vampires of my childhood." He took a long drink. "They actually exist. I'm surprised." He refilled his glass. "I'm not surprised very often. Usually, it's unpleasant. But this…"

"You don't think the fact that vampires are real is an unpleasant thought?" Erik put his glass down on the table. "And that they could kill us all?"

Gyorgi laughed softly. "I'm not afraid to die. I've fought many battles, faced death many times. In Afghanistan, China, Germany, Japan. My business takes me to many dangerous places, and the people that I deal with can be dangerous too." He placed his hands on the desk. "But I like a challenge. This – Valeria and her friends, it should be interesting to see what happens."

"*Interesting?*" echoed Erik. "They tried to kill me. They're deadly."

Gyorgi's ice – blue eyes stared at him. "And you are in love with one of them."

"That's different," Erik said. "Romana's –"

"Not like the others, hmm?" Gyorgi smiled. "She is a merciless killer like them. Do not doubt it." He sat back in his chair. "But you say she saved you from them, yes? And that she professes to love you." He stroked his chin reflectively. "Imagine having such power…immortality…"

"I'm not interested in that shit," Erik grated. "I just want to make sure she's okay."

"Oh, you aren't interested in living forever; the years leaving you untouched, never aging, or becoming sick, or…dying?" Gyorgi shook his head, amused.

The drummer gazed at him. *This dickhead wants to be one of them!* Aloud, he said: "Don't forget, that they have to live on the blood of mortals, and the Clan's rules are absolute; any one of them that breaks those rules are hunted down and destroyed."

Gyorgi's golden teeth flashed. "I'm used to living off other people. I need them to survive. We all need someone to survive." He waved his hand dismissively. "Don't worry, I'm not the slightest bit interested in becoming a vampire." He opened his jacket, and removed a gold cigarette case. Opening it, he took out a small lighter and a cigarette, lit it, took a deep drag on it, and exhaled a cloud of smoke. He put the lighter back, and returned the case to his jacket pocket. "Many people have tried to kill me, but have failed. I think even a vampire would find it impossible."

Erik looked at him closely. Gyorgi pretended not to be interested in the vampires, or even becoming one, but the drummer knew that he lied. He knew without any reservation that Valeria, and the power and eternal life that she and the Clan represented fascinated Gyorgi. By his side, even Sergei regarded the arms dealer through doubtful eyes.

There was a knock on the door. Gyorgi called out for whoever waited outside to enter. One of the heavies opened the door, and a man came in. Erik checked him out as he sauntered over to the desk. He looked Mexican, with dark olive skin and black hair, which was slicked back with oil. He wore faded blue denim jeans, and a black leather jacket over a white t-shirt. Converse hi top sneakers were on his feet, and a pair of Raybans hung down from the top of his t-shirt. He strode across the floor, exuding confidence, even arrogance. *Fuck, it's James Dean*, thought Erik wryly.

The newcomer halted in front of Gyorgi's desk. "Everything is ready, boss."

"Ramon," Gyorgi said, indicating Erik and Sergei, "These gentlemen are our passengers."

Ramon turned, eyeing them both. He folded his arms, and leaned back on Gyorgi's desk. His scornful glance swept over them, and a snide grin came to his lips. "Mister Rock and Roll," he said contemptuously, looking at Erik; "And The Bear." He snorted derisively. "What shithole are you goin' to now, Bear?"

Sergei returned his gaze. "Is nice to see you too, Ramon." He rose to his feet, drank the last of his drink, and put the glass down on the table. "I pay, you go where I say."

The Mexican's eyes flared, but he made no reply.

"Ramon is my pilot," Gyorgi said into the tense air. "Ramon, you will enjoy this. We go to see some vampires."

The pilot looked over his shoulder at his boss. Then he looked back at the two sitting on the lounge. He started to snigger, and then laughed outright. "*Vampires!* Are you fuckin' *jokin*? That's a good one, Bear! I might give you a discount for that!" He slapped his thigh, but subsided when he saw their faces. "You really mean it," he said, amazed.

"I have seen one of them for myself," said Gyorgi, "She was powerful and beautiful. She was definitely not human."

"There's many more where we're going to," added Erik, "unless you're scared, and we'll just have to get another pilot." He'd disliked the look of the Mexican, and now that he'd heard his arrogant bluster, liked him even less.

"*Fuck* you," Ramon hissed.

"Be still," Gyorgi said, quietly, but venomously. With a sneer on his lips, Ramon subsided, glaring at the pair on the lounge. Erik returned his stare, but Sergei smiled, and sauntered over to stand in front of the Mexican, who looked at him with undisguised contempt.

Without warning, the Russian punched Ramon in the stomach. The pilot doubled up, gasping, and fell to his knees. His glasses dropped onto the rug. He coughed and tried to draw breath. The two goons started forwards, guns appearing from nowhere, but Gyorgi raised his hand, and they stopped. Sergei grabbed Ramon by the collar of his jacket, and hauled him to his feet. Erik sat on the edge of the lounge, watching closely. What had Sergei done that for? What would happen now? He was aware of the two heavies standing just in front of him, and he'd seen their guns. He and Sergei were unarmed. He waited to see what would happen next, his heart pounding like the drums he pounded on.

His voice low and menacing Sergei said: "I remember last time I fly with you." He drew the still gasping Ramon in, until their faces were almost touching. "This time, I watch you." He flung the Mexican to the floor. Ramon looked up, hate filling his eyes. The Bear waited for him to say something, but the pilot just got to his feet, eyes burning with anger. He stood, his chest rising and falling furiously. They faced each other in the abrupt silence, each watching the other for any sudden move.

There was another knock at the door. The guard nearest it looked over at Gyorgi, who nodded, and he opened the door, to admit another man. This one was a tall and skinny teenager, wearing a black t-shirt that had the word Null blazoned across the front in glowing green letters. Black jeans clad his legs, and he had on industrial boots like Erik's. Thick-lensed glasses perched on his nose. His hair was a long and greasy brown. As he saw the standoff between the Russian and the Mexican in front of him, he stopped, standing in the middle of the room.

Sergei turned. "Bear!" said the arrival, and walked over to the Russian, a huge smile on his face. "Hey, dude, I haven't seen you in ages." He embraced Sergei. He looked at Ramon, still seething. "What's happenin'?"

The Bear smiled. "Nothing. Ramon and I, we have little chat." Ignoring the pilot, he spun him around, and with his arm around his shoulder, walked the man over to Erik. "Erik, this is Null. He is computer wizard."

Null goggled at Erik. "*Fuuck! Maschinekult!* You're Erik Davis. I've seen you guys play at The Crypt." He stared at the drummer, a fan-boy's feverish light in his eyes. The glasses made them look like they were the size of golf balls. He put out his hand, and shook Erik's vigorously, his grin threatening to split his face in half.

Gyorgi chuckled. "So, you have a big fan." He leaned back in his chair. "Did you want to see me, Null? Or did you want to meet the famous Erik?"

Null released Erik's hand, saying: "Uh, yeah. Dutchie said he's ready for you."

Gyorgi clapped his hands together. "Excellent." He rose from his chair. "Come, gentlemen." He came around the desk, and put his hand on Ramon's shoulder. His steely blue eyes pierced the pilot, and the Mexican blanched under the arms dealer's scrutiny. Erik and Sergei realised that Gyorgi was warning him not to cause any more disruption. Gyorgi smiled at Ramon, but his eyes were hard. He slapped him on the back, and then crossed the room, where he indicated that they should leave through the door, which one of the heavies had opened. Ramon stayed where he was, his face flushed with anger, his eyes fixed on Erik and Sergei as they left the room.

They filed out, going down the stairs, and followed the Georgian across the noisy warehouse towards a sealed-off room at the back. Erik found Null walking beside him, talking incessantly in a never-ending flow of words.

"And the drums on '*Cap It*,' are they electric?" he asked.

Erik smiled. "Yeah, there are electric drums on there, but we also added some garbage bin lids, metal drums, all sorts of shit that we sampled and triggered."

Null nodded enthusiastically. "Cool. I thought that's what all the crashin' and stuff was." He grinned at Erik. "I bet someone that's what was happenin,' but he said bullshit."

"Now you can tell him that you're right, Erik Davis himself told you." He pointed at the other's t-shirt. "Null?" he queried.

Null laughed. "Yeah. It means '*nothin'*. Wikipedia gives its meaning as 'of little or no consequence.' When I was at school, I was the nerd that all the jocks picked on. They said I was nothin'." He clenched his fist. "But I showed those fucks. I make shitloads of money through programmin' and stuff for Gyorgi. Most of them are in shit jobs, with naggin' wives and ungrateful kids, and insane mortgages." They both laughed.

The group stopped in front of a large metal door. Two guards stood to either side. At Gyorgi's nod, one of them turned and opened the door, and they went in. Inside was a shooting range, with targets ranged along a wall at the far end of the room, which was soundproofed. A table stood near the door, filled with pistols, rifles, and machine-pistols, and a stack of magazines. Gyorgi walked over to it, picked up a Mac Ingram, and a magazine. He fitted it, and turned to Erik.

"Have you fired one of these?" the Georgian asked.

The drummer shook his head. "Only a few old pistols; Webleys, Colts. No autos."

Gyorgi smiled. "You should enjoy this." He indicated the table. "When you told me of the nature of your friends, I ensured that we would have the weapons we needed to protect ourselves. Every bullet is a tracer." He addressed one of the goons who stood at the door: "Dim the lights."

The room became darker. Gyorgi cocked the machine-pistol. He walked to the firing line. Bringing the gun up, he thumbed the safety off, aimed, and pressed the trigger. With a chattering roar and a bright flare of light, the bullets spewed towards the target, each one of them drawing an incandescent line through the air. The target exploded as the hail of steel tore into it, disintegrating. He emptied the magazine, and then turned, a grin on his face. The acrid smoke hung in the air, filling their nostrils. He came back, leaning the gun on his shoulder. "I think even your vampires would find that a hot reception."

"Impressive," said Sergei.

"You must realise how difficult it was to obtain so many tracers," Gyorgi said. "It means that my price will be higher."

Sergei looked at Erik. The drummer had an amused look on his face, as though he'd expected something like this. Their eyes met, and the Russian could see that Erik would do anything to get Romana back. What was money? He nodded in response to the Bear's inquiring gaze. "Da," said Sergei, "We agree."

Gyorgi looked disappointed. "I thought that you would try to bargain."

"Sorry man," replied Erik, "I don't care about money, I just want my girl."

Gyorgi shrugged. "Very well. Here, try this for yourself. I know that Sergei is familiar with automatic weapons." He held the machine-pistol out to the drummer, who took it, and crossed over to the table. He picked up another magazine, and clipped it in. He walked back to the firing line, and grinned at the Bear. One of the Georgian's lackeys was setting up another target down the far end, so Erik waited for him to finish, inspecting the gun, familiarising himself with its operation. When the target was ready, Erik waited for Gyorgi's man to clear the firing range, and then stepped up, bracing himself. He flicked off the safety, and lined the target up. He squeezed the trigger, and the gun rattled again, the flash from the barrel blinding in the dark room. The tracers flared brightly as they ripped into the target, which was torn apart like the first target had been. Erik flicked the safety back on, removed the magazine, and walked back, grinning like a boy with a new toy.

Gyorgi laughed. "Good. That will do." He gestured towards the door. "Come."

They followed him out of the door, Erik giving the machine-pistol to the man who'd set up the targets.

7

The Clans

The room was dark. Stone columns led up to the high ceiling, vanishing into the darkness above. Carvings decorated them, composed of vampires hunting their prey, carved when Egypt was young. Gorgeous tapestries were hung around the walls, rich colours subdued in the dim light. Candles lent the room a gloomy grandeur, their soft light creating an amber glow that enhanced the darkness, rather than illuminating it. The carpet that lay on the floor had once been rich with colour, but now it was faded; its reds and yellows muted by the dust. The walls were of a yellowed marble, veined with black. Once, centuries ago, they had been a brilliant white, but the passage of time, and the candle smoke, had deadened their vibrancy.

A sepulchral silence reigned in this gloomy chamber. No sound echoed in that vaulted space. A thick dust was on the floor, and upon a raised stage at one end of the room, was a huge oval table, its dark wood also covered with the fine dust of centuries. A dozen chairs were set at this table, their once fine upholstery faded and worn. An atmosphere of neglect clung to everything in the room, as though it had been left to decay and rot, ignored by those who had once sat in those chairs.

At either side of the stage were heavy curtains, festooned with spider's webs, and coated with the ubiquitous dust. Set in front of them on either side of the stage were two statues, each of them vampires. One was a woman; her eyes wild, her hair a long mane that streamed behind her in an imaginary wind. Her face was terrifying. Her deadly fangs were displayed, ready to drink blood, and her arms were spread wide, as though she rushed to embrace her prey.

The other, a man, stood aloof, like some omnipotent god of destruction, his eyes filled with contempt, his arms folded in a representation of superiority. It was as though he gazed upon lowly mortals, and looked at them with disdain. His lips were set in a sneer, his fangs showing beneath the curling lip. The sculptor who had fashioned these two statues had given them such a lifelike appearance, they seemed ready to leap off the stage, and fly from the room.

Between these horrific images of vampiric power, upon the wall in the centre of the stage, was a record of the Clans, like that of a family tree. It began with two names at the very bottom of the record, and spread and branched out in ever-increasing branches as it went higher. Ten feet above the floor of the stage, it had widened to encompass the entire wall. The names set into the stone were inscribed in silver, dulled now also with the passage of time. Once, they must have shone out, their lustre shining in the candlelight. The names of the heads of each Clan were raised upon a reddish stone, so that, at a glance, one could tell who each of them was.

Halfway up this roll of names, there was an entire branch that had been erased; excised as though with hammer and chisel, torn from the wall. Each of the names had been obliterated in this manner, and the deep marks and scratches in the wall around them showed evidence of the frenzy in which they had been removed. Upon closer inspection, one of the chairs at the table had been smashed and torn as well; the back was gone, and the seat had been ripped up.

At the far end of the room was a pair of huge wooden doors, carved ornately with the figures of skulls that screamed. The dust hung on the massive metal bolts that were shot home, and cobwebs criss-crossed the portal, giving evidence that the doors had not been opened for a very long time.

Suddenly, the funereal stillness was broken by the sound of the bolts moving from their place. They slid slowly open with a loud scraping of rusted metal on metal, and then there came the dull creaking of the massive doors opening inwards. The spider webs were torn away as the doors opened wide, and met the walls with a dull thud. Dust rained down from the ceiling, and pattered upon the discoloured carpet.

Into the open doorway there came a procession of ten shadowy figures. All were pale of face, and their eyes were dead, like chips of glass, reflecting the candlelight, as they progressed along the floor and made their way up to the stage. They ranged themselves about the table, each going to their assigned place. They stood waiting.

Their heads turned as one as two forms stood in the doorway. The new arrivals paused, as though regarding the others, and counting their number. Then, they advanced across the room, and as they came into the candlelight, they were revealed as the very image of the two statues that were upon the stage. The vampires standing at the table bowed to them, their cold hands crossed above their unbeating hearts.

The man smiled coldly, and then took his place at the head of the table. His companion stood behind him as he seated himself. His cold gazed roved the faces of the ten gathered there, and he nodded to himself in satisfaction. His eyes lingered over the broken chair for a moment, and then he indicated that they should sit, and there was a scraping of chairs as they sat down. He looked down the room, and waved his hand. The doors closed.

He was tall and blonde, with blue eyes that were like the sea. He was Karl, the head of all of the Clans, a remnant of the Germanic tribes that had remained unconquered by the Roman Empire centuries ago. He had fought his way to the top of this vampire community, killing all who stood in his way. He was the very image of the Aryan superman. He was dressed in a dark grey Armani suit, but his face and penetrating eyes still held the wildness of the dark German forests, and the furs and skins that the fierce tribesmen had worn would have suited him better. It was easy to imagine him with a bloodied axe in his hand, fighting against the Roman legions.

The woman behind him was a Russian, known only as Irina. Her wild dark mane looked just like her statue. Her eyes held an animal ferocity that lay just below the surface. Even among her own kind, she was feared, for she was impulsive, and all there knew of her unwavering loyalty to her maker, Karl. More than once before, she had destroyed those who had gone against him. She wore a gothic red dress; she preferred to make a broad statement in her clothing, and she loved finery.

Now Karl's voice came; thick, with a guttural German accent: "So," he began, "you are all here." His cold smile came again. "Good."

"Why have you summoned us?" A tall thin man asked, his voice filled with irritation. He was Antonio Valetta, the head of the Italian vampires. His short dark hair was oiled, and a neat moustache adorned his upper lip. He also was clad in a smart suit, but unlike Karl, he had the look of a modern businessman. He was much younger than the German, only three hundred years old.

Karl's icy gaze fixed upon him. "You know why," he said roughly. "Romana has been found, and brought to us. She has agreed to Duvall's terms, as have we."

"Not *all* of us have agreed," said a gorgeous Indian woman. She was dressed in a black suit, and it and the long black hair that flowed down her back and her dark eyes accentuated the whiteness of her fangs as she spoke. Her name was Iranda.

"Yes, that is true," added a man to Karl's left. He was blonde, and dressed in a blue suit, and like the German, he also had an air of antiquity about him. He was Octavius Quintilius Flavius, from ancient Rome, and next to Karl was the oldest vampire in the room.

Karl looked at them in turn. "So," he said silkily, "You do not agree with my decision?" A sense of menace flowed from him. His eyes narrowed angrily.

"We did not say that," said Octavius. His gaze took in all of them. "We did not agree to bring the Abomination here. She is dangerous. Care must be taken."

"Of *course* she is dangerous," said Irina, her voice overflowing with contempt. "But so are *we*."

Karl smiled at her words. "Indeed," he said. "Duvall has promised me that she will pose no threat to us."

"And you believe him?" retorted Valetta. "A mortal?" He rose to his feet. His eyes swept over the gathering. "The same mortal who has been torturing and experimenting on us for years, and now you want to trust him to keep his word?" He folded his arms, and his stare was like ice.

Karl sneered. "The last time I looked, I was the leader of this Clan," he said, his voice low and ominous.

"That does not mean that you can make decisions without our consent," said Iranda.

Now Valetta smiled. "Yes," he added, "you must –"

Karl's fist crashed onto the table. *"Must!"* he roared. "I must do *nothing*! This group has only survived because of me. *I* am the leader of the Clans." His eyes filled with blood, and his anger radiated from him in waves of palpable energy.

Iranda and Octavius subsided, knowing that they had pushed the volatile German too far, but Valetta seemed not to realise the danger. He unfolded his arms, and leaned forwards, his hands splayed out upon the tabletop. "There are those of us who think that you have made a grave error in involving this Duvall in our affairs." He glanced at the others, seeking their support, but Karl's angry outburst had made them uneasy.

Irina fixed him with a steely gaze, her eyes also filled with crimson. Her body was coiled like a spring, and hatred for the Italian suffused her face.

Karl yawned theatrically, patting his mouth. Then his reddened orbs pierced Valetta through. "So," he said menacingly, "you question my authority to rule?" Every atom of his being became filled with dangerous pent up force, and all of them sensed that he was like a snake about to strike. Unconsciously, the other vampires shrank away from Valetta, knowing that the German's hate was boiling over.

Suddenly realising that he'd gone too far, the Italian stood erect. "N-no –" he began.

Irina's eyes flashed, and the Italian exploded into flame, shrieking. He fell backwards, stumbled, and dissolved into ash that filled the air of the chamber with a grey cloud.

The Russian smiled, her fangs displayed. She hissed in satisfaction. She'd never liked the annoying Italian, and now he was well disposed of. She swept the group with a menacing glance, waiting for another of them to oppose her maker, but they all sat silently, their faces unreadable.

As the ash drifted down and mixed with the dust of centuries, Karl rose to his feet. "Are there any other objections?" he asked. No one replied. "No? Good. Let us continue." At his back, Irina watched them all closely, but her sudden fierce attack had quieted any spirit of rebellion.

Karl waved his hand once more, and the doors opened ponderously. The group at the table turned their attention to the doorway. Framed in the entrance were two figures. They began to walk towards them, and when they came into the light of the candles, the onlookers realised that it was Romana and Gerald. They strode down the carpet, and came to a stop before the stage. The atmosphere in the room became tense.

One of the vampires, a French woman, leapt to her feet. "You dare to bring *that* here!" She pointed at Romana. Her eyes were gorged with blood, and her fangs were bared in a display of anger. Her agitation raced through the group like a brush fire. Others rose to their feet; their protesting voices joining hers in a bedlam of noise.

"*Sit down!*" bellowed Karl. He fixed them all with a deadly gaze. They subsided, returning to their seats. All of them stared at Romana, who hadn't moved or spoken. "Romana is here as our guest," Karl said, his voice dangerously calm. "We will treat her with respect."

"*Respect?*" Iranda said with revulsion. "It was her kind that tried to destroy us!"

"Oui," added the French woman, "We cannot –"

"If you defy me again, Jeanette, I will dispose of you as I disposed of that fool Valetta," Karl said icily.

Jeanette's eyes narrowed in anger, but she made no reply.

"They make a good point," said a blonde man. He was Edmund Drake, Gerald's father, and Maker. Hundreds of years ago, he had been an English Earl. Now, he still had the affected air of English nobility, although he didn't wear the finery that Gerald clad himself in. He indicated Romana with a flick of his hand. "Are we certain that we can trust this – *Abomination?*" His tones were foppish, as though he sat listlessly at a garden party of the sixteen hundreds, bored like all of the other aristocrats who sat around him, filled with ennui.

"I have given my word," Romana said.

"*Your word?*" echoed Jeanette. "What could *your* word be worth, when—"

Romana stepped forward, her eyes blazing. "I am not here to listen to you fight among yourselves," she said angrily. She swept the group with an icy glare. "It is *your* word that is to be questioned. For centuries you have hunted me, because of my kind, and what they did to you. Not once in all of that time have I sought you out. All I wish is to be left alone."

Jeanette sat there smouldering with hate. How *dare* this creature come in here and speak to them as though they were young fledglings! She should be taught who was master here.

Romana fixed her with a freezing glance. "Take care, Madame Fleur. Your thoughts are dangerous. I could destroy you all, and you know it."

"*You?*" exploded Edmund. "I think you value your powers too highly!"

"You are welcome to put them to the test," Romana said menacingly.

"Hold, Edmund," said Octavius, raising his hand imperiously. He studied the girl before them. Looking deep within, he saw great reserves of strength, and something else...the gift of seeing the future?

Reading his thoughts, the girl said: "Yes. It was my mother's power; she was a Romani Gypsy, and she passed it on to me. I can foresee what is to come."

"What is to come is that you will give Duvall your blood, and then you will be our prisoner, never to know freedom again," Iranda said arrogantly.

"Do you think so?" Romana replied. "I can see a future where there are no Clans, and all vampires will be hunted down and wiped out. Mortals will learn of our existence, and be afraid. And what men fear, they destroy." She smiled a grim smile. "With their fire and their science, they will come, and you will all burn."

"And where is your place in this world without vampires?" asked a tall black man. He was Kunda-Bele, and had once been a witch doctor in darkest Africa.

"I do not know," she said. "I cannot see my own future, only that of others."

Edmund snorted derisively. "How disappointing." He laughed.

The others joined in, all except Kunda-Bele, Octavius, and Karl. The German had been searching Romana's mind, and what he saw struck him with fear. The girl did possess such powers that she boasted of; she *could* kill them all. The fools that sat there were oblivious of what danger she posed. Only the three of them realised that Romana was such a threat to them.

"It is not wise to discount the visions of one who can see," said Kunda-Bele, his rich bass tones cutting through the laughter. He stood up, and bowed to the girl, acknowledging her powers.

"*What?*" cried another of the male vampires, "Do you believe this mumbo-jumbo she spouts?" He was French; Claude deMontforde was his name, he was an arrogant member of the Clans, always argumentative and outspoken.

The African turned to him. "Mumbo-jumbo?" he echoed. "Do you think *my* powers are not real?" He gestured at deMontforde, and began to chant in primitive tones.

DeMontforde gasped, and his hands went to his throat. He began to choke, his eyes bugging out of his conceited face. The laughter died off, as they all stared at the struggling figure, and watched him slide out of his chair, and fall to the floor. The group began to plead for Kunda-Bele to stop, but he continued to chant, his face a mask of primeval hatred. The voices clamoured, and the Frenchman choked and gasped, writhing on the dusty floor in the grip of the magic that he had discounted.

Irina watched, her face filled with pleasure. She hated deMontforde, and was relishing his suffering, enjoying it with a sadistic delight. She'd never seen Kunda-Bele use such a spell before, and watched with great interest, but without any feeling, as though she was seeing a demonstration, or a play.

"*Enough!*" Karl roared. Kunda-Bele stopped chanting, and his hands fell to his sides. The Frenchman staggered to his feet, his eyes filled with hatred, focussed on the tall African. Kunda-Bele returned his gaze, his face set like stone. Silence fell. "No more of this," said Karl. Kunda-Bele sat down, ignoring deMontforde's stare. Karl fixed him with a withering glance, and he too sat down, knowing that he'd gone too far, and knew that the German would allow no more disruption. Karl smiled to himself in satisfaction as the Frenchman sat cowed by the threat. He returned his attention to Romana. "You are strong, little one," he said. "And you have courage. I admire that." He walked around the table, and came down to stand in front of her.

Romana looked into his eyes unflinchingly. "I have come as I promised. Show me Abdullah."

The German smiled. "All in good time. Please allow me to introduce the leaders of the Clans to you." He pointed them out, one by one, starting from one end of the table. He indicated a Japanese woman, dressed in a rich blue silk business suit. "This is Mariko Sato." The woman made no response, but sat there staring at Romana, her face an inscrutable mask, with the unemotional expression of the East.

"Next to her is Robert Lacey, once an American." Lacey had the look of a cowboy; lean, and rangy, with sandy hair. He was clad in denim jeans and jacket. He nodded curtly to her. "Then," continued Karl, "there is Edgar Benson, formerly of England, who fought in the trenches at the Somme." Benson gave her a faint smile. She could imagine him in his British Army uniform, racing through the mud, as shells exploded around him.

"And of course, Jeanette Fleur." The German smiled, but the Frenchwoman gave Romana a stony stare. "Next to her is Iranda, from India, and Claude deMontforde." The two glared at the girl with undisguised hatred. "Edmund Drake, once an English lord." Drake sneered at her. "Octavius Quintillius Flavius, formerly a citizen of ancient Rome." Octavius bowed his head in greeting. "And Kunda-Bele, who used to enjoy his status as a witch-doctor in Africa two hundred years ago." The tall African also bowed to her.

"There is also my companion, Irina," said Karl, indicating the wild-haired Russian who still stood behind his chair. She locked eyes with Romana, and the girl knew that she was waiting for an excuse to attack her.

"Finally," said Karl, "there is myself; Karl, the leader of the Clans. Once I was one of those stubborn Germanic tribesmen who Octavius and his Legions failed to defeat all of those centuries ago." He chuckled. "I much prefer this century."

"There are two empty chairs at your table," Romana said.

"Ah," replied Karl, "one of them was a member who I had a... disagreement with."

A disagreement. An understatement, she thought wryly. Romana knew what had happened, for she'd sensed the argument, and the death of Valetta, because she'd been sending her thought into the chamber, wondering what to expect from her enemies. In her mind, she'd watched it all unfold, and told herself to be very wary of the Russian woman as well as Karl.

"That accounts for one absentee. Who sat in the broken chair?" Romana asked.

"The broken chair?" echoed the German. "Who do you think?"

Romana noticed the sudden intense interest that came over the vampires seated before her. They all stared at her attentively, to see what her answer would be. Her seemingly innocent question appeared to have great significance to them. Her gaze went from the ruined chair to the wall behind the table, where the record of the Clans was displayed. She looked at the names, her eyes travelling upwards, until they came to the obliterated station. None of the names were legible, but she had a feeling that she knew what they had been. "My father," she said.

Karl applauded her. "Very good." The sound of his hands clapping filled the chamber. "You are indeed psychic."

"Why are their names removed like that?" she asked.

"Why do you think?" answered a harsh voice. She looked up, and again met the vindictive gaze of the Russian. "They betrayed us! They created *Abominations*, and let them live, even though they knew the law. *Death!*" Irina's blood-filled eyes glared at her.

"And now their creation comes to us," said Jeanette. "Can we allow her to live?"

"No!" cried deMontforde, "She must die!"

Karl whirled, and moved in a blur of motion. He snatched up both Claude and Jeanette as though they were rag-dolls. He tossed the Frenchwoman from him with a powerful heave, and she spun through the air the length of the room, to crash against the heavy doors. She slid to the dusty floor, and lay stunned. Gripped tightly in his other hand, Claude whimpered. Karl took deMontforde's head in both of his hands, and twisted it savagely. With a sickening snap that reverberated in the chamber, the neck broke. An instant later, the corpse disintegrated into dust.

Karl swung about and glared at the others. Like a primeval image of some ancient god of death, he stood before them, anger burning from his every pore. *"Are there any others who would defy me?"* he roared. His blazing eyes challenged them, but the vampires, even though they had powers of their own, shrank before this display of terrible destruction. A faint sound drew all eyes to the door, where Jeanette had struggled to her feet, and stood with a shocked look frozen on her face. She had seen de Montforde's ghastly end, and now she trembled to see the mindless rage that they had awoken in the German. Karl stretched out his arm and made a beckoning gesture, and she rose into the air and was drawn swiftly towards him, as though she were a fish he was reeling in, until she was dangling in midair before him. She goggled at him, knowing that he could destroy her in an instant.

"Will you obey me?" he asked, his voice cold.

Held in the grip of his power, she could only nod in acquiescence, for she couldn't find her voice.

He dropped his hand, and Jeanette fell to the floor. She knelt before him, her head bowed in acknowledgement of his awful strength. She finally spoke: *"I will obey,"* she whispered hoarsely.

His face wore a look of satisfaction. "Good. Return to your place."

She rose to her feet, and walked slowly back to her chair. She sat down, not meeting the other's eyes. As Karl returned his attention back to Romana, Jeanette flashed him an evil look. She would bide her time. *One day*, she thought, and then cut off that thought, unless Karl sensed what burned in her mind. She met Romana's gaze, and knew that she had sensed her treacherous notion. Her eyes narrowed in hate.

"Now," the German said, controlling the anger that still flowed through him, "we can continue." He waved his hand a third time, and those heavy portals groaned open. He fixed his gaze upon Romana, who turned to face the sound, as all of the others looked towards the open doors. Something was rolling into the chamber. Was it a cart of some kind? As it came into the candlelight, they saw that it was an electric wheelchair, driven by a man who was little more than a skeleton. Pain ravaged that face, in lines that were scribed deep, and the eyes showed that every movement, every breath, was made in agony. Behind him to either side, were two armed men, carrying strange looking chrome plated rifles, his bodyguards. He rolled up to the stage, and stopped. His eyes hadn't left Romana; he'd stared at her intently since the moment he entered. She returned his stare, sizing him up as he studied her in return.

"Greetings, professor," said Karl.

"This is too much!" Attention turned to Edmund, who'd leapt to his feet. He pointed first at Romana and then at Duvall. "First you bring that – *thing* in here, and now you allow a mortal to enter, where no mortal has been for centuries, save to serve us as food!"

"I must agree, Karl," said Octavius. "We did not wish for this mortal to come to us here."

"You did not wish it?" Karl said softly. His gaze roved the group at the table in turn. He folded his arms.

They all watched to see if the German would explode into violent action. The atmosphere became tense, until even the mortals could sense it. Irina stared at the others like a predator ready to strike, waiting for one of them to make a foolish move. Duvall's guards raised their weapons, and pressed studs on their sides, and a red light on them changed to green. They stared at the vampires; sweat beginning to bead their faces. Nobody moved.

"It is done," said Karl, matter-of-factly. He unfolded his arms and gestured non-chalantly. He stepped down from the stage, and stood before Duvall. The tension was broken. "Professor, allow me to introduce you to your saviour. This is Romana."

Duvall raised a trembling hand, addressing his bodyguards: "Lower your weapons, you fools." The rifles came down, and they pressed the studs again. The green lights turned red once more. The bodyguard's eyes remained on the vampires, and one look told anyone that they would action their weapons and raise them instantly, if danger threatened.

The Frenchman's voice came, in a choking gasp, as though it were forced through his throat: "Finally we meet." Romana watched as a painful grimace appeared on his lips, and realised that he was smiling at her. His gleaming eyes devoured her, as though she were his next meal.

"I have come as I promised," she said. "Now bring me Abdullah."

"Patience, *ma chere*," croaked Duvall, "You will soon be with him." Again the contorted smile writhed on his pain-ravaged face.

8

Null

Erik laughed at Null's wide-eyed gaze. They'd been taken back to his loft, and now, after climbing the stairs, the hacker stared in wonder at Erik's firearms collection, his drum kit; everything seemed to be like a holy relic to the skinny tech. He walked rapidly from one thing to the next, his mouth open.

"*Fuuck* man," he said, "You've got some really amazin' shit here." He shook his head, still not believing that he'd actually been allowed to enter Erik's place. He felt as though he was inside a temple that was dedicated to the gods of industrial music.

Erik sat down on the lounge, and Sergei joined him. The Russian's grin mirrored the drummer's own. They watched, bemused, as the boy peered intently at everything.

"Maybe you charge entry fee next time, Da?" Sergei quipped.

Erik smiled. "Yeah. Might make good money."

Null heard, and came over, his face red. He stood in front of them, abashed. "Sorry," he said softly, "I didn't mean to come on all fan-boy." He lowered his gaze. "This is where you live…and I -"

"It's okay," the drummer said. "Don't worry about it." He stood up, and put his hand on Null's shoulder. "You're welcome here anytime."

The boy looked up, meeting Erik's gaze. "You really mean that?"

"Sure," Erik replied.

A wide grin appeared on the tech's face. "*Awesome*! Wow, I'm actually in Erik Davis's place, and I can come *anytime*?"

"Anytime. I'm not so famous that I need to lock everyone out. Wanna drink?"

The fixed grin was his answer. Erik walked over to the kitchen, and went to the refrigerator. He opened the door, and got out a bottle. Closing the door, he crossed the floor to a cupboard, and reached in, bringing out three glasses. He came back to the lounge-room, and sat down, motioning Null to a chair. As the boy sat down, Erik opened the bottle, and poured drinks for them all. As he gave a glass to Null, he was surprised to see tears in his eyes. "Are you okay?"

Null sniffed, rubbing his nose. "Yeah," he said, his voice thick with emotion. He took off his glasses, and wiped away tears. He looked up, his eyes red. "I'm sorry. It's just that *Kult* is my favourite band...You guys have kept me going...I wouldn't be here if it wasn't for you. I...ah, fuck, I dunno what to say." He sipped at his drink, and then put the glass down on the table. "I've been through some pretty heavy shit, and all the time, when I thought that I couldn't go on..." He faltered, trying to put his thoughts into words. "To have someone like *you*, who I look up to, care about *me*..." He put his head in his hands and sobbed.

Erik and the Bear sat amazed at this outburst. Erik stood up, and went to Null's side. He sat on the arm of the chair, and put his arm around the hacker's shoulder. He let the boy cry, and looked over at Sergei, who shrugged, and took a long pull at his drink.

After a few minutes, Null stopped crying, and grabbed Erik's hand. He looked up into the drummer's eyes, and said hoarsely: "I tried to off myself a couple of times, but both times, I either heard one of your songs, or saw a picture of the band. I dunno why, but it stopped me." He sniffed again. "You really saved my life."

Erik gave him his drink. "How old are you, Null?"

"Eighteen. I've been livin' hard, on the streets. I – I got into smack. If

Gyorgi hadn't took me in…"

"Your parents?" asked Sergei.

Null grimaced. "Dunno who my old man was. He left before I was born. Didn't want the responsibility, my mom said." He wiped his eyes and replaced his glasses. "She's a whore, though. He could'a been anyone – maybe someone from the club, or one of her lowlife friends who supplied her with drugs, and hung around." He raised his glass to his lips, drained it, and then put it down with a thud. Anger suffused his face. "She was always shootin' up with some fuck, or doin' crack. When I was really young, she'd say; 'I'm entertainin',' and send me outside on the street." He shook his head angrily. "*Entertainin'!* Huh! Even though I was little, I knew she was fuckin' those bastards." A faraway look came into his eyes. "Still, it was all of those nights that I spent on the streets that taught me what I needed to survive. One night, when I was fifteen, I just didn't go home." He focussed, and looked at them both in turn. "Then Gyorgi found me, and saw what I could do with computers, and gave me a place of my own, so's I could work for him."

"Is she still alive?" said Erik.

"Dunno. Don't give a fuck. She did nothin' for me." He smiled and indicated the Russian. "Bear here did more for me than that bitch ever did."

Sergei raised his glass and toasted the boy. "Is true," he said. "I bring plenty gifts for Null all the time."

Erik reached over and refilled Null's glass. "So what's your real name?"

"Null's good enough. I wanna forget that old life. It already seems like it was a thousand years ago." He picked up his glass and took a deep pull at his drink.

"And the smack?" queried the drummer.

The hacker smiled. "I got off it. Shit, *that* was hard. But Gyorgi helped me through it, and Bear here was always around to help too." He returned the Russian's toast. "They locked me in a storeroom at Gyorgi's warehouse, and made me go cold turkey. I hallucinated all the time, saw plenty of weird stuff; shit and spewed until I thought there'd be nothin' left of me. They came and fed me when I needed it, and cleaned me up. Took about a week, but I didn't know how long it was, I was so sick."

Erik saw Null through fresh eyes. He'd thought of the boy as just another rabid fan; mostly harmless, and hadn't expected to find such hidden strengths beneath such a bland exterior. "Well, Sergei," he said, "I didn't know that you had such a fatherly streak in you."

The Bear chuckled.

Erik put his hand on the boy's shoulder. "Null," he began, "have you thought about what our enemies are?" He fixed him with a serious gaze. "This isn't a game. These things are dangerous."

The tech nodded. "I know," he said, his voice firm with resolve. "I wanna help. Gyorgi and The Bear have done everythin' for me. I owe it to 'em."

Erik was impressed with the boy's courage. On the drive over, he'd told him of the desperate fight with the vampires on the freeway. Null's eyes had bugged out at the lurid details; it was obvious to the drummer that he had a vivid imagination, and that whenever he heard anything he was told, that imagination would create pictures in his mind. He slapped him on the back. "Okay, I guess you're coming along for the ride. Just what is it that you can do for us?"

Null grinned. Now he was on familiar ground. "I can break any secure alarm systems, and hack into anythin' you want." His eyes glittered, and Erik could see how much such illicit activity fired him up. It was like that with all of the hacker community; they found it a point of pride to break any code, open any lock. They saw it as a challenge, and every successful job brought them even higher cred with their peers.

"Da," added Sergei, "many times I see Null here do his work. He is the best."

Null blushed. "Ah, Bear, there's lots'a guys better than me."

"Niet. You are too modest. I tell Erik here you are genius. Is true."

The boy smiled. "I'm just good at what I do."

"Well," said Erik, "You'll be showing us your stuff when we get to the Duvall lab in Switzerland."

"Switzerland. I've never been there before." He scratched his chin. "I've never been *anywhere* before."

"Stick with us," the drummer said, "you'll go lots of places."

"This Duvall guy, who is he?" asked the hacker.

"Seems like he runs this lab that we're going to break into. Gerald told us that he's a scientist, and for many years, he's been capturing vampires, and experimenting with their blood, because he has some sort of spinal condition that's killing him. He thinks that their blood, which has incredible healing properties, will heal him. Not to mention that it appears that it also is what makes the vampires immortal."

"*Immortal*," echoed Null. "*Cool*. Imagine livin' *forever*, and havin' such power!"

Sergei raised an eyebrow at Null's response. Erik wondered, could the boy be attracted to the idea of immortality, as Gyorgi was?

"Anyway," Erik continued, "He also told us that a vampire named Abdullah is being held there, and Romana owes everything to him. He raised her from a baby, and taught her how to survive as a vampire. That's why she went; to save him, and to give Duvall her blood, in return for his freedom."

"Okay," said the boy, "but why does he want *her* blood? Hasn't he tried everythin' before, and not found a cure? What makes her blood any different?"

"She is most powerful vampire on earth," said the Russian.

"How?" The tech frowned in bewilderment.

"Romana was the last vampire Born, not Made." Seeing the confused look on Null's face, Erik continued: "When they give someone their blood, they call it *'Making'*, but they can also have babies, which are born like us. Centuries ago, they were allowed to have offspring. She was born to two vampires."

"Baby vampires?" said Null, amazed. "They can have babies? How come I never heard of that? Are there any more of 'em?"

"No," said Erik.

"How come?"

"They were too dangerous. It turns out that they were much stronger than their parents, and turned on them and destroyed them. The vampires are in groups called Clans, and they had a meeting, and decided to take out all of these young offspring. They called them Abominations. After that happened, they found a Chinese herbalist, who gave them some herbs that stopped the females conceiving. They made him one of them, so he could supply them indefinitely."

"Imagine bein' *born* a vampire. Whoa! What a trip. They'd be powerful right from birth." Null's eyes flashed. "No one would pick on 'em when they were kids, they'd tear 'em apart."

"Yeah." The drummer thought for a moment. *What did Gerald say? Oh yeah, I remember.* "They hunted them down, and killed them all. Or so they thought."

"Ah," said Null, snapping his fingers, "And this Abdullah dude hid baby Romana from 'em?"

"Da," said the Bear. "She live with him for long time in desert."

"But finally, the Clans discovered her, and sent Gerald to kill her. He's hunted her for hundreds of years."

Null screwed up his face. "So why would she go with him? If he's tried to kill her, he - I don't understand. That doesn't make sense."

"Yes, it does," Erik said. "She'd do anything to save Abdullah. She didn't even know he was alive, until Gerald told her."

"Bait," said the hacker.

"Da. Is what I think too," said Sergei. "They trap her using him."

The drummer shook his head. "We don't know that."

"You said this Gerald dude has been tryin' to kill her for hundreds of years. Why would he stop?"

"It was an order from the Clans," said Erik. "They told Gerald to seek her out, and offer her freedom, and Abdullah's freedom, in return for her blood, which Duvall would use to try and cure himself. In return, he would leave them alone."

Null laughed cynically. "Yeah, right. They'll just take some blood, and let her and her friend walk away? Bullshit. You can't trust 'em, they'll keep both of 'em once they've got 'em."

"Romana made the decision to accept their offer. She thinks that they'll keep their word."

"I do not like it," said the Bear. "These vampires, they hate us."

"Where did you get that idea?" A honeyed voice came from the balcony. Valeria stepped into the room, and sauntered over to where they sat. "We *love* you, especially your hot blood." Her green eyes swept over them, and her lips were set in a sardonic smile.

Sergei's eyes opened wide. He sat petrified as she gazed at them. Erik watched her closely; he knew that she was unpredictable, and could do anything. He looked over at the far wall, where his Very pistol hung. *Too far*, he thought. *Shit!* He fixed his eyes on her face, trying to read it.

Null stared at her voluptuous figure in amazement. The redhead turned her preternatural eyes upon him. She smiled wider, showing her deadly fangs. "What have we here?" she said silkily. With a blur of movement, she was by the boy's side, and she took him under the chin, and raised him into the air as though he was a doll. Her eyes filled with blood.

The drummer leapt up, but Valeria swung her reddened eyes to him, and he knew that he was helpless. She could kill Null at any moment, and he was powerless to stop her.

Reading his mind, she pouted. "You wound me, Erik," she said with a sigh. "I will not hurt him."

"What do you want?" Erik asked her, his voice flat.

"Can I not visit my friends?" she asked sweetly.

"We're *not* your friends," the drummer replied roughly.

She placed one hand over her heart, fingers spread wide. "Oh, but I am. I am looking out for your welfare. Gerald told me to make sure no harm comes to you."

Null hung suspended in her hand, shivering in fright. He felt the power in that hand, as hard as stone. He licked his lips, and sweat broke out on his face. He looked at Erik, his eyes pleading for his release.

"Am I not beautiful, Null?" Valeria said seductively, lowering him and bringing her mouth close to the tech's ear. "Is this what you desire, to be powerful and immortal? I could make you like me. I can see your thoughts; see the way you were beaten by those who despised you. I see all the pretty little girls that you wanted, but they were always out of your reach, because they thought you were disgusting." Taking his head in both hands, she turned him to face her. He stared into her blood-red eyes. "Ask me," she said sensuously, "and I will give you my blood." Her fangs appeared. "I know that you desire me."

In his head, the boy heard her thoughts, which were directed at him: *You know that you want me; you want to be like me, immortal. I can give you that.* He stared at her, his mind whirling with her offer. *Immortality! You know you want it.* She licked her lips lasciviously. *I can show you the pleasures that I have learned from over three hundred years of sexual adventures.*

He tried to speak, but in his terror, his tongue wouldn't work. His heart pounded, and he felt a stiffness in his loins. *Yes! Yes!* He thought; *I want to be like you! I want you!*

Valeria smiled.

"Leave him alone," said Erik.

Valeria put Null down in the chair. She stroked his head. "There," she said, holding up her hands, "he is not hurt." The blood faded in her eyes, and they returned to the green of before. A sly look appeared on her face. "I know what you are doing."

"What do you mean?" Erik exchanged a look with Sergei. The Russian sat terrified, sweating profusely.

"You wish to go to your Romana," she sneered. "Gerald would not like that." She narrowed her eyes. "Do not try to deny it, mortal. Remember I can read your thoughts like a book." She walked over to the wall where the weapons hung, and took the flare gun down. "However..." She toyed with it as she continued: "I will allow you to go."

"Why?" the drummer asked.

She turned her gaze to him. A feral light came to her eyes. "Because you will *die*, and that will break little Romana's heart. You will not stand a chance against the Clans." She opened the loading chamber. "This is loaded. That was naughty of you." She tossed it towards him. It spun through the air, tumbling over and over.

Erik's eyes were fixed on the spinning Very pistol. If he could only grab it and aim and fire, he could kill her. As it came close, he jumped up, grabbed it, and pulled back the hammer. He lowered it and aimed. Where Valeria had been was empty space. Sardonic laughter came echoing from the balcony. She'd moved swiftly even as she had thrown the gun.

"Goodbye, mortal. Go to your death!" her voice dissolved again into mocking laughter that faded as she took to the air.

"*Fuuuck!*" Null gasped out. "She's *gorgeous!*" He came and grabbed Erik's arm in a vicelike grip. "You didn't tell me she was so –"

"*Don't be a dickhead!*" Erik shouted.

The boy released him and staggered back, shocked. He gaped at the drummer.

Erik eased the hammer back on the flare gun, and his eyes burned into the boy. "That *thing* that you call beautiful would drain you dry. Don't be fooled. She's a killer! They hunt us for our blood." He stepped over to Null, grabbed him by the shoulders, and shook him roughly. "Do you know what they call us? *Cattle!*" He pushed the boy away, disgusted with him. A wild light was in his eyes.

Null stumbled over the arm of the chair and fell sprawling into it. He stared at Erik, amazed at his outburst. "But – I..."

"Erik," Sergei said softly, "Is not his fault."

The drummer's anger faded. "Shit," he said, "I'm sorry, Null." He held out his hand.

The tech stared at him. Finally, he took Erik's hand, and the drummer raised him to his feet. In the boy's eyes was a perplexed look.

"I know what you're thinking," said Erik. "How can I be in love with Romana, when she's the same as Valeria?"

"Yeah," Null replied, "It did cross my mind."

The drummer thought deeply. How could he explain the difference between the two vampires? *Ah,* he thought, *I know.* "It's like this," he said, "Romana will only take the blood of someone who's bad; an evildoer they call them, but Valeria has no regard for human life. Most of the others are the same, including Gerald and his friends. They'd happily kill us all, if they didn't need us to feed on."

"Is true," added Sergei, "these creatures do not care about us."

"But Romana?" asked the hacker.

"Romana?" echoed the drummer. "She's tired of them hunting her. She wants a companion. Romana's had them before. She just wants them to leave her alone."

"They can have a...*mortal* companion?"

Erik nodded. "Gerald implied that she'd had many. I don't care; I only want her to be with me, no matter how long that is."

"What about this Abdullah? Won't he want her to stay with him?"

"I don't know," Erik replied, doubt in his voice.

Silence fell.

Jeff Thomson

9

The Attack

The black helicopters whispered soundlessly through the night sky. There were four in all, Russian stealth machines, that didn't exist as far as American Intelligence knew, nor the rest of the world either. They were sleek, and fast, with the economic lines of a predator. Non-reflective ablative armour sheathed them, undetectable by any tracking system. Weapons pods were retracted into their smooth sides, waiting for the moment to unfold like deadly flowers, to cast their ordnance like seeds of death.

Seated within the lead helicopter were Erik, Sergei, Gyorgi, Null, and four of Gyorgi's fireteam. They all wore black Kevlar body armour over black camouflage fatigues, and had night-vision goggles slung around their necks. Their faces were blacked out, and they wore lightweight helmets, which had headphones and small microphones, so each member of the team could be monitored and could keep in constant touch. Each of them was armed with a machine pistol, every round a tracer. Erik also carried the Very pistol that Sergei had given him; he'd told the Bear that he didn't want to let any of the vampires near him. In addition to the firearms, they carried a number of phosphorus grenades; Gyorgi had assured them that they'd make short work of their enemies.

They sat in silence, each of them thinking of the mission ahead. Erik looked at the fireteam for the hundredth time. They were a mixed group, mercenaries from every nation, fighting for money. *And Gyorgi's got plenty of that,* he thought. But he wondered if any of them realised how dangerous their enemy was. Had Gyorgi even told them what they were up against? Did they even know that tonight they'd face creatures that to most people only existed in movies, or in the pages of novels? He met the gaze of one of them, a huge German; blonde, blue eyed; the perfect image of the Nazi superman. The man smiled a superior smile, and Erik knew that he looked at him with contempt. He looked away, out of the window and into the darkness.

Null sat tapping nervously at a laptop. He was nervous, but also excited. Would he meet Valeria tonight? Would she be there? She knew that they were coming, she'd told them that. He remembered how she'd demonstrated her power. An image of her effortlessly holding him in the air came to him. The thoughts that she'd sent him echoed in his brain. He wanted to be like her. Yes, he did, he wanted power and immortality, and to be at her side forever. And three hundred years of pleasure! Just thinking of all of the things that she could do to him made his heart crash in his thin chest, and he sweated in anticipation. He'd give himself up to her, and she'd make him her companion. Underneath the laptop, he had a painful erection.

"Are you all right?"

The tech jumped in surprise. At his side, the Georgian was sitting forwards in his seat and giving him a concerned glance.

"Uh…Yeah, I'm just thinkin' of how to break the security at the lab." He licked his lips nervously. A huge hand landed on his shoulder.

"Do not worry," said Sergei, sitting on the other side of him. "Gyorgi is good planner, and his men are best." He patted Null's shoulder, which made the boy bob up and down in his seat. "Stay with me, I take care of you."

Null smiled. "Thanks, Bear." He returned his attention to the laptop.

Gyorgi sat back and thought of the redhead too. *Such an amazing creature,* he thought. *I know she is attracted to me. How can I convince her to make me like her?* His mind was filled with the image of the gorgeous

Russian vampire. *To be with her,* he thought, *immortal and powerful. There must be a way.* His mind was filled with images of her voluptuous figure. The mission hardly concerned him; since he'd met Valeria, his own secret agenda was to become one with her, a companion that could be by her side for eternity. *Eternity! As an immortal. To live forever, while other men withered and died. Yes, that's what I want.* Outwardly, he showed no sign of his traitorous thoughts; all of the others only thought that he was working over the details of the mission in his mind. Only Sergei and Erik had doubts about him, but they couldn't be sure.

Erik took a sidelong glance at the Georgian. *I wonder what you're thinking?* the drummer thought. *Will the lure of immortality make you join sides with the enemy?* The Bear caught his eye, and they shared a look that told Erik that Sergei hadn't forgotten their suspicions. He gave Erik a smile, which told the drummer that he shared his thoughts, and Erik knew that he'd keep an eye on the arms merchant. Erik nodded, and indicated with a glance Null, as he tapped away. The Bear nodded imperceptibly. *Yes,* thought Erik, *we'll have to watch him too.* He gave Sergei thumbs up, and then sat back and waited for the chopper to arrive at their destination.

"Yes," said Gyorgi, speaking into his mic. "Good." He addressed the others: "We have reached the last marker. Now we split up, and we continue with one chopper to the hill above the lab, while the other two swing around behind it." He grinned. "Now the fun begins. Check your weapons."

They all examined their weapons, making sure that everything worked correctly. Null cocked his machine pistol nervously, his face a mask of concentration. Finally, after fumbling with the weapon for several minutes, he put it down at his side, satisfied that it was ready to use. Gyorgi leaned over, picked it up, and flicked the safety on.

"We don't want any accidents, do we?" he said to the tech. He handed the gun to Null, giving him a stern look as if to say; *Make sure that you do it right.*

The boy went red. "Fuck. Sorry man."

The German across the cabin sneered. *Oh,* thought Erik, *I bet Superman doesn't like that.* He'd checked his own weapon, and laid it across his lap. He glanced down; making sure the safety was on. He looked up, and met the mercenary's sardonic gaze. *Fuck you Naziboy,* he thought fiercely. He gave Naziboy a smile.

The helicopter suddenly lurched wildly, throwing them all about. Gyorgi yelled in his mic, and equipment tumbled about the cabin as the chopper thrashed erratically. They hung on to their safety harnesses grimly as the machine spun out of control. Getting no response from the pilot, Gyorgi cursed, and gestured to one of the fireteam. The man struggled up out of his seat, and staggered across the gyrating floor to the hatch that separated the cockpit from their cabin. Just as he reached it, it was flung open, and the vicious face of one of the vampires appeared in the opening. The mercenary gaped in astonishment, and then reached for his gun, but the vampire rushed forwards with impossible speed, and slashed the man's throat. Blood sprayed all over the cabin in a red fountain as the mercenary fell to the floor. Null screamed in terror, and the others desperately scrambled for their weapons. The vampire leapt at Gyorgi, but the Georgian had drawn his pistol, and he fired it at point-blank range. The vampire shrieked, and turned to ash as the tracers burned through him.

The outer door was suddenly ripped open and the cabin was filled with howling wind, and two more of the terrible creatures appeared. One, a female, entered swiftly, slashed Naziboy's harness, grabbed a fistful of his shirt, and with a negligent flick of her hand threw him out of the gaping doorway, to fall headlong into the night sky, dropping to the ground that was far away. The other, a male, dashed forwards, but Erik fired a short burst, and he followed his companion; blazed fiercely for a moment, and then disintegrated into ash that was blown all around the cabin that filled their eyes with grit. The female snarled, baring her fangs, and threw herself at Erik, but Sergei neatly shot her through the forehead. She joined the other two in dissolution.

Gyorgi flung himself out of his seat, and clawed his way into the cockpit, which was a bloody shambles; the two pilots were dead, their blood covered everything, and streaked the canopy. An alarm shrieked incessantly. The altimeter spun wildly as the chopper fell from the sky. Gyorgi slapped the release on the pilot's harness, tossed the corpse away, and threw himself into his seat, grasped the control column and heaved at it urgently. *It's no use,* he thought grimly, as he desperately sought to control their mad descent.

The other helicopter fared no better. As Gyorgi struggled frantically, the vampires attacked it, ripping open the outer doors. The pilot and co-pilot died quickly, their throats torn out; their hot blood sprayed the cockpit with gore. Taken by surprise, the fireteam reached rapidly for their guns, but only one man got off a frantic burst, and tracers sprayed wildly in the cabin, cutting down men and vampire alike. Several rounds pierced the fuel tank, and instantly the chopper blossomed into a huge ball of flame, exploding in a thunderous detonation. One man was blown clear and fell, a blazing torch, but the others were consumed by the conflagration. The debris of the helicopter tumbled downwards, spinning and burning, lighting up the darkness.

Gyorgi watched the ground coming quickly towards them. The machine's spin was under control, but he knew with a sense of finality that their fall was unchecked. Suddenly, a huge hand covered his own, and he looked up to see the Bear, adding his vast strength to his own. They pulled on the stick together, and almost succeeded, but just as they thought that they could pull out of the dive safely, a copse of trees raced up out of the darkness. They ploughed into them, smashing and scattering branches everywhere, and the chopper's rotor blades screamed and spun off wildly. The machine crashed to the ground, tumbling over and over across the snow, raining equipment as it went. It plunged along, until it finally came to rest, half buried in a snow bank.

A minute later, Null sprang out of the open hatch, and stumbled away from the wreck, sobbing uncontrollably. The experience of the attack, and the crash had frightened him out of his wits. He'd thought that their infiltration of the enemy's lair would have gone smoothly, like some movie where the good guys always triumph. His eyes were wide with shock, and his trembling legs only carried him a short distance before he collapsed on the snow, bawling.

Another figure stepped out; the last member of the fireteam. He stepped quickly over to the wailing boy, and pulled him to his feet. Null's gaze didn't register his presence. The man cursed, and then struck the tech across the face with a stinging slap. "Pull yourself together!" The boy immediately stopped crying, and stared at him, tears running down his face. He coughed several times, and gulped in a huge lungful of air.

"I – I'm okay," he said shakily. His glasses had vanished in the crash, and his eyes burned in the cold air.

Inside the helicopter, Sergei and Gyorgi lay sprawled in the cockpit. Sparks ran across the instrument panel. A small tongue of flame began, and fire started to spread. The Georgian groaned, and sat up in the pilot's seat. He saw the flames, and suddenly he was aware of the smell of fuel. He hit the harness release, and fell out of the seat. He grabbed Sergei by the shoulder and shook him roughly.

"Sergei! Get up!" His voice crackled with urgency.

The Russian shook his head to clear it, and rose with difficulty. He looked at the fire, and nodded to Gyorgi. "Da! Out we get!" He held out his hand, and Gyorgi took it and pulled the Bear to his feet. They staggered to the hatch, climbed over the sprawled bodies that lay in the cabin, and stumbled out into the snow. They saw the other two, and hurried towards them.

"Get down!" shouted the arms merchant, waving his arms frantically.

Behind them, the cockpit flared brightly beneath the snow as the fire spread rapidly. In moments, the fuel would ignite, and turn the chopper into blazing fragments.

Null whimpered like a puppy, and dove to the ground, trying to bury himself. The man with him dropped, and covered his head with his hands. As Sergei and Gyorgi came up to them, the Russian stared at the boy and the mercenary. He looked back at the helicopter in horror. *"Erik!"* he bawled. "Where is Erik?" He shrugged Gyorgi's arm off, and turned and ran back towards the wreck. *"Erik!"* he screamed.

"Sergei!" The Georgian raced after him. He grabbed Sergei's coat and spun him around. "He's dead! The fuel –"

With an angry cry, Sergei tried to shake him off. Gyorgi turned and shouted to the mercenary, as they struggled. The man leapt to his feet, and came and took Sergei's arm. The Russian snarled, and kicked out, catching the man on the shin. He gasped in pain, and let the Bear go. Then, his teeth set in rage; he unslung his weapon, and stepped up and struck the Russian across the temple with it. Sergei fell to the snow, stunned.

Something in the chopper ignited with a dull whump, and the mercenary and Gyorgi both dropped flat. The helicopter exploded violently, sending burning pieces of wreckage screaming through the air. A great wave of superheated air bloomed outwards.

Gyorgi rose to his feet. He stared at the burning debris. The flames flickered brightly in the night, and a huge column of black smoke poured skyward. The mercenary stood up beside him.

"Sorry, Erik," Gyorgi said. He looked down at the prostrate Russian. "Give me a hand," he said. They started to pick the Bear up, but a shattering scream interrupted them. They turned to see Null, who pointed beyond them, his eyes wide with terror. They spun around, to see several vampires hurtling through the air towards them. The man's machine – pistol came up, and he sprayed the creatures with a long burst. They shrieked and instantly blazed fiercely. He whirled to face two others. As he aimed at them, a heavy blow sent the gun spinning from his hand, and the next second; his head was grasped from either side by powerful hands. A savage twist followed, there was a sharp crack, and Gerald let his corpse fall.

Two of the vampires took Gyorgi's arms, and he looked over at the boy, and saw that Null was also pinioned. *At least he's stopped screaming,* Gyorgi thought. The tech was so terrified, that he couldn't make a sound, but just stood trembling in the vampire's vice-like grip.

Gerald's blood-filled eyes bored into Gyorgi. The foppish vampire walked slowly over and stood before him, his arms folded imperiously. Gerald looked down at Sergei, and then his deadly gaze came back to the arms merchant. He smiled wickedly. "Welcome to Switzerland," he said dryly. "Where is Romana's little playmate?"

Gyorgi looked into Gerald's eyes unflinchingly. He indicated the burning helicopter with a toss of his head. "In there." He smiled wryly, his gold teeth flashing in the firelight. "Why don't you go and look for him?"

Like a flash of lightning, Gerald's hand cracked across Gyorgi's face. He slumped in his captor's arms, and then slowly brought his head up. He smiled, knowing that he'd aggravated his enemy. Blood ran from his lip, which Gerald had split with his blow. He spat it into the snow, his gaze fixed on the vampire's face.

Gerald took his chin in his hands. "You think you are brave," he said, his voice low and menacing. "We will soon see how brave." He removed his hand, and licked the Georgian's blood from his fingers, staring into Gyorgi's eyes like some evil predatory beast. "Little Romana will not like it that you allowed her pet to die. She will be most upset with you." He pointed back the way that they had come, and Gyorgi saw another column of smoke. Below it was a reddish glow. "The professor is not pleased also. Your other machine crashed into his facility, and he has no alarm systems, no cameras, or any of his electric fences. He told me that he would make you pay for the destruction that you have wrought." He addressed his hunters: "Take them." Gyorgi and Null were lifted into the sky by the other vampires, who flew towards the distant fire, and Gerald knelt and picked up the Russian's heavy body as though it were a doll. He gazed once more at the burning helicopter, and then he followed the others.

A moment later, as they disappeared into the night, there was a rustling in the trees where the chopper had crashed. A figure stumbled into the fire's glare. Erik stared after the shrinking figures, until he lost them. "No security, eh?" he thought out loud. "Thanks blondie, that'll make my job a bit easier." He walked over to the corpse of the mercenary. The vampires hadn't bothered to take the dead man's weapon, and Erik knelt and picked it up. He went through the pockets, and also took the ammunition belt. Several grenades that were clipped to the jacket went onto his own. He stood up, cocked the machine - pistol, and walked over to the wreckage. Seeing that there was nothing there for him to salvage, he looked over at the dim glow. "Well, better get going." He trudged in the direction of the laboratory. Flakes of snow drifted down. "Great," he grumbled, walking towards the distant fire as the snow began to fall.

10

Abdullah

The group walked through echoing corridors that smelt sharply of disinfectant. Bright fluorescent lighting made everything stand out luridly. At the head of the group was the electric chair of Professor Duvall. Following him were his two bodyguards, chrome rifles at the ready. Behind them were Romana, Karl, and the heads of the Clans. No one spoke; the only sounds were the click of their footfalls upon the polished linoleum floor, and the light humming of Duvall's chair as they proceeded.

Romana's face was thoughtful. Duvall had promised to take them to see Abdullah. *He was alive!* She thought gladly. How many years had it been? Forty years since that day in the oasis, when they'd come and taken him, and she'd thought he'd been killed. Forty years, the time that he'd been tortured and used by this demon for his blood and its unique properties. Her eyes narrowed in anger as she thought of all of the days and nights that Abdullah had been subjected to this so – called professor's experiments. *There will be a reckoning,* she thought grimly.

"But not until we get what we want," said Karl at her side, reading her thoughts.

She turned her gaze upon him. "What *you* want?" she said, anger infusing her voice.

He smiled. "This is a much greater matter than you realise," he said. "If we allow Duvall to obtain the blood that will save him, he will stop hunting us down, and he will even provide us with the technical equipment at his disposal. We will become even more powerful."

She stared at him. "*More* powerful? You are vampires: immortal creatures with the strength of a score of men. What do you need with science?"

He returned her scornful glance. "It will allow us to integrate with this century. Many of us are old, and our ideas are also. We must understand this age that we find ourselves in."

He stopped talking as Duvall's chair came to a halt. They all stood before a huge metal door, which had a keypad embedded in its centre. The professor nodded to one of his guards. The man came forwards, and tapped out a code on the keypad. There was a soft chiming sound, and the door opened, sliding away into the walls. The chair rolled into the vast room that was revealed beyond the doorway. It was dim, but as Duvall hummed forwards, lights began to turn on, flickering as they became active. The group proceeded inside, and came up to the Frenchman, who was looking through a large window at the far end of the room. Beyond the window was darkness. But as the lighting came fully on, they could see that there was a figure that was chained to a wall within.

"*Abdullah!*" cried Romana. She rushed up to the glass, and peered inside.

The Arab hung slackly in his chains. His head was slumped down upon his chest, his long black hair covered his face, and they could see many metal tubes that snaked out of the wall, and disappeared into his arms and neck. Livid bruises covered his skin, bluish in the light. He was dressed only in a loincloth; his chest and arms and legs were bare, as were his feet.

Romana whipped about. "What have you done to him!" her eyes filled with blood, and she bared her fangs. Unconsciously, the other vampires dropped into a fighting stance. The two guards activated their rifles, and targeted the seething girl.

A harsh croaking sound came from the thing in the chair. They realised that Duvall was laughing. "He has been assisting me with my research," he wheezed. "He has not been permanently damaged." He rolled over and stopped in front of Romana. He gazed up into her predator's eyes, unfazed. "But unless you behave, and help me…" the evil voice tailed off. The Frenchman smiled, a twitching of his mouth.

Quivering with anger, Romana choked out: "I have told you I will give you what you want." She tore her crimson eyes from the hated professor, and stared longingly at the pitiful form in the other room. Tears of blood ran down her face. "Release him, I beg you!" she turned back, and an imploring tone came to her voice: "Please – I will give you my blood. Do not hurt him any more."

The creature in the chair nodded in satisfaction. "Good," he said throatily. "But in case you are thinking of not behaving…" he pointed, and her eyes followed the gesture, to see long silver tubes that were set in the ceiling above Abdullah, that were focussed on his body. They reminded her of the rifles that the guards carried.

As though he read her mind, Duvall said: "Yes, they fire the same naphthalene incendiary pellets that these rifles use; only theirs are larger and more effective. You see the dark patch behind your beloved Abdullah?" He chuckled. "They have been used more than once, when one of your kind became…unmanageable."

They all looked, and saw the blackened wall, realising that he meant that other vampires had hung there, and had been obliterated by the gleaming barrels.

"How many?" asked Karl, his voice suddenly harsh.

Duvall slowly wheeled to face him. He regarded the Clan leader with a quizzical gaze. Finally, he said: "I don't remember. Ten? Twelve?"

The German scowled. He exchanged a glance with the other vampires. All of them were enraged at the Frenchman's flippant answer.

Duvall noticed their anger. "May I remind you why we are here? You agreed to my terms; in return, I will cease my experiments, and will not hunt you again." He stared into the German's angry face. "You will receive the technological weaponry that you desire, and all of my expertise." He spun around, ignoring Karl, and addressed Romana: "Do you wish to speak to him?"

The girl took in the angry group of vampires at his back. *Good*, she thought, *maybe you will see him for the evil thing he is*. She caught Karl's eye, and was gratified to see that there was doubt written on his face. "Yes," she said. As Duvall rolled over to a keyboard that was set into the wall below the window, she stared at the German.

We must agree with him, he sent to her, *it is the only way*.

No. He must be destroyed. Her lips set in a hard line. She knew that the others had heard her thoughts. *You can all see what he has done to Abdullah*, she sent to them all. *He cannot be trusted to keep his word. It could be any of us hanging there*. She was pleased to see that they all were shocked and furious at the treatment that the Frenchman had dealt out to one of their kind. *How many has he destroyed?*

It does not matter. We must agree to his terms, Mariko sent.

Yes, added Octavius, *we need his weapons*.

No, sent Kunda – Bele. *We cannot allow him to hunt us and use us for this...*The African glared at the oblivious Duvall, who, with the guards, heard none of this exchange.

We will discuss this later, sent Karl to all of them.

There was silent assent.

"Here," said Duvall to Romana, gesturing her to come to his side. She came to the window, and the professor handed her a microphone. She looked at it, and thumbed the switch on its side. "Abdullah?" There was no response from the figure that hung upon the wall. "Abdullah?" she repeated. Still no sound came to them from the speakers that were fed from the other room, and the Arab gave no indication that he'd heard her. She turned to Duvall, her lips set in anger.

"Let me go in to him," she said.

The professor raised an eyebrow. He seemed to consider her words.

"If I try to do anything…" she pointed at the guns in the ceiling.

His eyes narrowed. "Very well. But if you play me false – "

"You will incinerate me, I know. I only wish to speak to him."

The Frenchman nodded. He flipped a switch on the panel, and a door set into the window rose into the ceiling. He indicated that she should enter. Romana walked into the room, and strode towards Abdullah. She stopped in front of him, and looked at the tubes more closely. The bruises that covered the Arab's body were strange; strange that they should be there at all, because the vampire blood that coursed through his veins should heal any wound in moments. *"Abdullah?"* she whispered, pity for her mentor filling her.

The head slowly came up, and his rheumy eyes focussed on her. At first they were blank, but then she saw the light of intelligence, and finally understanding, come into them. *"Romana?"* he croaked. Amazement sat there on his face as they stared at each other.

She stepped up to him, and lovingly stroked his face. Tears of blood welled up in her eyes, and ran down unheeded as her feelings overwhelmed her.

He smiled at her for a moment, but then he trembled. *"Go!"* he said shakily, "Get away from here!"

"No," she said. "I have come to save you."

"You cannot," he said. "Leave me –"

"Well, well." Duvall's voice came tinnily from speakers in the ceiling. "Not the happy greeting that you were expecting?"

The Arab glared at the Frenchman. He strained at his chains, to no avail. "Come in here," he said menacingly, "and I will greet *you*…"

Duvall shook his head. "Another time, perhaps." His rictus of a smile appeared on his twisted visage. "But your lovely Romana speaks the truth. She *has* come to save you." He indicated the vampires that stood behind him. "Thanks to the advice of your friends here, I have come to understand that she has the blood that I need, and once I have taken it, your – assistance – will no longer be required, and you can go free."

Abdullah laughed once, a bark of derision. "You will *set* me free?" He spat on the floor. "I know not to trust you. Your lies have brought Romana here, for –"

"Please!" The Frenchman held up his hand, cutting off the Arab's diatribe. "I don't care if you believe me or not, but I *will* allow you and Romana to go; once I have her blood. When I have completed my work, I will be immortal, and will never need to hunt your kind again. I will have become like you."

"Like us?" Abdullah echoed disdainfully. "You could *never* be like us. Not with all of your science. You do not understand us at all." He drew himself up proudly. "We are hunters; predators of the night, beautiful and deadly. We go on, age after age, becoming more powerful as the centuries pass."

"Yes," Duvall agreed, his eyes shining fervently, "that is what I want. Immortality. And I will have it. Romana, visiting time is over."

"No," she said defiantly. She stood in front of the Arab. "Come and get me."

The professor glared at her.

She smiled. "Or perhaps your lackeys could come to take me." She raked Karl and the vampires with a baleful gaze. "Let them try; I have destroyed many of them over the decades."

The vampire's eyes filled with blood at this taunt. Mariko hissed with anger. They all started forwards.

"Stop!" shouted Duvall. "You fools, she wants you to try. She knows that you are no match for her."

The advance halted. They stood there, quaking with impotent rage.

"He is right," Karl gritted. *Why do you do this?*

To prove a point, the girl replied. She turned to Abdullah. "I will die with you." She turned back to face the group gathered at the doorway. "It seems that you have no choice but to destroy the both of us. Use your flame guns. Burn us." She folded her arms insolently. "Or let us both go. *Now.*"

"No, Romana," said the Arab, "I do not want you to do this."

Without turning, she said: "He has no choice. He will not risk losing what he wants."

"There is more than one way to make you obey," croaked the Frenchman. He beckoned to his guards. They crossed the room to a cabinet. One of them opened it, and took out two guns. He handed the other to his comrade. They both checked the weapons, and came back to stand in the doorway, sighting the girl in the other room.

Romana was puzzled. Why would they chance killing her? Surely Duvall would not allow... Suddenly, she realised exactly what the rifles were. She'd seen others like them, many years ago, at the oasis, when Abdullah was taken... With an angry hiss, she rushed forwards, her arms outstretched, and her hands ready to rend and tear. Her fangs were displayed threateningly.

The rifles coughed. The girl felt the impacts of their darts, and staggered. She looked down, and saw them sticking into her. She screamed in hatred, and came on. The guns coughed again, and she stumbled and fell to her knees. Through a dull haze, she could see the Frenchman smiling in satisfaction. Romana tried to rise, to reach him, and rip out his throat... She fell heavily, and slipped into oblivion.

The professor rolled into the room, and came to a stop. "Four darts," he said. "Impressive." He looked up as Abdullah roared. "Don't worry; we'll take care of her." He summoned his guards. They came in, and warily picked up the unconscious Romana. As the Arab snarled and struggled in his chains, they carried her from the room.

"I hope she behaves herself, for *both* your sakes." Duvall spun about, and hummed out of the room. The door came down, and the room was sealed.

Abdullah met Karl's gaze. His eyes implored the German. *Help us!*

As the professor opened the outer door, and they followed the guards with their unconscious burden, Karl looked at the Arab. For a long moment, the two regarded each other. Finally, as the others filed out, the German looked away, and went in their wake. The door closed, and the lights dimmed, until Abdullah was in darkness again, a darkness that was mirrored by the thoughts that filled his mind.

11

Erik the Hero

Erik stumbled through the snow, his teeth chattering with the cold. He shivered violently as he plodded along. The snow was falling heavily now, and the deep drifts that he encountered hampered his progress. He peered through the blinding flakes that swirled around him, searching for the tell - tale glow of the fire from the helicopter that had crashed into the laboratory, but the fire had either died, or Duvall's men had put it out. He hoped that he was headed in the right direction; he knew that if he became lost, he would die from the cold. He staggered on doggedly.

An eternity later, he tripped over something, and fell. He slowly rose to his knees and looked at the obstacle. It was Naziboy. He'd fallen a long way when the vampire threw him from the chopper. He lay sprawled on his back; his blue eyes stared blankly into the night sky. A look of surprise was frozen on his face. Erik crawled over to him. The mercenary had a machine – pistol on him. The drummer divested him of it, added it to the others that were slung around his neck, and went through the German's jacket pockets for ammunition clips. Several grenades were attached to his belt. Erik took these also.

He looked into the dead eyes. "Sorry man," he whispered. He closed the eyes, brushing his hand down over the frozen face. "I guess I've gotta be the hero now." He stood up, and looked ahead. "I hope I'm goin' the right way." He stumbled away, and was soon swallowed up in the falling snow.

In a small cell in the facility, Gyorgi, Sergei and Null sat silently, each of them lost in their own thoughts. Sergei mourned his friend; he and Erik had been close for many years, and now the Russian had lost the drummer. He stared at the wall, hoping that it wouldn't be long before the vampires came and killed them all. What were they waiting for?

Null was petrified with fright. The attack on the helicopters had scared him out of his wits. He was curled up in a foetal position on the cold floor. He moaned to himself, his eyes squeezed tightly shut. Gyorgi had tried to stop him from moaning, but the tech hadn't even shown that he realised the other two shared the cell with him.

Gyorgi waited patiently. He knew that an enemy who didn't kill you outright wanted something from you. He wondered what it was. *I didn't see Valeria,* he thought. *I wonder if she is here.* Would she make him an offer to become like her? He looked at the boy. *He's too young and naïve,* he thought. *She wants a companion who's smart and cunning. That's me.* He smiled to himself.

There were sounds at the door. Gyorgi and the Bear looked up, and the door opened, and three of the creatures entered. They regarded the mortals with hungry eyes that were filled with blood.

"Get up," said the leader, indicating Gyorgi.

The Georgian rose. "What do you want?"

The vampire sneered. "Karl wants to see you." He beckoned to his comrades. "Take him." The two came forwards, and one of them took Gyorgi's arm in a vice – like grip. "The boy too." The other one went over to Null, and lifted the boy up as though he were a toy. Null's eyes were clenched shut, and his moans became a whine of terror. The vampire cuffed him, and the tech fell silent as he slumped unconscious in his arms.

"Go," the leader said. The two vampires left, taking the arms merchant and the tech with them. The remaining vampire fixed Segei with a piercing gaze. "You were not wanted," he said. "Perhaps Karl has no use for you."

The Bear stared into those terrible blood – red eyes. For some strange reason, he felt no fear. Now that Erik was dead, he didn't care about anything at all. "My friend is dead," he said flatly. "Kill me too."

The vampire smiled, showing his deadly fangs. "Not yet," he said.

Outside, Erik fell face down in the snow. He knew he couldn't go much further. He felt warm, and realised that his body was giving up. *Why not,* he thought. *Just go to sleep...Some fuckin' hero I turned out to be...*He lay there, the cold sapping his strength. *If only the fire was still there to show me the way.* He looked up, despair filling his heart. "I'm sorry," he croaked. Suddenly, he saw a tiny bright red point of light. "What the fuck?" With a supreme effort, he staggered to his feet. He stumbled towards it, and as he got closer, realised that he saw the light of a burning cigarette as someone drew on it. He circled the man who stood there, who was oblivious of his presence.

"'Go check the perimeter,'" the man grumbled to himself. "As if anyone would be out in this fuckin' snow..." He stomped his feet, trying to get warm.

Behind him, Erik fumbled his knife out of its sheath. He slowly approached the guard, his heart pounding. *If only he doesn't turn,* he thought desperately. He closed in on his victim, amazed at how unaware the man was.

At the last moment, as he reached to take the man's neck and plunge the knife into his back, he tripped and fell against his quarry. With a shout of surprise, the guard turned, trying to unsling his weapon. The drummer leapt forwards, and the knife punched into the man's chest. He fell backwards, and the snow was stained with his blood. Erik gasped, and stared at the bloody knife. Then he looked down at his handiwork.

"Fuck!" He trembled with shock, and fell to his knees. *Just like in the movies,* he thought madly. He giggled insanely. Minutes later, he came to

his senses. *"Shit."* He crept closer to his victim. He grabbed the chrome rifle, turning it over in his hands. He admired the beauty of its shape, and wondered what the thing fired. Examining it closely, he found the release for the magazine, and ejected it. Peering into it, he saw small plastic pellets, shaped like flu capsules. He scratched his head in perplexity. A smell of naphtha came to his nostrils. *Naphthalene, eh,* he thought. *Cool, incendiary pellets. Just like paintball, only with fire.* He replaced the magazine, found the arming button, and activated it. He looked about, but there was no one there; only he and the dead guard. Suddenly, he started, as he saw a fence, and beyond it a building, with a door. He smiled grimly. He got up, slung the rifle over his shoulder, and took the corpse by the heels. He dragged it behind a snow – drift, and then he held the rifle at the ready, and approached the door. "Here I come, ready or not," he said. He tried the handle, and cautiously pushed the door open. He peered inside. No alarm went off, and no one challenged him. With the gun held ready to fire, he ventured inside.

The vampire stared at Sergei. "Do you know what I am thinking?"

The Bear grunted. "I do not care. Erik is dead." He looked down at the floor.

The vampire snarled. "Do I not frighten you?" he hissed.

Sergei looked up. His eyes held a grim fatalistic light. "Not any more. You kill me anytime."

The creature bared its fangs. "Perhaps I will. Karl told me to do with you as I would." A wicked smile appeared on his face. "Stand up."

The Russian shook his head. "You make me," he said defiantly, fixing his enemy with an insolent glare. He folded his arms.

The vampire's face contorted with fury. He snarled again, and made to come over and wrench Sergei to his feet, to rip into his throat with his deadly fangs and drain the Russian's blood. A slight sound at the door made him turn, a curse on his undead lips. A soft pneumatic puff came from the doorway. He exploded into flame, shrieking as he burned. The Bear cried out, and shielded his face behind his hands, feeling the heat lapping him in waves of superheated air. The vampire disintegrated into ash.

"Wow," came a voice, *"I love it!"*

The Bear lowered his hands, and stared at the speaker. He gaped in amazement.

Erik stood in the doorway, a huge grin on his face. "Sorry I'm late."

The Russian slowly rose from the floor, goggling at the drummer. He shook his head. *"No,"* he said, "Impossible! You are *dead.*"

"I mightn't look too good," the drummer said, "but I'm not dead yet."

Sergei shouted joyfully. *"Erik!"* He rushed over, and crushed the drummer in his bear – like arms. He cried openly, shaking with wracking sobs. He drew back, and gazed into Erik's eyes. "I think I lose you," he choked.

Erik patted him on the back. Tears welled up in his eyes and ran down his face. "I missed you too, man." He gazed into the cell. "Where're the others?"

Sergei wiped the tears from his eyes. "Taken."

Erik nodded. He leaned down, and placed the naphtha rifle against the wall. He unslung two of the machine – pistols from around his neck, and presented them to the Russian, who took them. He picked the rifle up again. "Let's go," he said.

Sergei ejected the magazines of the guns, checked and replaced them, and nodded. "Da, is time for payback." He slung the straps over his shoulder, took a gun in each hand, and cocked both of them. He flicked the safeties off.

The drummer smiled. "Here." He gave Sergei several grenades, and then turned and peered out of the door. The corridor was empty.

"This way," Sergei said. He paced down the corridor like a panther, Erik following in his wake. Everything was as silent as a tomb. No – one challenged them, no alarm sounded. Reddish bulbs that were fixed in the ceiling dimly lighted the corridor.

Infrared? Erik thought. He hoped not. They padded silently through the empty corridor, until they came to the laboratory where Abdullah had been held.

Holding up his hand to indicate they should stop, Sergei went over to the door. He shook his head as he looked at the keypad. "Null would open him in second." He placed his hand on the door, and then stepped back in shock as the doorlock was activated. He quickly grabbed Erik and hustled him into a room across the corridor. They both ducked down behind a table as the door opened.

Several of the vampires emerged: Karl, Octavius, Kunda – Bele, and Mariko. Abdullah, who was fitted with some sort of restraining device, followed them. Like the rifle that Erik had taken from the guard, it shone like it was made of chrome. A collar around his neck was attached to a plate that was strapped to his chest by two large bands that were clasped around his back. Two manacles were clamped on the front of the plate, which his wrists were locked into. Two of Duvall's guards followed him, armed with the naphtha rifles that they trained on the prisoner. Bringing up the rear of this little group was Romana; her head bowed upon her chest, her long hair obscuring her face, walking beside Duvall himself, who rolled along in his chair.

Erik made to rise, but Sergei pulled him down, shaking his head. The drummer gritted his teeth, but subsided. They looked at the others from under the table, only seeing their feet.

Karl halted, and the others stopped. He turned and addressed the Frenchman: "This is not acceptable," he said, and his voice shook with anger. His eyes were blood – red. The vampires with him were also angered; they looked at the professor with undisguised rage in their blood filled eyes. Abdullah smiled to himself. The two guards regarded the vampires apprehensively. One of them licked his lips nervously, and swung his rifle away from Abdullah, and covered them. The other guard noticed his companion's action, but kept his own weapon fixed on his prisoner. Sweat began to bead their faces.

"What is this?" croaked the thing in the chair. "We have made a deal."

"We do not *like* your deal," Karl said venomously. "You said that we would have the weapons once you had taken Romana's blood." He stepped towards them, and the man covering them involuntarily backed away. "You have her blood. We want the weapons. *Now.*" He clenched his fist.

Fuck, Erik thought, she did give him her blood. He stared at the feet, wishing that he could see their faces. He glanced at the Bear. The Russian shook his head again. *Wait,* he mouthed silently.

Duvall's harsh croaking laugh came to them. "For an immortal," he said, his voice filled with pain, "you are impatient." He was wracked with a coughing fit. He took a handkerchief and wiped his mouth, and then said: "I will give the weapons to you, but first I must ensure that Romana's blood is indeed the cure I seek."

"Do you think we *lied* to you?" said Mariko.

The Frenchman waved his hands in negation. "No, no," he wheezed.

"Then, *professor*, we will *take* your weapons." Karl's tones dripped with sarcasm. His gaze flicked between the two guards, gauging them. He could smell their fear. The one closest to him was petrified. He had only to leap forwards, and the man would be dead. *But the other?* He thought.

I will take care of him, sent Mariko.

Karl sensed her tensing to spring. He smiled wickedly. "Perhaps we *will* just take them. We have given you our part of the bargain, it seems to me that you are no longer required." He fixed the crippled Frenchman with a deadly gaze. "Do you think that your men here can kill us all before we are at your throat?" He chuckled evilly. "If you are dead, you can no longer hunt us."

For an answer, Duvall reached into his coat, and brought out an object that he held up for them all to see. It was a remote.

"What is that?" asked Octavius.

"Do you see the capsule that is at the bottom of the plate which your friend is shackled to?" Duvall said.

The German frowned. He peered at Abdullah, and he saw the capsule.

The professor pushed a button on the remote, and Karl saw a green light appear. He looked back at the Frenchman, his eyes narrowed in anger.

"Yes," said Duvall, "it is an incendiary device, one which contains the same naphthalene accelerant as these rifles do." He indicated another button on the remote. "If I press *this* button, we will all be incinerated." He held his hand close to the remote.

Karl barked a laugh of contempt. "You will not do it."

The Frenchman brought his thumb closer to the button. "No?" he said.

Kunda – Bele, Mariko, Karl sent, *take the guards. I will deal with Duvall.*

Romana's head came up. Her hair fell away from her face. "No, Karl," she said. She walked unsteadily forwards, until they were face to face. "I have given this mortal what he wants; now you must honour your part of the bargain." Her face was fixed with determination. "I *know* that he will honour his word. He will leave you in peace."

"Peace!" Karl spat. His voice was low and deadly. "Do you know how many of us he has hunted down and used for his disgusting work?"

Romana shook her head. "No," she said calmly, "but I do not think it would equal the number of mortals that we have killed over the centuries." Her gaze swept over the vampires. "Think," she said to them, "once this has been done, you no longer have to fear this mortal. You will be stronger than ever before."

"Fear?" echoed Mariko. She snorted with contempt. "We do not fear him."

The girl smiled knowingly. "I know better." *Your thoughts show that you lie,* she sent.

The Japanese sneered. *Do I?*

Yes. You are all afraid of Duvall and what he represents. Romana turned her gaze back to Karl. *You know I speak the truth.*

The professor coughed for attention. "My arm grows tired. Will you honour your word? Romana is correct; if you agree to our original bargain, there will be no need for me to carry out my 'disgusting works'. His face twisted into a smile. "Well?" His arm shook with the strain of holding the remote.

Karl turned to the others. *We will accept. If he tries to cheat us...*He showed his fangs.

Octavius nodded. *I agree.*

Kunda – Bele's dark face was set like stone. *I also,* he sent grudgingly. *But I did not like this from the start.*

Mariko? The German inquired.

She stared at Duvall, and then fixed the two guards with a deadly gaze. She could see the fear in their eyes, and the pounding of their hearts awakened the thirst within her. *It would be so easy to take them.* She showed her fangs, and almost laughed as the nearest guard gulped in terror.

No. I forbid it. Do you disobey me? Karl bent his own fierce eyes on her.

What of the others? Mariko sent. She stared back in defiance.

They will obey. I am the Clan leader.

Erik brought the gun up, and pressed the stud, arming it. *"We've got to do something,"* he whispered.

The Bear's huge hand closed around his arm. *"Niet. Wait."*

The vampires suddenly became aware of their presence. They'd been so intent on the situation before them that they hadn't realised that the drummer and the Russian were close by.

Your pet is here, Karl sent to Romana, a wry smile appearing on his face.

Romana tensed. *Erik? Gerald told me he was dead.* She sensed the two hiding behind the table. Relief flowed through her as she identified them.

"Well?" Duvall repeated. "I do not wish to hold this all day. Do we burn here, or carry on as agreed?" Although he'd heard none of the vampire's thoughts, he knew that they were communicating, and arguing. He also knew from his experiments that they had some sort of telepathy; it was another of the things that he'd receive when he completed his work, and was cured. He would be strong; stronger than any man, and his body would no longer be some crippled thing wracked with pain, condemned to sit in his chair.

He realised that Karl was chuckling. "Something is amusing?"

The German turned back and faced him. "Yes." He didn't elaborate. "We agree to your terms."

"Good," the professor replied. He pressed another button, and the capsule was deactivated. He lowered his arms, and placed the remote on his lap. "Come." He rolled forwards, and Karl stepped out of his way. The others glared at the Frenchman contemptuously, but they also stepped aside, and Duvall continued down the corridor. Octavius, Kunda – Bele, and Mariko met Karl's eyes, and he nodded. The vampires turned and followed the chair.

Karl began to follow them, and Romana came up and walked alongside him. *Well, your pet is more resourceful than Gerald thought,* he sent. *Perhaps he will assist us?*

Romana smiled. *I am glad he lives. He is a good man, and has come to help me.*

Why? The German sneered. *Because he loves you? What of Abdullah?*

I am here to save him, she sent, *but Abdullah knows of my feelings for Erik.*

Feelings! For this mortal? Then you have chosen him to be your companion? Karl shook his head in disbelief.

Yes, she replied.

Karl looked back over his shoulder, where the two guards were walking at either side of the Arab. Abdullah strode along, his face unreadable. *What do you think of this?* Karl sent. No answer came from Abdullah, and Karl turned and looked at Romana. *So you come and save your mentor, but will take this mortal as your companion instead of being with him?* Karl laughed, and the more nervous of the guards gripped his rifle tighter. The German smiled at his reaction. *You are a fool. Mortals are weak, and he will betray you.* Romana paced along silently, and gave him no answer. Karl shook his head once again, and looked down the corridor at the professor's chair. *That is the only mortal that we have feared, and soon we will fear him no more.* They walked after the group.

Behind them, Erik and the Bear rose to their feet, and slowly and silently crept around the table. Sergei went to the door and peered down the corridor in both directions. When he saw that it was empty, he motioned Erik forwards. Holding his finger to his lips to indicate quiet, he slipped down the corridor in the direction that the others had taken. The drummer followed.

Duvall stopped in front of a door. He activated a keypad on the arm of his chair, and the door opened, revealing a large open space beyond it. The Frenchman rolled inside, and the others followed suit. In the room was a landing bay; doors open to the outside, and several of the institute's helicopters. A dozen of the professor's men stood there, armed with the naphtha rifles. They were guarding several cases that were stacked on the concrete floor. Standing across from them was a group of vampires, Gerald and Edmund at their head. Each group was watching the other intently. As they entered the room, Karl and the others noted that the men's weapons were activated, and were trained on the vampires, who stood there with blood – filled eyes.

"What is this?" he enquired.

The leader of the men came towards them, and stopped in front of the professor's chair. "Sir. Our *friends* seem to be eager to take the weapons that you promised them. I didn't want any - *accidents* - to occur, so I told my men to guard them." he glanced quickly at Karl, fear in his eyes.

The German fixed his gaze on the man, and smiled to himself as he watched the sweat come out on his brow. He looked over at the two groups that were ready to leap into action. The vampires were tensed to rush forwards and attack, and the men were waiting to open up on them with their deadly weapons. Neither group would back down. It was a standoff.

Karl stepped towards them, and several of the men swung their weapons around and covered him. His anger flared immediately. *"You dare!"* he hissed venomously. His eyes became crimson. He whirled upon the professor. "What is this?" he repeated.

Duvall merely smiled, and rolled towards his men. He beckoned, and the two guards pushed Abdullah and Romana after him. He came to a stop, and turned his chair around as the two men escorted them to the rear of the group. Now all of the vampires were on the other side of the hanger, and targeted by the naphtha rifles.

"Well," said Duvall, "this *is* an interesting situation." He steepled his gnarled hands in front of him. His eyes glittered, and his lips twisted with wry humour.

Karl glared at him. "So," he grated, "you betray us." He bared his fangs. "You never meant to give us the weapons." His red gaze swept over the men at the professor's back. "You only wanted to lure us here, so you could destroy us."

"Very good," said the professor, as though he were congratulating a young child who had solved a problem. "You are correct."

A look of hatred flashed across Karl's face, but then was replaced by a smile.

The professor frowned.

"You do not consider the many others of the Clans who are not with us. You may destroy us, but they will come, and they will destroy *you*." The German folded his arms.

Duvall sneered. "Let them come, I have dealt with them before." He leaned forwards in his chair. His voice throbbed with triumph. "Now that I have the blood of the most powerful vampire on earth, I will use it to cure myself, and *I* will be so powerful that I will fear no – one!" He turned to the leader of the guards. "Prepare to fire." He looked back at the vampires. "I am sorry, but our conversation is at an end."

The vampires snarled in impotent hate. Several of them appeared ready to attack, even though they knew they would be shot down in the attempt.

The leader of the guards stepped to one side of his men. He raised his hand. "Ready –"

"I wouldn't do that if I were you," a voice said from the doorway.

Every eye in the hanger swung to face the speaker. Erik stood there, the naphtha rifle trained on the creature in the chair. "Stand down, or the professor gets a taste of his own medicine."

Duvall's tortured laugh came. "Well, here comes the hero." He turned his chair to face the drummer. "You are Erik, I take it?" He nodded in answer of his own question. "I am impressed. You survived the crash, and braved the snow to find us. It must be very cold out there, and you endured it just to come for your girlfriend." He sneered. "How touching."

"Erik!" Romana cried. She made to go to him, but one of the guards pressed his rifle against her throat. At her side, Abdullah snarled a warning, but the other guard who covered him ensured that he couldn't do anything. The Arab turned his crimson gaze on the man, who flinched, but held his ground.

"It'll be a lot hotter in here, if you don't agree to let her and Abdullah go." Erik glanced at the two groups. "Where are Gyorgi and Null? I want them released as well."

"Oh, I *am* sorry," Duvall said mockingly, "but I gave them to your friends there." He indicated the vampires with a negligent wave of his hand. "And you *know* what they wanted them for." He chuckled evilly.

Erik gritted his teeth. *No! I let them die,* he thought. His finger tightened on the trigger. "You bastard."

"*Fool!*" cried Duvall. "What did you expect? It is what *they* do!" He raised a trembling arm and pointed savagely at the vampires. "They are your enemy, not *me!*"

The drummer shook his head. "No," he said roughly, you're more dangerous than them."

Erik, Gerald sent. *He lies. Your friends are unharmed.*

The drummer glanced at the foppish vampire, who nodded.

It is true, sent Karl. *We have not harmed them.*

How can I believe you? Erik replied.

You must trust us, Gerald sent.

Trust you? I don't know if I can.

Then we shall all die here, sent Octavius.

"Well?" Duvall asked, annoyance in his voice, "do we stand here forever, or can we come to some agreement?"

Erik stared at the professor through the rifle's sight. He noticed a door behind the knot of men at Duvall's back open stealthily, and the Bear stepped silently into the hanger. He slowly crept up on the men. "There's only one thing I'll agree to; let Romana and Abdullah go." The drummer thought: *Come on Sergei!*

Very clever, sent Edmund. He smiled wickedly.

"No," the Frenchman said. "I have need of them. But if you put down your weapon, I will allow you to leave."

The Russian was closing in on the two guards who covered Romana and Abdullah. Suddenly, he kicked a can that lay on the floor in his path, and it clattered across the hanger. The guards were galvanised into action. The men at the back of the group swung around, and covered Sergei. The vampires made to rush forwards, but the other guards covered them.

"*Shit!*" Erik yelled.

One of the guards who had him in his sights made as if to fire, but the drummer beat him to it; he shifted his aim from Duvall, and squeezed the trigger. The naphtha rifle spat, and the man instantly turned into a shrieking, blazing torch. Panicked, the other guards opened fire, and three vampires flared brightly as the pellets did their deadly work. The other creatures rushed forwards in a blur of speed, and four of the men went down in a welter of blood. In seconds, the hanger was a mad chaos of fire and death as the guards fired wildly, and the vampires attacked recklessly.

Erik leapt back into the corridor as a hail of pellets peppered the doorway where he'd stood, exploding onto flame. He risked a quick glance into the hanger bay, snapped off a few shots, and then ducked back as another salvo hammered into the wall behind him.

The Bear dropped to the floor as several men fired at him. He rolled his bulk swiftly, and took cover behind some drums. He peered around them, and the chatter of his machine – pistols added to the bedlam as he returned fire. One of the guards went down as Sergei's bullets tore into him. The men scattered, and sought cover.

Abdullah tore the throat out of the man at his side, and turned to help Romana. He didn't need to; the girl had struck the guard down, and rushed over to him. "Help me," Abdullah said. He strained at the manacles, and Romana added her strength to his, pulling with all her supernatural might.

Duvall had been thrown from his chair by the rush, and was crawling to safety. He reached cover behind the stacked weapon crates, and turned to stare out at the melee. He saw the Arab and Romana struggling with the restraints, and he snarled inarticulately. He still held the remote in his hand. Forgetting the girl's usefulness to him in his blind rage, he activated the detonator on the remote, held his finger above the button, and then stabbed it down savagely.

12

Escape

Erik checked the magazine on his rifle. He had no idea how many pellets it held. It seemed almost empty, so he searched the pockets of his jacket for another. When he'd found it, he placed it on the floor, ready for use. He moved to the side of the doorway, intending to keep firing at Duvall's men. Suddenly, a heavy explosion rocked the whole building, and he slid to the floor. Shaking his head groggily, he peered around the door. The hanger was filled with acrid white smoke, which made his eyes water immediately. Men and vampires both stumbled dazedly, concussed by the detonation. He searched the hanger for Romana, but she was nowhere to be seen. Abdullah too, had vanished. Puzzled, he looked everywhere, but he couldn't see them. Where were they? The last time he'd seen them, they'd been trying to get Abdullah out of his restraints.

His blood went cold. *The capsule!* He thought wildly. *Duvall must've detonated it!* "*No!*" he cried in anguish. *"Romana!"* He leapt to his feet, and ran recklessly into the hanger. As soon as he left the safety of the doorway, he was fired upon. He fell to the floor as pellets burst into flames around him. He covered his head with his hands as the fusillade bracketed him. Miraculously, none of the storm of shots hit him.

"Erik!"

The drummer looked up and glanced over to where the voice came from. It was Sergei, who fired at the men who pinned him down. "Quickly!" he yelled, and fired another burst. Erik jumped up, and raced over to slide behind the drums where the Russian had taken cover. Seconds later, pellets whined and blazed around them.

"Thanks, man," Erik panted.

The Bear grinned. "Is okay." He winced as a hail of fire flared around their position. "These bastards pin us down." He peeked around the drums, and fired a short burst. He ducked back as an answering torrent of pellets came. He met Erik's gaze grimly. "I think we die this time."

The drummer nodded. "I think you're right." Suddenly, a light of desperation came into his eyes, and he gripped the Russian's jacket tightly. "Sergei! Have you seen Romana? That explosion…"

"Da. The capsule…" he faltered. "Duvall, he blow it up."

"No," Erik whispered. He released Sergei's jacket, and slumped down.

Sergei took his shoulder in one massive hand. As more shots burst around them, he said: "I am sorry, Erik. I know you loved her."

Tears ran down the drummer's face, and he bowed his head. Suddenly, he looked up. "Sergei! Listen!"

"What?" the Russian asked. And then he realised what Erik meant. Apart from the crackling of fires, and the cries of wounded men, the hanger was silent. Why weren't they being fired on? He motioned Erik to stay down, and slowly raised his head and peered over their cover. No shots came, so he rose to his knees and looked across and saw that the guards had been joined by reinforcements. The vampires; those that survived, were gathered together and were being covered by these men.

Duvall was seated back in his chair, and surrounded by guards. The Russian saw the professor touch a stud on the arm of the chair, and his amplified voice rang out: "Give up. Drop your weapons where we can see them, or I will order my men to kill you both." The guard's rifles came up, and they fixed Sergei in their sights. He glanced down at Erik, who nodded wearily. They came to their feet, tossed their weapons on the floor, and held their hands up. At a gesture from the professor, they walked forwards.

They came to a stop in front of Duvall. He gazed at them contemptuously. "Well," he said acidly, "your little rescue attempt failed."

"What happens now?" Erik asked icily. "Are you going to shoot us?"

"Perhaps," Duvall replied. "You have caused much damage to my facility. Maybe I could find a way to prolong your suffering."

Erik fixed him with a steely gaze. "I don't give a fuck. You killed Romana, so you'd better kill me, or –"

"Erik!"

The drummer stared in amazement as Romana stepped out in front of the vampires. He gaped in astonishment, and tears of relief flowed down his face, cutting furrows through the grime that smeared it. Ignoring the guards, he ran over to the girl, and took her in his arms.

"I thought you were dead!" he choked.

"No," she replied. "Abdullah and I managed to break the manacles and throw the restraint away from us before Duvall detonated the capsule."

The Arab nodded to the drummer. Erik started to thank him, but Abdullah held up his hand.

"I do not need your thanks, mortal. Romana is precious to me also." He pierced Erik with his gaze. "Remember that. Protect her."

"Oh, I don't think he'll be able to," Duvall said derisively.

They turned to see the guards formed up in a firing squad, their weapons aimed at the group. One of the guards pushed Sergei forwards, and he stumbled and came to a stop in front of Erik and Romana.

"Aren't you forgetting something?" Erik said.

The professor raised an eyebrow. "Yes? And what would that be?"

"Romana is precious in more than one way; you need her blood. You can kill *us*, but *she* is too important to you."

A twisted smile appeared on the face of the creature in the chair. "Well, as to that, I have managed to synthesize her blood. I can make as much of it as I like, so she has become redundant." He spread his hands.

"But you can't be sure if her blood will cure you," said Erik. "If you kill her, and it doesn't, you're back to square one."

"My science is more accurate than that." He nodded to the leader of the firing squad.

The man shouted out an order: *"Ready!"*

"So," Karl said venomously, "you will kill us all."

"Yes," Duvall answered. "Surely you know I cannot leave such dangerous enemies as you alive?"

"What of the Clans?" Octavius said. "When they know of your treachery, they will come and slay you."

Duvall laughed, a strangled sound. "As I have said earlier, I have dealt with them before." He motioned for the leader to continue.

"Aim!"

The drummer grabbed Sergei by the arm. "I'm sorry I got you into this," he said.

The Bear grabbed his hand. "Is all right, Erik. I die with my friend."

A withering blast of machine - gun fire came from the open hanger door, mowing down the firing squad. Dumb with amazement, they stared across the floor, to see Ramon and his fire team, guns blazing as they rushed forwards. Demoralized, the guards scattered and were shot down as they searched for cover. Duvall spun away in his chair, and several of his guards ran after him.

"Get him!" yelled Erik. He ran forwards, and picked up a naphtha rifle. Whirling, he snapped off the remaining pellets at the fleeing group. Two of the men at the rear exploded into flames, but the Frenchman and five of his men escaped through the door. It clanged shut behind them.

"After them!" Karl cried, and several of the surviving vampires leapt into the air, and hurtled towards the door, avengers seeking the blood of the traitor. They attacked the door ferociously, tearing at the steel with their talons. With a shriek of tortured metal, the door fell to their assault, and they poured through the opening.

"They will not get far," Karl said.

Ramon sauntered over to them as his fire team made sure the area was secure. His machine – pistol was resting on his shoulder, and a smile was on his face. "Just in the nick of time, eh? How's that, Bear? We even?"

The Russian shook his head. "Not quite. I let you know."

The Mexican laughed. "Good to see you too." His gaze went to Karl. "So, these guys are the vampires, eh? Cool."

Karl looked the pilot over. He couldn't sense any fear from this man; he realized that Ramon was so full of himself, that he didn't even consider anything else. He smiled. "Yes, but we are much *cooler* than you think." He stepped right up to the pilot, and reached out and touched his face.

Ramon recoiled at the ice – cold touch. He stepped back a pace involuntarily.

"In fact," the German went on, "you could say that we are as cold as ice." His smile widened, to show his fangs.

The pilot's bravado fled, as the horrific nature of the creature that stood before him penetrated his bluster. He stared at Karl in shock.

"You do not have to fear me," the German said silkily. "For the moment, we are allies."

Octavius came forwards. "Karl." *You do not need to frighten him.*

Karl turned. Their eyes met. "Yes, of course." He motioned to the other vampires. "Take up our weapons, it is time for us to go." He addressed Romana: "My dear, I hope that you have chosen wisely."

Romana returned Karl's gaze. She came and put her arm around the drummer. "I have. You have what you want. I have what I want."

The vampire's eyes narrowed shrewdly. "Do you?" He glanced at Abdullah knowingly, and then he spun around, and strode over to the crates.

Octavius watched him walk away, and then gestured to a group of vampires who stood with some surviving guards in their grasp. They presented them to Erik and Sergei. "What do you wish to do with these?"

Erik looked at the men, who were all wounded. The vampires stared at him; he knew that they wanted the men for themselves, to take revenge and to drain them dry. The drummer knew he couldn't leave them to the vampires, no matter what they had done. "We'll bring them with us," he said.

Octavius smiled. "As you wish." He gestured, and the vampires released the men, and then they walked over to where Karl was ensuring that the crates contained what he wanted. The guards stood there, amazed that they were still alive.

"So, Ramon," said Erik, "how did you survive the attack on the choppers?"

The pilot grinned. "Well, when those things attacked, and I saw one of the choppers go down, I got the hell out of there, and ran just above the trees. I circled for a bit, and then I saw an explosion and a fire. It was snowing; there were no vampires in sight, so I took a chance and came in to check it out. Turned out to be the lab, where one of our birds went down. It must've taken out the security grid, 'cause I couldn't read anything on my 'scopes, so we landed, and came in. When we heard guns, and saw how this door was wide open, we decided to join the party." He smiled widely. "Pretty good, huh?" He laughed at the grim look on Sergei's face; the Russian had listened to his story without any show of interest. Ramon shook his head. He knew that the debt he owed to the Bear wouldn't be paid so easily. Suddenly, it struck him that not everyone was there. "Hey, where's Gyorgi?" he asked. "Did he –"

"No," said Erik. "He wasn't killed, but he and Null…"

"They are with them," said Sergei, nodding in the direction of the vampires.

Karl heard them, and came back across the floor. "Your friends had an

– *inclination* - to join us."

"*Join you?*" Ramon echoed disbelievingly. He shook his head. "Bullshit. What the fuck does *that* mean?"

Karl fixed him with an evil glare. "It means that they wish to have immortality, and great powers like us." His reddened eyes gazed deeply into Ramon, who felt like they were plumbing the very depths of his soul.

The pilot flinched. He brought his gun up, and cocked it. "Back off!"

The German smiled wickedly. "I am sorry," he said mockingly, "do I *frighten* you?" He took a step forwards, and Ramon fell back nervously.

Sweat beaded the Mexican's face, and he shivered with fright. Still, he kept the vampire in his sights. He gulped, and said: "You don't fuckin' scare me."

"No?" Karl said, his voice low and venomous. "I could take that toy away from you, and kill you before you could even take a breath."

"There is no need for this, Karl," said Romana. "Leave him be."

"Leave him alone," Erik said.

Karl's gaze swept over them. He stared at them contemptuously, and then looked back at the sweating Ramon. He shrugged. "As you wish," he sneered, and turned to walk away.

Ramon blew out a breath, and lowered his weapon. In a flash of speed, Karl rushed over to him, struck the machine – pistol from his hands, and took the Mexican in a deadly embrace, his fangs close to Ramon's pulsing jugular. He looked out at the others, his blood – filled eyes daring them to intervene. Ramon's fire team all brought their guns to bear on the vampire and his captive.

"*Stop!*" Octavius cried. He strode over, watching the men carefully, well knowing the power of their weapons. "Release him, Karl."

Karl stared at them. "But this mortal offends me. He does not understand the power that we possess. He thinks that what he sees of vampires in movies is what we are. He has no conception of the true nature of our people. The centuries that we have ruled from the darkness mean nothing to him; the great effectiveness of the Clan's manipulation of puny mortal civilization is unknown to his limited intellect. He belittles us." He bent Ramon's head back, exposing the Mexican's neck. "For that, he should die."

"No," said Abdullah. He stepped in front of the pair. "There has been enough death this day. Release him."

He and Karl stared fixedly at each other.

Within the complex, Duvall and his guards were traversing the corridors as fast as the professor's chair could go. They came to a door, and as he wheeled up to it, three of the men turned, and looked back down the corridor, their weapons raised and ready to fire. The professor reached towards a keypad set in the wall, and tapped out a code. The door opened, and he drove through, and two of his guards followed him inside. As the others turned to follow, the pursuing vampires rushed at them. At the sound of their screams, one of the men inside the other room punched the keypad in the room, and the door closed, leaving their companions to an awful fate. The muffled sounds of carnage came dimly to those who had escaped.

Duvall wheeled over to a console. He lifted a cover, and pulled out a key that hung on a chain that was around his neck. He inserted the key, and turned it. An alarm shrilled, and red lights blinked rapidly, filling the room with a lurid red glow. He turned and drove over to another door and opened it using the keypad that was there. When the door opened, he drove through, and his men followed. The door shut.

The standoff in the hanger was rudely interrupted by the alarm. Everyone looked about in confusion. Octavius strode over and grabbed one of the guards. "What is this?" he demanded.

The man gulped in terror. "I - it's a - self destruct alarm!"

"How long!" yelled Erik.

"Five minutes."

"Out!" Karl roared. He flung Ramon to the floor, and rushed over to the crates. "Take them!" The other vampires flashed over to the crates swiftly. Karl looked over at the group of mortals. "Until next time," he said scornfully. He rose into the air, and the others followed, lifting the crates from the floor with ease. They flew out of the hanger like streaks of lightning.

"The chopper!" Sergei cried. He picked the stunned Ramon up, and ran towards the open door. The others raced after him. They pelted through the snow, as the alarm howled behind them.

"Where?" the drummer gasped.

"Over there," one of the fire - team answered, pointing ahead of them.

They raced towards the black machine, panting with exertion as they staggered along. The guards had followed, stumbling in their wake. They came up to the chopper, and Sergei wrenched the hatch open. He flung Ramon inside, leapt in, and picked the stunned pilot up, and manhandled him into the cockpit. He dropped the Mexican into the pilot's seat, and slapped him roughly, trying to bring him around.

Erik got into the chopper, followed by the fire – team. Abdullah and Romana followed, but as the guards attempted to board, one of the fire team cocked his machine – pistol, and aimed it at them.

"Not you bastards." His face was grim.

"Please!" One of the men standing in the snow begged. "Let us come!"

"Fuck off!" the man with the gun snarled.

The men outside stared into the helicopter, their only hope to escape the destruction of Duvall's facility. In desperation, they made to jump into the compartment. The alarm shrilled in the air, a reminder that their time was rapidly elapsing.

"Back!" cried the gunman. He flourished the weapon in their anxious faces. "I'll shoot anyone who tries to get on."

"Let them in!" Erik yelled.

"No! They killed Tony. Let 'em die."

In the cockpit, Ramon started to come to his senses. "Wha –?" he shook his head groggily, and gazed around in bewilderment. "Where are we?"

Sergei shook him. "The chopper. Take off!"

The Mexican regarded him dazedly. "What's that noise?"

"Is alarm for destruction of base. Quickly! Get us away!"

Ramon stared at the Russian, a confused look on his face. Suddenly, that confusion was wiped away as he finally understood the import of Sergei's words. "A bomb? Shit!" He turned to the controls, throwing switches rapidly. The engine fired, and the blades began to turn as he rushed through the take – off procedure.

At the hatch in the rear, the sound of the engine and the turning of the blades made Duvall's guards surge forwards, terrified that they'd be left behind. The man inside with the gun snarled and fired, cutting two of them down. The others backed, anger and fear contorting their faces.

"Stop it!" Erik cried.

With a suddenness that stunned Erik, Abdullah reached out and grabbed the man with the machine – pistol. With a twist of his hands, he broke the man's neck, and flung him outside the chopper. He beckoned to the shocked guards. "Come!"

As one, they leapt inside, as the drummer stared at the corpse that lay in the snow. He turned to admonish Abdullah, but the vampire fixed him with his eyes. "No time for such stupidity."

Shaken, Erik merely nodded, and then turned away.

From the cockpit, Ramon yelled: *"Hang on!"*

The helicopter sprang into the air with a sickening lurch, and sped away just clearing the trees surrounding the laboratory. They hurtled through the air, as the seconds remaining for the countdown bled away.

Suddenly, there was a bright flash behind them, and moments later, a thunderous roar proclaimed the destruction of Duvall's facility. The shockwave rushed towards them, and struck the chopper, sending it tumbling and reeling drunkenly through the air. Ramon gripped the control column, his knuckles white with the strain of his attempt to control their mad plunge. Finally, the helicopter flew in a straight line, as they flew out of the turbulence. The Mexican activated his mic, speaking to the cabin. "We made it!" he turned to Sergei. "Not bad, huh?"

The Bear smiled. "Da. You do good." He held out his massive hand.

The pilot stared at him, surprised. He knew that the Russian hadn't forgiven him. Or had he? He grinned and held out his hand. "Even?'

Sergei nodded. "Da."

They shook hands firmly. Behind them, Erik went to the window and looked back, to see a massive fireball climbing into the sky. He flinched as someone put an arm around him. He turned to see Romana. She took his face in her hands, leaned forwards and kissed him.

She gazed into his eyes. "I want to explain –"

He held up his hand, silencing her. "It's okay. I know what you're gonna say." He faltered. "Uh – You and Abdullah..." He took her ice – cold hands in his own.

She smiled, and laughed. "It is not like that. I owed Abdullah my life. I came to free him, but it is you I love. He is my mentor, but I have chosen you for my companion."

He stared into her beautiful face. A stunned look came to his own. *She loves me?* He thought, amazed. He'd thought that she'd gone off to be with Abdullah forever. His mouth opened in surprise, and he took a deep breath, feeling his heart thundering in his chest. He sighed in relief. "You love me?" he said, astounded. His voice throbbed with emotion.

"Yes," she said. "Do you doubt me?"

"No, no. It's just that – when you went away, I thought –"

She silenced him by placing her hand over his lips. "It is you that I want to be with." She took him in her arms.

He put his arms around her, and hugged her hard body. Over her shoulder, he met the Arab's gaze. As he watched them, an unreadable expression came to his vampire face. Erik stared into those eyes, wondering if Abdullah would honour his word. The guards that had escaped with them had crowded along the seat, sitting as far as they could get from the vampire. The helicopter fled into the night.

On the ground far below them, Duvall watched the helicopter until it disappeared from view. He smiled to himself, and turned to the man beside him. "Now I can begin. They have no idea that I am alive."

The guard frowned. "Can you be sure of that, sir?"

Duvall nodded. "Of course I am sure. They are too wrapped up in each other to consider my survival."

"And the other vampires?"

"They are no longer a threat. Once I have perfected the transmutation, I will be immortal, and then my army will follow. They will not dare to oppose me. Besides, I left them a little surprise that should discourage them."

The guard looked back at the burning ruins behind them. "But the laboratory?"

"Its destruction was necessary. You know that I have other facilities, Claude." He turned his chair to face the Mercedes that awaited them. "Now we will go, and begin to create the most powerful army that the world has ever seen. Come." He drove his chair over to the waiting car, and his men assisted him inside. Claude got into the seat beside him, and closed the door. The car started up, and then drove away into the night.

13

Home

Erik twirled his sticks, showing off. The insistent throb of a new song began, and the crowd screamed. Elektra and Nick both leapt into the air, and came to the floor on the downbeat. A savage riff ripped into the club as *Maschinekult* exploded onstage; Jon's bass pumped thunderously, and Suzi ripped through a rapid-fire barrage of arpeggios. Elektra's voice soared and wailed. Erik kicked the song along with industrial precision. The crowd in front of them leapt about and pumped fists in time. Mouths gaped as the chorus kicked in, and they all sang along, screaming at the top of their lungs.

The drummer looked out over the sea of faces, and saw Romana and Abdullah. They stood silently at the bar and watched the band play. Abdullah was dressed in a green silk suit, and wore a black satin shirt. Many women had checked him out, impressed. Romana wore a gothic inspired corset over a full velvet dress that was a deep red. Her hair was swept up, and a necklace in the shape of a black widow nestled between her breasts. She'd also been stared at; she was the most stunning creature in the room.

Are you sure he is the one you want? Abdullah sent to the girl at his side.

Yes, she replied. *I know that we can be happy together.* She gazed at Erik, her eyes filled with love.

The Arab turned to her. "Then I am satisfied. I will go to Karl and tell him I will join them. I will make him promise that he will leave you alone." He put his hand on her shoulder. "I will leave you now." He dropped his arm, and salaamed.

As he turned to go, she grabbed his arm. "Please wait. I want you to meet the band, and to say goodbye to Erik."

"Is that necessary?" He looked up at the stage. *A mortal! To be my Romana's companion.* He scrutinised the drummer, looking deep within. *He has strength, and he is brave. Perhaps...*

"And he loves me," said Romana. "I am certain of that."

"If he ever hurts you..." Abdullah left the unspoken threat hanging.

She smiled. "He would not." She laughed. "Anyway, he knows that you would come and deal with him if he ever tried. He is afraid of you."

"Me? Why would that be?" A wry grin came to Abdullah's face. "Very well. I will wait."

She put her arms around him and hugged him tightly. "Thank you."

The band finished the last song. They came to the edge of the stage, and linked arms and bowed. Amid the howls for more, they turned and walked off. The lights came up, and after a few moments, the crowd began to reluctantly disperse, all but those who tried to get backstage.

"Let us –" Romana began, and stopped, as they both felt another presence in the room. She and the Arab turned, to see two figures approaching them.

Gerald and Valeria stopped in front of them. "Well," said the blonde dandy, "I like your suit, Abdullah. You have good taste." Valeria smiled at them, saying nothing.

"Thank you. What are you doing here?"

"Yes," added Romana, "What do you want, Gerald?" She clenched her hands into fists, and anger radiated from her.

Gerald raised his hand. "There is no need to get angry. I was sent by Karl to speak to you."

"Speak?" echoed the girl. "What about?"

"He wishes me to tell you about Duvall's treachery."

"Treachery?"

"Yes. The containers the weapons were in were fitted with explosives, and once in the air, they were detonated, killing many of our people. He had no intention of letting us have them."

Romana saw the anger in his eyes; the hatred that Gerald now felt for the Frenchman. He had betrayed their trust. "Perhaps he never wanted you to have the power that they represented." She shook her head. "I do not understand why Karl wanted them in the first place; we are powerful ourselves, *we* are weapons. Why should we need guns?"

"She is right," added Abdullah, "We are perfect killers without his toys."

As he said this, Valeria smiled. She stared at the Arab with interest.

They stopped talking for a moment, as the crowd meandered past them, some of them glancing at the group in curiosity. They waited until it was clear, and then Gerald said: "You are right. Why *would* Karl want them?" A smile that held humour in it was on his immortal face. "It is a mystery."

The light of understanding came to Romana's eyes. "He did *not* want them."

Gerald grinned openly, showing his fangs. He nodded. "Yes. Very good, my dear Romana. You are quite correct."

"Why this game then?" asked Abdullah. "If he was not interested in obtaining such things –" He stopped as he realised that Gerald and Valeria were both staring at the girl at his side. He turned to her.

"He only wanted me," she said. "The weapons were only a decoy. Karl only wanted to get to Duvall."

Valeria smiled. "She *is* smart, as well as pretty." She laughed.

Romana glared at her.

Abdullah stepped forward. "And why would he want to do that? Surely not to rescue me?"

One of the security guards came up to them. "Time to go, folks. Please make your way to the door."

Romana smiled at him. "We have been invited backstage."

The man looked bored. "Oh, yeah? I wasn't told about it. The club's closed, and you have to leave."

Valeria sauntered over to him. The guard gazed at her with interest. She ran a finger down the front of his shirt. As he looked into her eyes, she grabbed his tie. As he felt the strength in her hand, a look of confusion spread over his face. What was this? He turned to catch the eye of two other security men who were ushering the last of the punters out of the door. With a flick of his eyes, he signalled them for help.

"*Valeria.*" Gerald warned.

She dropped the tie, and turned to face the blonde vampire. "You never let me have any fun," she pouted. She patted the guard's tie down flat as the other two arrived.

"Trouble?" asked one of them.

"These wise guys –" began the guard.

"There you are!" Peach hurried over. "Romana, Erik's been looking for you. Bring your friends backstage." He addressed the first guard: "It's cool, Tony, these are Erik's guests."

The man considered the roadie. "It'd be nice of him to let us know," he said sourly.

Peach spread his hands apologetically. "Sorry, man. You know how crazy it is after a gig."

The guard shook his head, and then sent them away with a cursory stab of his thumb towards the stage door. "Okay. Get goin' then. Come on, boys." He and his companions walked over to the door, to make sure that everything was secure. He looked back at Valeria once, and then turned away.

"I think he likes you," Gerald said.

The redhead smiled wickedly. "I could eat him for breakfast."

"Lead the way, Peach," Romana said.

They followed the roadie across to the backstage door, and entered.

They walked along the passage, and came to the door to the green room. Peach opened it, and gestured to them to go in. Inside, there was the usual group that hung around the band, talking, drinking, and generally congratulating them on another awesome show.

Erik saw Romana and came over. He stopped as he saw Gerald and Valeria. He flashed Romana a quizzical look.

"It is all right," Gerald said, his tone soothing, "I am not here to cause trouble."

"Oh yeah?" the drummer replied. "I've heard that one before."

Valeria sauntered over to stand in front of him. "We are only here as friends. Don't you want to be friends?" She devoured him with her eyes.

"Some friends," Erik said, his voice filled with contempt.

"Is everything okay?" asked Peach. He stood behind Valeria and Gerald, and the drummer could see that he had one hand in his jacket pocket, where he knew the roadie kept his flick knife.

Without turning, Valeria said: "What do you intend to do with that toothpick?" She stared at Erik, but her attention was focussed on Peach.

The drummer raised his hand. "It's cool. I think she means what she says."

"Of course I do," the redhead purred. In a flash, she reached out and touched Erik's face. "We don't want to hurt our friends." She stroked his face, her touch icy, but gentle.

The roadie whipped out his blade, and met the drummer's eye. Erik shook his head slowly.

Romana stepped forwards. She glared at Valeria.

Gerald came and put his hand on the redhead's shoulder. Valeria smiled at Romana, and dropped her hand. Peach returned his knife to his pocket. He looked at Erik, who inclined his head to indicate the bar. Peach shrugged, and walked over to the main group.

"Ro!" Suzi came over, and hugged the girl. She stepped back, and her gaze met Abdullah. She gazed in open admiration at the Arab. "Hey, who's this?"

Abdullah bowed. "I am Abdullah."

The keyboardist smiled, and held out her hand. "Suzi. Come and have a drink."

The Arab looked at Romana.

Go on, she sent.

Abdullah reached out and took Suzi's hand. She smiled and led him away to the makeshift bar, where she poured them both a drink.

Erik watched in trepidation as the Arab downed his swiftly. Suzi chugged her drink, and then poured for them again. Erik turned to Romana. "Is that okay?" he asked, glancing at Gerald and Valeria.

"We *can* eat and drink," she said, "but it holds no sustenance for us."

"It is dry and tasteless," added Valeria, her lip curling in disgust.

The drummer smiled wryly. "Dining on ashes, huh?"

The redhead glared at him.

"You are a poet," said Gerald dryly.

They fell silent as Elektra broke away from her fans and came over to them. She looked at Gerald and Valeria, and raised an eyebrow at the drummer.

"It's okay, boss," he said, "What happened before –"

"– was just a misunderstanding," said Gerald. "Please allow me to apologise for my conduct." He stepped forwards, and took Elektra's hand, and kissed it.

The singer stared at him strangely. Who *was* this weirdo? She'd seen all sorts of freaks at gigs, but he acted and spoke as though he was in one of those old time movies. He was dressed like someone out of a play. "Uh – no problem. Glad you could catch the show." As he released her hand, she turned, flashing Erik a look that said: 'what a freak.' "Come and have a drink." She smiled and left them.

"I could drink them all," Valeria said, eyeing the others hungrily.

"You said you wouldn't cause any trouble," the drummer said. He regarded the two vampires warily.

"We will not," said Gerald. "I spoke the truth. We are here as messengers. I told you of Duvall's treachery."

"I am surprised that you took him at his word," said Romana. "Even after you knew of all of the terrible experiments that he had performed on our kind, you trusted him. It was a mistake."

"Yes," said the blonde dandy, "but you do not know all of it." He glanced at Erik.

"What you have to say to me can be heard by Erik also. He is my companion."

Valeria laughed. Gerald smiled deprecatingly. "Very well. Duvall is creating an army of immortals, using the samples of your blood. He has managed to make more of it somehow, using his science. These creatures will be as powerful as you are, and will answer only to him. Can you imagine how unbeatable such an army will be, armed with his weapons?"

"How do you know this?" Romana asked.

"We sent some assassins after him," said Valeria. "After what he had done to us, he deserved to die."

"He killed three of them, but sent one back to us as both a message, and a warning," Gerald added. His eyes filled with anger. "She came to us, broken and beaten, and told us about the things that he was making, and she said that he was watching us, and had told her to tell us not to interfere with him again."

"When she had told the Clan leaders this, she burst into flame, and was incinerated right before our eyes," said Valeria. Her face was set like stone. "No mortal has ever dared to do such a thing before."

"She had been fitted with one of the Frenchman's infernal devices," said Gerald. He paused and thought for a moment, and then continued: "Karl has asked me to come to you to ask for your help. If you join with us, your strength could be a great asset. We could destroy this threat once and for all."

"I am sorry that this has happened," said the girl, "but I am no longer involved. I gave him what he wanted to save Abdullah. My part has been played."

"Hang on," said Erik. They all regarded him. "If your blood allowed this Duvall guy to create these – *things* – then you have to help them. You owe them."

Gerald stared at the drummer admiringly. "You surprise me, mortal. Why would you think that Romana should help us, when you are afraid of us?"

"It's the right thing to do," Erik said. "Think, Romana, if you hadn't given your blood, this wouldn't have happened."

She frowned. "You *agree* with them? You want me to help them?"

He nodded. "Yes."

"You were right to choose this one," said Valeria. "He is smart as well as brave." She stared at Erik. "Handsome, too. If I wanted a companion…"

Gerald held up his hand. "Enough of that." He gave Romana an imploring look. "Will you help us?"

The girl's gaze swept over them. She couldn't sense any subterfuge in either of them. Could they be speaking the truth?

You know that we are, sent Valeria.

You must help us, Romana, Gerald sent. A beseeching look came to his face.

"Aloud, please," she said.

The redhead smiled wryly. "You want us to grovel before your companion?"

"No. I only want him to hear everything."

"That *is* everything. I have told you all. It only remains for you to decide if you will help us." Gerald stood waiting expectantly.

Romana turned to the mortal at her side. "You really think I should help them?"

Erik nodded. "Yeah. I know it's probably the last thing that you want to do, but I still say that you owe it to them." He glanced at the two vampires. "I know that you couldn't live with the fact that it was your blood that allowed Duvall to make such monsters."

"*Live?*" echoed Valeria, her voice amused.

"You know what I mean," said the drummer.

"Well?" asked Gerald.

"I will consider it. Allow me to give it some thought. I will tell you tomorrow what I decide."

"Decide quickly," said Gerald. He turned to Valeria. "Shall we have a drink?"

"Of course," the redhead replied. "For appearances sake." She held out her arm, and he took it, and they walked over to the bar, where Suzi and Abdullah were matching each other drink for drink.

Erik shook his head. "Enemies one day…"

"Do not be fooled by their words," Romana said. "They are only friendly because they need me. They could indeed kill everyone here, and you know it."

"But they won't."

"No. But I believe that I can trust them." She looked into his eyes. "At least until we have settled with the Frenchman once and for all."

"Then what happens?"

She put her arms around him. "What do you *want* to happen?"

He stroked her beautiful face. "I want us to be together, just the two of us."

She smiled. "I have something to tell you."

"Yeah?"

She watched him carefully, not knowing how he would react to her news. How could she tell him? She thought deeply for a moment, but realised that the only way was to tell him straight out. "I am with child. *Your* child."

"*What?*" "How?"

"I thought you knew how babies were created?"

"Yeah, but, but - what about those herbs that you told me you take to stop that from happening?"

She shrugged. "I ran out of them." She stared deeply into his eyes. "You are not pleased?"

"Uh – yeah! You just surprised me, is all." He hugged her. "That's great! Do you know if it's a boy or a girl?"

"I do not know. Does it matter?"

"No." He paused. Concern came to his face. "Will you be okay to go and help the Clan in this state?"

"I am not an invalid. I have conquered much greater difficulties than this."

"I'm going too, then," he said.

"I was hoping you might." She looked over at the others. "We should join them, they are wondering why we are standing over here."

"Come on then." He put his arm around her, and they walked over and joined the party.

14

The Truce

Erik took a deep pull at his drink and regarded the group gathered in his lounge room. After the gig, they had come back to his loft to discuss the finer points of the truce that Gerald and Valeria had come to see Romana about. It was strange to see them standing there, talking. Not so long ago, they had both appeared here as dangerous enemies; but now... He shrugged, and listened. Sitting to his left was Sergei, and he watched and listened to the vampires, his face uneasy. He and the drummer had spoken about the alliance on the way, and the Russian wasn't convinced that the offer was genuine, or that Gerald and Valeria would keep their word. It wasn't his business, but he wanted to help Erik anyway he could. After the drummer had saved him from certain death at Duvall's laboratory, he felt deeply his debt to his friend. And Sergei *always* paid his debts. He leaned back in the chair, and Erik turned and met his gaze. The drummer raised an eyebrow, as if to say: 'What do you think?'

The Bear shrugged. He knew that anything could happen.

"The only thing that will happen is that we will find Duvall, and destroy his army," said Gerald, reading the human's minds. He smiled dryly at them. "You do not have any faith in us, do you?" At his side, Valeria mirrored his smile, her green eyes staring at Erik contemptuously.

Erik drained his glass, and put it down on the table. He met the vampire's stare. "Would you?" He rose to his feet, his gaze never leaving the pair. "I don't like the idea of Romana going with you to meet the Clans alone, after what happened before."

"We don't care what you don't like, mortal," said Valeria coldly.

The blonde dandy shook his head. "I do not understand you. First you convince Romana to help us, but now, you do not want her to come with us. Why?"

"I'll tell you why," Erik said.

"Please do," Valeria purred.

The drummer ignored her. "Because she was almost killed when she went with you. Duvall –"

"– only wanted her blood." Gerald finished. "He did not want to kill her."

"Yeah, and now he's got it, and can make more of it whenever he wants. That means she's dispensable." He walked over and stood before them. "And I don't think he'll hesitate to kill her if he gets the chance." He folded his arms, waiting for Gerald to reply.

Gerald smiled. "You impress me, mortal. When you first met me, I could feel your fear. Now...you have faced that fear." His eyes hardened. "But do not believe that I will not slay you if you get in my way."

"Gerald," Romana said warningly.

He smiled, and turned to her. "Do not worry, my dear. I will not hurt your pet." He turned his gaze back upon the drummer. "If he insists on coming with you, I will not argue. But..." He raised his hands and shrugged in a very human gesture.

"But if something happens to me, you won't hold yourself responsible," Erik finished.

"Oh, he *is* clever," Valeria said sarcastically. "We did not even have to spell it out for him." Her eyes held amusement in their depths.

"Don't worry," the drummer replied, "I know you won't go out of your way to protect me. I can look after myself."

"I am sure you can," said Gerald. "But if we take you along, you will slow us down."

"And Karl was very insistent that we come to him quickly," Valeria added. "He is not one to – *disappoint*."

"Yeah, Romana told me what a big, happy family the Clans are. What with Karl killing anyone who upsets him, I'm surprised that there are any of you left."

"He is not to be trifled with," Gerald said. "He is used to being obeyed without question. He and Octavius are the oldest and strongest among us, but Octavius was a Roman, and a civilised one at that. Karl was a barbarian, and his people were used to taking power by killing all who stood in their way."

"He is the leader of the Clans," said Valeria, "As such he *must* be obeyed."

"Even if it means he gets you all killed?" Erik snorted derisively. "Even the dumbest soldier wouldn't follow so blindly –"

Valeria's eyes filled with blood, and she leapt forward, only to be grabbed from behind by Romana and Gerald. She bared her fangs at the drummer as they held her struggling form inches away from him. He gaped at her in shock.

"Release me!" She shrieked.

There was a click.

"That is enough."

They all turned to see Sergei standing by the wall, pointing the Very pistol at them. "Such bickering is stupid. Behave yourselves." He was calm and focussed. "Erik, sit down."

The drummer gazed at him, still in shock. "What?"

"Sit!"

Erik stumbled back, and fell into the lounge, amazed at his friend's composure. Sergei was petrified of the vampires – wasn't he?

"Good. Now, Valeria, will you behave, or do I shoot you?"

The three vampires gazed at him. The redhead relaxed, and Gerald and

Romana released her and watched her cautiously. She glared at the Russian.

"You *dare* threaten me?" She said icily.

"Da. I kill you if you do not listen."

She folded her arms. "Listen to this fool?" She indicated Erik with a contemptuous nod.

"Da. Erik save us all. If not for him, we would all be dead."

Gerald stared at the Russian. "You surprise me, mortal. Not long ago, you were terrified by our very presence, but now, you threaten us. Where is your fear?"

Sergei smiled. "Is gone. I was ready to die in Switzerland, killed by one of your kind, and prepared myself. But Erik saved me, and now – I do not know why, but I do not fear you. I am soldier again." He met the drummer's eye, and Erik was surprised to see the coolness there in his friend's gaze. Sergei winked at him.

Romana smiled. She walked over, and gave Sergei a hug. The Russian kissed her forehead.

"How nice," Valeria said dryly.

"Now we sit and talk nice, da?" He motioned the vampires towards the lounge.

Valeria exchanged a glance with Gerald.

Let me kill the fool, she sent to him.

No, he sent, *let us humour him.* He walked over to the lounge, and sat down at Erik's left. He looked at Valeria expectantly.

The redhead shook her head in exasperation, but went and sat on one of the chairs. She leaned back, crossed her long legs, and folded her arms. "Well? Are you happy now?" she said sarcastically.

The Bear nodded. "Da. Please continue, Erik."

Romana came over and sat on the lounge on the drummer's right. Erik glanced at the two vampires sitting at either side of him, and then said: "Well, I want to go with you. I promised Romana that I would." He thought for a moment. "And I'd die for her if I had to."

Romana put her cold hand on his knee, and he covered it with his own. They exchanged a loving glance.

"How romantic," Valeria sneered.

"But you do not have much to offer us," Gerald said. "A lone mortal –"

"Wait," said Sergei, "I come too, to look out for Erik. I have Gyorgi's weapons and helicopters." He came and stood at the table, and picked up his drink from where he had left it. He drained it, and then put the empty glass back down. "That is worth something, da?" He eased the hammer back on the Very pistol, and lay it down on the table. He met Valeria's cold stare, as if he challenged her. The redhead gave him a grudging look of respect.

"He is right, Gerald," Romana said, "Facing Duvall without these modern weapons is suicide, especially now that he has created this immortal army. We must have Erik and Sergei's support."

Gerald stared at The Bear. His eyes glazed over as his mind went back over the centuries, recalling all of the foolish mortals that had tried to kill him and his kind. Until Duvall had invented the naphtha weapons, most of them had been unsuccessful. But now...

"Yes," said Romana, reading his thoughts, "You know they must come. It is the only way to defeat Duvall."

The blonde vampire looked over at Valeria. She shrugged.

`If they want to come and die*, she sent, *let them*. She gazed at the two mortals, and smiled wickedly.

"Very well," Gerald said aloud, "Come if you must." He looked at the drummer and the Russian in turn. "But I will not guarantee your safety; you will have to look after yourselves." He rose to his feet, and Valeria followed suit. "But we are leaving at dawn. We will not wait for you if you are not ready."

"Is okay," Sergei said. "I call Ramon, he is waiting." He pulled his phone out of his coat, and punched in the pilot's number. When Ramon answered, he walked over to the window, talking rapidly.

"Cool," Erik said. "Another chopper ride."

"Let us hope that it is less eventful than the last," said Gerald.

"Yeah," Erik agreed. He stood up. "I'm gonna pack some clothes." He walked into the bedroom.

"So, Romana," Valeria said, "Your pet will come with us after all."

Romana gave her a look of contempt. "He is resourceful. He saved us all at Duvall's laboratory."

"And he *loves* you," the redhead said sarcastically.

"Yes. He does."

"But it is foolish. You know that he will die, and you will go on, immortal." Valeria shook her head. "I prefer one of our own kind as a companion."

"Until you tire of them," the girl said coldly.

"I do get bored so quickly," Valeria said, yawning theatrically and playing with her hair. She turned her green eyed gaze upon Romana. "But you yourself have had many other mortals as your companions over the centuries. What do you see in such pitiful creatures?"

The girl stared at her. "I see their acceptance of me; they do not care what I am. Even when they know that I will go on after they die, they love me and want to be with me, however long that lasts." She touched her belly. "And now I have a child by Erik. I will love and care for it."

"Why did you do this, Romana?" Gerald asked, his face aggrieved.

"My supply of contraceptive herbs ran out. I wanted him, and I wanted a child." She met his hurt gaze. "It was my own decision."

"It was stupid." The blonde vampire rose to his feet. He looked down at her. "You should not have done this."

"Why? It has nothing to do with you, or The Clans."

"Oh, but it does. Think, Romana, if Duvall finds out about this child, surely he will want it." He paused. "And what do you think Karl will say?"

"Karl?" Romana echoed.

"Yes," Valeria added, "He will not allow you to give birth to this child. In his eyes it is just like the Abominations. You know Karl and the other Clan leaders are obsessed with the purity of our people."

"How can you say that? Erik is no vampire. Very likely it will have no powers at all, and just be human. Duvall will not have any use for it, and Karl will not have to trouble himself."

Gerald shook his head gravely. "No. It has happened before. Every time a mortal and one of us has had offspring, the Dark Blood is always stronger than the human blood."

"Once Duvall learns of the child, he *will* want it," Valeria added. "Its blood will be powerful, and he will stop at nothing to get it."

"I do not care about such things. I only wish to be left alone."

"But others do care," said Valeria coldly, "and it is they who will seek this child out, and take it from you."

The girl slowly turned to face the redhead. "They can try."

The Bear came over. "Is good. Ramon he is waiting for us." He noticed the tension in the three vampires. "What is wrong?"

Romana exchanged a glance with Valeria and Gerald. *Do not say anything*, she sent to them both.

The blonde dandy stared at her, knowing how futile it would be to change her mind. *Very well*, he sent in reply. He sat down, resignation written on his pale face.

The girl turned again to Valeria, who only shrugged and nodded. *If that is what you want.*

It is. Romana stood. "Nothing," she lied. "I will go and see what is keeping Erik." She walked into the bedroom.

"Well, comrade," Valeria said, "you join us once again." She gazed at him, her pale face showing puzzlement. "I still cannot understand how you could master your fear." She smiled. "I am impressed."

The Bear smiled in return. "Make no mistake, I watch you for tricks."

"Tricks?" She pouted. "I would not do that to you. We are friends?"

"Only for short time," he answered. "I only come for Erik and Romana."

Erik and Romana sat on the bed. She put her hand on his knee.

"Are you certain of this? You have seen how dangerous and merciless Duvall is. If you become involved –"

"I became involved the minute I saw you. I meant what I said in there, I'll die for you."

"I know. I do not want to lose you. Be careful."

"You won't." He put his hand on her belly. "You're the one who has to be careful."

She smiled and covered his hand with her own. "I will be. Come, it is time to leave." She stood up, and he looked up at her.

"You're the most beautiful creature I've ever seen." He stood and hugged her hard body to him. "Don't let Duvall or Karl destroy you."

She broke from the embrace, and gazed into his eyes. "Never. It will take more power than they possess to destroy me." She took his hand. He picked up his bag, and she led him into the lounge room.

"Are we ready to go now?" Valeria asked sweetly.

15

The Dark Thirst

Duvall walked along the diving board. He breathed in the warm sultry air with relish. Coming to the end of the board, he paused, and looked about. The Caribbean surrounded him on three sides, and behind him was a large palatial residence, fringed by palm trees, and backed by a cliff that soared high above. He was dressed in board shorts, and his body glistened with sweat. On his left wrist was a communication device that extended from his wrist almost up to his elbow. It had a display screen, and a keypad. He glanced at it, and entered a series of numbers. He looked at the graphics that were called up, and a smile of satisfaction came upon his face. He cleared the screen. Gone was the crippled thing that had sat wracked with pain, confined to a wheelchair. Now, thanks to the blood that he'd obtained from Romana, he was built like an athlete, his body strong and handsome. He leapt into the air, diving gracefully down into the crystal water. He clove the surface, barely making a splash, and plunged down towards the bottom of the pool. When he reached it, he turned about, and with a strong push of his feet, he rose to the surface. As he broke through into the air, he saw someone standing at the edge of the pool. With powerful strokes, he swam to the edge, and raised himself out of the pool in one fluid movement. The man standing there handed him a towel, and as he rubbed himself dry, he said:

"Christian. What is it?"

"I'm sorry to disturb you, sir, but we have a problem." The speaker was dressed in a light blue suit, and his voice was cultured like that of an English butler. He was tall, blonde, and exuded a sense of calm. He was immaculate; even his nails were neat and polished, and his shoes glistened in the sunlight. One got the impression that nothing could fluster him. The heat didn't seem to bother him in the slightest.

Duvall frowned. "What sort of problem?"

Christian coughed into his hand. "Two of the Immortals, sir."

The Frenchman tossed his towel onto a lounge that was close by. He went and sat on its companion. "The same as before?"

The butler nodded. "I'm afraid so, sir."

Duvall scowled. "Bring them to me."

"At once, sir." Christian hurried off.

Damn, Duvall thought, *that makes fifteen. I must find a way to solve this.* He sat luxuriating in the heat, but his mind was as cold as ice as he considered the defect that had made him destroy so many of his super soldiers. He sat up as Christian returned, followed by the two individuals in question, themselves escorted by four armed men.

"Well. What have we here?" He stood and regarded the two prisoners, who stared back at him unflinchingly. He folded his arms as he waited for an answer.

The man on the right replied: "We have come to ask for our freedom." His eyes were like glass, as was his companion's. They were both clad in black combat fatigues. On the right breast of their shirts a four-digit number was displayed in bright yellow. Each of them had the aura of the predator. Their escorts covered them with naphtha rifles. Their hands were bound behind their backs with manacles.

"Freedom?" The Frenchman echoed. "I'm afraid that is not possible. You knew what you were volunteering for. You are my soldiers. My Immortals."

The other man spoke: "We want to live as we want. Free, to be hunters.

Not fed a weak substitute for the blood of men." He glared at Duvall.

"I'm afraid that I cannot allow you to be free. You will live forever. What more could you want?"

The first speaker glanced at his companion, and an unspoken agreement flashed between them. They flexed their arms, and strained against their bonds.

"Look out!" One of the guards cried.

With a metallic snap, the manacles were broken, and the two captives exploded into violent action. With a sweep of his arm, the first Immortal struck down two of the guards, and sprang upon a third. The last guard gasped in terror, and tried to fire his weapon, but the safety was on, and he was too terrified by the sight of the other prisoner rushing towards him, eyes filled with blood and fangs bared, to take it off. In a moment, those fangs sank into his neck.

Christian staggered back, appalled. Duvall activated his wrist computer. He punched in the number on the first Immortal's shirt as that individual turned with a snarl. As he leapt at him, Duvall stabbed his hand down on a red glowing button. In mid – leap, the Immortal instantly flared into bright incandescence, shrieking as he incinerated. His companion dropped the corpse of the guard, and rushed the Frenchman with an animal cry of fury. As Duvall desperately punched in the Immortal's number, he slammed into him; they stumbled over the chair, and plunged into the pool.

"My god!" Christian cried, aghast. He stared down into the pool, its water roiling and heaving with the violence of the struggle going on in its cool depths. He tried to see what was happening, but the sun glaring off the surface blinded him. "Do something!" he turned and yelled at one of the guards, who was rising shakily to his feet. The man picked up his naphtha rifle and ran to the pool's edge. He peered into the glare with slitted eyes.

"I can't see anything!" he gasped. He swept his rifle back and forth in a futile attempt to locate the Immortal.

Suddenly, a head broke the surface, and the guard cried out, and levelled his weapon. As he pulled the trigger, Christian slammed the barrel upwards, and the incendiary shell screamed over the pool, to explode against a palm tree.

Duvall gave Christian a grim smile as he swam towards them. "I'm glad you have good eyes."

Christian helped the professor out of the pool. "What happened?"

"I broke his neck. I am nearly as strong as they are, remember?"

"I – I'm sorry, sir," stammered the guard. "I thought –"

Duvall cut him off with an impatient flick of his hand. "Clean this up."

"At once, sir." He checked the other guards. All were dead.

The Frenchman regarded the scene with a cold eye. He *must* find a way to solve this problem. He picked the towel up, and dried himself, as his mind worked on his dilemma.

A group of guards ran up, attracted by the sound of the explosion.

"Are you all right, sir?" panted their leader. They swept the area with their rifles, alert for any danger.

"It's all right, sergeant. I was merely having a - *conversation* – with two of my Immortals." He turned to Christian. "Bring me the results of the last test. I'll be in my quarters."

"Certainly, sir." Christian watched him walk off; admiring how cool the professor seemed, after what had just occurred.

"Must have been one hell of a conversation," the sergeant remarked dryly.

"It did become a bit heated," Christian said.

The sergeant smiled grimly. "Bates!"

"Yes, sergeant!"

"Fetch some body bags for these men, and have them taken to the morgue."

"Yes, sergeant!" the guard hurried off, as his companions cleaned up.

In the cool air of his quarters, Duvall padded barefoot into the kitchen, and opened the refrigerator. He took out a bottle of orange juice, walked over to a cupboard, and took down a glass. He poured himself some juice, and drank down it in one long swallow. He rinsed the glass in the sink, and placed it in the dish rack.

He walked into the bedroom, and his gaze took in the two forms that lay on the rumpled sheets of the bed. Two island girls, their dusky nakedness enticing, lay sprawled. He'd made love to them both until they had collapsed from exhaustion. He smiled to himself. There were other benefits to Romana's blood, aside from its healing properties. He felt as rampant as a teenager. In fact...

He walked over to the bed, as his blood pooled in his loins. In moments, he was erect. He reached out and touched the nearer of the two girls. She was cold. He looked closely, and saw that she wasn't breathing. He checked her pulse. Nothing. The girl was dead; her glassy eyes stared at the ceiling. He glanced over at the other girl, and as he did so, some sense woke her. She screamed and scrambled away from him, falling out of the bed, to hit the floor with a thud.

"No, no, *please!*" she gasped at him. Her eyes were wide with horror, and her breasts heaved convulsively as she panted like a frightened animal. She backed away from him, until she came up against the wall. She held her arms in front of her face, as though she could shut out the vision of him standing before her.

Duvall stepped towards her, and the girl screamed in terror. He snapped the board shorts open, and let them fall to the floor. The girl stared at his manhood, and began to wail. He stepped closer.

"Sir?"

The Frenchman turned with a snarl. "*What is it?*"

Christian stood in the doorway. Behind him in the corridor, two men stood waiting, staring at the wall, and deliberately averting their gaze from the drama in the room. He took in the scene before him. Ignoring the terrified girl, and Duvall's nakedness, he said: "Mister Harrow has the results of the last test for you, sir. Ah, he says that he has found something strange, and asks if you would come and see him in the lab."

The professor's eyes narrowed. "Did he now? How interesting." He glanced down at the girl for a moment, and then turned his gaze back to Christian. "Very well. Let me dress, and I'll come with you." He went over to the walk – in wardrobe. He turned, saying: "Give her to the men, and have Marta come and clean up the room. And have two fresh girls brought here tonight."

"Yes, sir." He beckoned the guards into the room.

The girl broke into heavy sobs as Duvall walked into the wardrobe, and picked out a clean shirt. As he dressed, he heard her being led from the room, sobbing. He pulled on a pair of pants, and then walked back out into the bedroom. One of the guards was manhandling the other girl's corpse into a body bag. He straightened as Duvall came in.

"Carry on," he said with a negligent wave of his hand. "Now, Christian, let us go and see what Harrow has found."

Christian turned and walked out into the corridor, and Duvall followed him. They walked for some time in silence, passing several doors. They came to a large window, and the professor held up his hand to halt them as he stopped and looked in. Christian stood motionless at his side, and looked as well.

Inside was a huge room, filled with black clad figures. All were perfect specimens of manhood. *No*, thought Duvall, *not men, **supermen**!* He turned to his companion. "Marvellous, aren't they?" He turned back and watched the men as they ran through combat drills; unarmed, armed with knives, and at the end of the vast space, others were firing naphtha rifles with deadly accuracy. His army of Immortals! Their reflexes were ten times that of any ordinary human, and they were as strong as a dozen men. He watched them moving. They moved like the vampires did; bursts of speed that flashed from place to place. Any attack that they carried out on a human would be lightning swift and deadly. "No one can stand against them. They are the perfect soldiers." He smiled to himself.

"Except for our little problem, of course," Christian said.

The Frenchman turned to him again. His smile fell. "Yes, unfortunately, not so little a problem. I *must* solve it. I can't afford to lose more men to the Dark Thirst. I don't understand why it happens to some, and not to others."

"Ah, - Mister Harrow wanted to ask you something about that, sir." Christian looked uncomfortable.

"Well, what does he want to know?" Duvall said irritably.

The other man looked into the window, and then back at the professor, not meeting his eyes. "He wanted to know...I don't quite know how to say this, sir..."

"Out with it!" Duvall fumed. "What is it?"

Christian licked his lips nervously. "Ah, he wanted to know -" he went on in a rush, "- if you had felt any of the same – *impulses* – sir."

"*Me!*" the professor said angrily. "Of course not! The *fool*! Come with me." He stomped down the corridor towards Harrow's laboratory. Christian trailed along in his wake, taking long strides to keep up with him.

They came to a large metal door, flanked by two guards armed with naphtha rifles. They saluted Duvall, who strode up to the door, and entered his password into a keypad that was set into the wall. A chime rang out melodiously, and then the door hissed open. The professor entered with long, impatient strides, and Christian hurried after him. The pair walked between tables covered with instruments, where several white-coated technicians laboured, peering into microscopes, and studying readouts on computer monitors. They all turned as Duvall swept by them, but none met his eye as they saw the rage that was building in him, and turned quickly back to their work.

At length, they came up to a short man who was sitting at a desk reading a report. He had grey hair, and wore thick glasses, which made his eyes seem huge as he looked up, and saw them approach. "Ah, professor," he said in a piping voice. He smiled warily, seeing Duvall's dark mood. He met Christian's eye, and Christian shook his head warningly.

Duvall stopped in front of the desk. He folded his arms, and regarded the man with an imperious gaze. "How *dare* you accuse me of having the same defect that has cost me my soldiers," he fumed. The anger in him was boiling over.

"S - sir?" Harrow stammered. He rose to his feet, licking his lips nervously. "I – I did no such thing. I –"

"*Silence!*" The Frenchman roared. The small sounds in the laboratory immediately ceased, as though they had been cut off with a knife. The other workers turned and watched the drama unfolding.

"Christian told me that you thought I might have the same – *problem* – that we have seen in some of my Immortals," Duvall said, his voice low and dangerous. His eyes narrowed. "Do you deny this?" he asked silkily.

Harrow took out a handkerchief, and mopped his sweating brow. He stared into his employer's flinty gaze. "Uh – No, no," he said, his voice trembling. "I – ah, found something unusual, and I thought it would be prudent to – ah – perhaps, I mean, - *test* - you, sir."

The Frenchman regarded him. "Test?" he echoed.

The scientist picked up the sheets of paper he had been reading. He nodded. "Yes, sir. It's all in here." He held out the report. The paper rustled in his shaking hand.

The professor snatched the sheets, and studied them, looking up from time to time, and impaling the unfortunate Harrow with his glare. As he read further, the import of Harrow's discovery was brought to him with a shock. He finished reading, and looked up, and met Harrow's worried gaze.

"Are you certain of this?" The anger drained from him.

Harrow nodded again. "Yes, professor. I ran the tests five times. Each result was the same."

"What is it, sir?" Christian asked.

The professor held the papers up. "This shows that the synthesized Dark Blood will always overpower any attempt to subvert its nature; anyone who has been infected with it will eventually turn into a vampire."

"Everyone?" said Christian. "All of the Immortals?"

"Yes," said Harrow, "All of them that were made with the synthesized blood. It's only a matter of time. It's very tenacious; it destroys all the systems in the bodies of those it infects, changing their blood, and filling them with the urge to feed on normal human blood. It has overwhelmed every serum and formula that I've tried; nothing will work. It will have its way with these men; every last one of them will be eventually turned into an unstoppable monster that thirsts, and that thirst must be slaked."

"*My god!*" cried Christian, aghast, "there are three hundred of them! What does this mean?"

"It means we must find some way to solve this, or they will turn against us," said Duvall grimly. "They will all be uncontrollable, like the two this afternoon, and the others before them." He dropped the sheets onto the desk. "They will be as dangerous as the vampires – no, even more dangerous, as they are armed with my weapons." He looked at his wrist computer. *With one master command,* he thought, *I could incinerate them all.* A sudden thought came to him. "What about those who were made with original vampire blood?"

"They don't appear to be infected, sir. It seems that it is only our synthesized blood that has the effect on them." The scientist steepled his hands before himself, giving the impression that he was praying. "Sir," he said hesitantly, "there may be a way to solve this."

Duvall turned his gaze upon him. "Yes?"

Harrow blanched before his stare, and lowered his hands. "Uh, yes. I was thinking, that if I could perhaps obtain more of the original blood, I believe I could find a cure."

The Frenchman smiled. "Obtain more of the original blood," he echoed. "Interesting. What would this achieve?"

"I believe that the – *defect* – is contained in the subatomic structure of the original sample, sir. I think that it was caused by a fault in the synthesizing process. If I could get more of it, I am fairly sure that I could solve the problem." He thought for a moment, and then continued: "I have isolated the elements that cause this effect, and I believe that I can remove them, and so eliminate the danger of the synthesized Dark Blood turning our subjects into vampires."

"But you must have the original blood; Romana's blood."

"Yes, professor."

"It's certain that she won't be interested in supplying us with any more," said Christian.

A cunning smile came to Duvall's lips. "Then we must find some way of convincing her to give us what we need. Good work, Harrow. Continue your work. Come, Christian."

"Thank you, sir," the scientist said, relief in his voice. He'd seen first hand how the Frenchman hated failure, and knew how those that failed paid the price for that failure. He watched the pair walk out of the laboratory. The other workers returned to their various tasks. Harrow sat down, and turned to a computer terminal. He switched it on, and waited for the machine to boot up, his face thoughtful.

Duvall and Christian exited the laboratory. They walked in silence for a while, progressing through the corridors. Christian glanced at the professor from time to time, knowing that the Frenchman was deep in thought, his mind working. But he knew that Duvall didn't like to have his thought processes interrupted, so he kept quiet. At last, as they came outside into the warm Caribbean sun, Duvall turned to him.

"I have it."

"Sir?"

"We must bring Romana here, yes?" He blinked in the light; his eyes began to sting.

"Harrow must have her blood."

"Yes, so that my Immortals can be cured of the Dark Thirst." The sunlight glared brightly, and his temples began to throb.

"And you also, sir," said Christian tentatively.

"Yes, yes, myself as well," Duvall said irritably. He nodded to himself. "I know how we can bring her here." His head began to pound. He could feel his blood rushing through his veins. *What was this?* He put a hand up to his throbbing temple.

"Sir?"

The Frenchman smiled shrewdly. "We need to get a message to her. We will tell her that there is a danger to her unborn child; something happened when her blood was taken, the synthesizing process caused some - *unexpected* - complication. Yes, that should bring her to us. She won't risk any harm coming to her baby." The light burned into his eyes, and a sudden dryness came to his throat.

Christian looked sceptical. "Do you really think she will believe that, sir? She is very intelligent."

"It won't matter. When it comes to the safety of their offspring, I have seen that any female becomes irrational. She is no exception. She will believe it, and she will bring us what we need; her blood." The sunlight was painful now. He had to get out of it. He shook his pounding head.

Christian stared at him, his face filled with concern. "Are you all right, sir?"

Duvall gazed back at him. "Eh? What? Of course. It's the sun, it's too damned bright. I'll be in my quarters. See that you contact Romana, and tell her what I said. She will come, you'll see." He stared at Christian, and was suddenly aware of the blood that pumped through his veins. He could sense it pulsing; hear it moving through the man's jugular, a hot tide of life that he suddenly wanted to drink. Christian's heartbeats came to his abruptly hypersensitive ears, thundering loudly. He staggered.

"Sir!" Christian went to grab him.

"Back!" Duvall cried. His eyes filled with blood. *I must get away from him,* he thought frantically.

Christian backed away, staring in horror at the change that was taking place before him.

"Just do as I say!" Duvall growled, and turned and rushed towards his quarters.

Christian shuddered as the professor fled. *My god!* He thought. *It's begun.* He took his phone out of his jacket pocket and punched in a number. When his call was answered, he said: "I must talk to you at once. It's the professor. He's been affected. Yes, it happened right in front of me. I don't know. I don't think it's occurred before. He went to his quarters. No. All right, I'll send some guards. I'm coming to you right now. Good." He hung up, his face thoughtful. *Where do we go from here?* He put his phone back in his jacket, and strode away, his stride purposeful.

Duvall staggered to his door, the blood thundered in his throbbing veins. His heart pounded like a drum, filling his ears with its tumult. His hands went to his hammering temples, attempting to stop the torture. He groaned like an animal. His throat burned with the lust to slake itself on human blood. *No! Not me! This can't happen to me!* He grabbed the door handle, turned it, opened the door and stumbled into the room. Someone gasped in shock as he entered. He looked up, and his blood red eyes met the terrified stares of the two girls that he'd ordered Christian to provide for his evening's entertainment. They stood gaping in open-mouthed horror at him, their eyes bulging from their sockets. And their blood – it called to him. He rushed at them, and they both screamed in terror.

Christian and Harrow stood in one of the laboratory's storerooms. Christian had asked the scientist to speak with him where no one could hear them. Harrow took off his thick glasses, and cleaned the lenses with his coat. Christian knew that it was a habit of his; one that he carried out when he was unsettled. And Christian's tale of Duvall's awful transformation had definitely unsettled him, to say the least.

"What can we do?" Harrow said, his voice trembling.

"We have to take charge of the project," Christian said. "The professor is unable to carry on."

"Ha, ha, ha!" The little man laughed nervously. "Are you suggesting that *we* take over? That's insane!" He put his glasses back on, and goggled at Christian, his eyes filled with fear. He pointed a trembling hand at Christian. "You've wanted this all along. You're jealous of the professor's newfound power; you want the Immortals to serve you."

Christian snarled angrily. "Don't be a fool! We have to *do* something. If the professor has become like the others that fell victim to the Dark Thirst, it won't be long before he's out of control. *Control* - that's it! We have to get his wrist computer, so we can have the power to destroy the others."

"What about him? He hasn't had a micro explosive implanted."

"Naphtha rifles can deal with him," Christian said grimly.

Duvall stood above the corpses of the two girls, staring down at them in horrified fascination. He'd attacked them both, draining them of their blood, which now burned in his veins like a rich wine. He felt like a god; a grim god of death, filled with the power to destroy. The blood filled him with unbounded energy. *My god!* He thought. *I had no idea of the **power!*** He stared at the bodies, and felt an overwhelming sense of superiority. These soft, weak things were far below him now. The Dark Blood that coursed through his veins had given him ultimate power; power that he would wield. Now he was one with the Immortals who had succumbed to the Dark Thirst. He would lead them, an unstoppable army; they would conquer and subdue all who stood in their way. He saw himself as their leader, a leader who had more strength than any other puny mortal who had tried to rule the world. He *would* rule it, and any fool who attempted to stop him would be crushed without mercy.

The door opened. He came out of his reverie. Four guards stood there, naphtha rifles aimed and charged. "What is this?" he snarled.

The guards took in the appalling scene in the room. The first man stepped forwards. "Sir. Please come with us." His weapon held the professor in its sights.

Duvall glared at them. "By whose authority?"

"Mister King, sir. He wants you to come to Mister Harrow's laboratory."

Christian, eh? The Frenchman thought. "Do you remember who I am?" he said icily.

"Yes, sir. But Mister King is – *concerned* – about your current state, and he asked us to bring you to Mister Harrow so he could conduct some tests on you."

"Tests?" Duvall echoed. "Why?"

"They think that you've been affected, sir." The man's eyes shifted to the corpses on the bed. He returned his gaze to the professor. "Please, sir."

The Frenchman stared at the guards, his mind racing. He must escape them. But the unwavering barrels of their guns were fixed upon him. He nodded in feigned acquiescence. "Very well, lead the way." He walked slowly towards them. The guns followed him, ready to unleash their deadly pellets.

The first guard backed out of the room, and into the corridor. As Duvall reached the door, he moved swiftly, and slammed the door. He spun around, and raced towards the window. The door was kicked open, and the guard leapt into the room. He fired at the rushing form just as the professor dove forward and smashed through the glass. The naphtha pellet exploded into flame, filling the room with unbearable heat that forced the guards to back away.

The first guard reached for his radio. *"Mister King!"* he cried, "He's escaped, sir! Broke through the window, and he's headed into the forest."

"Fools!" Christian's voice bellowed from the radio. *"Go after him!"*

"Yes, sir!" He closed the connection, and gestured to his men. "You heard him! Let's go!" He ran into the room, and across to the window, and leapt out. He brought up a tracking device that he wore on his belt. He activated it, and scanned for the professor. An image that came up on the small screen showed him the direction that the fugitive had gone. He ran towards the forest, eyes on the scanner, and his men trailed after. In moments, they had disappeared into the trees.

Duvall ran, smashing heedlessly through the undergrowth. He plunged through branches that whipped into his face that left small cuts there. In seconds, they had gone, thanks to the regenerative power of the Dark Blood that burned within his veins. He ran faster than any human being could ever have run, and within minutes, he was many kilometres from the buildings. He suddenly halted.

Why am I running? He thought. "They are the ones who should fear me," he said aloud. He looked about himself. He was alone, deep in the forest. He knew that the guards were even now tracking him. A smile came to his lips. *What if they find me?* He brought up his wrist computer. Punching in a command, he accessed the tracker that the guard was using to find him. They were coming, but Duvall knew that it would take them a lot longer to traverse the distance than he did. *I should make it easier for them.* Running back the way he'd come, he smiled in anticipation of the fresh blood that was coming his way.

The four men advanced through the trees, weapons armed and covering themselves in every direction. They followed the guard who had the tracker, searching for the professor.

"He's close," he whispered. *"Get ready."*

He raised his hand and clenched it into a fist; they stopped, squatted down, and swept the area with the naphtha rifles.

"Where?" One of the guards said softly.

"Just ahead, there's – Damn!"

"What's up?"

The first guard was fumbling with the tracker, cursing under his breath.

"What's wrong?"

"This fuckin' thing's just shut down!"

"Well, turn it on again!"

The man flicked the switch on and off in frustration. When it didn't turn back on, he banged it with the heel of his hand. "I can't!" he gasped.

"Shit! Where is he?"

"I don't –"

"There!" one of the other men cried, jumped to his feet, and fired. The pellet struck a tree, and exploded into flame.

The second man stood and grabbed his rifle away from him. "Dickhead!" he bawled, "wait until you see a target!"

The last man in the line suddenly gurgled something unintelligible. They turned to see him fall, his jugular spraying a fountain of blood. A shadowy shape sped away from them, its progress whipping the branches.

"Fuck!" forgetting his admonition of his colleague, the second man peppered the forest around them with a scattering of shots. The pellets burst into flame, creating an inferno among the trees.

They squinted into the fire, rifles searching. The glare from the flames was blinding, the heat stifling. For what seemed an eternity, they scanned the burning trees, but no sight or sound of their attacker came to them. Sweat poured from them in the heat of the blaze; dripping into eyes that stung, and blinked furiously to clear their vision.

Rushing among them again, the figure struck the third man with a slash of its outstretched hand. Its nails, sharp as a razor, took the guard's head off, and as his blood sprayed like the first victim, the corpse fell to the forest floor. Duvall was a flash of impossible speed as he dodged away from a volley of shots that merely added to the conflagration around them.

"Christ!" The second man ran, flinging his weapon aside. He raced back towards the compound, his heart in his mouth. He'd only gone a short way, when the dark figure ran across his path, and lashed out at him. He staggered and stumbled to a halt, and swayed for a moment. Then, with a hiss, his blood leapt high, and he fell.

The last man saw his demise, crouching in terror, the tracker forgotten in his hand. He swept the trees with eyes that were wide with horror. The trees burned with a fierce crackling, and the light of the flames blinded him. Suddenly, he was aware of someone standing behind him. He groaned, and turned slowly.

Duvall stood over him like an angel of death. He raised his wrist, showing the terrified guard his computer. "Did you forget I have an off switch to your little toy?"

The man goggled at him, his mouth agape.

With a flash of fangs, the Frenchman rushed at him.

The guard's scream ended in a choking gurgle.

16

Valeria and Sergei

Erik watched the clouds rush by through the window of the small jet he sat in. They were flying at ten thousand feet over the Caribbean. Romana had received a message from Christian, and they were on their way to Duvall's island. There had been much debate and argument about her decision to go and give more of her blood to the professor, but in the end, she couldn't be talked out of going, especially when Christian had told her of the danger to her unborn child. He had been very apologetic, telling her that they had had no idea that the synthesising process could have had such a dangerous side effect. He had assured her that their scientists had solved the problem, and that there would be no risk in her giving another donation. He also explained the problem that had arisen concerning the Immortals. The experiment was a failure. Without exception, he had said, every one of the volunteers had eventually turned into a vampire, uncontrollable, and dangerous. These men had been – *retired* – but there were now hundreds of them, and it was inevitable that they would all turn out the same way. If she came to help, perhaps she could convince the Clans to take charge of them? Duvall no longer wanted to create his army; the failure that had come about as a result of the defect in synthesizing her blood, and the transformation his men had undergone, making them useless to him, had decided him to abandon the project. Christian had promised her that no harm would come to her baby.

The memory of the message went through the drummer's mind as he absently gazed out at the passing clouds. He didn't believe it. He didn't think that Duvall would have asked for assistance from Romana, and something about Christian bothered him. The guy had spoken in an ingratiating tone, and Erik *never* trusted anyone who tried to suck up to him. *Romana shouldn't trust **him** either,* he thought gloomily. *And as for Duvall...*

A hand touched his arm. He turned to see Romana gazing at him. She smiled.

"Do you suspect everyone of being false?"

Knowing that she'd read his mind, he gave her a wan smile in return. "Only people who try to kill me," he said dryly. "Look, I don't like this. Duvall hasn't been truthful to you right from the start; he was only interested in your blood, and didn't care about anything else. I don't trust him."

She put her hand on his arm. "I do not trust him either. But if there were any danger to our child, would you allow that danger to be a threat, just to spite him? Would you deny him his request, and risk our baby's life?"

"No," he said. He covered her cold hand with his own. "I'm with you. I'm just not ready to trust someone who tried to kill us. Who is this Christian guy? I don't like him either, there's something flaky about him."

"He is Duvall's servant."

The drummer shook his head irritably. "I know that. Why did he get in touch with you, and not Duvall?"

Romana shrugged. "Perhaps the professor is busy with his work."

Erik pulled a wry face. "Huh! No, something smells about this, Romana."

"And how would you know that, mortal?"

He looked up, and into Valeria's green eyes. The redhead leaned against the seat back that was in front of him, and regarded him languidly, her arms crossed in front of her breasts. A black dress that accentuated her curves looked to Erik as though she had been sewn into it. It came off her shoulder and was cut nearly down to her navel, displaying a lot of her whiteness.

She'd been walking up and down the aircraft's aisle, bored. She gave him a condescending smile.

"I just think it's fishy, that's all," he said defensively.

Her smile widened. "So you think we are wasting our time?" she asked.

"It is my time to waste," Romana said coldly. She fixed Valeria with a freezing stare.

"You didn't have to come along," Erik said.

Valeria stood up straight, and a mock expression of hurt came to her face. She uncrossed her arms, and put her hand on her undead heart. "Oh, but I wanted to come. I want to help you, Romana, you and your – *companion.* She accented the word as though she were speaking of an unruly pet.

"Valeria."

She turned. Gerald sat across the aisle, watching. His eyes held a warning. The redhead held his stare for a long moment, and then bowed to him. "I wish I were flying," she said, irritation in her voice. "I hate these mechanical contraptions. I want to feel the wind in my hair." She turned abruptly, and the split in her dress showed her long legs in a flash of pale flesh. She strutted away on her high stiletto heels down the aisle towards the cockpit.

"My apologies," Gerald said.

The drummer regarded the blonde vampire. He raised an eyebrow. "You're being considerate today."

Gerald smiled disarmingly. "Come now, Erik, we should all try to get along." He glanced down the aisle, and watched Valeria come to a halt beside the empty seat next to Sergei, who was sitting up front. She said something to the Russian, and smiled at him. She felt Gerald's eyes on her, and looked back at him. *Behave yourself,* he sent. Still smiling, she sat down next to Sergei.

"Get along?" the drummer said. "I didn't do anything. It was her –" he stopped as Romana grabbed his arm and squeezed it warningly.

"Keep her under control," she said to Gerald.

"Of course I will, my dear Romana," he replied. "Valeria is headstrong; she always was, you know that."

"Yes," she said sarcastically. "I remember. She was always difficult for you to manage." Her eyes were like glass. "Why did the Clans allow her to remain one of your hunters? I thought that they had to obey all orders immediately without question? I can recall many times when she has disobeyed you."

Erik felt as though he was sitting between two duellists. The anger radiating from Romana was palpable. He caught Gerald's eye, and the dandy regarded him for a moment, and then returned his gaze to the girl.

"I will tell you why," Gerald said. "Her voice was one of the loudest when it came to the decision to hunt you. She is very - *particular* – about the purity of our blood. Her own Maker –"

"Yes, yes, I know," Romana interrupted him irritably. She leaned across Erik. "Just make sure she does not cause any trouble. Remind her why she is here."

Gerald gave a slight bow. "Certainly. We are the messengers of the Clans; she knows that. We are only accompanying you to hear what Duvall has to say."

"Then remind her that the best way to hear what someone has to say is to *listen*. That means that she does not speak." Romana sat back and closed her eyes. The discussion was ended.

Gerald looked at the drummer. "Of course, my dear." He held Erik's gaze for a moment, and then he turned to look out of the window.

Sergei raised his glass of vodka to his lips, and took a deep pull. Valeria sat beside him, regarding him with a smile on her face. He was wearing a brightly patterned Hawaiian shirt that was all green and blue, and covered with palm trees and pineapples. An ancient pair of Levi's that had faded to a light blue and a pair of red Converse running shoes completed his outfit. He slowly turned to face her.

"Something is funny?"

She reached out and touched his shirt. "This." Her green eyes flickered with amusement. "I have not seen you so – *colourful* – before. I like it."

"Thank you," he said, wondering what she was up to.

She stroked his beard. "But this…" She shook her head in mock sorrow, and her lips turned downwards. "You should shave it off."

"Why?"

Valeria took a long lock of her hair and twirled it absently. It made her look like a little girl. "Because you would look better." She leaned forward, and took the glass out of his hand. She brought it to her lips, and then, as though she were remembering her manners, she asked: "May I?"

The Bear nodded. "Please."

She grinned, showing her fangs, and then drained the glass. She made a face. "Awful. But quite stimulating." She gave it back to him. "I am sorry. Would you like another?"

"Da." He regarded her curiously.

Valeria rose sinuously, and walked over to the small area where a steward sat. He was reading a magazine, but looked up as she stood in front of him. "Can I help you?" he asked solicitously.

"A bottle of vodka," she purred.

The steward put down his magazine. "Uh, okay." He went to the small bar fridge, and opened the door. He took out a bottle, and went and handed it to the redhead.

"A glass?"

"Oh, of course." He went to a cupboard set into the bulkhead, opened it, and got out a glass. He turned and gave it to her.

"Thank you," she said, and strutted back and sat down next to Sergei. She opened the bottle, and poured him a drink. Then she filled her own glass. They drank; the Russian kept his eye on her, puzzled at this unusual behaviour.

"You do not think I can be civilized?" she asked, reading his mind. Her green eyes gazed languidly at him.

"I am – *surprised*," the Bear replied, choosing his words carefully.

She smiled. "Do you know where I come from?"

"The Motherland."

"Yes, but *where*? And when?"

He shook his head.

A far away look came into her eyes. "I was born in 1899 and lived in Moscow. My parents were of noble birth. I enjoyed riches and privileges that most Russians never know. My father doted on me as though I were a princess. There was nothing that he would not give me. We lived in a world that was elegant, and filled with happiness. We did not concern ourselves with the peasants. They existed to serve us." She turned to him. "Until 1917."

"The Revolution?"

"Yes," she said softly. "Everything changed. Our world was torn apart. The Bolsheviks destroyed anything and anyone that did not fit into their ideology. We were driven from our house, and we fled the mobs. Others were not so lucky. During the long war with Germany, our country had suffered much, but we, the nobility, had ignored such suffering; it had not touched us in our little world. But now that world was gone, and the harsh reality of Russia's desperate situation came upon us like a kick in the face."

Sergei regarded her with new eyes.

"So we fled. There was no place for us in the new Russia. We heard the awful news of the overthrow and execution of the Tsar and his family. We were shocked and stunned." She fell silent for a moment, and then she raised her glass and emptied it in one long draught. She screwed up her face at the vodka's taste. Gazing at the empty glass, she said: "I used to love the taste of vodka." The corners of her mouth turned downwards. "Now, it is disgusting. Only blood satisfies my thirst."

"How did you become a vampire?" Sergei asked.

She gave him a wan smile. "I was coming to that, tovarisch. I thought you would like to hear the story."

"Da. Please continue."

"We were escaping from the chaos that had fallen. In three cars, we hurried towards Poland; relatives were there, they would take us in. It was snowing, and driving in the snow was difficult. My mother, father, and two brothers were with me in the lead car, and our servants followed in the others. We passed through the bleak landscape like fugitives. We *were* fugitives; the Bolsheviks considered us enemies of the state." She paused, remembering. They sat for what seemed a long time.

Sergei regarded her in a new light. He'd no idea that Valeria had suffered so much. The revolution had been bloody and brutal. He'd read enough about it, and his uncle Mikhael had often told him horror stories of that time when he was a child.

She gave him a smile. "Thank you for your sympathy."

He looked away, abashed. He took a long drink. He started as she put her hand on his leg. He turned to her. "Must you always do that?"

She held him in her green eyes. "I apologize. It is normal for us. I will not do it without your approval again." She removed her hand. "May I continue?"

He nodded.

"As the sun was going down, we came to a crossroads. The dying sun painted everything red; the whole world was like blood. I shivered, as though it was an evil omen. We stopped, and Nikolai, our driver, got out. He looked at each of the roads, obviously puzzled. My father got out of the car and joined him. Towards the east there were long black clouds rising from the frozen earth. Something burned there, and I was suddenly afraid. At the side of the road there was a field, and a derelict farmhouse and barn.

They looked forbidding in the ruddy light. The driver and my father were talking together, their heads close, and their voices low, so that we couldn't hear them. My youngest brother Ivan asked mother when we were going to arrive, his voice petulant. He was only six, and didn't understand the situation we were in. He'd been told we were going on a holiday. She told him to be still. Her eyes were on father and Nikolai; she knew with sudden certainty that they were unsure of which way to go. Suddenly there was a shout. We looked, and saw a group of men hurrying towards us from the east. As they came closer, we could see that they were from our army. They were dirty and unshaven, and their clothes were ragged." She stopped.

Sergei picked up the bottle, and filled his glass. He sipped at his drink and waited for her to continue.

"Their leader walked up to my father and Nikolai," she continued, her voice empty and cold. "He stood there looking my father up and down, contempt in his eyes. I can still hear his voice as he said: "You're going the wrong way, comrade." He smiled, showing yellowed teeth. His men laughed, and stared at our cars greedily."

"What do you want?" my father asked, keeping his voice neutral.

'The man pointed at the cars. "We need those. Tell your people to get out."

"How dare you speak to the baron like that!" Nikolai said, outraged at his insolence.

'The man took out his pistol, and shot Nikolai in the head. Mother and I screamed, and my brothers gripped her in terror. Ivan started to cry. The servants in the other cars cried out in horror.

"*Sergeant!*" the officer bellowed.

"Yes, Captain?" answered a huge man.

"Get these – *people* – out of those vehicles." He spat into the snow. He gave father an evil smile.

"Yes, Captain Orlov." He beckoned to his men, and they came forwards.

They reached us, and threw open the doors.

"Out!" the sergeant yelled. They levelled their rifles at us. We were dragged from the cars, to stand shivering in the falling snow. Ivan, and Alexei, my two brothers, held on to mother for dear life, their little eyes staring wildly at the evil soldiers surrounding us. The servants stood there in shock, their frightened gazes telling of the terror that gripped their madly beating hearts.

'The sergeant grabbed a handful of my hair, and dragged me close. His eyes were bloodshot, and I could smell his sour breath. He gazed at me hungrily, and then turned to the Captain. "Look, sir! She's a real beauty!" His men laughed. He suddenly yelled in anger, and let me go. Alexei had run up and kicked him in the shin.

"Let Valeria go, you pig!" Alexei screamed.

"No, Alexei!" mother shrieked.

'The sergeant gave a roar, and snatched a rifle from one of his soldiers. He plunged the bayonet that was fixed on it deep into Alexei's chest. My brother gaped in surprise, and then fell to the snow, which was immediately turned red by his blood.

'Mother screamed, and tried to go to him, but Ivan was holding her legs and crying, and hampered her. Father ran to Alexei's side, and knelt down. The boy was dead. "How dare you!" He clenched his fists in fury. Tears of anguish ran down his face. He picked Alexei up, and held him to his chest, which became wracked with sobs.

"Your world is finished, comrade," said the Captain, who had walked up.

"Sir!" shouted one of the soldiers, "Look!" He held up two bottles of vodka that had been in the last car. He tossed them to his comrades, and then reached inside, and brought out a wicker basket. "Food too!" The soldiers cheered.

'Captain Orlov looked me up and down, and then turned his lustful gaze upon my mother. He smiled, and then looked over at the barn. "It seems we have all we need for a party." He gestured imperiously. "Bring the food and drink. And the women," he said suggestively.

'Father's head snapped up. "You animal!" He came to his feet in a rush, and went for the Captain. His hands went around Orlov's throat, and they fell to the snow. Several soldiers rushed in, and dragged my father off, and held him. He struggled in their arms as Orlov staggered to his feet.

'The Captain's eyes were filled with hate. "So," he said. "So." He pulled out his pistol, and shot father in the chest. The two soldiers released him, and he fell to the snow, his blood joining Alexei's.

"*Gyorgi!*" mother screamed.

'With an angry cry, she heaved Ivan away, and plunged towards Orlov. Two of the soldiers grabbed her, and at the sight of their mistress bring manhandled by the filthy brutes, the servants leaped at the soldiers; punching, kicking, and the girls scratching at their tormentor's eyes." She stopped with a shudder.

Segei reached out tentatively, and put his hand on Valeria's shoulder. "I am sorry," he said.

Valeria turned to him. Tears of blood welled in her eyes, and then flowed down her cheeks. She grabbed his hand with cold hard fingers. "Thank you."

"No more," he said softly. He was shocked at the emotions pouring from her. He'd only seen her as a dangerous killing machine; now he could see that she did indeed feel, and feel deeply. He wiped her tears away with his hand.

She smiled. "But I have not finished. And I want to. I want you to see why I am a 'killing machine.'" She took his hands in hers.

"Go on," he said.

"Shots were fired; the soldiers went mad, shooting and using their bayonets. Our servants fell, but not before they had killed four of the soldiers with their bare hands. Ivan was bawling, screaming as the horror went on. When the servants were all dead, he was still screaming. But not for long. Captain Orlov went up to him, and shot him in the back of the head. Silence fell. Only my mother's sobs filled the air, as she cradled my father's body. I lay in the bloody snow, and stared in horror at the death around me.

"Sergeant," the Captain said.

"Sir?"

"Bring those vehicles over to that barn. We will have our party."

'The men let out a ragged cheer.

"Bring them," Orlov ordered, indicating mother and I. He walked to one of the cars, and sat in the back seat like the Tsar. One of his men jumped in, started it, and they drove towards the barn. Soldiers climbed into the other cars, and followed. Two soldiers came to me, and hauled me to my feet. Two others went to mother, and dragged her off father's body. They pushed us roughly after the cars. Mother had fallen silent.

'Inside the barn they took out the food and vodka, and ate and drank like it was their last meal on earth. We were thrown to the ground, and two soldiers watched us as the others feasted. Then two others took their place, and they went and joined the riotous mob that was roaring and singing. And then, when the food and drink were gone…

'The Captain staggered up to us, leering drunkenly. The sergeant was with him. His men crowded around expectantly.

"Now," said Orlov, "the entertainment." He grinned evilly. "Strip them."

'Soldiers fell upon us, tearing our clothing away. I screamed and fought, but mother was still silent. She lay there passively, her eyes vacant. One of the soldiers struck me, and tore the last of my clothing away. Then they held us down.

'The Captain undid his pants, and fell upon my mother, grunting and thrusting. She stared at the roof of the barn silently. The sergeant grinned at me, and took me. A sharp pain tore me open, and I screamed as he heaved on top of me. When they had both finished, they got off us, and the Captain said: "Enjoy yourselves, boys."

'The soldiers raped us both, in a nightmare of pain and suffering that seemed to go on for a thousand years. There were sixteen of them. When they had had their fill of us, Captain Orlov and the sergeant came up to us. They looked down at us, contempt in their drunken eyes.

"Thank you for your hospitality, ladies," Orlov said mockingly, bowing. He turned to the sergeant. "Get rid of them," he said, and walked away.

'The sergeant gestured to one of the guards. "Give me your rifle."

'The man handed it to him. The sergeant cocked it, and took aim at me. I waited for him to shoot, to feel the bullet tearing into me. I stared back at him with hatred blazing in my eyes. He suddenly smirked, and stabbed me with the bayonet. The cold steel ripped into my belly, and I gasped in shock. He walked over to mother, and bayoneted her. Then he turned to me, and said: "No quick death for you. It will take hours for you to die. Use them to think of what your kind have done to Russia." He spat at mother, and then at me. He tossed the rifle to the soldier, and turned away to walk over to the cars, which were being started up. The two soldiers followed him. All of them clambered into and onto our cars, the men outside hanging on like fleas on a dog. The engines revved, and they drove away, leaving mother and I to bleed to death.

'I crawled over to her. "Mother," I gasped, shaking her. Her eyes were like glass. She was already dead. The bayonet must have pierced her heart. Or perhaps she just willed herself to die. I crawled across the floor, until I reached the door. I pulled myself up and looked out. The corpses on and around the road lay in the snow, which was falling from the darkening sky more heavily. The cars were just disappearing from view, heading back the way we had come. Suddenly, I heard a howl. It was answered, and I saw grey shapes loping towards the bodies. As I stood there with my blood running between my hands, the wolves appeared out of the snow, and fell upon the bodies, ripping and tearing. Several of them looked towards me, and with a howl, they came on. I was rigid with terror. The wolves broke into a run, and I slid to the floor. After everything I had suffered, I was now to be eaten alive!

'The lead wolf leapt at me. I closed my eyes. I had no breath for a scream; my blood was draining away, I had no strength to fight or run. I waited for those terrible fangs to rip into me. Suddenly, there was a heavy thud, as though something had dropped onto the snow. An awful crack came to my ears, like the sound a branch makes when it breaks. Another came, and with it a yelp that was cut off, and I opened my eyes.

'A dark figure was among the wolves, smashing them into the snow with its bare hands. It took a wolf by the throat, and broke its neck with a snap of its wrist, and then tossed another high into the air with a sweep of its arm. The wolf tumbled over and over, yelping in terror, and crashed to earth with a dreadful sound of snapping bones. The last two turned and fled, but the figure leapt after them. With lightning speed, it grabbed them both, and drove their heads together. The skulls splintered with the shock, and the wolves' brains were dashed upon the bloody snow.

'The form stared out at the wolves on the road, and roared a challenge, blood and gore dripped from its hands. The wolves snarled, but backed hurriedly away, frightened off by the deaths of their comrades. In moments, they had vanished.

'I gaped at the figure as it walked back to me, and squatted down before me. It was a man. He was very handsome, with black hair and pale skin. His eyes were as red as the blood everywhere around me. He was dressed in a long black coat, and tall boots were upon his feet. *Vampyre!* I shuddered. He smiled, showing his deadly fangs.

"Yes," he said, reading my mind. He reached out and touched my hair. "Beautiful." He stared into my eyes. "But you are dying, koshka."

"D – don't hurt me," I managed to gasp out. I was getting cold. I couldn't feel my legs.

"Your blood is nearly gone. If I leave you, you will die." He leaned forwards. "But I can give you life. *Eternal* life."

'I shook my head. *"No,"* I said weakly. The cold made its way up my chest. My hands were freezing, and my heart was slowing.

'Suddenly, he took his wrist in his mouth, and tore it with his teeth. Black blood welled out. He held his wrist in front of me. "Drink."

'I flinched away, horrified.

'He grabbed the back of my head, and forced his wrist against my mouth. Without intending to, I gulped some of the horrid stuff down. And then... an awful need sprang up inside of me; I wanted to drink his dark blood more than anything in the world. I grabbed his wrist with both hands, and my hungry mouth sucked and sucked. Everything faded away, and the only thing in the universe that existed was the sensation of his blood burning within me. I could feel it filling me until I thought I would burst.

"Good, good," someone said, far away.

'Then, suddenly, it was taken away. I fell to the ground, thrashing and convulsing. My body felt as if it was on fire. I screamed. I felt the wound in my stomach close. I got to my knees, and looked up. He was standing over me, with his hand out. I took it, and he helped me to my feet. I stood before him, immortal as he was, and a vampyre.

'I struck his hand away. "You had no right!" I yelled at him.

'He smiled. "I know," he said mildly. "But I could not let such a beautiful creature die." He regarded me. "Now you are my companion. We can roam the world forever."

'I turned away from him. "I do not wish to go with you." I walked over to my mother's body, and knelt down. I stroked her hair. "Can you do the same for her? Can you make her one of us?" I stared into her glassy eyes.

'He was suddenly at my side. "No," he said. "She is truly dead, as is your father and all of your friends."

"Then leave me here with them, and go."

"You will be forced to seek out living blood."

"No. I will stay here and die with them. I will not kill anyone."

'He chuckled. "You haven't felt the Dark Thirst yet. It is overpowering, and will make you hunt." He knelt at my side. "You can avenge them."

'I turned and faced him. "What?"

"The ones who did this, they haven't gone far."

"You can – *sense* – them?"

'He nodded. "Yes. You and I could go and pay them a visit. We could make them pay for this." He indicated mother.

'Rage exploded within me. Avenge them! Avenge them all! Yes! That is what I wanted. I leapt to my feet. "*Yes!*" I cried. "Take me to them." They would pay dearly for what they had done. He and I would be angels of death, exacting an ultimate and terrible revenge for the outrage they had committed.

'He stood, smiling. "Come," he said. He strode to the door. I followed him. He turned and rose into the air.

'I stood staring, amazed. "How do you do that? Can I fly?"

'He grinned. "Of course, koshka. Imagine it, and you can."

'I thought to myself: *I will fly. I will fly.* I closed my eyes, concentrating, forcing my will to lift my body into the air. Nothing happened. Laughter opened my eyes. I glared at him. He smiled down at me, his arms folded.

"You're not listening, koshka. I said *imagine*."

'I pictured myself floating in the air. Like a feather, I rose until I was floating before him. I grinned at the success of my feat.

'He applauded me. "Good. Easy, isn't it? The imagination is the most powerful force on earth." He held out his hand, and I took it. "Now, your next lesson." We flew over the snow, away from the barn, and over the road. The bodies lay under a light covering of snow. The wolves would return, and feast on them, once they knew we had gone. We plunged through the air, the ground far below us rushed by in a blur of speed. It was exhilarating. I looked over at him, and we shared a grin.

'Then, he pointed ahead of us. I looked down, and saw our cars, and the soldiers standing about them. The lead car had obviously broken down, for there were two men looking at the engine. We hurtled towards them.

"Don't be afraid," he said. "Their bullets can't hurt us."

'We dropped out of the sky, and landed among them. Cries of terror rose into the air. He released me, and rushed at a man. He sank his fangs into his throat, drinking deeply. I grabbed a soldier, and sank my own teeth into his pulsing jugular. His blood filled me like the finest wine. Shots rang out, and I felt little shocks, like pin – pricks that stung my immortal body with momentary twinges of pain as the bullets hit me. It was like being bitten by ants. The pain vanished immediately. I laughed madly. The soldiers were firing wildly, some of them shooting their own companions. Others fled screaming, throwing their weapons away.

'My companion tossed the man's corpse away, and was suddenly in amongst them, striking them down with his rock hard fists. Skulls smashed, and blood and brains sprayed about, as he butchered them without mercy. I leapt at the others, my own hands dealing death. Soldiers flew through the air, and were smashed against the blood-spattered cars in an orgy of destruction. The gunfire and screams ceased, and we stood amongst the bodies.

'My companion leapt into the air, and pursued the ones who had run. He chased them down, and slaughtered them mercilessly. He caught the last man, and flew back and flung him before me. It was the sergeant. He looked up at me, terror in his eyes.

"Now let me entertain you," I said savagely. I took him by the neck, and wrenched him to his feet. I threw my right hand forwards, and punched him in the chest, tearing through his coat, his uniform, and right through his ribs. He screamed. I ripped out his heart, and flourished it before him.

I swear that for an instant, he was still alive, and gaped at it in horror. Then the light fled from his eyes, and I dropped his body to the bloody snow.

'A small sound came to us, like someone had gasped, and the sound had suddenly been choked off. Our blood – filled eyes turned upon the last car. I walked over to it, and peered through the gore – caked windows. I seized the rear door, and with a wrench of tortured metal, I tore it from the car and heaved it away. It flew twenty feet and crashed to the ground. I leaned inside the car. There were two figures huddled in there, their faces like terrified children. I reached in, and grasped the coat of the one nearest me. As though this had shocked him out of his terror, he drew a knife and plunged it at me. I gripped his hand in my own cold hard fist. He stared, stunned at my unnatural strength, and I took his knife and rammed it under his chin. His eyes rolled up into his head, and I tossed him to the snow.

'I leaned in, and dragged the other man out of the car, and threw him to the ground. It was Captain Orlov.

"You! – You!" he gasped. "Impossible!"

'I stood over him like Death himself. I glared at him, hatred emanating from every atom of my immortal body. He cringed, and tried to look away, but he was mesmerised by my eyes. I showed him my fangs, and he gulped in terror.

"Take him, koshka," said my companion.

"No," I said. "He deserves an awful death. For what he did to my family."

"Listen, Koshka."

'My supernatural hearing brought to me the sound of the wolves, back at the farmhouse. I smiled wickedly.

"Yes," I said. I hauled Orlov to his feet, and rose into the air. He cried out. My companion joined us.

"This way," he said, and sped away. I followed, with Orlov gibbering in terror as we rushed over the landscape far below. We came to the farmhouse, and the wolves looked up at us warily. Most of the bodies had been eaten, their pitiful bones were scattered across the road. I slowly floated downwards, until I was only twelve feet above the pack. They retreated, but watched us cautiously. Orlov looked down, and suddenly realised what I was about to do.

"*No,*" he gasped.

'I dropped him. He fell onto the road, and scrambled to his feet. "You can't!" he cried. The wolves regarded him, and began to close in. I rose again into the air, so that the wolves wouldn't consider me a threat.

"Please!" Orlov begged.

"You have a weapon, Captain. Die like a man." My eyes burned into him.

'He stared about himself wildly, gaping at the wolves as they closed in on him. He took out his pistol with a shaking hand. He trembled, and held it up, trying to steady his hand. The wolves came closer. There was a sharp report, and one of them fell dead, shot through the head. The other wolves scattered, and retreated. My companion applauded.

"Good shot, Captain," he said, as though he was watching some sporting event.

'The wolves came back warily, watching the terrified man in the centre of their circle of death. They snarled at him, and closed in. He fired twice, but this time, he was so rattled, he missed. The lean forms backed away each time, but then came closer when none of their number was hurt.

'Orlov cast a quick glance up at us. "*Save me!*" he cried.

'I regarded him with hate filled eyes. I remembered what he had said to Father when he had shot Alexei, and gave him back his own words: "Your world is finished, comrade," I said coldly.

'He goggled at me, his eyes wide with terror. The wolves snarled, and closed in. Orlov stared at them, trembling. Then he put his pistol to his temple. He closed his eyes, and pulled the trigger. There was a click. The pistol was empty. He opened his eyes, and lowered it, and stared in horror at the oncoming wolves. He screamed as they leapt, and dragged him down. The screams ended as fangs tore out his throat, and the wolves ripped him apart. We watched, my companion and I, and I felt a deep sense of satisfaction at the Captain's death. My family had been avenged.

"You are satisfied?" came a voice, interrupting my reverie.

'I looked over at my companion, and nodded.

"Good," he said. "I am Arkady."

"My name is –" I began.

'He held up his hand, cutting me off. "You are Koshka. Your old life is gone. Now you are immortal, and I give you a new name." He held out his hand. "Come, Koshka."

'I took his hand, and we flew away, away from my mortal life, away from my family, and into a new life as one of the undead, a drinker of blood. A girl who would be eighteen for all of eternity."

She stopped talking. Sergei stared at her, and saw a single tear of blood run down her pale cheek. He reached out, and wiped it away.

"I did not know," he said softly, "that you have suffered so much." He stroked her hair.

She smiled. "Thank you." She held his hand in her own cold, hard hands. "Now do you see why I am the way I am?"

"Valeria, all men are not like those animals."

"Every mortal man that I have encountered has been the same; lustful, greedy, and only interested in themselves. They deserve to be killed, and I kill them."

"No," he said. "There are good men also. Do you think *I* am like that?"

"No," she said softly.

"And Erik? He is good man too."

"He is a fool."

"A fool? Why?"

"Because he thinks that Romana loves him. She has had many mortal companions over the centuries. She will cast him aside like all the others."

"Did she have children with any of them?"

"No."

"Then that would be a good reason for her to stay this time, da?"

She regarded him with her green eyes. "Perhaps."

He changed the subject. "So, you and – *Arkady* – you continued to live in Russia?"

"Yes, for a long time. He had taken a mansion for himself that was far from any city or town. He taught me how to use my powers. We hunted, and loved, and our life was good. For twenty years, we existed like that, and then…" She trailed off.

"Yes," The Bear prompted. "And then?"

"Then, I became pregnant. Arkady was upset. We had been using the herbs that our kind use to guard against such an event, but for some reason, the last batch that I had used did not work. He had told me of the Clans, and of their law against offspring."

"And he thought that they would come for the baby."

She stared into space. "No. One day, when the child was one, four vampire hunters appeared, led by Gerald. They came to the mansion without warning. We confronted them on the front steps." She paused for a moment, remembering, and then continued. "'You know why I am here, Arkady,' he said. Arkady nodded, and came over to me."

"What is this?" I asked. "What do you want?" I had never met another vampire before; Arkady and I had kept to ourselves.

"Ask him," Gerald said. He gestured to his hunters, and they made to go inside.

'I blocked their path. Glaring at them, I said; "You will not take our child." Arkady took my arm.

"Koshka, please."

'I stared at him. His guilt was written all over his face. I did not need to read his mind, or theirs, to know what had happened.

"Yes," he said softly, "I sent for them."

"Why?" I said, appalled.

"It is the law," Gerald said.

'I turned and fixed him with a withering gaze. "Your law, not ours. We are not members of your Clan."

"That doesn't matter. The Abominations must be destroyed. Out of our way." His eyes met Arkady's.

'Before I knew what was happening, Arkady had grabbed me in a vice – like grip. The hunters rushed past me as I screamed in fury. Gerald watched me without expression. Arkady was much too strong for me to break free. In a few moments, the hunters returned, one of them holding my son. He held him out to Gerald, who took him.

"*No!*" I screamed. "Don't do this!"

'Gerald's eyes filled with blood. He held me in his gaze for a moment, and then his fangs sought my child's throat. I screamed. He drained the pitiful little thing, and then cast it to the ground. He concentrated, and the corpse ignited. It burned brightly for a moment, and then the fire died, leaving a small pile of ash, that blew away. Nothing remained of my child. I ceased to struggle, and stood staring in horror. Tears of blood ran down my face. Arkady released me.

"The law has been obeyed," Gerald said. He nodded to Arkady, and walked down the steps. His hunters followed. At the foot of the steps they turned, and he said: "Remember."

'I pointed a trembling hand at him. "I will remember *you*," I hissed savagely.

'He smiled, gave me a mocking bow, and then, as one, they took off, and flew away.

"Koshka." Arkady put his hand on my shoulder.

"Don't touch me!" I shrugged his hand away angrily. "How could you - "

"I had no choice! They would have found out about the child, and the same thing would have happened."

'I glared at him. "So," I said savagely, "obeying their law is more important than the life of our child. You disgust me."

"Koshka, please -"

"No, Arakdy, I have heard enough. I do not want to speak to you ever again. Goodbye."

'His mouth dropped open in astonishment as I rose into the air. His eyes beseeched me, but I ignored their imploring gaze. I looked once more at the home that we had had, and then I turned and flew away as fast as I could." She stopped talking, lost in her memories.

"Did you ever see him again?" Sergei said.

"Yes. For five years I hunted alone, travelling from place to place. I met a few other vampires, but I didn't stay with them. The mortal world had been plunged into another war, and it was easy to hunt isolated soldiers as they performed sentry duty. The Nazis had conquered all of Europe, crushing all who attempted to stop them. One night, as I was flying over a forest in Germany, I saw lights on the road below me. I flew lower, and saw that it was a big car, a Mercedes. Three men were in it: a driver, an officer, and a guard, all clad in black SS uniforms. I smiled to myself, and flew ahead of them and landed in the middle of the road. The Mercedes raced towards me where I stood waiting in the cone of the lights. The car screeched to a halt. The guard got out. The other two watched, perplexed looks on their faces. The forest was quiet around us, as if it waited with bated breath. The idling engine was the only sound.

"Was ist?" the guard said. He frowned at me.

'I smiled, and walked towards him.

'He brought his machine pistol up, and cocked it with a metallic click.

"Halt!"

'I bore down upon him. He fired at me, and the gun hammered loudly into the still night. The bullets patted me like the blows of a child's fist, and I laughed at the sensation. My dress was torn to shreds under the spray of gunfire. He emptied the magazine at me as I continued to close in on him. He gaped in amazement as he stared at the wounds on my body closing and healing before his stupefied gaze. The driver cried out, leapt out of the car, and pelted for the trees. I reached the soldier, and slashed his throat with a flick of my wrist. His blood fountained into the air, and he collapsed. I looked over at the officer, my eyes filling with blood.

'He sat transfixed. He had not even attempted to pull out his pistol. He stared at my pale flesh that was revealed through the shredded dress. He gaped unbelievingly at my stomach, my breasts, which should have been bloody and ripped apart. "Gott im himmel! Was bist du?" *God in Heaven, What are you?*

'I leapt into the car, and looked down upon him. "Der Engel des Todes." *The Angel of Death.* My fangs found his throat, and I drained him dry. As his blood filled me with delicious warmth, I looked at his dead face. He was the personification of the Nazi superman; blonde, blue eyes, and had the figure of an athlete. He was dressed in the uniform of a Sturmbannfuehrer. I looked at the tattered remains of my dress and smiled. I ripped it off, and stripped him, dressing in his warm clothes. With a flash of my nails, I tore the insignia off. Even his boots fitted me. "Danke, Herr Sturmbannfuehrer." I gave him a mock salute. The Mercedes purred on, oblivious of the death that was in and around it.

'I got out of the car. I could still sense and hear the frantic driver as he ran sobbing through the dark trees. I shrugged. I would let him go. I had had my fun, had drunk, and had nice new clothes. I rose into the night sky and flew away.

'A little later I saw a group of vampire hunters pursuing another figure. Intrigued, I flew after, and followed them, and they came to earth just at the forest's edge. The fugitive ran into the trees, and by the way he stumbled and staggered, I knew he was nearly done. The hunters gave chase, sensing the end. I landed, and saw a blonde figure order the other hunters to follow the quarry. Sensing me, he turned. Yes, it was Gerald.

'He smiled. "Well, well," he said, "imagine meeting you here." His gaze took in the uniform. "Have you joined the SS?"

"No. But they have stylish clothes. I – *obtained* – them."

'He read my thoughts, and saw what I had done. "I see. Yes, they do suit you."

'I came up to him. He watched me warily. "I see you are still doing the work of the Clans," I said. "A bit harder to chase someone than to kill an innocent baby, isn't it? Especially when they can turn and fight."

"Yes," he said. "Although it is a much finer sport."

"Sport?" I echoed.

"Oh, yes. It is a fine sport to hunt one of our own; one who has defied the law, not once, but twice."

'I gazed at him, puzzled. "What do you mean?"

'At that moment, there was a rustling in the trees. He turned slightly, keeping one eye on me. With a cracking and snapping of small branches, the hunters emerged, dragging their prey. They hurled the fugitive to the ground before Gerald.

'He looked up. It was Arkady. His clothes were ripped and torn, and he was filthy. He stared up at the blonde dandy. He was exhausted, and unaware that I stood there. I felt pity for him.

"You've given us quite a chase," Gerald said.

"Finish it," Arkady said grimly.

'Gerald smiled, showing his fangs. "Oh, no, not yet. Look who has come to see you." He gestured, and Arkady looked. He gaped at me.

"Koshka!" he gasped. "Are you one of them?"

"Yes," Gerald said, interrupting my reply. "She knows that you broke the law a second time, Arkady. She is here to see that you receive justice."

'Arkady stared at me, shock written on his dirty face. *"No,"* he whispered. He shook his head in disbelief.

'I regarded him, my Maker, my saviour; the one who had brought me into this not - life, this purgatory. The one who had allowed Gerald and his hunters to destroy my child. My pity at his awful state fled before an inferno of hatred that exploded inside of me. I bared my fangs at him. He flinched away from me. I turned to Gerald. "Kill him!" I rasped, my voice harsh.

'He smiled, and gestured to his hunters. They fell upon Arkady, and their fangs sank into him. Moments later it was done. Gerald's hunters rose, and stepped away from him. My old companion sprawled there, the unholy life that had animated him gone forever.

"You may finish it," Gerald said.

'I turned my gaze from Arkady's corpse to him. "Finish it?" I echoed.

"The fire." He regarded me closely. His hunters were still in a heightened state of awareness, and I realised that they were waiting to see what I would do. I could feel their eyes on me.

"You *do* know how to do it?" Gerald said.

"Yes, of course," I replied.

'He raised his eyebrows, and gestured at Arkady. "Well, then."

'I looked down at the body, remembering everything that Arkady had done for me, how he had taught me, protected me, loved me.

"That is all gone," Gerald said.

"Yes," I said softly. I concentrated, and the fire rose in my eyes. I sent it out, and into Arkady. He flared into appalling brightness, and in seconds, burned into ash.

"Good," Gerald said. He folded his arms. "Now, what do we do with you?"

"Me?"

"You are not a member of the Clan. This is a problem. You must either become one of my hunters, or we must destroy you."

"What! How could you even *think* I would join you, after what you did to my child!"

'He shook his head. "You know that happened because you and Arkady broke the law. *'No offspring.'* That is Clan law. The Abominations must not be allowed to live."

'I glared at him. His hunters spread out, surrounding me. "I am not one of them."

"No, my dear. But you did give birth to one. That is almost as bad." He smiled. "But you have shown me that you can be ruthless." He gestured at the pile of ash. "If you can show me that you can be a loyal hunter, I believe that I can speak to the Clan for you, and they will allow you to live, just as long as you obey me, and be one of us."

'I looked around at the circle of hunters that had fixed their blood – red eyes upon me. They would like to destroy me, and were only held in place by Gerald's will. If he gave the order, they would fall on me like rabid wolves.

"But I do not *want* to give that order, my dear." Gerald held out his hand. "Join me." He glanced at the others. "Or die. Make your decision."

'What choice did I have? I came to him.

"Kneel."

'I went to my knees before him. He placed his hand on my head. "Do you swear to serve me and the Clan for all eternity, to hunt down those who break Clan law, and to destroy the Abominations wherever they may be found, knowing that if you fail, or be a traitor to our cause, you will be slain without mercy?"

"I swear."

'He removed his hand from my head, and held it before me. "Kiss the symbol of the Clan."

'He wore a ring. I leaned forwards, and kissed it. He smiled.

"Rise."

'I rose to my feet.

"Welcome, Koshka –"

"I held up my hand. "No, I am no longer Koshka."

'He gazed at me, puzzled.

"My name is Valeria."

'He smiled. "Welcome, Valeria. Come, I will take you to the Clan."

'We rose into the air, and his hunters followed.

A small chime sounded. The 'fasten seatbelts' sign was lit. They were coming in for the final approach to Duvall's island. The plane banked, and prepared to land. They both fastened their belts.

Sergei took Valeria's cold hands in his own. "Thank you for telling me your story." He smiled.

She regarded him. "So you do not fear me any more?"

He shook his head. "Niet."

She returned his smile. "Good." She lay back and closed her eyes.

The undercarriage came down with a thud, and the plane sank lower. With a jolt and a rumble, they landed. Sergei stared at her white face as they taxied along the runway.

17

The Immortals

The plane came to a stop. They undid their belts, and rose up out of their seats. The steward that had given Valeria the bottle walked up to the hatch and opened it. Then he lowered the set of steps and stood back. The passengers filed down the aisle, and stopped at the open hatch, looking out. A group stood there on the tarmac, all dressed in black combat fatigues. They were all armed with the chrome naphtha rifles that Duvall had created.

Sergei motioned Valeria to precede him. The redhead sashayed down the steps, her voluptuous figure drawing the eye of every member of the group that waited. The Bear followed her, and then Romana and Erik, with Gerald bringing up the rear. They walked up to the group, and stopped before them.

Their leader stepped forwards. "Welcome. I'm Matthew." His glance flicked over them rapidly, and lingered on Romana. He smiled, showing his fangs. "It's a great honour to have you with us," he said to her. He stared at her fixedly. "You're pregnant."

"Yes," Romana replied.

"To *him*," Matthew said, pointing at Erik.

"That's right," the drummer said.

"Where is Duvall?" said Gerald.

The leader shrugged, and waved at the jungle. "Somewhere in there."

Romana's gaze swept the group. "Why is he not here to meet us?" She regarded the leader, her eyes widening, as she read his thoughts. "He has become one of us."

"Yes," Matthew said. "Your blood changed him."

Gerald glanced at Romana, and then looked back at Matthew. He stared at him for a long moment, reading his thoughts. "I see. So you are now in charge here."

"I am."

Sergei and Erik looked warily at the Immortals.

Matthew smiled. "Don't be afraid. As long as we get what we want, you won't be hurt."

"And what would that be?" said Erik frostily.

Matthew indicated Romana. "Leave her with us, and you're free to go."

Erik stepped forwards. "What if we don't *want* to leave her?"

The Immortal's smile became wider, and his fangs gleamed in the sun. "Do you think you could stop us from *taking* her?"

There was a click. The naphtha rifles came up, and were actioned. The Immortals behind Matthew fixed their sights on The Bear.

Matthew turned his attention to Sergei, who was pointing a pistol between his eyes. "Pitiful. You know mere bullets can't hurt us."

The Bear nodded. "Not normal bullets, da. But these are special."

The Immortal's eyes narrowed. He stared at Sergei, reading the Russian's mind. His smile fell. His eyes filled with blood.

"Da," said Sergei, "every bullet is tracer."

"Sergei!" said Valeria. She looked ready to leap into explosive action.

"Is all right, darling. Matthew does not want to burn, eh, Matthew?" He grinned at Matthew.

"You would only get one shot off, fool," Matthew sneered. "My men would turn you into a torch in a second."

"Is true. But you would not know. I am good shot. I make sure of you first."

They stared at each other. Matthew glared at Sergei, and Sergei stood there calmly, his finger curled around the trigger. The Immortals stood like statues, their rifles glinting in the sun. A century seemed to pass by.

"This is foolish," Gerald said. "We agreed to bring Romana here, so more of her blood could be taken. We did not agree to leave her."

Without taking his eyes from Sergei, Matthew said: "That deal was with Duvall. We *want* her."

"No deal," Erik said.

Romana stepped forwards. "I will stay. But you must let them go."

The drummer grabbed her arm. "No, Romana!"

She turned to him. "I am what they want. I agreed to come. Leave with the others. They will not harm me." She put her cold hand against his cheek. "Or our baby."

"Yes," said Matthew, "we won't hurt them. She'll be safe. We just need more of her blood."

"Because your science failed." Gerald shook his head. "You couldn't make Romana's blood in your laboratory."

Matthew shot the blonde dandy a look filled with irritation. "It was tried, but the scientists couldn't make it work. Every time, it changed the subject. They became vampires, and eventually became uncontrollable, and we had to destroy them. We must have the original."

"Why? So you can make an army of Immortals?" said Valeria.

Ignoring the redhead's question, Gerald said: "Why didn't you change?"

"I was made from original vampire blood. It doesn't seem to have the same effect as the synthetic blood."

"And that's why you need Romana's blood," said Erik.

"Yes," Matthew said. "Now, please step back onto the aircraft, and we'll allow you to leave."

"No," said Sergei. "Not unless Romana comes too."

Matthew glared. He waved his men forward. They advanced a step, their rifles covering the whole group. Valeria snarled. Against so many armed with the deadly rifles, what could she and Gerald and Romana do?

"Back!" The Bear cried. "Back, or I shoot!"

Matthew smiled, and stepped towards them. His men followed. Erik braced himself. Gerald, Valeria and Romana readied themselves to spring. Sergei prepared to fire.

In a rapid chain of explosions, Matthew's advancing soldiers disappeared in gouts of flame. The others were thrown to the tarmac. A wave of heat rushed over them. Erik looked up, to see that all of the vampires had been destroyed. Matthew alone remained. He rose to his feet, only to be hit by something that rushed at him. He was flung across the runway, and smashed into the plane by a blow that would have killed any ordinary human. In a flash, Duvall stood over him, and dragged him to his feet.

Erik and Sergei gazed at the Frenchman in amazement. The change that he had undergone was incredible. They hadn't known what to expect, but their faces showed that they hadn't even imagined that he could have become the superhuman creature that now met their eyes. The others, however, merely took his appearance in their stride. They cautiously approached. Erik went over to where the guards had been, and picked up a couple of the naphtha rifles that lay on the smoking runway. He came over, and offered one to Sergei. The Bear put his pistol away, and took it. They both advanced, watching the two vampires by the aircraft warily.

Duvall was holding Matthew in a vice-like grip. He shook his head ruefully.

"I'm disappointed in you, Matthew," he said. He brought up his left arm, and displayed the wrist computer. "I thought you would have found a way to turn my toy off by now."

Matthew stared at him with hate-filled eyes. "We're working on it," he said, his voice flat and unemotional. His gaze moved to the others.

The Frenchman turned. "Welcome. I'm afraid there's been an – *incident*. Harrow and Christian have turned against me, and have tried to take control."

"Yes," said Gerald, "but they aren't in control now."

Duvall smiled. "No. The fools. They thought that they could tell the Immortals what to do. Ha! Impossible."

An alarm sounded.

"Time to go," Duvall said. "Goodbye, Matthew." With a snap of his wrist, he broke Matthew's neck. The body dissolved into ash.

Several shouts rang out, and they turned to see a group of Immortals rushing towards them, firing as they came. The deadly naphtha pellets exploded around them.

"Scatter!" Duvall shouted, taking Romana's arm and leaping into the air.

"No!" Erik cried. Gerald grabbed him, and they took to the air. Valeria snatched Sergei by the collar, and they too rushed into the sky. A thunderous explosion blossomed behind them as one of the pellets struck the jet and turned it into a blazing wreck. The Immortals gave chase, splitting up and following the three separate groups. Naphtha pellets flew around the fugitives as they hurtled over the jungle.

"Take me to Romana!" yelled Erik. *"Now!"* He turned to see his beloved rushing away from him.

"Fool!" Gerald cried. "We must flee and hide."

The drummer snarled. *"Gerald!"*

"No, mortal. This is the only way. Duvall will not harm her."

Erik looked back at their pursuers. They came on, firing. The pellets whizzed all around them, but luckily, none had hit them. *Wait a minute!* Erik thought. He gazed at the rifle in his hands, and then looked ahead.

They were approaching a mountain covered with trees. "Gerald!"

"We are *not* going to Romana!"

The drummer shook his head angrily. "Go lower."

The vampire read his mind. He smiled. "Good. I see. Yes." They plummeted towards the mountain. Their enemy hurtled after them, still firing.

Erik gasped at the sudden spurt of speed that Gerald put on. "*Jesus!*" the wind hammered at him, and his stomach churned as he watched the ground rapidly approach. "T – those trees," he managed to say.

The vampire swept down among the trees, flew through them, and then came to a jarring halt. It was as if they had hit a brick wall. He turned, and they hung in mid air. Erik brought the rifle up as the Immortals came down among the trees. He fired off a rapid fusillade as the vampires suddenly stopped in surprise, fooled by the pair's manoeuvre. They exploded into flame as the pellets tore into them. The echo of the detonations reverberated through the jungle and faded. Gerald landed, and gave Erik an admiring look. "That was a good idea," he said.

"Thanks. I do come up with the occasional one."

Gerald smiled, showing his fangs. "Indeed."

"What now?" the drummer said.

"Now, we hide." He regarded Erik. "Don't worry, I know Romana will be safe."

The drummer looked back the way they had come. "I hope you're right."

They moved deeper into the jungle, seeking refuge.

Valeria and Sergei hurtled over the treetops, naphtha pellets seeking to turn them into ash. The Immortals gave pursuit, three of them plunging after the two fugitives. The Bear turned his head, and saw that they were beginning to catch up.

"Valeria!"

"I know."

Sergei looked down at the trees that flashed rapidly by. He gritted his teeth. *"Take me down!"* he cried.

"No!" Valeria replied.

"Trust me. Look into my mind!"

Valeria read his thoughts. She grinned wickedly. "Yes! Get ready!" They dived towards the trees. As they swept over a clearing, the redhead dropped Sergei onto the grass, and raced away. He stood and shook his fist at her retreating figure.

The Immortals flew over the Russian. Their leader cried: "Leave him! After her!"

Sergei watched them as they rushed past him and went in pursuit of Valeria. *Now, my dear,* he thought, *do not fail.* For what seemed an eternity, he stood, blinking sweat out of his eyes. *Come on! Where are you?* He fixed the trees in his sights, ready to fire.

Valeria exploded out of the trees in front of him. Hot on her heels came the Immortals. The Bear fired quickly as they appeared, and two of them vanished in roiling clouds of flame. Valeria turned as the last one came on. She rushed at him, and knocked his rifle away with a sweep of her hand. They grappled in midair, each seeking the other's throat. They fell to the ground, and rolled along the grass, tearing at each other like the predators they were. Sergei raced up, but couldn't see how he could help her. Valeria pinned the Immortal to the ground, and her fangs ripped into his neck. She drained him, and tossed her head back in ecstasy as his blood flowed through her. Her hair whipped about her like a lion's mane. She fixed Sergei with her blood-filled eyes. Valeria rose from the corpse, and advanced upon the Russian.

"Valeria! It's me!" He stepped back, shocked at the bloodlust that still gripped her. She came on, and bared her fangs at him. *"No!"* he cried, *"get back!"* He brought up the rifle, but she leapt forward and ripped it out of his hands and flung it away. She grabbed him by the shoulders, and stuck her tongue down his throat in a passionate kiss. He tasted the Immortal's blood. She ripped his shirt off, and pushed him to the ground. With an urgent tug, she removed his trousers and boxers. The Russian felt a fire building within his loins. As Sergei stared at her in amazement, she unzipped her dress, and tossed it away. She stepped out of her black panties, and took off her bra. It followed the dress. Valeria dropped down and straddled him. She took his hardness in her cold hand and guided him inside her. He gasped as he entered her, and Valeria rode him fiercely. Their mingled cries echoed in the jungle depths.

Romana and Duvall raced over the jungle, with four of the Immortals hurtling along behind them. Romana glanced back at their pursuers. She turned to the Frenchman, puzzled.

"They are not firing at us! Why?"

He smiled. "You are too important to them," he said. "They wouldn't dare destroy the blood that they seek. I however – "

"Yes. They are afraid of you."

"They should be." He held up his wrist computer. "With this, I can destroy them all. They haven't found a way to deactivate it, and I have turned off all of their sensors and alarms. Once we evade these fools, I will deal with Christian and the others."

"We must evade them first."

He nodded. He looked ahead. They were approaching the other side of the mountain that Gerald and Erik had flown to. "Romana, when we reach that mountain, I will turn aside and wait for our pursuers. You continue on; they will want to catch you. I will then attack them from behind. When you sense my assault, turn and come at them. Don't worry, they won't fire at you."

She met his gaze. "Very well."

"Be ready," he said, as they closed in on the tree-clad mountainside. They flew down and flashed low over the trees. *"Now!"* He plunged to the right, and vanished. Romana continued ahead, and the Immortals followed. The four of them were closing in. Their leader frowned as he saw they were chasing only one fugitive. *Where was the other one?* A scream answered his thought. He glanced back, and saw Duvall and one of his men struggling in midair. A cloud of ash that was drifting downwards had obviously been another. He snarled to the Immortal at his side.

"Shoot them both!" He raised his naphtha rifle, and actioned it.

The other Immortal turned, and cocked his rifle. Then he lost his head. Literally. Romana had turned and sped towards them, and her talons had slashed through his neck. He turned to ash as she grabbed the leader's rifle, and they grappled as they dropped towards the ground. As the trees rushed up to meet them, she drove her fingers through his chest. He joined his companions. Romana stopped her headlong fall, and gazed upward.

Duvall was drifting down to meet her, having disposed of his opponent. He grinned. "You are both beautiful *and* deadly." They hung over the trees.

"Thank you. Now what?"

"Now, we go and pay a visit to Christian. I will see if there are any more Immortals looking for us." The Frenchman activated his computer.

"I thought you said you had deactivated the sensors?"

He smiled. "For Christian and the others. Only I have the use of them."

"Good. Find the others, and we will leave this place."

He considered her for a moment. "Romana?"

"Yes?"

"Do you really want to rejoin your friends?"

She met his gaze. "Yes. Why do you ask me?"

He looked at the display screen. There was no sign of any other searchers. "I can see where Erik and Sergei are. They are not far." He deactivated the computer and turned to her. "Think for a moment. We – you and I – are the two most powerful vampires on earth. With our combined strength, and my weapons and technology, we could rule the world. You have no need of your companions." He looked at her belly, which was starting to show. "When your children are born, we will have established an empire of Immortals, with you and I as the rulers. Your children will join us, and we will show them all of the skills we possess, and teach them how to use their powers." His eyes flashed. "Many mortals have thought to have dominion over the earth; you and I have the power and strength to do so. *Think of it!*" He clenched his fist in emphasis. "An army of Immortals will do our bidding; mortals shall serve us as slaves, or be our cattle. Our empire will last forever."

Sarcastic clapping interrupted Duvall's speech. He and Romana turned to face the applause. Erik and Gerald stood there; the drummer was covering the professor, and Gerald was the one clapping. The blonde dandy grinned, showing his fangs. "Oh, yes," he said derisively, "that sounds fabulous. You could be a queen, Romana." He stopped his applause, and lowered his hands.

The Frenchman's eyes narrowed dangerously. He stared fixedly at Erik. "You *dare* threaten me?" he hissed.

The drummer gave him an icy smile. "You know how effective these rifles are against vampires, don't you, professor? Just use your little toy there to tell us where Sergei and Valeria are, and we'll be going."

"Just like that?" Duvall said. "What about the Immortals?"

"I believe the Clan will be interested to hear that they are no longer under your control," said Gerald. "We will deal with them."

"*Fool!*" the Frenchman cried. "They are far more dangerous than you know."

"Oh, I don't know," said Erik. He smiled. "We seemed to have no trouble disposing of them. Now, professor, we'd like to know where our friends are."

"Wait," Romana said.

The drummer glanced at her, and then turned his attention back to Duvall. "What for? Your deal with the professor here is off. We don't need to be here anymore. Let's get Sergei and Valeria and go home."

Gerald fixed his gaze on her. He raised an eyebrow as he read her thoughts.

"Yes," Romana said. "*I* am responsible for the creation of the Immortals. It was my blood that made them. Now that these mortals and their science have failed, I have to help to destroy them." She turned to Duvall. "That *is* what you are going to do?"

"Yes," the professor said. His face was blank.

"No," the drummer said. "We can't trust him, Romana. It's all *his* doing, his crazy plan of taking over the world with his army of vampires. How can we know that he's telling the truth?" He slowly lowered the rifle.

The professor turned his eyes upon Erik. "You can't understand, mortal. I *can't* lie to them, they can read my mind, and see any subterfuge. Correct?"

"Yes," Gerald agreed. "He speaks the truth."

"Oh, so now you *don't* want to take over the world?" Erik said mockingly.

"There is no need. I have become what I wanted to be. I am immortal."

"What about your little speech just now?" Erik said, unconvinced.

Duvall shrugged. "It doesn't matter. I know that Romana will not join me." he looked at the girl regretfully. "It is a shame. Now, I must go and destroy the Immortals, and deal with those who betrayed me." He met Romana's gaze. "Will you help me?"

Romana nodded. "Yes."

"Romana," Erik said, "let him go. It's not your problem."

"Erik, it is. I must help him. Why do you not understand?"

"Perhaps his mortal brain is too feeble to understand," Duvall said. He grinned at the drummer, showing his fangs. "If he were one of us – " He took a step forward.

"*Fuck that!*" Erik stepped back involuntarily. He brought the rifle up swiftly, and covered the professor. "Take one more step, and I'll burn you down!"

"But you would be able to read my mind," the professor said reasonably. "You would know that I speak the truth." He spread his hands imploringly.

"I don't care. I don't want to be a vampire."

"You don't know what you're missing," Duvall said. "Look at me. Remember how I was; crippled, tortured by pain, condemned to exist in a chair for the rest of my miserable existence. Now, I am a god! Apart from your lovely Romana here, I am the most powerful vampire on earth. I have no need of an army. It is obvious that Romana's blood is too strong to control; the Immortals will all turn into creatures that will not accept orders from anyone. Those fools Christian and Harrow don't realise that they have no chance of controlling them." He held up his computer. "In here are the master codes to destroy the entire island. There is a nuclear device that will vaporise everything, including the Immortals." He gave them a grim smile. "But first, I will deal with those who betrayed me. I want to kill them myself. Will you help me?"

Romana stepped up to the drummer, and made him lower the rifle. She put her cold hand to his cheek. "I must do this, my love. If you do not want to join us, I will understand."

Erik shook his head. "I don't like it." He gave Duvall a hard stare. "If you even *try* to do anything – "

The professor held up his hands. "I know, you will 'burn me down.'"

"Well," Gerald said, "that's settled. We can go and find the others, and finish this."

Duvall activated his computer. He tapped in a series of numbers. He nodded. "This way." He started off.

Romana and Gerald turned to follow. They stopped when they realised Erik hadn't moved. The drummer watched the figure of the professor with a frown written on his face. The two vampires shared a glance and then walked after Duvall; Romana turned and gave the drummer an imploring look. Erik stood for a moment more, and then finally came after them.

Valeria buttoned up the shirt she'd taken from the dead Immortal and given to Sergei. Luckily, he'd been large, and the shirt fit The Bear well. The Immortal's pants had also gone to the Russian, and now he looked like a soldier again. His Converse trainers looked out of place, but he'd refused the Immortal's boots. One of the naphtha rifles was slung over his shoulder, and the webbing belt that held the clips for it was strapped around his waist. Valeria brushed some leaves from the shirt, and stepped back, gazing at Sergei admiringly. She nodded in satisfaction.

"That looks good on you," she said. She smiled, and grabbed his beard. "But this – " The redhead gave him a mock frown. "I do not like it. It must go, my love."

Sergei drew her into an embrace. "Must it?" He leaned down, and kissed her.

A discreet cough interrupted them. They turned to see Duvall, who stood with a smile on his face. Romana, Gerald, and Erik were with him. The vampires were smiling, but the drummer looked puzzled. The redhead and The Bear came over to them. Sergei's arm went around Valeria's shoulder, and she leaned into him.

"Hello," said Sergei, "is good to see you, my friends." He grinned.

Erik stared at Sergei, taking in his clothing. He looked into the clearing, and saw the shredded remains of his Hawaiian shirt.

"What happened to your shirt, man?" Erik looked at the pair, wondering at Sergei's closeness to Valeria. Where had the Russian's fear of the vampire gone? He glanced at her, and saw the satisfied look on her face. *Oh.*

"Is only shirt, Erik. I have plenty." His eyes twinkled.

"So," Gerald said, "You are both all right."

"More than all right," said Valeria. She grinned.

"Well," said the professor, "shall we go?"

"Yeah," said Erik. "Let's finish this."

"We can fly in," Duvall said. "I will show you a spot where we won't be seen."

Romana took Erik by the arm. Valeria did the same with Sergei.

"Here we go again," the drummer said. They took to the air, and headed towards Duvall's compound.

A short time later, they lay upon a hill overlooking the compound. They looked down, watching the Immortals going to and fro. No humans were seen. They watched for a while, and then they crawled back from the edge, and talked together, their voices low.

"It seems the mortals are all held prisoner," Gerald said.

The professor nodded. "Yes, I told you; Matthew and his followers rounded them all up, and confined them in the laboratory." His gaze took them all in. "It is the perfect time to strike."

"There are guards still patrolling the perimeter," Erik said.

Duvall gave a negligent grunt. "We can handle them. I told you, they have no sensors."

"None but their own," said Romana.

The professor turned to her.

"Remember they are all vampires. They can smell mortal blood, and can sense others of their kind: us." She glanced at Gerald and Valeria.

"She's right," the blonde dandy said. "They are still dangerous even without their technology."

The redhead smiled wickedly, showing her fangs. "Oh, I don't know. They don't seem to be very successful as vampires. We killed all of those who pursued us." Her eyes swept the group. "I agree with the professor; attack now, kill them all, and set off his bomb."

"Thank you, my dear," Duvall said.

"I don't know," Erik said, "there's still a lot of them. What do you think, Bear?"

Valeria's enthusiasm had seemed to affect Sergei. He grinned. "I say attack. Surprise is on our side. They not expect us to do that, da?" Valeria hugged him.

The drummer frowned. "I think it's still a risky move."

"Of course it is," Valeria said, "but we can't just sit around and wait for them to find us."

Erik turned to Romana. "What do you think?"

She regarded him, and then she looked at the group. She turned her gaze back to him. "I think they are right, Erik. We have a chance to destroy them. We should take it."

He stared at her belly. "What about you? Are you in any condition to fight?"

Romana put her hand on his shoulder. "I will be all right. I am not an invalid."

"What about the baby?" His face was marked with concern.

She smiled, and touched his hand gently. "There is time."

"No," he said, shaking his head. "I don't want you to do this."

"I must, my love. You know my feelings about this."

"We will look after her," Duvall said.

"Yes," added Valeria, "we will protect her, and her baby."

"No," Erik said. "*I'll* protect her." He raised the naphtha rifle.

"You should stay here," Duvall said. "The Immortals are too fast for you. And there are too many. Sergei can stay with you."

"Niet," Sergei said. "I come too."

Valeria took his face in her cold hands, and turned him to look at her.

"No, my love. Duvall is right. You should stay here with Erik."

The Russian took her hand away. "Niet," he said again, "I go with you."

"Do you want to leave Erik here all alone?" she said.

The Bear looked at the drummer. He shook his head. "Very well. Erik is my friend. I stay with him." He fell silent.

"You can cover us from here," Duvall said. "There are four guards on patrol. We will silence them, and then make for the laboratory." He held up his computer. "The code for the destruction of the facility is in here; once we have taken care of Christian and the others, I will activate it. We will then have ten minutes to clear the blast zone."

"That will be easy," Gerald said.

The redhead grinned. "Yes. These Immortals rely too much on technology. We can kill them easily. They have no real idea what it is to be a vampire. And then, you can deal with your friends."

"We will come back for you both," Romana said. She hugged Erik.

They crept back to the edge of the cliff, and peered downwards. Activity in the compound had ceased. The four patrolling guards were the only movement. Duvall nodded in satisfaction.

"Romana and I will take the two on the east side. Valeria, you and Gerald will deal with the two on the west side. We will meet at that door over there." He pointed. "Agreed?"

They all agreed. Then, without another word, they moved off, descended the hill, and began to work their way towards their respective targets. Erik and Sergei watched them go.

The drummer cursed softly. "I don't like it, Sergei. I still don't trust that slimy Frenchie."

"We must, Erik. Is only way." He patted the drummer's arm.

Erik turned to him. "What if he turns on them? We can't do anything."

The Russian stared downwards, his gaze fixed on Valeria and Gerald. "We must trust him. Now he is vampire, he can't lie to them. They would know."

Erik snorted. "I'm not convinced of that." He turned and watched Romana and Duvall close in on one of the guards. The professor leapt forwards, and took the Immortal's head in his hands. A quick wrench, and the guard turned to ash. Duvall caught the guard's naphtha rifle before it could hit the ground.

"Not bad," Erik said grudgingly.

Duvall turned and looked back. He made a bow.

The drummer smiled in spite of himself. The professor had heard him. He and Romana moved towards the other guard, stealthily advancing until they were close. This time, it was the girl who disposed of the Immortal. She stepped up behind him, and snapped his neck. He joined his companion. She grabbed the guard's rifle as Duvall had done. She looked back, and Erik saw her fangs as she grinned.

"Nice work," he said, knowing that she had heard him as Duvall had.

The Bear was watching Valeria intently. She and Gerald were approaching the first of their targets. They exchanged a brief glance, and Gerald went forwards, until the unsuspecting guard was close. The blonde vampire stepped up to his victim; his hand flew out like a striking snake, and punched through the Immortal's chest from behind. The guard disintegrated, and Gerald caught his rifle with a flourish. He and the redhead proceeded towards the last guard. They stealthily approached him as he stood scanning the forest. He seemed to be more alert than his companions. Valeria and Gerald slowly made their way towards him. As she rose to her feet to move up and dispose of the Immortal, Gerald grabbed her arm and stopped her. The guard had reached for his radio, and had clicked it on. He spoke into it, but received no reply. His face became puzzled, and the watchers realised that he was trying to contact the sentries that they had dispatched. He stood for a moment, obviously wondering about the lack of response from his comrades, and then activated his radio again.

Valeria exploded out of her hiding place, and rushed towards him. He turned towards her, shouting something into the radio. He dropped it, and brought his rifle up as the redhead closed in. Erik realised with a sick feeling that she was too far away from her target. The guard would fire before she reached him.

"Niet!" Sergei cried, and leapt to his feet. With one swift motion, he swung up his rifle, sighted, and fired. The Immortal, startled by the Russian's cry, turned towards them, and was incinerated as the naphtha pellet hit him and exploded with a concussion that roared like thunder. An alarm sounded.

"Fuck! That's torn it," the drummer yelled. *"Sergei!"*

The Bear was running down the side of the hill, racing towards Valeria and Gerald. The compound below Erik suddenly erupted with running figures. Immortals poured out of the doors, and headed towards the source of the explosion.

"Shit," Erik cursed. He pressed the activation stud on his rifle, and fired shot after shot into the mass of advancing guards. The pellets exploded into balls of flame, bringing fiery death. As he poured his fire into them, the drummer saw his companions run towards the Immortals, their own weapons sending a hail of pellets into them. The compound became a sea of flame. He leapt to his feet, and ran down the hill to join his friends.

Erik came panting up, and jumped down amongst them. The concentrated fire from the Immortals had pinned them down behind a rise of earth outside the compound wall. They fired back, and ducked down as the naphtha pellets flew around them.

"We've got to get out of here!" Erik cried.

The vampires exchanged a glance. Gerald nodded. "Yes. Go."

Valeria and Romana moved to the left, and Gerald and the professor headed to the right. Their attention was fixed on the guards.

"What are you doing?" Sergei asked. He ducked as another barrage of pellets exploded around them.

"I believe it is called a flanking manoeuvre," Duvall said. "Keep their eyes on you." He and Gerald raced off into the trees. The redhead and Romana sped off in the opposite direction.

"No! Wait!" the drummer cried. He cursed, and turned to the Bear.

Sergei was firing as fast as he could. His rifle spat pellet after pellet, and the Immortals that had pinned them down were now taking cover. Erik joined him, and emptied his rifle at them as well. *Where are they?* He thought.

Duvall and Gerald sped towards the Immortals, closing in from the side. Valeria and Romana rushed in, and in seconds, the compound became the field of savage combat, as the Immortals abandoned their weapons, and attacked.

Erik and Sergei leapt to their feet, and ran towards the fight. Only ten of the guards remained, and they were no match for the strength of the other vampires. Romana ripped the heart of one of them from his chest, and danced away as he disintegrated into ash; Valeria snapped the neck of another, and leapt onto his comrade, and bore him to earth, her fangs buried in his neck. Duvall grabbed one of the Immortals, raised him high, and then brought him down across his outthrust leg, snapping his spine. As the Immortal joined his comrades, Gerald took the head off one guard, and then spun on his heel and slashed another's throat open with a flick of his wrist. Erik and Sergei shot the other four Immortals, who disappeared in an inferno of naphtha.

"Excellent!" Duvall cried. "Now, to the laboratory!" They ran for the door. Sergei and Erik paused only to pick up some fresh magazines for their weapons, and hurried after them.

As they reached the door, Gerald held up his hand in caution. They moved to either side of the wall. The blonde vampire kicked in the door, and rapidly turned away as a storm of shots spewed from the opening. Gerald slipped inside, followed by Valeria, and the sounds of close combat came from the corridor. Several screams burst into the air, and then there was silence. The others outside stood waiting, their attention fixed on the opening.

Gerald appeared. He bowed, and indicated that they should enter. "Please join us," he said with a smile.

The group entered the building, stepping over the rifles that the Immortals that Gerald and the redhead had dispatched had dropped on the floor. Sergie and Erik picked them up, and then they continued down the corridor, looking into the open doorways on either side, wary of attack. All except Duvall. He strode forwards confidently, heading for the laboratory. The others followed in his wake.

"Slow down!" Erik cried. "They could attack us from any of these rooms."

"No," the professor said, "they are all dead."

"How can you be so sure?" the drummer said.

"He is sure," Romana said.

"Yes," Gerald added, "the Immortals have all been destroyed."

"Only Christian and Harrow remain alive," Duvall said. "But not for long."

They followed him until they came to the door of the laboratory. No guards stood there. Duvall went up to the keypad, and entered his password. A flat tone rang out. The professor smiled wryly.

"What is it?" The Bear asked.

Duvall turned to them. "Christian has changed the password. At least he thought to do that."

"Can't you override it with your computer?" said Erik.

The professor shook his head. "No."

"Is there another way in?" Gerald asked.

"No," Duvall said. "Only this door."

"Why don't we just take off, and blow this place to hell?" the drummer said. "That'd take care of them too."

The professor shook his head again, and held up his wrist computer. "I'm afraid that can't be done. It seems that they have finally managed to block any commands that I send from this." He glanced at the others meaningfully. "This door must be opened."

"Very well," Gerald said. He walked up to the door, and reached out and touched it. He drew his arm back, and punched the door, which rang like a gong. He drew his arm back, and struck the door again.

Valeria joined him, and together they rained heavy blows upon the door. Sergei and Erik stepped back, and watched the two vampires attack the metal portal, amazed at the strength of their blows. The door slowly began to show the results of the impact of their hard fists. Metallic thunder echoed in the corridor as each punch smashed into the door.

How long can they keep this up? Erik wondered. He felt Romana's arm go around his waist. He put his arm around her.

Until the door is opened, she sent to him.

The blonde dandy and the redhead stepped back. Without any word or thought exchanged between them, Romana and Duvall took their place. They hammered at the door, their fists slamming into the tortured metal, turning into blurs as the speed of their blows increased. The sound of the impacts sped up, until it was like the sound of jackhammers. Erik and Sergei retreated down the corridor, their hands held over their punished ears. They gaped at the power that Romana and Duvall were demonstrating. The door was collapsing under the barrage of undead flesh.

With a shriek of tortured metal, Romana tore a wide gap in the door, exposing its inner workings. She and Duvall stepped up, and began to rip them out. Metal levers and pneumatics littered the floor as the pair tore the mechanism apart.

Gerald and Valeria joined them, and grabbed the edge of the door. Exerting their supernatural strength, all four of the vampires heaved. The portal groaned open with an almost despairing scream of tormented metal. The door came off its massive hinges, and they tossed in onto the floor, where it fell heavily.

The vampires stepped into the laboratory. Erik and Sergei followed, their rifles sweeping the room. They advanced cautiously. A litter of papers covered the floor, and instruments had fallen from tables and lay scattered everywhere. The monitors showed flickering displays of charts and breakdowns of blood analysis, but there was no one there to read them. The room was empty. The only sound was the quiet hum of the air conditioning.

Duvall strode up to Harrow's desk. The scientist's chair lay overturned on the floor, and the drawers on the desk had been opened and rifled. Filing cabinets behind the desk appeared to have also been hurriedly emptied of all of Harrow's research. Everything seemed to show that Harrow had taken all of his notes and papers and fled. The Frenchman stared at the disarray in anger. And then, without warning, he brought his heavy fist smashing down, and the desk splintered and broke in two.

An alarm sounded.

"What's that?" The drummer cried, yelling to be heard over the incessant wailing.

Duvall bared his fangs. "The self destruct system has been activated. We have ten minutes to escape the blast radius." His eyes filled with blood. *"Christian,"* he hissed. He gazed around the laboratory, and then turned to them. *"Come!"* He whirled, and raced towards the doorway. The others sped after him. They ran through the corridors, and burst out into the compound.

Without a word or glance, Romana and Valeria grabbed Erik and The Bear, and the group leapt into the air. As the wailing siren faded behind them, they hurtled away from the island. The drummer turned and watched the island recede as they rushed through the air. In moments, it faded to a speck, and disappeared. There was a flash, brighter than the sun. Erik closed his eyes against the glare. A huge mushroom cloud mounted skywards. Seconds later, the roar of the explosion thundered out.

The group flew onwards, heading towards the mainland, as the island, and the facility on it, which had housed all of Duvall's work, was vaporised in the inferno of atomic fury.

18

Home Again

The television announcer's voice filled the room. Sergei, Valeria, Duvall, Romana and Erik sat in the drummer's lounge room, watching images of the mushroom cloud flash on the screen. The footage shuddered and moved jerkily. It was obvious that all of it had been taken on mobile phones or hand held cameras.

"The nuclear blast that destroyed the island facility of the Duvall Biological Laboratories earlier today was the result of a reactor core meltdown, a spokesman for the company said. Christian King, the executive who was Professor Duvall's administrator of the facility, was luckily away on a business trip for the professor when the tragedy occurred."

The scene changed to a shot of Christian, surrounded by reporters all holding microphones towards him. He was dressed in one of his immaculate suits, and his manner was unflappable in the face of all the media attention.

"Mister King," one of them asked, "are you certain that Professor Duvall is dead?"

Christian gave them a sorrowful look. "I am afraid so. He was working in the laboratory when the reactor exploded. All of the workers who were with him also perished. It was a dreadful accident."

"What of the professor's research?" another asked.

"It was saved. Professor Harrow had sent all of the updated materials to our facility in Paris." He paused, and wiped a tear from his eye. "I thank god that his life's work was not destroyed."

"Very nice," Duvall said dryly. "Such feeling."

"Mister King, will the professor's work be continued?"

Christian looked directly into the camera. He nodded emphatically. "Yes. Professor Harrow and a team of experts are even now examining all of the data. Professor Duvall's work will continue, a fitting legacy for such a dedicated man of science. I know that he would be proud that Professor Harrow has taken up his research, and that the fruits of his work will one day be of benefit to the entire world." He smiled. "Thank you, gentlemen. Good day."

The television was switched off. Erik put the remote down on the table.

"A pretty speech," Gerald said.

"Empty words," Duvall said. "He is only interested in the synthetic blood and the power that it can give him. He knows that Harrow can create an army of Immortals."

"Reminds me of someone," the drummer said.

Duvall turned to face him. "I no longer need to have such an army. Look at me. Do you remember the crippled thing that I was; doomed to exist as only half a man, reliant on science to keep me alive? Now, I am immortal. The dream I had of the Immortals is now just a fading memory, and I now see it as a futile exercise. Christian thinks that he can take that dream and rule the world. He is a fool."

"A fool with all of the tools needed to create that army," Valeria said.

"Da," added Sergei, "we know he can do this."

Gerald rose to his feet. "They must be stopped. I will go and inform the Clans of this development."

"Wait, Gerald." Romana also stood. She looked at them all in turn. "I think we should deal with Christian and Harrow ourselves."

"Why?" Duvall asked. "Karl has hundreds of vampires at his command. Am I correct, Gerald?"

The blonde dandy nodded. "More. Thousands. They would overwhelm Christian and his toys."

"His *toys* nearly killed us all," Romana said. "Don't forget that."

"If the Clans become involved, how can we be sure that Karl won't take those weapons for himself?" the drummer said.

Gerald waved his hand dismissively. "We know he only used that deal as a pretext to get into the laboratory and destroy it."

"Did he?" Valeria said. "Can we be sure?"

Gerald regarded the redhead.

"You know she could be right, Gerald," said Romana.

"Yes," he replied, "she *could* be. There is no way to know."

The drummer got to his feet. "No, there isn't, but we've got to make sure he doesn't get his hands on any of them." He looked at them all in turn. "We know how dangerous a threat the Immortals are; imagine how much more dangerous they'd be with the naphtha rifles, and all of the stuff that Christian and Harrow can put their hands on. And if Karl takes them…" He walked over to the kitchen door, and turned. "I'm getting a drink. Anyone want one?"

Valeria smiled, showing her fangs. "Do you have large quantities of fresh blood in your kitchen?"

Erik reddened. "Shit. Sorry, I forgot."

"You should blush more often, mortal," the redhead said. "It gives your face such a nice colour."

"*Valeria.*"

She turned and met Gerald's icy gaze.

"Do not worry, I am only joking." She smiled sweetly.

"I would like drink, Erik," said Sergei.

The drummer nodded, and went into the kitchen.

"So, What do we want to say to Karl and the Clans?" Romana said. "Let us deal with these mortals, and do not interfere?"

Erik returned from the kitchen, a bottle of Stolichnaya in one hand, and two glasses in the other. He went up to the Bear, gave him a glass, and poured him a drink. He went and sat down, and poured himself one. As he placed the bottle on the table, Gerald said: "I do not think Karl will like your proposal."

"And how do you know that, Gerald?" came a voice from the balcony.

They all turned as Karl walked into the room, followed by several vampires. They were all dressed in expensive suits. Karl's barbarian figure looked out of place clad in such finery. Beside him stood Irina, looking as though she had stepped out of a Tim Burton film, dressed in her usual gothic red dress.

Romana, Gerald, Valeria, and Duvall instantly braced themselves for a fight. The room was filled with tension. Erik and Sergei came to their feet slowly, their eyes fixed on the newcomers.

Karl smiled. "There's no need to be alarmed." He spread his arms wide in a gesture of peace. "We're only here to talk." He looked around the room, his gaze taking in Erik's collection of weapons that were displayed upon the wall. His stare lingered on the naphtha rifle, which gleamed in the light. He finally turned to the drummer. "Nice collection."

"Thanks," Erik said warily.

"Will you not invite us in?" the German said reproachfully.

The drummer looked at Karl's companions, and then met the vampire's stare. "Do I have a choice? You all treat my place like Central Station."

Karl laughed. "Very good, mortal. I like you." He took a step forward, and everyone in the room tensed. He stopped advancing. "I assure you, I mean no harm." He regarded them. "Read my thoughts."

Gerald and Romana stepped forwards and stared at Karl. Valeria and Duvall gazed at the Clan leader with them. After a few moments, the blonde dandy nodded.

"You are satisfied of my intentions?" Karl asked.

"Yes," Romana said.

"Good." He advanced again, and stood before them. "I will go along with your suggestion, my dear," he said to Romana. He held up his hands as Gerald began to speak. "The threat that Christian and Harrow represent should be dealt with. We cannot allow them to create an army of Immortals."

Erik met the vampire's gaze. "So you can promise us you have no interest in obtaining the weapons that Christian has?"

Irina swept over, her dress rustling. She fixed the drummer with a steely glare. "He has already told you, mortal. Do you doubt his word?" She indicated Romana and the others. "*They* do not doubt. They can read his thoughts, and are certain that what he says is the truth."

Karl put his hand on her shoulder. "My dear, please." *There is no need for this.*

She turned to him, and they stared at each other for a long moment. The drummer realised that they were exchanging thoughts.

Yes, they are, Romana sent to him.

I hope they agree, he replied.

The German looked over at Erik. "Yes, we do agree. Does that please you?"

"Yeah, it does. That's if you can keep the promises you make."

Karl laughed. "Yes, I can." He came up to the drummer, and held out his hand. "Perhaps you would prefer to shake my hand, and seal my promise that way?"

Erik regarded the vampire cautiously. *What was he trying to pull?* He wondered.

I am only trying to show you that my word is good, Karl sent to him.

The drummer smiled wryly. *Ok, but I'm keeping an eye on you. If you try to trick us –*

" – you can 'burn me down' with your new toy," Karl said aloud, cocking a thumb at the naphtha rifle. He grinned. "Yes, I know what happened between you and Duvall before."

"That was before we became allies," Duvall said coldly.

Karl slowly turned to him. He gave the Frenchman a thin smile. "Allies?" he echoed. He took a step forward. His eyes filled with blood. "We know how *you* treat your allies," he said flatly. "We haven't forgotten how you dealt with us. Such treachery – "

"Karl." Romana said, stepping between them. Karl turned his attention to her. "We need him, Karl."

They faced each other for a long moment. The tension in the room rose as they stood like statues, their eyes locked. Irina's wild eyes were fixed on Duvall. The other vampires that had accompanied her and Karl tensed themselves for a fight. Romana, Valeria, Gerald, and Duvall did the same. The Bear and Erik shared a glance. With his eyes, Sergei indicated the rifle that hung on the wall. The drummer shook his head. It was too far away. The vampires could move so quickly that they wouldn't have a chance of reaching it. He licked his lips nervously, as he realised how he could break the impasse.

"Okay," Erik said. He reached out and grabbed Karl's cold hand, and shook it firmly. "I trust you."

The German turned to him. He slowly smiled. "Very good, mortal. You are smart. For your kind." He gave Romana an indulgent smile. "And now, we will leave you. Just let us know what you intend to do." He fixed Duvall with a freezing gaze. "If you want to deal with him, it's no concern of ours." He glared at Duvall. "Know this, Frenchman, we'll be watching." He turned to leave, but stopped as he met Irina's gaze. She had a sardonic smile on her face. "Ah, yes." He addressed Erik and Sergei. "There are some friends who wish to speak to you." He gestured at the balcony doorway.

Two figures entered. They walked across the floor, and stood before the group. Erik stared in amazement. Sergei glanced at him, and then turned his attention to the newcomers.

Null and Gyorgi stood there. The boy radiated confidence; he met their eyes proudly, whereas before, he had been riddled with low self-esteem, and had been reluctant to look anyone straight in the eye. Gyorgi looked the same as they remembered; he was dressed in his fine silk suit, but when they looked at his face, they could see the strength of the immortals there. Both of them exuded the aura of the vampires that the drummer and the Bear had encountered.

"Hey, dudes," Null said, waving and smiling at them. His fangs gave him a predatory look. His black garb seemed more fitting than before. Now that he possessed the perfect vision that the vampires had, he had no need of the thick glasses he'd worn before. It took Erik and Sergei a few moments to realise what was different about him.

"Hey," the drummer said, "you're a handsome guy without those glasses."

Null grinned.

"Sergei," Gyorgi said.

Sergei shook his head, a wry smile on his face. "So, you are not dead."

"No. I am *undead*." The Georgian grinned. "I am pleased to see you."

"They have both joined us," Karl said.

"Obviously," Erik said dryly.

Null came up to him. "It's awesome, Erik." His face was alight with fervour. "I can do anything." He winked at the drummer, and then vanished in a flash, appearing and disappearing for a moment in each corner of the room in rapid succession. In an instant, he stood in front of Erik again. "You shoulda seen how I took out those fucks that once treated me like shit." His eyes burned into the drummer. He raised his right hand, and clenched his fist. "They were no match for me. Some of 'em begged me not to kill 'em. But I drank 'em all up, all the same." He laughed.

"Look at you," Erik said, shaking his head in wonder. "You're a rock and roll vampire." He held out his hand. "I'm pleased for you, man."

The boy shook his hand. "You could be like us, man." He spread his arms wide. "Immortal, powerful." He glanced at Romana. "You're already the companion of the most powerful vampire on earth. If she made you one of us –"

"Erik does not want to join us," Romana said.

Null met her gaze. "Why not?"

The girl put her arm around the drummer. "It is his choice."

The boy shrugged. "Well, that's okay, I guess." He put his cold hand on Erik's shoulder. "You don't know what you're missin'." He grinned. "You're still my favourite drummer anyway, man." He slapped Erik on the shoulder.

"What about you, Sergei?" asked Gyorgi. His eyes took in Valeria's voluptuous curves, and then met the Russian's gaze. "You have a lovely companion. You would make a powerful vampire." He looked at Valeria again. "Such a beautiful creature needs a powerful vampire at her side."

The redhead stepped forward, and draped herself over Sergei. Her eyes blazed.

The Bear smiled. "We are talking about it."

"And have you decided what you will do?"

"Niet. I think some more about it."

Gyorgi smiled. He leaned closer. "Don't take too long," he said. He stared at Valeria suggestively. Sergei braced himself. The room went deadly quiet. Seconds passed by as slowly as an age as they faced each other.

"Such a touching reunion," Karl said, breaking the silence. He bowed to them, saying: "We will leave you now. Come, Gyorgi, Null." He gestured imperiously.

The Georgian took one last look at the redhead, and then turned and walked over to Karl. Null winked at Erik, and followed. They all crossed the floor, and went out onto the balcony. In moments, they had gone.

"Fuck." Erik said, releasing a pent up breath. "Just once, I'd like to have a quiet night." He wiped sweat from his brow.

"I do not think that will ever happen," Gerald said. "At least Karl did not go into a rage. He is very dangerous. As for Irina…"

"Yeah," the drummer said dryly, "we all know how much of an uncontrollable bitch she is." He shook his head. "How did you guys ever live so long, with characters like that around? I would've thought you'd have killed each other off hundreds of years ago."

"You have the wrong impression of us, mortal," Valeria said. "True, there are those amongst us who must be dealt with carefully. But after the passage of so much time, and the simple fact that we must tolerate each other, because of what we are, we do exist together."

"Though not always in harmony," Gerald said frankly. "Karl has destroyed many who dared to stand against him. And Irina is more unpredictable than he is." He thought for a moment, and then continued: "The Clans came about because as solitary hunters, we did not have the support of any other vampire, and were easy to surprise when we lay in our coffins. Many of us were killed by mortals this way." He gestured at the lounges, and they all sat down. "It was Octavius and Karl who began the task of creating the Clans. The Roman had the knowledge and experience of a senator of the Imperial Senate, and had seen the benefit of such an organisation. It was he who sent messages to us, and brought us together. A great meeting was held, and he put forward the idea that we could form the Clans, and divide the world up into areas that they would rule; the idea being that the most powerful vampire in that area would be that Clan's leader." He glanced at Romana. "There were those who were opposed to such an idea; they wanted to remain as they were; free to do as they pleased, without bowing to another's orders."

"My father was one such," Romana said.

The blonde dandy nodded. "Yes, he was against Octavius's proposal. He said that we should make ourselves companions, and in such a way, we could have the protection that their presence provided. He said we did not need groups like the Clans." He turned to Erik. "You may have noticed also, that we crave a companion. It is a lonely existence, being a vampire. We do not change, and the world does. Many destroy themselves, worn out by the centuries of sameness."

"What happened to Romana's father?" the drummer asked.

Gerald smiled thinly. "Nothing. There were many there who agreed with him. Karl was furious, but Octavius prevented him from beginning a conflict that would have turned vampire against vampire. It was decided that those who wished to exist as Romana's father had suggested, could do so. Others wanted to form the Clans, and nominated leaders for the different areas that the world was divided into. Both sides thought that their way was right. Each group was allowed to go their own way."

"But not for long," Valeria said.

Gerald nodded. "No. Karl stirred up those who wished to form the Clans. There was war, a war among the immortals. The mortal world had no idea that it was happening. Thousands of us, who had been in existence for centuries, were destroyed. After several centuries of this destructive conflict, Octavius arranged a truce. We gathered again, to discuss what should be done. There was angry debate. There were those who still wished to be left alone, to be free of the Clans. Octavius tried to make them see that his way was the right one. They argued for days. It seemed that they would depart, without anything being changed. But Karl betrayed the truce, and he and his followers fell upon them, and they were annihilated. Apart from Octavius, he was the most powerful among us, and after that, none dared defy him."

"How could Romana's father have survived?" Erik asked.

"There were some who surrendered. Romana's father was one of them. They were a pitifully small number. Karl forced them to pledge allegiance to the Clans. They were split up, and accepted into different Clans, and were watched carefully."

"No wonder he hated Karl," the drummer said.

"There was more to it than that," Romana added. She smiled at Erik as he yawned cavernously. "But that can wait for another time. You are tired. Go to bed."

Erik yawned again. "Ok," he mumbled sleepily, and wandered towards the bedroom.

"Sergei, are you staying?" Romana asked.

"Da. I sleep on couch."

The vampires all exchanged a glance. Valeria kissed the Russian. Gerald addressed Duvall: "Professor, will you join us?"

"Please, call me Phillipe. I will join you."

They made their way to the balcony. Romana turned. "Tell Erik I will see him later."

The Bear nodded. "Ok. I see you too," he said to the redhead.

They were gone. Sergei shrugged, lay down on the couch, and in moments was fast asleep.

19

Christian

The Duvall Biological Research Facility in Paris was immense. It took up several blocks. Passing tourists snapped away with their cameras, marvelling at the unique structural design of the main building. Several arches overflew each other, intertwining in a maze of marble. Obviously influenced by the Spanish artist Dore, it was a triumph of modern architecture. A large statue of Philippe Duvall stood before it. It showed the scientist with one hand on his heart, and the other hand was stretched out, as though he were attempting to grasp the secrets of the universe. On the fifth floor, a lone figure stared out at the passing throng and shook his head.

Christian turned away from the window, and paced back to the large desk that faced the room. He sat down in the large leather high backed chair, and glanced at the monitor on the desktop. He frowned, and sat back, steepling his fingers in front of himself. Christian looked up, and gave his attention to the other figure in the room.

"So, what you are saying, Harrow, is that this 'defect' cannot be purged from our soldier's blood?"

The scientist nodded gravely. "I am sorry, sir. Professor Duvall – " he stopped as Christian bristled at the name. "Er – we tried to solve the dilemma before, sir, but it is somehow written into the DNA of the blood; in the very smallest subatomic particle, in fact."

"I see," Christian said. His lips turned down.

Harrow licked his own lips. "Er – the research team is still investigating *every* avenue, sir. We hope that we may still find a way to negate the – er – defect."

"You *hope*?" the other echoed. He sat forward, and he tapped his right forefinger on the desktop, emphasising his words. "If we don't find a way to solve this problem, Harrow, the army of Immortals will be useless." He sat back, and shook his head. "You and I know how dangerous they are when they are out of our control. We *must* find a solution to this problem."

"What if there *is* no solution, sir?" Harrow opined. "There may be no way to – "

"That's enough," Christian said harshly. He glared at the little man. "Get out," he said coldly, and turned to the monitor, ignoring Harrow.

The scientist gave a perfunctory nod, and stalked to the door. He opened it, and left the room. The door slowly closed behind him.

Why am I surrounded by such fools? Christian fumed. He stood up, and strode over to the window. He stared at the statue. *Is this the way that you felt about Harrow and his crew of incompetents?* A wry smile came to his lips. He laughed once. "Well, you don't have to worry about *anything* now, do you?" He sobered. "No, you have no worries at all now, do you, my former master? Where did you go when you were vaporised in the destruction of the island? Not to heaven, I'll wager; a scientist like you doesn't believe in it. What *did* you believe in? Even Einstein said he wanted to know the mind of God."

The phone on the desk chimed. Christian crossed the floor, and pressed the button.

"What is it?"

His secretary's voice answered: *"Excuse me, sir. Mister Ashton is here to see you."*

"Excellent. Send him in, Miss Lee."

"Yes, sir."

As Christian sat down in his seat, the door opened, and a man strode in. He walked like a panther; silently, his feet softly touching the floor briefly, as he padded up to Christian's desk. He looked as though he were ready to spring into action; coiled like a spring before its release. He wore a dark grey silk suit, and was tall and spare, with light blue eyes that were the colour of the sky outside of the window. White hair that was cropped short in a crew-cut crowned his head. He stopped in front of the desk, and smiled.

"You summoned me, sir?" His voice was soft and high, almost like a woman's.

Christian returned his smile. "Yes, Daniel. I have a job for you."

The other's smile became wolfish.

Christian held up his hand. "Not an assassination."

Daniels' smile fell.

Christian laughed. "I'm sorry. All I want you to do is bring someone to me."

Daniel almost pouted. "I'm not an errand boy, sir. Send Phillips."

Christian shook his head. "This job requires your special skills, Daniel." He leaned back in the chair. "You might even find it a real challenge," he said suggestively.

Daniel raised one snow-white eyebrow. "Oh, yes? And why would that be?"

Christian's face became enigmatic. He gazed at the other man.

Daniel frowned. Then he snapped his fingers. "The vampire! You want me to bring her to you!" He practically bounced on the spot.

Christian nodded at his eagerness. "Yes. Of all of my employees, I trust you the most. That idiot Harrow and his team are going around in circles; the defect that was discovered before still has no solution, and I believe that the answer will only be found in her blood." He sat forward, and placed his hands on the desk. He fixed Daniel with a penetrating stare. "We *must* have her, Daniel. At any cost."

Daniel's smile returned. "And if there is anyone with her?"

Christian thought for a moment. "I'll leave that up to your discretion. Kill them if you want, but don't leave any evidence that can point back to us." He got out of the seat, and walked back over to the window, and gazed out.

"When should I leave, sir?" Daniel asked.

Without turning, Christian answered: "Now. There is a car waiting for you. It will take you to your apartment, where you can get your equipment, and then it will take you to the airport, where one of my jets is waiting. Miss Lee will give you all the information that you need."

Daniel nodded. "Very good, sir." He turned, and walked up to the door, opened it, and left as soundlessly as he had come.

"Now," Christian mused, "I will have you, my dear. Your blood will give me the ultimate army." He looked down upon the mass of humanity that passed below him. He smiled to himself. "Poor fools. They have no idea…" He turned away from the window, and walked over to a bar that was ranged against one wall. He picked up a glass, and placed it on the bar, opened the glass cabinet in front of him, and took out a bottle of Johnnie Walker. He opened the bottle, and poured himself a drink. He raised it to his lips and drank deeply. He closed his eyes in satisfaction as the fiery liquor burned its way down his throat. When he'd finished it, he poured himself another, and walked back to the window. Once again, his gaze went to the statue of Duvall. He raised his glass in a toast. "Here's to you, Phillipe. Without your tireless years of research, I wouldn't be about to create the most perfect and powerful army the world has ever seen. It's a pity that you didn't live to see it. Immortals; under my control, armed with the most deadliest weapons that have ever been devised." He drank. "Not bad for an uneducated boy from Liverpool, eh?"

His mind went back; back thirty years. Back to when he was fifteen years old. He'd gone to France with friends; they had travelled all around the country, going from place to place. All of them were living from day to day, none of them had much money, and survived as best as they could. They had told him it would be a great adventure. But on the days when his hunger became a painful hollow in his stomach, he wished he'd never come. Which were most days. This went on for a few weeks; the group straggled from town to town, tired and hungry. Their money had run out, and they had descended to the level of vagabonds.

One night, as they huddled on dilapidated chairs around a small fire in a derelict building, Toby, the leader of the group, had proposed a plan. Christian could remember the words as though he'd heard them only yesterday.

"Listen," Toby had said, "we can't go on like this. I've got an idea."

They all stared at him expectantly.

"Let's roll someone." He grinned.

This suggestion was met with disapproval. "No way, man," said Jean, the youngest of the group. Some of the others agreed.

Andy stood up. He was as old as Toby, and pushy. "Yeah. Let's do it. Who cares about the Frogs, anyway? We gotta eat. That means money."

"We can't do it," Christian said. "We'd be caught and arrested."

"Fuck you, pretty boy," Toby said. "You're too chicken to do anything."

Andy laughed. "Yeah, Chrissy is a coward."

Christian glared at him. "I'm not a coward. I'm just talking sense."

"That's right," Jean said, "we'd be caught. Christian's right."

He gave her a look of appreciation. He'd always liked Jean, but was too unsure of himself to do anything about it. She smiled at him.

Carla and Warren were the other two members of the group. They looked undecided. Christian appealed to them.

"What do you think?"

Warren was a weedy little boy, who wore thick glasses. He licked his lips. "I dunno. We haveta get food somehow." He gazed at the others indecisively.

"Carla?"

Carla was a tall, willowy blonde with huge breasts and incredible blue eyes. Both Toby and Andy vied for her attention. Christian knew what her opinion would be, even before she spoke. Her eyes shone with excitement.

"Let's do it," she breathed. Her teeth flashed in a wide grin.

Christian shook his head in exasperation.

"Stay here if you're scared, pretty boy," Toby sneered. He waved the others on as he walked to the doorway.

Christian stepped up and grabbed his arm.

Toby rounded on him, and punched him in the chest. Christian slammed into the wall, and slid to the ground. "Outta my way, coward." He stepped through the door. After a moment's hesitation, the rest followed him. Andy laughed as he passed Christian.

Only Jean had remained behind. She came over to Christian, and helped him rise. The girl wiped blood from his split lip with her handkerchief. She helped him over to one of the chairs and lowered him into it. He doubled over with a fit of coughing.

He looked up, and she stepped back in fright as she met his burning gaze.

"*Dickheads!*" he hissed. He clenched his fist in impotent anger. He rose to his feet, trembling with fury. He was ashamed to have been humiliated in front of Jean.

The girl reached out to him tentatively. She'd seen his filthy temper before. She really liked him, but it was the one thing that stopped her from taking their friendship to another level.

"Christian, calm down." She took one of his hands.

He gave an inarticulate cry, and pulled away from her. He turned and picked up the chair. He whirled it in the air, and smashed it against the wall. He kicked another chair across the room.

Jean backed away as his rage exploded.

The boy stormed out of the room, and went in pursuit of the others. Jean raced after him, knowing that in his angered state, he was likely to do something stupid. She caught up with him as he spotted the group as they were going down one of the town's dark alleyways. Jean reached out and grabbed his collar.

"*Christian!*" she hissed, not wanting the others to hear.

He whirled around, and took her by the shoulders. He shook her like a rag doll. His face was a grimace of hate. "No, Jean!" he husked. "I've had enough of Toby and Andy. I – " He gaped at her, and dropped his arms. His anger vanished as he realised what he had done. He lowered his gaze in shame. In a moment, his shoulders shook as he began to cry.

Jean stared at him, still shaking from his rough treatment. She gazed at him in pity, and went and slowly put her arms around him.

"Shhhh, It's all right." She patted his back gently.

He sobbed as she held him; ashamed and embarrassed at his anger, but relishing her touch.

"What are they doing?" Jean said.

Christian raised his head. "What?"

The girl stepped away from him and pointed. "Look."

The boy turned, and saw the others hiding behind an ancient stone wall. Coming down the road was a solitary figure, unaware of their presence. Toby and Andy were readying themselves to leap out on the newcomer. Warren and Carla stood back watching. Even from where they stood, Christian and Jean could see that Warren was holding back. He stood hiding behind the blonde, who was obviously itching to see her two rivals do their thing. The shadowy figure came closer, and the two toughs inched towards the edge of the wall. The night was dark, and they were well hidden.

Christian made to go down and warn the stranger, but Jean pulled him back, into the shadow of a tree.

"Jean! I've got to warn him!" he whispered hoarsely.

"It's too late," she said. "Look!"

Christian looked down the road. Toby and Andy had leapt out from behind the wall, and were confronting the man. From this distance, he couldn't hear what they were saying, but obviously they were demanding money. The man laughed.

The two boys looked at each other. Toby pulled out his knife, and brandished it. Andy showed the stranger the length of pipe he was holding. He swung it into his other hand with a meaty thwack. They meant business.

Then the moon came out, and shone down clearly. The road was lit up, and Toby and Andy stepped back as the light exposed their victim. Andy dropped his pipe. The man opened his mouth, and showed them his fangs. *Fangs?* Christian thought. *What the fuck?* At his side, Jean gasped.

In a move too fast for them to see, the man leapt at Toby, slapping his knife away with a blow of his hand, and those fangs were buried in the boy's neck. Andy stood there petrified as his friend was drained of blood. The vampire dropped Toby's corpse to the road, and his blood-filled eyes regarded the trembling youth. Andy wet his pants. It was the last thing he did on earth. The vampire punched him in the chest. As the others watched in horror, he withdrew his bloody hand, and Andy's heart was gripped in his fist. Andy fell.

A shrill scream pierced the night. The creature's head whipped around, and his terrible eyes bored into Carla and Warren. They were backing away from the awful scene before them, arms around each other like little children. He dropped Andy's heart, and bared his fangs at them. Carla screamed again, and the vampire leapt towards them. With a sweep of his hand, he struck them both to the ground. He took Warren by the neck, and held him up kicking in the air in front of him. Warren tried to scream, but could only make small gulping sounds. With a contemptuous flick of his wrist, the vampire broke the boy's neck. The terrified girl screamed a third time. The vampire dragged her to her feet, and sank his teeth into her pulsing throat.

"Fuck!" Christian ejaculated.

The vampire whirled, and dropped Carla's body. Its blood-filled eyes regarded Christian and Jean where they stood trembling. In a flash of speed, it was before them. Jean shrieked, and fell to the ground. She wrapped her arms around the boy's legs, and held on for dear life. Christian stared at the thing, his heart crashing in his chest.

The vampire looked like a young man. He was unnaturally handsome, reminding Christian of pictures he'd seen of angels. His skin was pale and taut, and his hair was long and brown. He was tall and slim, and Christian could see that his hands that had dealt death were long and slender like those of an artist. His predatory eyes narrowed as he looked at the two before him. He studied them for a moment; the only sound was their terrified breathing. Christian was too scared to move or speak. The girl shuddered at his feet; her horror had overcome her. She stared at the vampire, her eyes wide with terror. Her fingernails dug into Christian's flesh through the material of his jeans.

Finishing his scrutiny, the vampire smiled. "So," he said, his voice mellow and cultured, "you did not want to join your friends, and try to – *roll* – me?" He said the word as though he were tasting an unfamiliar thing.

Finding his voice at last, Christian gasped: "N-no."

The vampire smiled again. The boy shivered. "Good. You can see how they fared. I warrant they were very surprised."

"I-I guess they were." Christian stared into those crimson orbs.

"You do not want to join them in death?" the creature asked.

Christian shook his head.

The vampire smiled. He looked down at Jean, studied her for a moment, and then looked back at the boy.

"She does like you. But your temper, she does not like that."

Christian licked his lips.

The creature looked deep into his eyes. "Yes," he said finally, "I can see the rage within you." A look of desire came to his white face. "Show me your rage."

The boy gaped at him. "What?"

"Your anger. Show it to me."

Christian stared.

The vampire reached down, and before Christian knew it, he had torn Jean away from him, and hurled her down the road towards the bodies that lay there. She fell among them, rolled along the road, and lay still. The vampire stood before him, a smirk on his face.

"*Bastard!*" Christian cried. He balled his fists, but made no other move.

The vampire sneered. "*This* is your anger? Your *fury*? Ha! You are as weak as your friends." He turned his back on the boy, who trembled now not from fear, but from anger at what the monster had done to Jean. The vampire walked towards the girl, and glanced back over his shoulder. "Perhaps I should *enjoy* her," he snickered, and turned away. In a flash, he was standing over Jean's prone figure. He reached down, and lifted her like she was a rag doll. The vampire brought her neck close to his fangs, and then he turned and fixed Christian with his blood-red eyes. He smiled wickedly, and made to sink his fangs into Jean's neck. All the while, he stared at the boy, challenging him.

Something in Christian snapped. He screamed in rage, and rushed towards the creature. He saw the pipe Andy had dropped, and scooped it up. He raised it high, and plunged headlong at the vampire, who stood waiting, a smile on his face. He'd dropped Jean as soon as he'd seen the boy's attack. Christian struck at him, but he wasn't there. The boy stumbled. A mocking laugh came from behind him.

"That's better!" The creature bared his fangs. "Here I am!"

The boy raced towards him, his weapon raised. He swung with all of his might, and fell to the ground, for the vampire had moved again with lightning swiftness.

More laughter grated in Christian's ears. As he got to his feet, he glared at the vampire with loathing, and then launched himself at him. The boy swung, and his momentum spun him around, and he crashed to the road amidst the bodies.

Howls of delight exploded in the night air. The vampire roared with glee.

Christian staggered to his feet. He was covered in his friend's blood. He lowered the pipe.

"What's this?" the vampire said. "Are you giving up, boy?"

"What's the point?" Christian panted. "You're too fast." He dropped the pipe. "Go ahead and kill me."

"No," his tormentor said. "I am enjoying myself." He pointed at the pipe. "Pick it up."

The boy stared at him defiantly. "Fuck you."

The creature's eyes slitted in anger. "Pick it up," he repeated, his voice menacing.

Christian folded his arms.

The vampire sneered. "Very well. Now you will die."

Suddenly, the night became brighter than the day. The vampire snarled, and covered his eyes. The two of them were bathed in white light that blinded them both. Christian dropped to the ground, and groped about for the pipe. His seeking hands closed over it, and he came to his feet. As the vampire cowered under the assault of the light, the boy rushed towards him. As he raised his weapon to strike, the vampire sensed him. He turned towards the boy, baring his fangs. Too late. With a mighty swing, Christian struck at him, delivering a blow that would have killed a mortal man. But the vampire merely turned his head with the blow. He turned back to face the boy, and with horror, Christian saw a deep gash that the pipe had made in his enemy's skull close up before his unbelieving gaze.

There was a soft sound, and a dart appeared in the vampire's neck. He pulled it out, looked at it curiously, and tossed it to the ground. Two sounds like the first echoed in the night. Two more darts sank into the pale flesh. The vampire staggered, swayed, and then fell to the road. Christian stared in amazement at the prone form.

"Are you all right?"

The boy started in shock at the sound of the voice. He turned, shading his eyes against the glare. He could dimly make out the shape of a man standing there.

"That's enough, Claude. Shut off the lights, and arrange transport for our quarry."

"Yes, sir."

The light immediately dimmed. Christian blinked furiously; the red image of the afterglow swam in his vision. He sensed rather than saw someone in front of him. He raised the pipe threateningly.

"It's all right. I won't hurt you. You don't need that." The voice was soothing and cultured.

Christian lowered his weapon. Two men went past him, and he turned to see what they were doing. They were wearing white coveralls, and one of them was carrying some kind of pack. They stopped at the unconscious vampire, and knelt down. Then the man with the pack opened it, and he took something out. His companion assisted him. Looking closer, the boy could see that they were strapping the creature into some sort of harness.

"You are a brave lad."

Christian turned. The man stood before him. He was wearing the same coveralls. He smiled at the boy, and pointed at the pipe in his hands. "I've never seen anyone take on a vampire with a pipe before."

Christian looked at his weapon. "It didn't do much good against him," he said ruefully. He dropped it on the road.

"No matter. It was a very brave thing to do."

"Brave?" Christian snorted. "It was dumb. I got angry, and…" His voice faded. A look of horror came to his face. *"That thing was going to kill me,"* he whispered hoarsely. He trembled with shock.

"I'm afraid so. Just like your friends."

"Jean!" Christian cried. He spun around, and rushed to the girl's side. He fell to his knees, and lifted her. Her head fell back at an unnatural angle, and the boy dropped her, and gaped open mouthed. Her neck was broken. Hot tears welled up in his eyes, as he stared at her, and then he gazed at the bodies that lay in the road. That thing had slaughtered all of his friends! It was impossible! Vampires didn't exist; they were only dark creatures that moved stealthily through books and movies, weren't they? Christian felt a hand on his shoulder, and looked up.

The man was there, comforting him. His face was sad. "I'm so sorry. It's an awful thing to lose the ones you love." A look of concern appeared on his kindly face. "Are you all right?"

Christian's vision was blurring. His rescuer's face grew dim. The boy swayed, and collapsed. He was dimly aware of the man picking him up, and carrying him into a field, where several helicopters stood waiting. He was put on board one of them, and then the man and the others boarded. The engines were started up, and as Christian fell into unconsciousness, they flew off into the night.

Christian finished his drink. He stared at the statue. "That's how it all began, wasn't it, professor? You saved me, and took me under your wing. Education; the finest clothes, and a position of power in your organisation all followed." He smiled. "Now it's *my* organisation." He turned and went back to the bar, and refilled his glass. Then he walked back to his desk, and sat down. He savoured his whisky as his mind worked. Finally, he finished his drink, and placed the glass on the desktop. He nodded to himself, reached for the phone, and pressed the button for his secretary.

"*Yes, sir?*"

"Get me Karl, Miss Lee."

"*Yes, sir.*"

He leaned back in his plush chair. He knew the vampires were unpredictable, but he had decided to take a chance, and accept the Clan leader's offer. Unbeknownst to Romana and her little group, he'd made a deal with Karl, one that should prove to be very lucrative. He could dispose of the other vampires later, after he had her blood, and that fool Harrow had solved their little problem. He smiled with satisfaction.

20

Karl and Octavius

Karl walked into his private study. Here was his inner sanctum; a place where he could relax, and not be concerned with the affairs of the Clans. *The Clans,* he thought, *whose foolish idea was it to create them? Ah yes, Octavius.* He shook his head. He'd much rather preferred being a hunter, alone with Octavius his mentor. Those had been much better days, filled with the excitement of the hunt and the kill; hot spurting blood that made his immortal body sing. Octavius had created him, and had shown him the ways of the vampire. Then the Roman had come up with the idea of the Clans. Karl had argued with him, but it was pointless, Octavius was determined to unite all of the vampires on earth. It was the reality of the decline and fall of the Roman Empire that they witnessed that gave Octavius the idea. He'd seen how powerful the Romans had been. And yet, they still fell. He told the German that the vampires would follow, joining the Romans in destruction. Every mortal's hand was turned against them; they were the enemy of mankind, and had to unite and stand as one, or fall alone.

Stupidity, Karl thought. *We should have remained as we were, and not concerned ourselves with others.* He crossed the richly carpeted floor, and sat down at the huge desk that stood against the far wall. He gazed at the bookshelves that filled every wall, packed with ancient tomes; books that any mortal scholar would have died to possess. He'd read them all; the texts of dark magic, the histories of empires that were now forgotten and buried beneath the dust of centuries. Everything that the mortals did was doomed to fall, to die and vanish. Their history was filled with such destruction and conflict; he was amazed that they still existed. *They should have died out centuries ago,* he mused.

And yet ... and yet, somehow, they continued to exist, to thrive and fill the planet with their useless selves. The only way that they were useful was to provide the blood that the vampires needed. They were but cattle for the immortals.

He smiled. If he had his way, the great majority of them would be destroyed, and only a relative handful would be allowed to remain alive. They would become slaves, to be fed upon, while the immortals would rule the earth. *Perhaps we could arrange hunts,* he thought, *to keep our predatory instincts alive.* He smiled to himself, showing his fangs.

The door opened. He gazed at the figure in the doorway.

"What is it?" he asked tonelessly, irritated at the interruption of his musing.

Octavius entered the room, and closed the door behind him. He was the only one that Karl would tolerate in his sanctum. Still, the German didn't like this invasion of his privacy. He regarded the Roman sourly.

"Karl." Octavius stared at him for a moment, and then he smiled. "Still dreaming of an empire of immortals?"

"And if I am?"

Octavius crossed the room, and sat in a chair that was in front of the desk. He shook his head. "You know it is foolish. All empires fall. We have seen it ourselves. The Roman Empire –"

" – was made up of mortals. Flawed, weak. We are not like them."

"We are more like them than you realise."

"No." the German leaned back in his chair. "We are destined to rule this world. The mortals are only there to serve us. Once I have Romana's blood, we will use it to make ourselves the most powerful vampires on earth. No other immortal will dare stand against us, and the mortals will be culled to a manageable number. We will take their world, and make it our own."

Octavius regarded him silently. Then, he spoke, his voice low. "Do you not remember the treachery of Duvall? How can you believe that his successor will not treat us the same way? They are not to be trusted."

"I *don't* trust them," Karl said. "But we need their weapons. This is a technological age, Octavius, and their science is dangerous to us. Better if we take it for ourselves, than allow them to use it against us."

The Roman sighed. "What use do we have of such toys? We *are* weapons. We are the hunters, and they are the prey." He thought for a moment, and then went on: "For centuries, it has been so; they have never been able to destroy us. But it is only through our united strength that we can stand and defy them. If it were not for the Clans, if we were only solitary hunters, they would seek us out and annihilate us. It is through the strength of the Clans that we continue to exist."

"Bah! The Clans have outworn their usefulness." Karl leaned forward. "Think, Octavius. If you and I are the only ones to share Romana's blood, we will be the ones who can dictate to those fools how things will be. We will no longer have to listen to their petty bickering. You and I will be the strongest, and none will defy us."

The Roman shook his head. "No, Karl. You are wrong. If we do not share her blood with them, they will join together and destroy us. United—"

The German slammed his huge fists on to the desktop and leapt to his feet. His eyes filled with blood. Octavius could feel the anger radiating from his massive body. Karl fixed him with a freezing gaze.

"Do you defy my decision, Octavius?" His voice was low and menacing.

Octavius regarded him warily. He knew that in this state, Karl was dangerous. The German's rage could explode at any moment, and even though Octavius was the older vampire, he knew that Karl's strength was equal to his own.

"No," he said cautiously. "I only want you to consider the alternatives."

"There *are* no alternatives," Karl said. He sat down. "We will take Romana's blood, and we will take the mortal's weapons. I won't change my mind."

"You are obsessed with these mortal weapons. Why is that? We are powerful without them. Why must you have them?"

Karl sat back in the chair, and relaxed. He gave his maker a grin. Octavius smiled to himself. He was used the German's rapid mood swings, but every now and then, even after all the centuries that they had spent together, he could still be surprised and amused.

"Let's not argue about such things, Octavius. I just want to make sure that we have the same advantage that this mortal Christian has; I haven't forgotten Duvall's betrayal. On the contrary, I remember every last moment of it. I remember how, when we had obtained the weapons, and were returning here, that many of us were incinerated by the containers that he had sabotaged. He had wanted to destroy us even then. The only use he had for us was to make himself immortal." He smiled. "But now we know that he was himself destroyed by his own bomb. Ironic, isn't it?"

"Yes," the Roman agreed.

A phone began to ring. Karl reached into his jacket pocket, and took out his mobile. He flipped it open and placed it to his ear. "Yes?" He listened for a moment, as Octavius watched and wondered who the caller was. Karl glanced at him, and saw his interest. He smiled, and punched the button for the speaker. Then he laid the phone on the table.

"Are you there?" came a voice. *"Karl?"*

Christian! Thought Octavius. He stared at Karl perplexedly.

The German held up his hand for silence. "I'm here. What do you want? Have you considered my terms?"

Terms? What was this about? Wondered Octavius.

"I have. I agree to them."

"Good. Then we'll meet at the suggested place?"

There was a moment's silence. The two vampires waited for Christian's reply.

"Are you sure that you've made the Clan leaders understand my proposal? Do they agree?"

Karl met Octavius's puzzled gaze. "They agree. All is arranged."

The Roman looked at him, wondering what he had done. What was this proposal that Christian had suggested? He knew that Karl hadn't told any of the Clan leaders anything about it. He hadn't even known that Karl had been in contact with the mortal.

"Very well. We'll meet as we discussed. Midnight?"

"Yes."

"Good. I'm looking forward to meeting you."

"And I you. Until later, then." Karl closed the phone, and put it back in his pocket. He met the Roman's inquiring gaze.

"What is all this about?" Octavius regarded Karl suspiciously. *What had he done?* He wondered.

The German leaned back in his chair. "It's all right. I have the situation under control."

"I see," Octavius replied doubtfully. "Tell me."

"This mortal who has taken over Duvall's work wants to form an alliance with us. He will give us the weapons we want, and in exchange, we are to supply him with an army; an army of immortals."

Octavius stared, incredulous. "And you have agreed to do this? After everything that has happened?"

Karl nodded. "Yes," he said flatly.

The Roman sat forward. "This is dangerous, Karl. These mortals are not to be trusted."

Karl brushed the Roman's words away with an angry sweep of his hand. "This mortal is not Duvall. He *needs* us."

"To be his own personal army? The Clan leaders will not agree."

"I haven't told them. It's my own decision."

Octavius frowned. "You cannot do that. All proposals must be put to the Clan leaders, and only when they have agreed, can such proposals be accepted."

Karl's mouth turned downwards. "They are fools. Fools who are stuck in the old ways of centuries passed away. Think, Octavius. Think of the fact that the world changes, and we do not. We go on, century after century, unchanged, immortal. But we don't realise that we need to have a connection to the times that we find ourselves in. These weapons can obliterate us. Never before in the long history of our people has a mortal weapon been such a threat. We must have them for our own safety. We must join with this mortal, give him his army, and save ourselves."

The Roman sighed. "No, Karl."

"No?" Karl echoed. "Are you questioning my decision, Octavius?" His eyes filled with blood.

The Roman regarded Karl with trepidation. Now was when he was the most dangerous. His unpredictable mood swings made dealing with him difficult, and Octavius had seen many who had defied Karl fall victim to his blinding rage.

"Think, Karl," he said imploringly. "This mortal demands something from us that we must not give. If he has this army, he will become our most dangerous enemy."

Karl shook his head. "No. He will have to rely on us. Only our people can be of use to him in this situation." He fell silent, and the blood receded from his eyes.

Octavius looked deeply into those eyes. "What is it that you are not telling me? Is there something else to this that I should know about?"

Karl rose to his feet. "No. I've told you everything. Now I will inform the Clan leaders of the deal that I've made."

Octavius stood. He fixed the other with a piercing gaze. "I think there is something else. Something that you do not want to tell me."

Karl came around the desk, and they faced each other.

"There is nothing," Karl said tonelessly.

The Roman searched Karl's face. He sent his thoughts probing into the German's mind. His thoughts were blocked. Karl was not allowing him to read his mind.

"I know you better than that, Karl. I made you, and I know how you think." He watched the German closely, waiting for the explosion to come.

Karl's eyes blazed. His face became grim.

"Get out of the way," he said gruffly.

The Roman merely folded his arms, standing his ground.

'Not until you tell me what you are hiding."

The blood returned to Karl's eyes.

"I know there is something else," Octavius said.

The German stared at his maker. A minute went by. The two of them remained as motionless as statues.

"Very well," Karl finally said. "This mortal requires something else from us."

"Yes? And what would that be?"

Karl hesitated.

"Tell me."

"He needs – *test* – subjects to continue working on our blood."

The Roman stared at him aghast. "You would give him more of our people? You would sacrifice them to his science?" His voice was disbelieving. "You would not –"

A wordless exclamation of fury erupted from Karl. "It's the only way he'll agree to let us have the weapons." He bristled with anger.

"The Clan leaders will not allow – "

"*Enough!*" Karl bellowed. "I have decided to accept this proposal. Now get out of my way." He strode forward, intent on brushing Octavius aside.

But the Roman stood his ground. Karl grabbed him, and they grappled together, two of the oldest and most powerful vampires on earth. Each had the strength of twenty mortals, and even though Octavius was the eldest, the German's brute strength matched his own. Karl's fangs gaped from his mouth, as he tried to tear Octavius's throat out. The Roman held him at bay. They smashed into the heavy wooden desk, and it disintegrated into flying splinters. One of the chairs was sent tumbling across the floor, to crash against the wall. They staggered about the chamber, each of them struggling to gain the upper hand.

Octavius was only trying to overpower his protégée, but Karl was in deadly earnest. The Roman realised with a shock that Karl was trying to destroy him. Suddenly, the German broke away from their savage embrace, shoved Octavius across the room, and began to summon the power of fire. Octavius felt the gathering of force, and picked up the other chair, and hurled it at his opponent. Karl raised his hands, and threw the chair aside, and it smashed apart on the floor. Not giving him a chance to summon again, Octavius rushed at Karl, and they slammed into the wall heavily. Cracks spread out from the point of impact, and dust from centuries ago fell from the ceiling.

Octavius knew that he had to overpower Karl, or be destroyed. They exploded away from the wall, each of them with their hands closed about the other's neck. They stumbled about the floor, kicking the wreckage in all directions. Both of their eyes were filled with blood. On the Roman's face was frozen a look of grim determination. But Karl's visage was that of a demon bent on destruction. His animal-like brutishness emanated from every atom of his undead body. He roared in frustration as Octavius held off his assault. Any other vampire would have fallen to his attack, but the Roman had taught him, and knew all of his methods, and anticipated everything that Karl did.

Again Karl broke away, and they regarded each other with baleful glares. Octavius watched his creation closely, knowing that Karl had only broken off his attack to try something different and unexpected. The German searched his mind for a way to take Octavius down. But, search as he might, he could find no way that he could overpower his maker. He knew that Octavius could match any attack that he made upon him. They were locked in a stalemate from which there was no escaping. Escaping! That was it! Suddenly, he knew he must escape from the Roman. Karl hid his thoughts from his opponent, lest Octavius realise what he was going to do, and try to stop him. He must reach Irina, and together they could gather others to them who were in agreement with his desire for Christian's weapons. He kept his eyes on the Roman, watching to see if Octavius would attack. Like statues they stood, each ready to explode into savage action.

The door opened.

Karl whirled and rushed towards it. A figure stood in the doorway, about to enter the room. The German grabbed it by the shoulders, and threw it at Octavius. The Roman was hurtling across the room, attempting to grab Karl. The other vampire collided with Octavius, and both of them smashed into the wall. Karl raced out into the corridor, and sped away.

The pair got to their feet.

"What is this?" Mariko shrilled. She grabbed Octavius by the arm.

He turned on her, his eyes blazing. "No time!" he gasped. "We must stop Karl!"

He made to pursue the German, but Mariko held him fast. He rounded on her, exasperated.

"What is happening?" the Japanese demanded.

"Karl has made a deal with the mortal that has the weapons." He stopped, knowing that his words were too slow, and sent his thoughts towards her. Her oriental eyes closed, as she saw the events of before pass before her. She heard everything that had been said, from the beginning.

The words that had been exchanged during the phone call made her eyes flash open, and the vision of the ensuing struggle brought her fangs into view. She snarled.

"He would not *dare!*"

"He *would.* Quickly, we must stop him!"

The two vampires rushed to the door. They looked down the corridor, in both directions. Without a word, Octavius went to the left, and Mariko sped down to the right. He sent his thoughts out to Kunda-Bele.

The African's face appeared in his mind. *Octavius? What is the matter?*

Swifty, the Roman shared the same thoughts that he had shared with Mariko. *Stop him! Don't allow him to leave!*

Kunda-Bele nodded. *At once. We will find him and chain him.*

Be careful. He is enraged. Tell everyone to meet in the council hall.

Very good. The contact was severed, as Kunda-Bele alerted the others. Their thoughts blazed in Octavius's mind as the hunt began.

As he hurtled down the ancient passageway, Octavius's mind reeled. *Karl,* he thought, *what have you **done?*** His mouth was a severe line. He knew, with complete certainty, that Karl was now the most dangerous enemy that the Clans had ever faced. Now he would be an outcast, and the Clan leaders would insist on hunting him down and destroying him. Octavius also knew that there were many vampires that agreed with him. This could lead to a split in the community. If Karl could draw to him all of the vampires that were unhappy with the Clan's leadership, it could even ignite a war!

That must not be! He thought furiously. *There has not been such a thing for centuries! We must stop him.* The sudden realisation of what he had to do exploded in his mind. *I must stop him.* He reached the door to the council chamber, and pushed it open as he strode inside. Hundreds of vampires were within. But there was no sign of Karl. He turned as another arrived. It was Mariko.

"No sign of him?" she asked.

He shook his head.

"He escaped," Kunda-Bele said, coming up to them. "By the time we had raised the alarm, he had gone."

"Gone to raise an army," Octavius said grimly. "Armed with the weapons that Duvall created, and now his successor has them. That is what he and this mortal agreed upon. There are many who will join him." His gaze went around the room, searching the vampires that were there. Irina was not one of them. There were several other missing faces, and he knew that Karl had already begun to find his supporters. Now, Karl must be destroyed. But were they powerful enough to do that, especially with the mortal's deadly weapons in Karl's hands? He closed his eyes and thought deeply, as the others looked on. After long moments, he opened his eyes and regarded Kunda-Bele and Mariko.

Smiling grimly, he said: "I have a proposal."

21

Romana and Ashton

Ashton stepped out of the jet and made his way down the steps to the tarmac. A black limousine was waiting for him. The driver was standing by the right rear passenger door. He opened it, and Ashton got in. Two men who had followed him were carrying bags that contained his equipment. They opened the boot of the car, deposited the bags, and closed the boot. The driver got in and sat waiting. Ashton looked at his watch. Five thirty AM. He glanced out of the window. The sun was beginning to rise.

A good time to hunt the undead, he mused, *when they are asleep.*

The driver looked at him in the rear view mirror. Ashton nodded, and the driver started the car and put it in gear. They drove over to a gate in the wire fence that surrounded the airport. There was a man waiting for them. Without a word, he walked up to the gate and opened it wide. They drove through it, and left the airport behind. The gate was closed, and the man wandered off.

As they drove along, Ashton went over the information he'd been given about the target. He'd read all of the Intel that he'd been provided with, and had packed all of the necessary equipment to deal with her. He checked it off in his mind. One; the Supramesh net that was launched from a pneumatic gun; Two, the dart gun that fired the anaesthetic darts that were used to take the vampires down; Three, ten of the darts.

Surely I won't need that many? He thought. He'd seen them used on the vampires before. Usually it only took one, or two at the most to tranquilise them. This Romana was supposed to be strong, incredibly so for a vampire, but he didn't think he'd need more than, say, *three* of the darts? He smiled. *Still, better to have and not want, than want and not have.*

He gazed out of the window.

L.A. Such a grubby place, he mused. *Even Hollywood can't make it beautiful.* He knew most people thought that it was amazing; filled with stars and models. *Ha! There are more hookers than stars.*

"Ten minutes to target area, sir," the driver said.

"Good," Ashton replied. He began flexing his fingers.

Sergei opened his eyes. He yawned cavernously, and sat up. Sitting on the chairs around him were Valeria, Phillipe, and Gerald.

"He *is* like a bear," Gerald said.

"Yes," Phillipe added, "coming out of hibernation." They laughed.

"He's *my* bear," Valeria said, and came and kissed the Russian. She sat down and put her arm around him.

"How long are you sitting there?" Sergei asked. He rubbed his eyes with the back of his hand.

"For a few hours," Gerald said.

"Hours?" Sergei echoed.

"They want to be sure that you will be the perfect companion," Valeria said. "They want to know what you are really like."

"Perfect?" Sergei said. "But I not make my mind up yet." He blinked. "Wait. How can you know what I am like?"

They merely looked at him.

He snapped his fingers.

"You read my mind? While I sleep?"

Gerald nodded.

The Bear frowned. "I do not like it. Is – what you say? Invasion of privacy."

"They only want to be sure of you, my love," Valeria said.

The Russian folded his arms.

"What is verdict, then?" He asked. "Am I good man?"

Gerald and Phillipe shared a knowing glance.

"You have done – *questionable* - things," Phillipe said.

"Yes," added Gerald. "I am afraid we cannot say that you are a 'good man.'"

"Niet? This is your thought?"

"You are not a 'good man,'" Valeria said. "You are a great one!" She crushed him in her embrace while Gerald and Phillipe grinned.

"That is good. Arg! Valeria, you break me...."

She released him and sat back, crossing her long legs. Her green eyes glowed with love.

"Have you decided yet?" Gerald said.

Flustered, Sergei shook his head.

"Is big decision. I must think more."

"Do not take too long," Phillipe said. "Gyorgi would love to take Valeria for himself."

"Huh! That pig! I would never be with him." The redhead rose to her feet, and wandered over to the wall where Erik's collection hung. She ran a finger down the barrel of a Garand carbine.

Sergei stared at her, drinking in her loveliness. How could he refuse to be with such a beautiful creature? Forever...

"Yes, Sergei. Forever," Gerald said. "You are privileged, Sergei. Many vampires over the centuries have wished that Valeria had chosen them to be her companion. Think of it. You could spend eternity with her. We know you love her."

"Da," Sergei said, his eyes still on the gorgeous redhead. "This I know.

But, to be vampire –"

"It is wonderful, Sergei," Phillipe said. "You remember how I was? A pitiful sick creature doomed to live out my existence in a wheelchair. But now, look at me. I am immortal."

The Bear wrenched his gaze away from Valeria. He looked at both of them; seeing their glasslike eyes, their smooth, hard skin. He knew that they each possessed the strength of twenty men. They had a beauty that was not seen in mortal men. They were like marble statues come to life.

"And we are ageless, and will never sicken and die," Gerald said.

"Yes," added Phillipe, "if you became one of us, death would mean nothing to you."

Sergei glanced over toward the bedroom.

"Unlike Erik," he said. "I would go on, but he would age and die."

"Not if I have anything to say about it."

They turned to see Romana standing in the bedroom doorway. She came over and sat down on the lounge next to Sergei.

"You change his mind?" The Russian said.

The girl smiled.

"Not yet. But I will."

Erik came out of the bedroom and joined them. Romana moved over, and he sat down between her and Sergei.

"What is your thought, Erik?" Sergei asked. "Do you become vampire too?"

Erik shook his head.

"No, man. I want to remain as I am."

"That does not seem fair," Valeria said, walking back to the lounge. She sat on Sergei's lap and put her arm around his shoulder. "What about Romana, and your children?"

"I'll do the best I can for them," he said. "But it's too much, thinking of becoming -" He trailed off.

"Like us?" Gerald said.

The drummer nodded.

"So much shit has happened. I'm, I dunno, still processing it. I didn't even know you existed a few days ago. Since then, I've been through all sorts of stuff. It's crazy."

"That is not the real reason for your hesitation," Romana said.

The others looked at her. Clearly, they had been discussing the subject. Erik looked uncomfortable. He got up.

"I'm gonnna make some breakfast." He went over to the kitchen, and disappeared inside.

"I know why Erik is like this," Sergei said.

"Do tell," Gerald said.

"Is because of children."

"What do you mean?" Phillipe said.

"When Erik was boy, his father left. Erik had to look after his mother. She was sick. He could not follow his love of music. When she die, Erik finally could do that. Then, he had girlfriend who became pregnant. She wanted him to give up his music. He wouldn't. They argue a lot, but he wouldn't change his mind." Sergei stopped talking.

"What happened?" Valeria asked.

The Russian gazed at their expectant faces.

"She jumped off cliff. Erik was devastated. He blame himself." He smiled sadly. "Now he won't get involved with girl who has children, or anyone who wants them."

"But this is different, Sergei," Romana said. "If he becomes one of us, we can be together forever. I won't die. Neither will he."

"What of children? Will they age and die?"

"No," Gerald said. "If a vampire and a mortal have any offspring, the Dark Blood is always more powerful. The children will be vampires."

"I think all of this is too much for Erik to make any sort of decision,"

Phillipe said. "We should leave him and Romana alone to work it out."

"Da, is good idea."

They all rose from their seats.

"I wish you luck, my dear," Gerald said.

"We will return tonight," Phillipe said.

"Show me where you live," Valeria said to Sergei.

"Is not much. Dump, really."

"I want to see it anyway." She put her arm around him.

"Okay. Come on, then." He grinned.

"Thank you, my friends," Romana said.

She went with them down the stairs and opened the door for them.

"Until tonight," Gerald said.

They filed out into the street, and Romana closed the door and climbed the stairs. She went into the lounge room and sat on the lounge. She was lost in thought.

Erik came out of the kitchen carrying a plate filled with bacon, eggs, and toast.

"Hey, Sergei – "

He stared at Romana.

"Where'd they go?"

Romana came out of her reverie.

"They left to give us some privacy, so that we may discuss our dilemma."

"We've been talking about it for hours. I haven't changed my mind."

The girl frowned.

"Come and sit with me, my love." She patted the lounge in a very human gesture.

Erik came over, and put his breakfast down on the coffee table. He looked uncomfortable.

"Just gimme a minute, there's bacon and eggs cookin' on the stove. Lemme turn it off."

He went towards the kitchen. He turned and gave her a smile.

"Don't want to burn the place down." He laughed, and disappeared inside.

Romana knew he was just stalling. It was true: they *had* been talking for hours, but Erik wouldn't budge from his position. He was stubborn. He was adamant about his decision. Being a vampire wasn't for him. *How can he reject immortality,* she thought. *How can he reject* me?

There came the sound of plates clattering, and then something was smashed.

"Erik?"

There was no answer.

"Erik? Are you all right?"

She rose to her feet, and crossed the floor. She stopped as a man appeared in the kitchen doorway. He was pointing a gun at her.

"Who are you? Where is Erik?"

She peered past him, and saw the drummer lying prone on the floor. Rage burst upon her. Romana bared her fangs, and glared.

"If you have hurt him—"

The man smiled, and pressed the trigger. There was a soft sound, and a dart struck her in the chest. She looked at it, and then her eyes filled with blood. The girl threw herself at him. Five shots followed the first in rapid succession. She felt the impacts as tiny pinpricks. Romana staggered, feeling the drug overpowering her. She fell to her knees, glowering at her assailant.

Ashton holstered the dart gun, and raised the Supramesh gun. As Romana crawled towards him, he took aim and fired. With a sharp cough, the net leapt out and enveloped her in an unbreakable embrace. The girl fell to the floor.

She struggled, but the net was the strongest thing she had ever felt. It tightened around her as she tried to break free. Soon she couldn't move, and felt her consciousness slipping away.

Ashton approached her cautiously. Her blood-filled eyes still regarded him with hate, but he could see there was no way Romana could escape. He smiled in satisfaction, and pulled out his mobile. He punched in the number for Christian's secretary, and waited for an answer.

"Duvall Biotechnic Laboratory. How may I help you?"

"It's Ashton. Get me Christian."

"Of course, sir. Please hold."

A minute went by.

"Ashton?"

Romana hissed. *Christian! So this man was taking her to him... No! She must not let him...* Romana redoubled her efforts to break free. It was useless. The Supramesh was too strong, even for her.

"Target has been subdued, sir," Ashton was saying. "Please send the transport."

"Excellent work, Ashton. I'll send the jet to you now."

Romana seethed with anger. She thought furiously. How could she stop him? Her mind was clouding. The drug was dragging her down. If only her companions were here...

Yes! That was it! Focussing her muddled thoughts, she sent a message.

Valeria! Help me...

There was no reply. She summoned up the last of her fading strength.

Valeria...

An image of the redhead came to her.

Romana? What is it?

That was it. She was done. Romana sank into unconsciousness.

Valeria stood as though she were listening to an internal voice. She frowned.

"What is it?" Sergei asked.

"I do not know. Romana sent me a message, but then she faded away."

She shook her head. "Perhaps it is nothing."

The Bear looked thoughtful.

"Hmmm. Strange. Can you sense her now?"

The redhead concentrated.

"No. I cannot sense her at all. Perhaps she sleeps."

Sergei stroked his beard as he thought.

"Niet. I do not like it. Something is wrong."

Valeria smiled at him.

"She is pregnant, my love. Even a vampire's strength wanes at such a time. She must be exhausted, and is probably just asleep."

"Niet," Sergei said. "We go back."

"There's no need, I tell you. Wait. Call Erik. He will tell you that she rests. Will that satisfy you?"

"Da. I do it."

Sergei pulled out his phone and punched the drummer's number in. He stood listening to the number of rings. Finally, he cancelled the call.

"Twenty rings and no answer."

Valeria took his arm in hers, and they hurtled into the air.

Ashton dragged the unconscious Romana across the floor. He was about to pick the girl up when a small sound reached him. He pulled out the anaesthetic gun and cocked it. Leaving Romana at the head of the stairs, he crossed the lounge room, and came warily into the kitchen. With the gun held out before him, he swept the room. No-one was there. Erik still lay where he had fallen. Ashton stepped over him, and went to the window. He gazed out into the morning. Nothing.

There was another sound. He spun about, and saw Valeria rushing towards him. He fired. The dart took her in the chest, and she stumbled and fell to the floor. Ashton approached her cautiously. He prodded her with his foot, but she was unconscious. He smiled to himself.

Two for the price of one! What luck.

His gaze travelled over the redhead's body.

And such a stunner too! Christian will be very pleased.

He holstered his gun, and sauntered out into the lounge room to get Romana.

She wasn't there.

"Hello, comrade."

Ashton whipped about to face the speaker. Sergei stood in the kitchen doorway.

"Who the fuck are you?" Ashton grated. "Where is the girl?"

Sergei shrugged. As he did this, Ashton drew his dart gun. The Bear stepped to one side, and threw the kitchen knife he'd been holding. The gun spat a dart that missed him, and then the knife plunged into Ashton's hand. With a cry, he dropped the gun. Ashton grabbed the knife, and pulled it free of the wound.

The Bear was upon him. He crushed the smaller man in his embrace, and the knife fell to the floor. Ashton slammed his forehead into Sergei's nose. The Russian shouted and let him go, and staggered backwards. They faced each other in combat stances. Blood dripped from Sergei's nose onto the carpet. He wiped it with the back of his hand.

"Good," Sergei said. "I like good fight." He leapt forward.

They struck out at each other in a rapid series of strikes. Each attack was blocked or deflected. They jumped back to give themselves room.

"Not bad," Ashton said. "SAS?' Blood dripped down his fingers. He flexed his hand and realised that he'd lost some dexterity due to the knife wound.

"Niet. Spetsnaz," Sergei growled.

"Ah. From Russia with love, eh?" Ashton sneered. He stepped forward, and aimed a kick at Sergei's head.

The Bear caught his leg, and whirled Ashton around. The intruder hopped on one leg as Sergei spun him about. The Russian let Ashton go, and he flew through the air and crashed into the wall. Several weapons fell to the floor. Ashton grabbed up a Lee Enfield rifle that had a fixed bayonet. He lunged at Sergei.

The Bear dodged the deadly thrust, and grabbed the rifle's barrel. They struggled to take command of the weapon. Ashton tried several times to stomp on Sergei's instep, but the Russian stepped away from each attack.

Sergei grabbed Ashton's collar, and using a sweep kick, he kicked the smaller man's legs' from under him. As Ashton fell, Sergei used the momentum of his fall, and swung him high into the air. He brought him crashing down onto the coffee table, which smashed into pieces. The rifle clattered to the floor.

The Bear regarded his enemy. Ashton still breathed, but was unconscious. Sergei knelt and undid Ashton's boots, took them off, and used the laces to tie his ankles together. Then he pulled the intruder's belt off, and looped it around his wrists. Sergei inserted the tongue through the iron belt stay, and pulled it tight. He stood, and looked at his handiwork.

With a satisfied nod, he walked over to the kitchen, and opened the pantry door. He took out a bottle of Jack Daniels and went and picked up a glass that was in the dish drainer. He opened the bottle and poured himself a drink. He slammed it down. Another followed it.

There was a groan. Sergei turned and saw Erik sitting up and rubbing his head.

"Sergei? What's goin' on?" He asked, his voice raw.

The Russian got another glass from the cupboard, filled it, and took it to Erik, who drank it with relish.

"Thanks, man. What's goin' on?" He repeated. He stared at the Russian in surprise. "What happened to your face?"

The Bear pointed into the lounge room.

"You have uninvited guest."

Erik looked and saw Ashton. He cursed, and staggered to his feet. Sergei came and helped him across the floor. They stood looking down at the intruder. Erik swayed, and Sergei eased him down to sit on the lounge.

"Sorry, Erik. I break table."

The drummer waved Sergei's apology away.

"Don't worry about it. Who is this guy?"

"I would think he is one of Christian's men."

They turned to see Valeria coming into the room. She came and hugged Sergei, and then stared at the blood on his face.

"Are you all right, my love?"

"Da. You should see other guy." He grinned, and then winced.

"Let me clean that up for you," Valeria said, and went back into the kitchen.

"The other guy met his match," Erik said. "Nice work, Sergei."

The Russian came and sat down next to him.

"Is okay. No-one comes to my Erik's place and breaks in." He clapped his huge hand on the drummer's shoulder.

Valeria came back with a damp tea towel. She knelt, and wiped the blood from Sergei's face.

"If you were a vampire, this little scratch would heal in an instant," Valeria scolded.

"Where's Romana?" Erik said. He jumped to his feet. "If this prick –"

The Russian grabbed him by the leg.

"Is okay, Erik. I put her on bed. She is all right. This dog not take her." He released the drummer.

With a sigh of relief, Erik stumbled to the bedroom. He propped himself up in the doorway. Romana lay on the bed, unconscious, but safe. Tears welled up in his eyes. He staggered across the floor, and sat on the bed. Erik stroked her face, glad beyond measure that Romana hadn't been taken. Then his eyes turned to slits, and his mouth turned down. He rose to his feet, and came back into the lounge room. His face was grim.

"Wake this fucker up."

The Bear rose to his feet. He picked Ashton up, and then dropped him on the floor. The intruder groaned, and then opened his eyes. He stared at them, and then became aware that he was trussed up. He lay back and closed his eyes.

"Did Christian send you to take Romana?" Erik said.

There was no reply. The drummer kicked him in the side. Ashton cried out, and his eyes flew open.

"I asked you a question."

Ashton merely glared at him in silence.

"I make him talk," Sergei said.

"No," Valeria said. "Let me."

She came and stood over the prisoner, looking down. She stared fixedly into his eyes. She slowly opened her mouth and displayed her fangs. Ashton began to sweat.

"You know what I am," she purred.

The man swallowed.

"Yes."

"You hurt my friend. That is not a nice thing to do. You wanted to take her away."

Ashton licked his lips nervously.

"Do you agree?" she asked sweetly.

He nodded. Erik and Sergei watched in interest. *What is she going to do?* The drummer thought. *We need him alive.*

The redhead turned her lovely face towards him.

"Don't worry, Erik. I won't kill him." She returned her attention to their prisoner. "Not straight away." She allowed her eyes to fill with blood, and knelt down, her face inches from Ashton.

Ashton went pale. He writhed on the floor, trying to get away. His terrified gaze was fixed upon her. Valeria's mouth gaped open, and her fangs were displayed. The pair watching on the lounge could feel the terror that emanated from her victim as she came closer to his unprotected neck. The jugular pulsed there. The redhead could sense it pounding.

"*Wait!*" Ashton cried. "*Don't let her kill me!*"

He wrenched his eyes away from his impending doom, and stared at them wildly.

"*Save me! I'll tell you anything!*"

"Yes, you will," The Bear said coldly. "Did Christian send you?"

Valeria grazed his neck with her fangs.

"*Yes!!*" Ashton screamed. "*Make her stop!*"

"Are you alone?" Erik asked.

"N-no. My driver – he's two blocks away..." He gulped.

The redhead's sharp fingernails traced his pulsing jugular.

"Anyone else?" Erik asked.

Ashton shook his head. Valeria paused in her inspection and looked him in the eye.

"You lie."

He stared at her transfixed.

"No, It's true –"

"She can tell when you lie," the drummer said. "She can read your mind."

"I don't like it when you lie," Valeria said. Without warning, she poked the sharp talon on her index finger into Ashton's neck. He screamed as blood welled up around the wound. Valeria withdrew the nail, and then she bent closer and licked at the blood.   She sat back and licked her lips.

"Mmmm. Nice."

Ashton was too terrified to speak. He goggled at her in horror.

"There is someone else?" The Russian said. "Just nod."

The prisoner nodded furiously. His blood ran from the tiny wound and dripped onto the floor.

"Yes," Valeria affirmed. "Four men are coming in an aeroplane to pick him and Romana up." She rose to her feet, and stood silently for a few minutes. Erik and Sergei didn't speak, because they knew she was contacting Gerald and Phillipe. Ashton merely stared, out of his wits with fear. Finally, the girl turned and addressed the two friends.

"It is done. Gerald and Phillipe will take care of them."

"What about him?" Sergei asked.

"I don't care," Erik said. "Get rid of him, Valeria."

"With pleasure," she said.

Ashton's mouth fell open. He tried to speak, but was too terrified.

"No. He is mine."

They all turned to see Romana standing in the bedroom doorway. She walked slowly towards them like a hunting cat. Her gaze was fixed upon Ashton. She came and stood over him.

"So you would take me to Christian so he could experiment on me?" Her eyes blazed.

Ashton made no response. He stared mutely.

Romana allowed his fear to intensify. She could see that Valeria had terrified him. Now that he faced her, he was petrified.

"Erik, Sergei, you may want to leave," Romana said. "You don't want to see this."

Wordlessly, they rose to their feet.

"Have we missed the party?"

Gerald and Phillipe walked in from the balcony. They came and regarded Ashton. Phillipe shook his head.

"Well, well," he said, "welcome, Daniel. Imagine meeting you here. You *are* in the lion's den, aren't you?"

At the sound of his name, Ashton found his voice. He addressed Phillipe.

"Professor!"

"No, Daniel. I am no longer that man. Now I am an immortal, like my friends here."

"Unfortunately, *your* friends had an accident," Gerald said. "Their plane crashed into the sea." He addressed them all. "It's amazing how fragile these machines are. One piece can come off when they are in the air; say, the tail, and they drop like a stone." He smiled wickedly.

"Good work," Erik said. "Serves the bastards right."

"Do you have his phone?" Phillipe asked.

"I get it," The Russian said. He came and knelt at Ashton's side, and rummaged in his pockets. He brought out the prisoner's phone, and tossed it to Phillipe, who caught it deftly.

He brought up the last call.

Smiling, Phillipe redialled it.

"Duvall Biotechnic Laboratory. How may I help you?"

"Ah, Miss Lee. Can you put me onto Christian, please?"

"Who is this?"

"It's Russell, Mister Ashton's driver. I'm afraid we have a problem."

"Please hold a moment."

"Of course." Phillipe glanced at Ashton. "It *is* Russell, isn't it?"

Ashton nodded.

"This is Christian. What's the problem, Russell?"

"I'm afraid we've lost contact with the plane, sir."

"Yes, we have as well. What is Ashton doing? Put him on."

"I'm afraid he can't talk, sir."

"What? What's wrong with him?"

"He's bleeding, sir."

"Bleeding? What's happening?"

Phillipe didn't reply.

"Russell! Russell! What the hell is going on?"

"Hell," Phillipe mused. "Yes, you could say he is in Hell."

"What?"

There was silence on the line for a few seconds.

"Who is this? You aren't Russell."

"Oh, bravo, Christian. It's nice to see your expensive education wasn't a complete waste of time and money after all."

There was another moment of silence.

"Duvall. You're alive!"

"Actually, I'm one of the undead."

"But how? The lab, the explosion –"

"We escaped, obviously. Do you want to say anything to Daniel? Romana wants to drink him all up, and I'm afraid she's impatient."

"Mister King!" Ashton cried. *"Help me!"*

"Ashton! What –"

"Time's up, Christian," Phillipe said. "Don't worry, I'll send you a video of Ashton's last moments." He activated the camera on the phone.

Ashton began to scream. Romana knelt at his side. She turned her blood-filled eyes upon Erik and Sergei.

"Out. Now," she grated.

They quickly backed away, and went to the kitchen. As Erik made to shut the door, he saw Romana lean down and take Ashton by the neck. She slowly brought him towards her fangs as the other vampires watched. Phillipe was calmly filming the horrific event, and Chistian's voice was still coming from the phone's speaker.

The door closed, shutting out the frightful scene. The Bear put his hand on Erik's shoulder.

"We not look, Erik. We have drink, da?"

Sergei led the drummer over to the kitchen table, and made him sit. Then he went over to the pantry and opened the door. He took out another bottle of Jack. There was more booze in there than food. He went and got two glasses and walked over and sat down with Erik. The Bear opened the bottle, poured them both a drink, and gave one to Erik. They both drank them down fast. Sergei refilled the glasses, and they drank again.

All this time, Ashton's piercing screams were coming from the other side of the door.

They went on for hours.

22

The Proposal

Erik looked out of the window. He watched the clouds streaming past as the jet hurtled through the air. They were flying towards a rendezvous with the Clan leaders. After Romana and her friends had dealt with Ashton, she had come and led him and Sergei out into the lounge room. The vampires were sitting on the lounge and the chairs. There was no sign of Ashton. When he'd asked her what they'd done to him, Romana had only said that 'He had died like no mortal had died for over a thousand years.' None of the others had spoken. *What did that mean?* He wondered. *Had they* eaten *him?* He and The Bear had listened to Ashton's screams for hours. Finally, they had become intermittent, and then they had heard a long sigh. He'd looked at Sergei.

"Da," he had said. "Ashton is dead."

Half an hour later Romana had come to the door and invited them to join the group. She had explained that they were going to meet the Clans. Then she had asked Sergei to arrange the transport, and he had got out his phone and done his thing.

Erik was apprehensive, as all of their dealings with the Clans hadn't been successful. *Successful?* He thought wryly. *Shit, we're lucky to still be alive, after all the things we've been through.* He turned away from the window, and his gaze rested upon the sleeping Romana in the seat next to him. The drummer stared lovingly at her peaceful face. She was becoming more beautiful every day. *Maybe it's the baby?* He thought. *Hell, what do*

I know about kids? He'd always kept away from women who had either had them or wanted them. He hadn't wanted anything to interfere with his music. *But now...*He shrugged. Erik looked at her belly. It was starting to show. They'd argued about her joining the rendezvous, but she'd talked him down, saying that it was her duty to meet and arrange a truce with Karl and the Clans. He shook his head ruefully, and then stared at the back of the seat in front of them. *Anything could happen. If she gets hurt...*His brow creased with worry.

"Erik."

"Huh?" He turned back to see she was awake, and regarding him with a smile.

"Don't think so much." Romana put her hand on his arm reassuringly. "It will be all right."

"You listening to my thoughts?" He said, returning her smile.

"It is not hard. You think too much."

He laughed. "Well, I've never heard a drummer being accused of thinking before. I'll have to tell the band. They'll enjoy that." His face became serious. "I hope you're right. I don't trust Karl."

"Neither do I. But we must hope that we can bring an end to this conflict. If Christian uses the science that Philippe created, we are all in danger. Karl knows that it is in his best interests to join forces against him."

"And he will," a voice beside them said. They turned to see Philippe. "Excuse me." He held out a glass filled with Jack Daniels. "You could use this, Erik."

The drummer smiled and accepted it. He brought it to his lips and drained it. "Ah," he said with relish. "Thanks. I think I did need that."

Philippe smiled. "Romana is right. There's no need to worry. Gerald has told me that Karl and the Clan leaders are very concerned about Christian. They really need this truce between us. If he is allowed to create his immortal army, then the entire world is in danger."

The drummer nodded. "Yeah. I know. But I'm worried that Karl won't keep to his word. He's broken it before. And I don't like the idea of Romana being there. They could take her, and use her blood. It wouldn't be the first time." Erik immediately knew he'd said the wrong thing. "I'm sorry, I didn't mean that. Uh…"

Philippe waved his hand in negation. "It's all right. You *did* mean it. I'm not offended, Erik. Once I was the one who had mad ideas of an army of vampires. I was the one who wanted Romana's blood. But now - look at me. I have everything I worked tirelessly for many years to achieve. Now I have the immortality I craved." His face grew pensive. "I only wish that it hadn't taken all of those lives to obtain it. I can't remember how many vampires I destroyed in my quest." He became silent.

The girl put her hand on his arm. "It does not matter now, Philippe. You are one of us. The past is gone, and you cannot change it."

He looked at her. Erik could see that thoughts were being exchanged between them.

"Thank you," Philippe said. "Another drink, Erik?" He held out his hand for the glass.

"Yeah, thanks." He gave Philippe the glass, and the vampire turned and walked off to get him another drink. Erik shook his head.

"What is it?" Romana asked. She stared at him for a moment. "You don't believe he is sincere."

He turned to her. "I dunno. It's weird. One minute, he's the enemy, the next – " He shrugged. "Do *you* think he's sincere?"

"Yes. I have no doubts in my mind. We have shared thoughts, and he gave them to me without any sense of holding anything back. He speaks the truth, Erik."

The drummer smiled ruefully. "Well, it's hard to keep track of who's on our side. People keep changing sides. Were your people always like that?"

"I am afraid so," she replied. "The strongest amongst them is always the leader. But there are many others who always seek to be that one, and so they plot and plan. Allegiances change all the time. Only the Clan leaders have the power to control their own areas."

"It's like a Shakespearean play," he said. "Everyone is plotting against everyone else."

Romana laughed. "Yes. It is like that."

"Except for you. You weren't in a Clan. They hunted you. I can't imagine how you could have lived like that for centuries. It must have been lonely."

"Yes. It was. But now I have you. And we will have our children. I am happy. Are you happy, Erik?"

He put his arm around her. "Yeah. I am, I really am."

Philippe arrived with another glass, and held it out to the drummer. He looked at them and smiled. "You make a fine couple."

"Thanks," Erik said. He tossed back the drink, and then wiped his lips. "So, how is this truce gonna work? Are you sure Karl will go for it?"

"He will," said a voice from behind them. The drummer leaned out of his seat, and looked over his shoulder to meet Gerald's gaze.

Erik smiled wryly. "Do you guys listen to every little conversation?"

"No," the dandy replied, "but it is easy to hear you. And Romana is right. You think a great deal. Be assured that Karl will keep his word this time." He held up his hand as the drummer began to interject. "I know you have your doubts, Erik, but let me say again that Karl is sincere. This truce is of the utmost importance." He nodded towards Philippe. "If Philippe's weapons are used by an Immortal army, the Clans will be in as much danger as the mortal world."

"Perhaps more so," Philippe added. He turned to Erik. "You know that Christian is power hungry. He had to stay in my shadow whilst I was in charge; fretting, fuming, that he was not the one in the position of power. I know now that he hated that. He forgot all of the things that I did for him. I took him, an uneducated ruffian, and filled him with knowledge, and I turned him into a gentleman. How he hates me. Christian also hates the vampires. They are only a means to an end for him. Karl knows this too. He knows that he must have us as allies, or Christian will enslave those vampires that he has a use for, and destroy the rest. Karl would be one of the latter."

"All of us would be in that group," Gerald added.

"Yes," Philippe said. "Now that he knows that I wasn't destroyed along with the laboratory on the island, he'll stop at nothing to make sure of my destruction." He turned to the blonde vampire. "I know he has no use for you, either, Gerald. You're right; our survival depends on this truce, and we must ensure that Christian and his weapons do not become a threat. They must be eradicated."

"How do you feel about that?" Erik asked. "I mean, you worked for a long time to perfect those weapons, but now you agree that we have to take them out. Don't you feel some remorse?"

Philippe smiled. "No. I no longer need such toys. That life is ended. To allow Christian to have control over such an arsenal in the hands of an immortal army would be a grave mistake. We must 'take out' both the weapons and him."

The fasten seatbelts sign came on, and a tone sounded in the cabin.

"We're about to land. Please return to your seats and ensure your trays are in the upright position. Thank you for flying with us."

Erik smiled as Ramon's voice cut off. Philippe walked back to his seat, sat down, and put on his seatbelt. The others checked their belts. The plane banked to the right, and Erik looked down, watching the city whip past below them. In a few minutes, they had flown over it, and left it behind. They were heading towards a private runway, set far from any sign of habitation. Erik watched the flaps move and then he heard the landing gear come down with a thud. The engines whined as they slowly came lower over the field. With a slight shock, the wheels contacted the runway, and then with a bump they were down. The nose wheel came down, and the engines thundered for a moment, giving them braking power. As they slowed, Ramon taxied them towards some hangers that lay ahead. A group of people stood waiting. Several black limousines were behind them.

"Octavius," Romana said.

Erik peered through the window. The vampire was watching the jet approach. Was that apprehension on that immortal face?

"Something is wrong," the girl said. Her gaze was fixed on the Roman.

"Yeah," Erik agreed. "He's not happy about somethin'."

They rolled to a stop, and the engines powered down with a descending whine. There was a clatter as the seatbelts were unfastened, and Erik felt someone lean on the back of his seat. He turned to see Philippe gazing out the window.

"Yes, Romana," he said, "Something troubles him."

"Let us see what it is," Gerald said, standing behind him in the aisle.

They made their way towards the hatch at the front of the jet. Valeria and Sergei followed them. The hatch opened, and they walked down the stairs towards the waiting Octavius. At his side stood a Japanese woman, dressed in a smart suit. A dozen other vampires stood behind them.

"Mariko," Romana said to Erik, "the leader of the Japanese Clans."

Octavius came forward. For several minutes, the vampires stood exchanging thoughts. No words were spoken. The drummer began to get nervous. His gaze roved over the vampires, and rested upon Mariko for a moment. She glanced at him, looked at him and Sergei like they were a lower form of life, and then gave her attention to Gerald and Philippe. He looked from her to Octavius. *So, this is the oldest vampire in the world,* he thought. The Roman turned to him. His gaze seemed to pierce the drummer through. Erik began to sweat. *What's goin' on?* He looked over at the gathered vampires with trepidation. *Where's Karl?* He wondered where the Clan big shot was. Surely he would have come to meet them? He caught

Sergei's eye, and the Russian shrugged.

"Karl is no longer with us," Octavius said, reading the drummer's mind.

"What?" Erik said. "What do you mean?"

"The others know what happened. I will explain."

"There's no time," Mariko said, exasperated. She turned to Romana. "Why did you bring these mortals? Their presence is not required. They only serve one purpose."

"They are our companions," the girl replied. "And they have helped us in the past." She regarded the Japanese angrily.

Mariko's face was stone. "Have they," she said witheringly.

"Yes," Gerald said. "Without their help, we would all have been destroyed. Let me show you." He stepped forward, and he and Octavius and Mariko shared thoughts. After what seemed a long time, he said: "Now do you see why we brought them?"

"I do not care," Mariko said. "They should not be here. This is Clan business. Send them away."

"Wait, Mariko," Octavius said. "They could be helpful."

"I know of only one way that they could be," she said suggestively, and smiled, showing her fangs.

Erik licked his lips nervously. Were he and Sergei going to be killed by this bitch? Valeria's eyes blazed, and she moved Sergei behind her, and her body became tense.

Romana saw the redhead's move in the corner of her eye, and stepped forward. She stood in front of Mariko. Their eyes locked. "They are *not* to be harmed," she said coldly. She knew that Valeria would do something stupid if she didn't defuse the situation.

The Japanese stared at her haughtily. "Who are you to demand what we do? You are an *Abomination*; your kind threatened us with extinction, until we finally destroyed them. You dare to tell the Clans – "

" – I am here at your request," Romana broke in. She fixed the fuming

Mariko with a steely gaze. "If you do not want my help, I will leave."

The Japanese bristled. She stepped forwards. "You *dare* to dictate to us - !"

"Hold it!"

All attention turned to the jet. Standing at the top of the stairs was Ramon, and he had one of the naphtha rifles trained on Mariko and her companions. She stood and stared at the pilot trembling with rage, her entire body ready to leap at the interloper. But the rifle was a deadly threat, and she knew she would be ash before she could reach him and tear out his throat.

As if he read her mind, Ramon said: "That's right. You know what these babies can do, don't ya? Back off, or I'll toast you and your friends."

Mariko hissed like a wild beast, baring her fangs. The vampires behind her began to slowly move forward, but stopped when they could see that Ramon was watching them closely. With a few well-placed shots, he could destroy them all. They stopped and stood like statues.

"Mariko," Octavius said, taking her by the arm.

She turned blood-filled eyes on him.

The Roman shook his head. "Mariko, you cannot win."

She glared at him. "You think we should allow this *mortal* to threaten us?"

"Why don't you talk to us?" Erik said.

Octavius and Mariko turned their attention to him.

"That's what we're here for, isn't it?" Sweat beaded his face, but he concentrated on keeping his voice low and unthreatening. "If we don't help each other, Karl and Christian will create their army, and we'll *all* die."

The vampire's gaze seemed to penetrate every atom of his being. Without turning his eyes from them, he raised his voice and said: "Ramon. Put the gun down."

"Can we be sure these fuckers won't kill us?" The Mexican shouted.

"Yes," Octavius said. "You have my word." He gave Mariko a withering glance. She pulled her arm free, nodded subserviently, and stepped back. The blood left her eyes, but they could see that she was still angry. It was obvious, however, that the Roman was in charge, and Mariko deferred to his authority, even though she was still furious.

"Ramon?" Erik said. Now it was their turn to show that they could be trusted.

Octavius and Mariko waited to see if the Mexican would lower his weapon. *We should kill them all for this insult,* she sent to him.

He glanced at her and replied: *No. We must have Romana's cooperation, and these mortals are important to her.*

Yes, they are, Romana sent to them both. *Do not forget that.* She gave Mariko an icy stare. *Will you agree to obey Octavius? With Karl gone, he should be the leader of the Clans.*

Yes, he is. I obey his orders. The Japanese looked away from the girl, and up at the Mexican. *Can you make this fool put that thing down?*

Yes. The girl turned and addressed the pilot: "Ramon, put the rifle down. They will keep the truce."

Ramon stared down at the vampires. He shifted his feet nervously. "We've been told that before; look what happened."

Philippe turned and walked over to the steps, and began to climb towards the Mexican. "These are not the same vampires, Ramon. I know that they will honour Octavius's word." He spoke slowly, his voice soft. He advanced, step by step. "Now we must show that we can join with them without fear." He stopped right in front of the pilot, and reached out cautiously. Philippe took the barrel of the rifle, and pushed it downwards. Ramon slowly lowered the weapon, and Philippe took it from him. He turned and addressed the vampires below: "These mortals are to come to no harm."

"I said that they would honour my word," Octavius said, indicating

Mariko and the other vampires at his back.

"I believe you," Philippe said. "Well, Romana, is that good enough for you?"

"It will have to be," she replied.

"Well then," Philippe said, smiling, "now that we're all friends, take us to the Clans." He handed Ramon the rifle. "Perhaps it would be better if you stayed and watched the jet."

"Okay," Ramon said meekly. He took one more look at his friends, surrounded by the vampires, and then backed into the jet. The hatch closed.

Philippe walked down the steps and rejoined the group. "Shall we?" He gestured towards the cars.

Octavius smiled. "Of course." He turned and led the way to the waiting limousines. The others followed, Mariko enveloped in a surly silence. She pointedly ignored Erik and Sergei. The waiting vampires opened the doors and they got in. The doors closed, and the cars set off.

Philippe sat back in the luxurious seat, and stretched out his legs. Beside him sat Octavius, and with them were Erik and Romana. In the next car were Sergei, Valeria, and Gerald. Mariko had taken the last car for herself, refusing to travel with them.

The drummer looked Octavius over. "So you're the oldest vampire on earth?"

The Roman turned his undead eyes on him. "Yes. I have existed for two thousand years. I have seen the rise and fall of the Roman Empire, and watched much of your history unfold from the shadows."

"You must have seen some amazing stuff."

The vampire nodded. He smiled. "Yes. 'Amazing stuff.'" He stared at the drummer, his gaze seeming to pierce Erik through. "You do not fear me," Octavius said.

"That surprises you?"

"It does. Here you sit with three vampires, and you are quite at ease."

The drummer shrugged. "I guess I'm used to 'em."

Octavius laughed. "An interesting attitude. Of course, the lovely Romana would not allow any harm to come to you."

Romana addressed him: "Tell Erik what happened."

"Very well." He told Erik of the events that had led to Karl leaving the Clan, and how his confederates had joined him. Octavius explained how Karl had made a deal with Christian.

"Shit," Erik said. "And you think that Karl has gone to join this Christian guy?"

Octavius looked grim. "We believe he has."

"Christian is hungry for power," Philippe said. "He wants to rule over a world controlled by his army of immortals; themselves under *his* control. Poor fool. As soon as Karl sees an opportunity, he'll destroy him, and become the leader. He sees himself ruling the world for all eternity."

"And with your weapons at his disposal, he could do it," the Roman added.

"That must not be allowed to happen," Philippe said.

"What – " Erik began. His voice was drowned by the sound of two explosions. A heavy concussion hit the car like a giant fist, and a third explosion that enveloped the limousine deafened them.

The car lurched violently, throwing them against the windows. It shuddered, and then rolled over. They tumbled about as the limousine careered off the road, and smashed through some saplings at the edge. It came to rest on its roof.

Seconds later, one of the doors was torn from its hinges, and flung far from the car. Octavius and Phillipe leapt out. Romana was trying to drag the unconscious form of the drummer from the wreckage. The two vampires looked back down the road, and saw the limousine that had contained Sergei, Valeria and Gerald had suffered the same fate that their own car had. It lay on its side in the middle of the road, wheels slowly spinning. They looked further along the road, and saw the last car. It was burning. There was no sign of Mariko or the driver or the vampire bodyguards.

"Help me!" Romana cried. The stink of gasoline was sharp in the air, and she feared that the car would catch fire.

As they turned to help her, they became aware of the presence of others watching them. They whirled, readying themselves for combat. Surrounding them were a dozen of Karl's vampire soldiers, each of them armed with a naphtha rifle that was trained on them. Octavius and Phillipe froze into immobility. A chuckle sounded clearly over the sound of the burning limousine.

Karl stepped forward, and smiled. "Well, well. What have we here?" His gaze swept the pair, and then focussed on Romana. "You shouldn't be in there, my dear. It could catch fire."

The girl's eyes blazed. "Help me get Erik out."

"Why? He's only a mortal. There are plenty more of them we can feed on."

Phillipe went to help the girl.

"No, professor," Karl said. "Leave the mortal to burn."

Phillipe froze as two of the soldiers advanced upon him, weapons ready.

"Come, Romana," Karl said. He motioned for her to leave the drummer.

"No," she said flatly. "If he burns, then so do I."

The German stared at her. "Don't be foolish. He's nothing."

She returned his gaze defiantly. "He is everything to me."

"We can find you another companion. An *immortal* one."

"Karl," Octavius said, "you cannot win. The Clans will hunt you down. Give up your mad plans of conquest."

Karl turned on him. "You are no longer my master, Octavius. *I* am in command here, and I will do as I please."

The driver's door was kicked open, and the driver emerged. He looked around himself at the soldiers, and stood as still as Octavius and Phillipe when he saw the naphtha rifles.

"You would cause a war amongst our people?" The Roman asked. "You would set us against each other? Kill your own kind?"

"Yes," Karl said.

The Roman regarded him. "I do not think you will. This Christian is the enemy. He only wants to use us for his own ends."

The German stared at him for a long moment, and then he turned to the nearest soldier. "Give me your rifle." The vampire handed him the weapon. Karl turned his attention back to Octavius. "I will kill *anyone* who stands in my way." He brought the naphtha rifle up quickly, and fired. The driver disappeared in a ball of flame. He turned towards the car in the middle of the road. "Anyone!"

"No, Karl!" Octavius cried.

Karl fired at the underside of the car. The naphtha pellet penetrated the petrol tank, and the car turned into an inferno. He turned, and tossed the rifle to the soldier. As the car blazed behind him, he advanced upon Octavius until they stood face to face.

"Now you see that I am true to my word."

The Roman stared at him sorrowfully. "I should not have created you," he said softly, "you should have died with Varus's legion and the tribes that opposed him."

Karl smiled. "But I didn't, and I have you to thank. You are my Maker, Octavius. Join me, and we will rule this world." He held out his hand.

"No," Octavius said flatly.

Karl regarded him for a moment, and then lowered his hand. "Very well." He stepped back, and gestured to two of his soldiers. "Take Romana."

They advanced. The girl bared her fangs. "Try it, and you will die," she hissed. They halted.

"Be reasonable, my dear," Karl said. "There is nothing for you here."

"The father of my children is here, and so are my friends."

Karl turned his attention to Octavius and Phillipe. He nodded to his soldiers, and they aimed their weapons at the two immortals. "If she does not come with us, shoot them." He turned and walked up to the car. With lightning swiftness, he reached in, and pulled Romana from it. She struggled in his arms, but couldn't free herself. She had never fought such a powerful vampire before. Romana's efforts to free herself were futile. Karl dragged her away from the wrecked limousine. The girl stopped struggling, and subsided in his arms.

"You will not join me?" Karl said to Octavius.

"No."

"And you, professor?"

Phillipe shook his head.

"Very well," Karl said. "I am sorry, Octavius." With a movement of his head, he indicated that they should stand over by the car. They walked over to it as the soldiers formed a line. "Goodbye, Octavius." The rifles came up.

"No!" Romana cried, helpless in the German's crushing embrace.

Three rushing figures exploded from the trees, and tore into the soldiers. Valeria, Gerald, and Mariko were a whirl of fangs and claws. In seconds, half of Karl's soldiers were ash. Octavius rushed in to help, and a wild melee ensued in the middle of the road as vampire fought vampire.

Phillipe dragged Erik from the wreck, and turned to see if he could help. A soldier stood before him, his weapon aimed. There was no time for him to escape the rifle's deadly pellet. The soldier bared his fangs as his finger began to press the trigger. Phillipe waited for fiery death to take him, realising the irony of being destroyed by a weapon that he had created.

The vampire suddenly cried out in agony, and looked down at his chest in amazement. A long knife protruded from it. He disintegrated into ash, joining his fallen companions. The rifle clattered to the road. Sergei stood there grinning.

"Thank you, Sergei!" Phillipe cried. He leapt into the fight.

The Russian picked up the rifle, and turned to the struggling mass of immortals. He saw one of Karl's soldiers strike Valeria a stunning blow, and she fell. As the soldier moved in for the kill, Sergei fired, and the naphtha pellet turned the vampire into a pillar of fire. The redhead leapt to her feet, giving Sergei a grin. He nodded in acknowledgement, and watched for another opportunity to take another soldier down.

There was no need. Only friends stood there; all of Karl's soldiers had been destroyed. Their ashes were strewn all over the road.

"Karl!" Octavius cried.

They looked about themselves, seeking their enemy.

The German had vanished, taking Romana with him.

23

The Outcasts

Romana strained at her bonds. The chains that held her to the rock wall were new, but she had seen that the staple that they were attached to was old and rusted. She should be able to pull it out of the wall. Romana pulled with all of her strength, but the staple refused to move. The girl slumped back against the rock, defeated. Karl had flown a long way carrying her. He had brought Romana to a system of underground caves high up in the mountains. The girl had been chained, and left in the dark in one of the deepest caves. Why was she so weak? She would normally be able to tear such flimsy links apart like they were rotten cloth. Why had her strength left her?

"Perhaps it is because you are carrying two Abominations," said a smug voice.

Romana looked out into the darkness that surrounded her. A face, then a figure appeared. Karl walked slowly towards her. He stopped and stood in front of her.

"Now you see first-hand how these monsters drained our people of their strength." He smiled.

Romana lunged forward, intent on ripping the German's throat out. She bared her fangs, ready to sink them into his hated neck.

But it was to no avail. The chains pulled her up short of her target. Karl had judged the distance she could reach with meticulous care. They stood face to face, only inches apart. She raved against the chains for a moment more, and then fell back against the wall. Her eyes burned into him.

Karl chuckled. "There is still some fight left in you. Good."

"Come closer and I will show you how much," she snarled.

The German shook his head. "No, my dear. Soon Christian will be here. He's looking forward to seeing you." He grinned suggestively.

"You have betrayed our people," Romana said icily.

Karl's grin ran away from his face. "*Our* people?" He sneered. "You are an Abomination. *You* are not one of us!" He bared his fangs. "It was *your* kind who tried to destroy *us!*" Karl's eyes filled with blood.

Romana laughed. "Fool! You will give this mortal the army he wants, and when he has no more use for you, he will kill you!"

With an inarticulate cry, Karl leapt forward, and dealt her a savage openhanded blow. His talons tore through her cheek. Romana was too stunned to respond. She only stared at him in shock as the wounds instantly healed.

He grabbed her by the shoulders and slammed her against the wall. His grip was like a vice.

"You think you are so superior," he hissed. His eyes blazed with fury. "It was only the mingling of the blood of your makers that made you so. Your kind was wiped from the face of the earth because they were intent on destroying us. Now, we will avail ourselves of your blood, and *we* will be the superior ones."

She met his gaze with her own furious glare. "You speak of my kind with hatred and disgust, and then in the next breath, you admit you long to claim our blood for your own purpose. You are a hypocrite."

Karl laughed; a short sharp bark. "*I* am a hypocrite! *You* are the one who has taken a mere mortal as a companion. You taint our immortal blood even further with such a despicable act."

"That is no concern of yours. All I ever wanted was to be left alone. But you and your Clans have hunted me like an animal. I never bothered you;

why did you hunt me?"

He pushed her away, and stepped back out of her reach.

"You know why. It is the law. The Abominations were not to be allowed to exist. That was what was decided by the Clans."

"You said that they were hunted and killed because they were a threat to you. You said that they made war upon you, and that you faced annihilation at their hands." She fixed him with a freezing gaze. "That is a lie."

"A lie?" He echoed. "Why do you say that? Who told you it was a lie?"

"Gerald did."

"Ha! *That* dandy! And you believed him?"

"Yes."

The German smiled. "It was he who lied. There *was* a war."

"No." The girl shook her head. "There was no war. It was just an excuse to allow you to carry out your plan of eradication. You feared my kind for their great strength, but they were no threat. You told the Clans that they were, and manufactured false evidence to support your claims. They believed you, and the slaughter began."

"Ridiculous!" He stepped closer, and Romana could see the rage boiling within his hulking frame.

"It was Octavius who told the Clans of the danger. I had nothing to do with it. I supported him, of course, but it was not I who condemned your kind to death."

Romana's lip curled in disgust. "I know you lie. Octavius gave me his thoughts. I saw what happened in the council chamber all those centuries ago. Octavius opposed your idea, but you argued him down. You convinced the others that you were right."

The German regarded her coldly. "There was no time for you to share such thoughts," he said. "We were aware of all that occurred when you met them at the airfield, and when you were in the car. Octavius and your witless mortal did most of the talking, and Octavius did not speak of the

Abominations at all."

Karl's phone rang. He turned away from her, pulled it out of his jacket, and answered it. "Yes? Good. Yes, we have her. We are looking forward to you joining us." He listened for a moment, then: "An hour? Good, we will await you at the arranged spot. Goodbye." He returned the phone and faced Romana again.

"No need for me to ask who that was," the girl said dryly.

"Christian and his companions are coming. His scientists are very interested in meeting you." His gaze went to her belly. "And your children." He turned to leave.

"Wait," Romana said.

The German paused, and then turned back to her.

"Do not hurt my children." Tears of blood welled in the girl's eyes. "Let them live. Take my blood, but I beg you to leave them be." Her tears burned down her face.

Karl's lips turned downward. He looked at her with undisguised loathing. "Do you see how weak this has made you?" This *mating* with a mortal, it disgusts me. You are the most powerful vampire on earth; an immortal should have been your companion. Instead, you chose this weakling human." His face was a mask of revulsion.

"You do not even know if they will have the Dark Thirst. They may just be mortal, like Erik. They do not have the blood of two immortals, so they are no threat to you. They are not…Abominations." Her eyes implored him. "You do not need to experiment on them."

Karl smiled. "Oh, but professor Harrow and his colleagues are so eager to see what powers they possess. I have agreed to let them have them."

"No. I beg you. You have me. When they are born, let them go."

"You are in no position to argue. We can take your blood anytime we want, and also that of your children."

"I will kill anyone who tries," she said icily.

The German laughed. "You will try." His voice became low and menacing. "I do not care how many you kill. In the end, your blood will be ours. As will that of your children. Your resistance is useless." He spun on his heel and walked into the darkness. The sound of a heavy door opening came to her, and then she heard it shut with a thud.

Romana hung her head and sobbed. Her bitter tears fell upon the stony floor.

"How do you suggest we proceed? Once they have Christian's weapons, it would be foolish to attack." The speaker was Octavius. He addressed the gathered Clan leaders, and also sitting at the table with them were Erik, Sergei, Valeria and Philippe. Their presence had been a source of contention among the vampires, but when Octavius and Gerald had shared their thoughts, the mortals had been grudgingly accepted within the immortal's most secret chamber.

It was Erik's question that the Roman had replied to. The drummer's gaze took in all of the vampires sitting around them. He knew he had to convince them that they had to take Karl and Christian down.

"We have to get to Romana before Christian arrives. We've gotta get her out, and get rid of Karl."

"Do you know the size of his army?" Mariko said. "Many of our people have joined him. Once Christian joins them, they will be invincible."

The drummer glared at her. "I thought you were scared of nothing."

Mariko's eyes flashed. "Scared?" she echoed frostily. "Take care, mortal. Remember who you are talking to."

"We know where they are, Octavius," said Kunda-Bele. "The mortal is right. We should attack now."

The Roman considered this opinion. He was deep in thought for what seemed a long time. "Who agrees?" he finally said, meeting their eyes in turn.

"I do," said Kunda-Bele.

"And I," added Gerald.

"I too," said Valeria. She sat at Sergei's side.

"Jeanette?" Octavius said.

Jeanette regarded the drummer haughtily. Her gaze went from Erik to Sergei, and then she answered: "No." She sat back and watched silently.

The Roman nodded. "Edmund?"

"I agree with Jeanette. To face these guns that can incinerate us would be folly."

"Robert?"

"I'm not sure, Octavius." He glanced at Jeanette. "These weapons are deadly. We have to be very careful." Jeanette nodded slightly, and smiled. It was well known that they shared the same views on almost any proposition.

Octavius regarded them both. "Indeed we do. Edgar?"

"I've faced guns before. I think we should attack." He smiled.

"Not guns like these, Edgar," said Edmund. "It is not puny bullets that they fire, but flame itself."

The drummer listened to them in disbelief. "*You're* the ones who've guided the affairs of the world secretly for hundreds of years? You're like a bunch of old pensioners decidin' what fuckin' bus to take to bingo. We have to go, *now!*" He slammed his fist on the table.

The vampires leapt to their feet. Their eyes filled with blood, and several of them snarled, baring their fangs at the outrageous behaviour of the mortal before them. Mariko made as if to rush at Erik, and rip out his throat.

"*Hold!*" Octavius cried, in tones of command. The Clan members froze in their place, knowing the Roman's power. All but Mariko. She paced towards the drummer like a stalking predator, her gaze fixed upon him.

"Mariko," Octavius said in warning tones.

She ignored him, and continued to approach Erik, her body trembling in fury. "You *dare* to speak to us like that?" she hissed. She spread her arms wide, and her hands opened, displaying their deadly talons, and she readied herself to leap upon him.

Erik stood staring at her. *Fuck. I've done it now. I'm dead.* His heart crashed in his chest, and sweat ran in rivulets down his body.

Mariko attacked. With a blur of motion, Octavius was between her and Erik. He grabbed her by the throat, and bent her backwards. The other vampires still stood like statues. Mariko and Octavius were only a foot away from the drummer. He looked into Mariko's eyes. The crimson orbs were still fixed upon him in hatred, but she was powerless in the Roman's powerful grasp. She snarled in exasperation.

"Stop this, Mariko!" Octavius said. He shook her roughly. "I will destroy you." He bent her back still further, until it became apparent that if he continued, he would break her in half. "Will you behave?"

Mariko was gasping, trembling in his crushing embrace. She closed her eyes, defeated. *"I - will - behave!"* She whispered hoarsley.

"I will release you now," Octavius said. He slowly took pressure off her, allowed her to stand, and stepped back. He watched her closely, looking to see if she would try to attack.

Mariko regarded him with a cold gaze. She glanced at Erik, and then returned her attention to the Roman. Her face was a frozen mask.

"It would seem that I am no longer wanted. Clearly, you all prefer the company of mortals. Goodbye." Her gaze swept the Clan leaders with contempt. She turned and walked past Octavius. As she passed Erik, she bared her fangs at him. Mariko smiled evilly as the drummer started in fear. She stepped down from the platform, and stalked across the chamber. Reaching the huge doors, she looked back. She shook her head, and then opened the door and went out. The door slammed shut, and as the echoes of its closing reverberated around the chamber, dust fell from the ceiling. An uncomfortable silence descended.

"Well," said Gerald, "that *is* unfortunate."

Edmund rounded on his creation. *"Unfortunate!"* He shook his head in disbelief. "We know the size of the army that Mariko commands, and how strong it is. If she decides to join Karl…" He let his words hang suggestively.

"She will not," Octavius said firmly. All eyes turned to regard him. "Mariko knows that Karl and his followers are doomed. If he accepts help from Christian, sooner or later that mortal will destroy him. He also faces the combined strength of all the Clans. Either way, he cannot win."

"Wait, Octavius," said Jeanette. "We have not all agreed to your plan. There are those amongst us who do not wish to fight Karl."

"That much is obvious," said Kunda-Bele sourly.

"We have not agreed to join you, Octavius," added Edmund. "The loss of Mariko and her Clan is a serious blow. Can we expect to defeat Karl without them?" His glance swept all of them. "To say nothing of this Christian and his weapons. Do not forget, we must defeat him also."

"I'm afraid I agree, Octavius," said Lacey.

"Perhaps we should stay out of the fighting," offered Jeanette. "We could let Karl defeat the mortals, and by our non-interference show him that we are not his enemy. He will leave us in peace."

"Don't be so naïve," said Erik, regaining his poise. "Once Karl and Christian take out mankind, they'll come gunning for you."

"Your opinion is not required, mortal," said Edmund.

"Well, I'm gonna give it to you anyway," Erik continued. "You *have* to be involved. If you sit on the fence, you'll let Karl and Christian win, and then they'll come for you."

"We have never involved ourselves in the petty bickering of mortals," Jeanette said frostily, "and we do not care to do so now."

"Oh *yeah*," the drummer said sarcastically, "you've only manipulated us from behind the scenes. All of humanity's history is a result of your meddling. Maybe every war we've ever suffered was brought about by you."

"That is a lie," Jeanette hissed. "You mortals are warlike without our intervention. You have slaughtered your own kind often enough without our involvement."

"Enough," said Octavius crisply.

Jeanette fell silent, but continued to regard the drummer with distaste. Octavius sighed. He'd thought it would have been this way.

"It appears that we cannot come to an agreement on this matter." Octavius met the eye of each of the immortals. "Very well. Perhaps it is time to dissolve the Clans, and go our separate ways."

There was a collective gasp of disapproval.

"No, Octavius!" said Gerald, appalled. "The Clans have been united for centuries. We must remain so."

"I agree," said Kunda-Bele. "We must stay together. Only by remaining united can we stay strong, and support and protect each other."

The Roman put his hand on Kunda-Bele's shoulder. "Perhaps the time has come to change. We have remained the same through all the long years, unchanging, going on into eternity. But our thinking has not changed, either. We are products of a world long gone. Most of us have seen two or three centuries go by. Some of us are far older. It is a new world, filled with science that we cannot understand. We must adapt, or perish." He looked at them all in turn. "You must all decide what you want to do for your own groups." He turned and stepped down from the platform, and walked across the floor. He reached the door, opened it, passed through, and closed it behind him.

Erik regarded the staring vampires. *I bet they didn't expect that*, he thought, *I know I didn't. What are they gonna do now?*

"You are correct, Erik," Gerald said, reading the drummer's mind. "We did not expect Octavius to do that. He has always insisted on the Clans remaining united. What has changed his mind so much that he would ignore all the centuries that he has kept us together?

"Maybe Karl's actions are the answer to that," said Kunda-Bele. "Remember, he was Karl's Maker. Perhaps he thinks he is somehow to blame for Karl's betrayal."

"Yes," added Edmund, "I think you are right. Remember how they would often argue, but in the end, Karl would eventually support Octavius and whatever decision he made. Now, he has turned against him, and us, too."

"His indecision is dangerous," Jeanette said. 'If Octavius does not show Karl that we are not a threat to him, perhaps he *will* decide to destroy us." She glanced at the drummer. "This mortal could be right."

"You *know* I'm right," Erik said firmly. "You have to fight Karl."

"We don't have to do *anything* you want," Lacey said.

"Erik is right, and you know it," Valeria said. "Karl is merciless. He will wipe you out. You must attack first."

"Da," Sergei added, "to Valeria and Erik you must listen. You have been betrayed by these scientists before." He reddened, and glanced at Philippe. "I am sorry. I meant no offence."

Philippe smiled. "I'm not offended, Sergei. You are right. Christian will not allow us to sit on the fence. In his mind, if we aren't with him, we are against him. He will convince Karl that we are a threat, and they will destroy us."

"That's *if* they don't wipe each other out first," Lacey said.

Philippe nodded. "That *will* surely happen. Both of them are only interested in what they can get out of the other. Once they have it, they'll move against each other."

"But is that certain?" Edmund said. "I believe Jeanette is right. We must not involve ourselves in this struggle."

Kunda-Bele sighed. "It appears that we have a problem. For centuries, the Clans have always managed to agree. Now, though, this matter has divided us. Octavius is loath to lead us, Mariko has left us, and now we cannot decide what to do."

"Well," Erik said, "you'd better figure out what you're gonna do. Times runnin' out for Romana, and if you're not with us, we'll take Karl on ourselves." He turned to his companions. "Am I right?"

The Bear smiled. "Da. I come with you, Erik."

"Where Sergei goes, I go," Valeria said. "I will help you."

"You have my support, also," Philippe said.

They turned to Gerald. The blonde vampire regarded the Clan leaders. His face was blank. He'd served them for centuries, but he still loved Romana in his own way, even though he knew that they would never be together. He smiled at the drummer.

"I will join you."

"You are a fool," Edmund said.

Gerald turned to him. "It is my choice. I will help them."

Edmund gazed at him in disgust. "Do as you will."

Romana looked up as the door to her prison opened. In came Karl, followed by Christian and Harrow. Behind them was Mariko. The group walked across the cave, and stood before her. Harrow stared at her gravid belly in open interest.

"I have brought some guests for you, Romana," said Karl.

The girl glared at them in stubborn silence.

"Do you have no greeting to give us?" Mariko asked.

"Step closer and I will greet you," Romana said icily. Her eyes burned into the Japanese vampire.

Mariko smiled. "I do not think so."

"So you have joined Karl and his band of rebels," the girl said, reading her mind. "The Clans have finally gone their own separate ways. I am not surprised. For all of your talk about hating mortals, here you are in league with them. You are as big a fool as he is if you think you can trust them."

"It serves our best interests to join them," Mariko said reasonably. "We would rather be on their side, than have their weapons ranged against us."

The girl turned her attention to Karl. "So you will just give them my children, and let them take my blood?"

"That is right," Karl said, nodding. He stepped closer, knowing that both he and Romana knew the extent of the chain's reach. "You have been a thorn in the side of the Clans for centuries, Romana. Now we will be rid of you, and at the same time, we will obtain your blood, and will transfer its power to us." His eyes shone.

The girl laughed sourly. "You speak of the Abominations, and how they were a threat to you, and yet you admit to wanting their blood? I said before you were a hypocrite, and now I say it again." Her gaze strayed to the two mortals, who had said nothing. "What of you, Christian? Will you give Karl the only weapons he fears, trusting that he and his rebels will not fall upon you once you have done so, and have rendered yourself defenceless?"

Christian smiled. "Karl knows that his soldiers must obey, or I can destroy them all."

The girl probed his thoughts. A look of comprehension came to her face.

"I see. So you have fitted Karl's soldiers with an explosive device that only *you* control. Interesting. You have the same type of control unit that Duvall used. What is there to stop you from destroying the Immortals once you have attained your goal?" She glanced at the German. "Then you would have disposed of the vampires, and would rule the mortal world." She turned her attention back to Christian.

"Nice try," he said, folding his arms. "That won't happen. We need each other, and we both know it. It's true that Professor Duvall had the same unit, but his was lost in the destruction of the island. It was the only way for him to ensure control over the Immortals. It was a shame that it was destroyed, but luckily, there is another I can use. Karl trusts me with it. I've given my word that I won't use it against his soldiers."

"I believe I have found the enzyme that caused the defect that made them savage," Harrow said, looking up from his inspection of Romana's belly.

The girl ignored Harrow. "Philippe still has his control unit." She gave Christian a mock concern look. "Does that mean that he can override yours, and give the command for all of the devices to explode?"

"You're lying." Christian said doubtfully.

"No," Mariko said. "She tells the truth. I see it in her mind."

Christian turned to Karl. "Is this true?"

"Yes," the German said.

"Why aren't you concerned?"

"It is not important."

"Not important! Duvall has one of the finest minds on earth. He has all the knowledge of my weapons. If he can get to me, he can destroy *everything*." Christian's face reddened with anger. "And if he *does* have the original master control unit, we're in trouble. I have to change the access codes immediately."

"You overreact, I think," Mariko said. "One shot from one of your guns, and he will be ash."

"You have to get close enough to make that shot," Christian said acidly.

"Do you wish you had not joined us?" The Japanese said. She slowly turned and her gaze pierced him through. "Are you having second thoughts about our alliance?" Her eyes burned into him.

Silence fell in the cell. Harrow looked over at Mariko. He stared at her, and licked his lips nervously. Romana watched closely.

"No," Christian said finally. Sweat broke out upon his brow.

"Good," she said. "Remember your place, mortal. We have allowed you to join us because we have common goals. If you stray from that path, however..." She bared her fangs suggestively.

"There is no need for this," Karl said. "Harrow."

"Yes?"

"Bring your equipment. You will begin."

The scientist glanced at Christian, who nodded. Harrow turned and walked swiftly out the door.

Mariko advanced and stood at the German's side. She looked the girl over, her gaze lingering on Romana's belly. She looked up and met Romana's eyes.

"So now we will relieve you of your burden," she said smiling. "Your children will give their power to us."

Romana glared at her. "I will kill anyone who tries to take them."

"You will try," the Japanese said. "But in the end, we will have them. It does not matter how many of the mortals you kill."

"Can you be sure that they even have the strength of our blood?" Romana said. "Erik is the father. He is only a mortal. They may be like him."

Karl shook his head. "No. In every case, when one of us has mated with a mortal, our blood overpowers theirs, and the result is always a vampire. Your children have your blood, and they are like us."

Harrow returned, dressed in an operating gown. Following him was a small group of technicians, pushing several carts that were laden with equipment. Three sets of lights were set up, including a cluster of operating lights that were suspended over an operating table. A small generator was wheeled in, and the lights were connected to it. It was switched on, and the operating lights filled the cell with a blinding actinic glare. In moments, the cell was filled up with gear, and resembled a hospital room. Harrow and his technicians stood ready.

Romana surged forward against her chains, and snarled. The hatred that radiated from her was palpable. She spread her arms wide, ready to grab anyone foolhardy enough to approach. Her eyes filled with blood.

"Can you use the tranquiliser gun on her?" Christian asked.

"No," Harrow said. "It might harm the babies. We can use a sedative, but nothing too strong." He motioned several of his men forwards. They advanced nervously, staring at the furious girl. Both of them held hypodermics, which were filled with the sedative Harrow had mentioned. Each of them moved forward warily, watching the girl closely. First one, and then the other would inch towards her.

Romana glared at them, her blood-filled eyes flicking between them. She hissed like a wild animal.

Suddenly, the man on the left leapt at her, attempting to drive the needle into her arm. Romana was ready for him. She took his wrist in an iron grip, and dragged him towards her waiting fangs. The girl sank them into his throat, and tore it open. She hurled him away as the second man rushed in. Blood sprayed from the first man's ghastly wound, splashing off the ceiling, and covering everyone and everything in the cell with gore.

Romana's second attacker fared no better than the first. As he rushed in, syringe held high, the girl lashed out with her hand. She drew her talons across his throat. The technician grunted, dropped his hypodermic, and fell to his knees. He clapped his hand desperately across the wide slash that gaped in his neck, from which his blood spurted. He stared at her in wide-eyed shock as his life blood pumped itself into the air. Moments later, he dropped to the floor and joined his companion.

Romana bared her fangs at the other technicians, daring them to attack. Harrow and his remaining crew stepped back, shocked by the suddenness of her assault. They stared at their dead comrades in horror. A shocked silence fell. The only sound was that of the blood that dripped from the ceiling to splash upon the floor.

A low chuckling suddenly filled the silence.

"Bravo, my dear," Karl said.

"There are still some mortals left," Romana said. "Why not send them against me?"

"We can't allow you to kill all of Harrow's men, my dear," the German replied with a smile. "He would have no-one to use his machines," he said reasonably. He glanced at Mariko. She nodded.

In a flash of speed, the two vampires rushed forwards, and pinned each of Romana's arms. She screamed in fury, and attempted to bite them. As she raved against their combined strength, Karl called out: "Now would be a good time, doctor!"

Harrow and his technicians' stared open mouthed at the struggling immortals. As the German called out his name, Harrow started in shock. He suddenly realised that they had their chance, and motioned two more of his men forwards. They advanced cautiously, staring at the girl in terror. One of them gathered his courage and leapt in. He stabbed Romana with his syringe, and stepped hastily back out of harm's way. The other technician took his own chance, stepped in, and drove his needle home. He retreated and joined Harrow and the others.

Romana screamed and redoubled her efforts. She knew that once the sedative had taken effect, her babies would be torn from her, and then the vampires would kill her.

Karl and Mariko were hard pressed to restrain the struggling girl. Karl had never before fought an immortal that was so powerful. Even as they struggled to keep Romana from escaping, he was amazed at her strength. But he realised that the two needles had not been enough.

"More, doctor!" he cried.

"More?" Harrow echoed. "But you'll kill her!"

The German managed to flick an angry glance at Harrow. "*Now,* doctor!" he rasped. His reddened eyes pierced the scientist through.

Harrow swallowed nervously, picked up a hypodermic, and began to fill it. He put in double the amount that the others had used. He turned an enquiring gaze upon Christian.

"*Do it!*" Christian cried.

Harrow advanced towards the struggling vampires. Suddenly, with a metallic scream, the staple holding Romana's chain to the wall gave way. With a terrific surge, she leaped away from the wall, dragging Mariko and Karl with her. The girl grabbed the Japanese and hurled her into the air. Mariko flew across the room, smashed into the operating table, and knocked the light over. It fell against the generator, which gave off a bright fountain of sparks, and died. The room was plunged into darkness. The technicians scattered in all directions as their gear fell in disarray across the floor. Two of them were near the door. They groped in the dimness, found the door, opened it, and fled. Light from the corridor outside the cell made a strip of illumination down the centre of the floor.

Karl and Romana faced each other, each of them trying to tear out the other's throat. They staggered and stumbled about the room, stepping on the wreckage that had been Harrow's equipment. Glass and plastic shattered under their feet. Hands locked about each other, they danced a deadly dance in the dark. They passed through the light several times; in and out of the shadows as they fought savagely.

Suddenly, Romana broke free, and wrapped the chain around Karl's throat. She pulled it taught with all of her strength. The German gasped, and fell to his knees. He reached back, trying to loosen the girl's hold on the chain, but he couldn't grasp her wrists. She placed her knee into the small of his back, and pulled. The German was bent double.

The pain was unbelievable. Karl's vision began to fade. Was this how his immortal life would end? He began to black out.

The chain suddenly slackened, and its deadly embrace lessened. The German heard the other end of it hit the floor with a ringing cascade of links. Karl fell forward, and turned to see Romana swaying above him. Her eyes were glazed, and as he watched, her hands fell loosely by her sides. For a moment more, the girl stood there, and then she collapsed onto the floor. Six darts were in her back.

Harrow appeared, holding the tranquilizer gun. He looked down at the unconscious girl, and then turned to the German.

"I-I'm sorry," he stuttered, "b-but the sedative w-was useless. I h-had to..." He trailed off as Karl unwound the chain from his throat. He slowly rose to his feet and fixed Harrow with a deadly gaze.

"If her babies have been harmed - " he threatened.

" - it wouldn't be Harrow's fault," Christian interjected. He came into the light, and looked down at the girl. He put his hand on the scientist's shoulder. "Good shooting, Harrow. Now get this mess cleaned up, and get to work."

"Yes, sir." Grateful to escape Karl's gimlet-like stare, the scientist went to survey the damage to his equipment.

The German came closer to Christian. Christian faced his stare unblinkingly.

"He had no choice, Karl. You would have been killed, and Romana would have escaped."

Karl's anger subsided, but Christian could see that it simmered just below the surface. He would have to be careful.

"Perhaps you're right," Karl said. He turned away and went over to Mariko, who was just rising to her feet. The Japanese was checking herself for injuries. A deep slash in her face closed up as Karl stood before her.

"Let me have her when the mortal has finished with her," she said coldly.

Karl put out his cold hand and stroked her undead cheek.

"Of course you can have her, my dear," he said, smiling.

24

The Loss

The helicopters rushed through the sky. There were four of them; Russian Hinds. Somehow Sergei had obtained them at the last minute. Erik smiled to himself. His friend never ceased to amaze him. If Sergei couldn't obtain something, no-one could. He looked around the cabin. Sergei and Valeria sat across from him, Philippe sat to his left, and Octavius was on the drummer's right. All of the others in the cabin were vampires. The decision to attempt the rescue and attack Karl and his rebels had been made. But some of the Clan leaders had not agreed. Following the meeting, several of them had left, declaring their non-involvement. Jeanette had been stubborn in her refusal, not budging at all. Mariko could not be found, and was thought to have returned to Japan. The Clan had split over the issue. For centuries, the Clan leaders had deferred to the Roman's leadership. But now that the problem of Karl and Romana had been argued over with no agreement from all members, those who had not agreed to join had gone their own way. Nothing like it had happened in all of the Clan's long history. It was without precedent. Octavius had returned to the chamber to find that half of the Clan leaders had gone. He had merely sat down, and allowed the mortals to lay out their plans. Once this had been done, they had left the chamber to get themselves ready. He hadn't spoken since then, keeping silent as they boarded the helicopters that had appeared after Sergei had made a long phone call. Erik glanced at Octavius. What was he thinking? Did he feel remorse at the splitting of the Clans? Could he feel *anything*?

The Roman turned to him. "Yes," he said. "I can and do feel remorse. I led the Clans for centuries. Never before has there been an issue that has divided us like this has done. Even when we faced the crisis of the Abominations, we remained united." He glanced at the other vampires, and noted that they were listening intently. "We have always supported each other. Until now."

"What'll happen now?" Erik asked. "Will the Clans get back together once we've got Romana and have dealt with Karl?"

"I do not know. Perhaps the idea of the Clans has run its course. It may go back to how it was hundreds of years ago; each immortal fended for themselves. Sometimes they preyed upon each other. Many died, not having any other to depend upon. Some were killed by mortals, others decided to destroy themselves."

"Destroy themselves?" the drummer echoed. "Why?"

The Roman's eyes seemed filled with infinite sadness. "Can you imagine living forever?"

Erik shook his head. "No. But I guess that's something that a lot of people wouldn't mind. I mean, immortality's been a dream that the human race has had forever."

Octavius gave him a sad smile. "Yes, I know. But think of it for a moment. What if *you* could be immortal? Live forever; unchanging, never suffering from age or illness. Would that appeal to you?"

"It would be pretty cool."

"Pretty cool."

"Yeah. You'd never worry about death ever again. Just think of the things you'd see!"

"I *have* seen many things," Octavius said. He paused, and then went on: "What about your friends? What of them?"

"What do you mean?"

"Imagine if they were *not* immortal, like you. What would happen?"

The drummer thought for a moment. "They'd die."

"Yes. They would die. Imagine all of your friends dying, and you living on, year after year, decade after decade. Century after century. Imagine everyone that you had ever known and cared for, everyone that you had ever *loved* dying, and leaving you all alone in a strange world." The Roman seemed to be looking deep into Erik's soul. "And the world, it too would go on, but it would *change*. But you would not. You would remain the same, while everything and everyone around you succumbed to time. Eventually, everywhere that you had been, lived, and kept close to your heart would crumble into dust and ruin. The world would be so different, and you would be an alien in the time in which you found yourself."

"You could adapt, learn new things," the drummer said. "People learn things all the time."

"Indeed you could. But could you do that for *eternity*? Could you learn to adapt, to change how you thought forever? What would a man from the Middle Ages make of your world today? He could not understand it. He would feel alone and an outcast. His mind could not grasp the strangeness of what was before him."

"But you could make new friends," Erik offered.

"Oh, yes," Octavius agreed. "New friends. You could always do that. Surround yourself with companions who are like you. Of course. Like the Clans." He smiled sadly. "And what of love? What if you had a love that was not like you, a mere mortal, doomed to exist but for a brief while? She would die, and you would endure the passing of time without her."

The drummer gave him a wry smile. "I see what you mean. Is that why some of your people destroy themselves?"

"Yes. Immortality can be a great burden. There are those who cannot face their nature as an immortal. The world changes around them, but they do not. After centuries of that, they cannot stand to exist any longer. That is why the Clans were created; to provide support for each other against mortals, and companionship that can last throughout eternity."

Erik shook his head. "I guess I never thought of that. It seems like immortality is really a curse."

"It is," Octavius said. "At first, the idea of living forever is very attractive, but as the centuries go by, it becomes apparent that immortality is a great burden."

"But movies and TV shows make it so - "

"Romantic? Glamorous? Bah. I have seen most of these entertainments that you speak of. Vampires who fall in love with mortals, and deny their true nature; killers who mate with the very humans that they should feast upon. It is all rubbish; youthful fantasies that they sell to the ignorant masses. This is reality, Erik. We are beasts; beasts that hunt your kind without mercy. For centuries we have preyed upon mortals. You have seen for yourself what vampires are like."

"But what about Romana and I? She came to me, she told me that she wanted a companion, and that it had happened many times in the past."

The Roman nodded. "Yes, it has, but it is quite rare for one of us to remain with a mortal. Usually they are made into one of us, or..." Octavius tailed off, looking thoughtful.

"Or?" the drummer prompted him.

Octavius gazed at him intently. "Or the vampire grows tired of the mortal, and kills them, or abandons them. I believe you have told Romana that you do not want to be one of us. Where then will your relationship go? Will she stay by your side, watching you age, sicken, and eventually die?"

The drummer stared into Octavius's icy blue eyes. "I don't know. I don't think she'd kill me. I can't see her leaving me, either."

"You could become one of us," Valeria said. "Like Philippe. Maybe Sergei will join us too."

Erik looked over at the two of them. The Bear had his arm around the gorgeous redhead's waist. They looked very comfortable together. Maybe he would join them.

Phillipe smiled, showing the briefest hint of his vampire fangs.

"Yes," he said. "It is very good to be a vampire, Erik. Think; you and Romana could be together always. Immortal."

"You would never tire playing your drums ever again," Valeria said.

Erik smiled. "Now *that* would be cool." His smile faded. "I wonder if she's okay? If Christian or Karl hurt her..."

Octavius put his cold hand on the drummer's shoulder.

"Do not worry. They will not harm her. The children are what they want. At worst they will bring them into the world earlier than they were due."

"Don't forget they also want her blood, Octavius," Philippe said. "Romana is the most powerful vampire on earth. They want her blood for their super soldiers, and to make themselves more powerful. Once they have her children, they only need to drain her for what they need."

The drummer stared down at the floor beneath his feet.

"I am sorry, Erik," said Philippe, "but that is the truth of it. Christian and Karl are determined to carry out their mad scheme. Romana is the unfortunate victim, and so are your children."

"We cannot allow this to happen," the Roman said. "They must be stopped, and Romana rescued. When I think of an unstoppable army of Immortals under their command, I fear for what the world would become. We have preyed upon humans for many years, but we have never wanted to destroy most of them, and enslave the rest. That is madness."

Erik looked up. "They seem pretty crazy to me."

"Is all right, Erik," Sergei said. "We are with you. We help you get them back."

"Thanks man," the drummer said.

"We are all here to help you," Philippe said. "I know how much

Christian hungers for power. We cannot allow him to create an army of Immortals. We will stop him."

"Karl is a danger too," Octavius added. "It was he who first thought of obtaining your weapons. His ambitions have split the Clans; perhaps divided us forever."

Valeria leaned forward. "Romana will be safe, Erik. Karl will not kill her."

The drummer looked at her doubtfully. "I hope you're right."

They fell silent. The thrum of the engine and the whirl of the rotors overhead filled the cabin.

Romana opened her eyes. A dull ache throbbed in her belly. She was shackled to a frame like the one she had seen Abdullah in. She looked about herself; dimness surrounded her. The girl looked down and uttered a groan as she saw that her once swollen belly was now flatter. Harrow had taken her children! Did they still live, or had Christian and Karl merely drained them of the blood that they were so eager to obtain, and kill them out of hand? She strained against her bonds, but the frame was not as weak as the staple in the cavern had been. Romana inspected it. The metal of which it was made was shiny and new. She knew that there was no way she could break free.

The girl peered out into the shadows, attempting to see something; anything, but nothing came to her seeking eyes. She felt the room was vast; a sensation of a huge space came to her. It was clearly not the same place she had been held in. Romana sensed that it was deep underground; the feeling of tonnes of solid rock above her came to her.

She felt groggy. She remembered the sensation of being shot with several of the tranquilizer darts. How many had it taken to put her down? There was a metallic taste in her mouth. Not like blood, with its coppery tang; she had known that flavour for centuries. It must have been caused by the drug.

The girl cast her mind back. What was the last thing she remembered? Ah yes. Karl. She had been about to kill him when someone shot her. Romana saw an image of the German with the chain around his neck. She wished she had broken it. Her strength and speed had allowed her to create chaos amongst them. Her blood would allow them to be as powerful as she was. She must not let that happen. Romana knew that she must fight them until Erik came. She was certain that he would come and rescue her. But until that happened... She smiled grimly. Next time, she would make sure that she killed Karl, along with as many of his followers as possible.

"Are you sorry that you didn't kill me?"

Romana peered into the darkness. Light began to grow; dull orange at first, but then it blossomed into a bright glare that the girl closed her eyes and looked away from. She heard footsteps, and turned towards the sounds. Romana opened her eyes, and saw Karl standing there. Behind him was a huge open space, filled with chairs, and the chairs were filled with his followers. The vampires regarded her expectantly.

She looked about herself. The chamber *was* huge; she looked up and up. The rock ceiling overhead was far away. She and the German were on a platform that was raised above the floor where the vampires sat waiting. The room was long, too. It stretched into the distance, a long space that drew her gaze towards an immense door that lay on its other side. The girl could tell that the door was gigantic, because flanking it were two mortal guards, both armed with the naphtha rifles, and they were dwarfed by the portal.

She returned her gaze to Karl. He was bathed by the lights that were set up on either side of the platform. He stepped towards her.

"Well? Are you sorry?" He asked.

"Yes," the girl said coldly. "I wish I had managed to kill you."

Karl smiled. "Perhaps you are not as powerful as we thought."

Romana fixed him with a freezing stare. "Release me, and I will show you how powerful I am."

The German shook his head. "I am afraid not, my dear. Christian and his scientists wish to study you. We would not want you to come to any harm."

"*I* would not be the one who was harmed. If I had not been shot, I *would* have destroyed you."

Karl nodded. "Yes, you would have. Would that have satisfied you?"

"Only for a moment."

Karl chuckled. "A moment?" he echoed. "Ending an existence that has lasted for centuries would only give you such a brief sense of satisfaction? I'm disappointed. I thought your urge to destroy me was more important than anything else on earth to you."

"It was. But my children are more important. Where are they? Have you killed them?"

"No, Romana. They live. We will care for them, and guide them when they feel the Dark Thirst. They will become honoured members of our group." He came closer. "Of course, Christian and his scientist friend will be allowed to study them first."

Romana strained against her shackles. Her eyes filled with blood. She hissed at him angrily.

"I will kill you, Karl!" she raged.

"You embarrass yourself in front of my friends, Romana," Karl said. He turned and indicated the vampires with a sweep of his arm. "Don't you know why they are here?"

"I do not care," she replied acidly.

"You should feel honoured," Karl said. "They are going to drink from you. Harrow and his science hasn't perfected a serum from your blood. It's too unstable, and no matter what he tries, the soldiers that he makes are uncontrollable." He smiled. "But if the blood is taken directly from the source..." he trailed off suggestively.

Romana stared out at the ranks of pale faces and hungry eyes, horrified. "But there must be hundreds of them..."

The German stepped closer to her, and his face filled her vision.

"There are a thousand of them. They will be the first of legions of soldiers we will create. When they have drunk from you, they will give your blood to another thousand, and so on, until we have a vast army." He smiled. "But that is a lot of blood to be taken. I wonder how long it will be before you die from such blood loss?"

"What about Christian?" The girl said. "He and his scientist want my blood too. Do you dare to betray them, and risk them destroying you?"

The German shook his head. "There will be enough left for Harrow to experiment with. Besides, he has the children, and they will provide more."

Karl stepped back, and she saw that others had joined them on the platform. Mariko and Jeanette were in the forefront of the group. Lacey stood just behind them, in front of a dozen others.

"You said I could kill her," Mariko said irritably.

The German turned to her.

"And you will. But you will have to wait until my soldiers have all taken their fill. I will allow you to kill her then."

"We want to drink now," Jeanette said. She eyed Romana hungrily.

"You promised we'd be first," Lacey said curtly.

"You will. Patience. We must wait until Christian and his scientist are here."

"Why?" Mariko said. "They are unimportant. We will kill them once we have what we want anyway."

"That's right," Lacey added. "We don't care about them." He turned his gaze upon the girl, and his eyes filled with blood. "Give her to us *now*."

The vampires began to move forward.

"Stop!" Karl said. He stood blocking their way. "You will do as I say, or

I will destroy you."

"Can you stop us all?" Mariko said threateningly. She glanced at Jeanette and Lacey, and knew that they would support her. Long enough to get the girl's blood, anyway. After that...

They spread out, each of them taking up an attacking posture. The others at their back stopped and waited.

"Fools!" Karl hissed. He watched them closely, waiting for an attack. He shot a quick glance down onto the floor at the waiting vampires, and saw that they merely sat there. Karl met the eye of several of his captains who were sitting in the front row.

"Seize these traitors, and put them in chains!" he cried.

The captains watched impassively as the group of vampires close in on him. He realised that he had been betrayed.

"Why don't your soldiers help you?" Lacey asked. His voice was sarcastic. "I'll tell you why. They want what we want. They don't care about any army, they just want her blood. They can smell its power too."

"We will give them freedom," Jeanette said. "You only wanted them to be your slaves."

Mocking laughter rang out.

All eyes went to Romana, who was laughing at them all.

"I think they will not be satisfied with a little drink, Karl," she said. "They might want your blood as well. You are almost as strong as I am."

Jeanette laughed in turn. "She has a point, Karl. If you won't get out of our way, we will drain you as well."

The German sneered at her. "And then you will just take over, is that it? You are fools. You don't understand Christian like I do. He'll destroy you when he has the chance."

"Then we won't let him have the chance." Lacey said.

"Enough," Mariko said. "Will you give her up, Karl?"

"No," Karl said flatly.

Mariko and her companions exchanged a swift glance.

"Very well. Prepare to be destroyed with her."

The sound of the heavy door closing echoed in the vast space. All eyes turned to see ten figures advancing towards the platform. Christian and Harrow walked down the aisle, escorted by guards carrying naphtha rifles. They stopped in front of the platform, and the guards spread out. For a moment, no-one spoke.

"Well," Christian finally said, "this looks interesting. What's going on?"

"Nothing that need concern you, mortal," Jeanette said. Her blood-filled eyes took in the deadly rifles.

Christian regarded the group before him, let his gaze wander to Karl, and then he looked at Romana.

"I hope we're all friends here," he said. "Harrow has come to take one last sample of Romana's blood."

"I'm afraid there won't be any left," Lacey said.

"Oh?" Christian said. "Why not? She looks like she's full of the stuff. I don't understand what you mean."

"Foolish mortal," Mariko said icily, "we are going to take her blood; Karl's too." Her eyes burned with bloodlust.

Christian snapped his fingers. Four of his men stepped forward, and activated their rifles. They trained them on the vampires on the platform. The other four guards covered the vampires who were seated.

The scientist advanced. His eyes were cold.

"Now listen to me, and listen carefully. Step away from Karl and Romana, or my men will incinerate you."

Mariko hissed. "You *dare* to order us!"

"Who do you think you are?" Lacey said.

"I'm the one with the guns," Christian said. "Step away from them."

"You cannot kill all of us," Jeanette said.

"True," he replied, "but do *you* want to die? After such a long life?" He folded his arms and waited.

They stared at each other for what seemed an eternity.

"Harrow," Christian said, "go and take your sample." His gaze was fixed on the vampires on the platform.

The scientist stared at them; sweat breaking out on his face. He turned to Christian.

"A - are you certain they won't harm me?"

"They won't dare. Get up there and do as I say."

Harrow returned his gaze to the vampires. He swallowed, and took a step forward.

Mariko hissed and bared her fangs. Her blood red eyes pierced him through, and Harrow stepped back fearfully. The vampires exchanged a glance, and then turned as one and regarded the mortals hungrily.

Mariko and Lacey advanced. Their bloodlust was driving them on. They only saw Christian and his men as a hindrance that stood before them and their goal; the powerful blood that coursed through Romana's veins. They wanted it; they would risk anything to get it, even the fiery death that the naphtha rifles dealt. Jeanette advanced also, but she hung back a little; she still feared the weapons that the men bore. It meant nothing to her if Mariko and Lacey were killed. She had only her own survival in mind.

"Stop!" Christian cried.

The vampires crept closer.

"Fools!" Karl cried. He burst through the advancing immortals, and stood before them.

"Get out of the way, Karl," Lacey said coldly. "We've had enough of these mortals."

"No! *I* am the leader of the Clans! You will obey me!"

"You are the fool, Karl," Jeanette said. "We are no longer interested in holding onto that outdated arrangement. We will take Romana's blood, and we will take this mortal's weapons, and then no-one will dare to stand against us."

"You don't even know how to use them," Christian said.

Mariko's blood-filled eyes swept over the guards. "We will leave one of them alive to show us how your science works." She pointed at Harrow, who flinched and trembled. "Perhaps we will spare him also; he could be useful." She smiled wickedly, and looked beyond into the chamber. "Rise, my brothers and sisters. Slay these mortals, and Romana's blood will be yours."

There was a rustling as the vampires rose to their feet. The chamber was suddenly filled with a thousand pairs of blood red eyes. The guards stepped back, and the mortals unconsciously formed a circle, a circle that was immediately encroached upon by the horde of immortals.

"Back! Get back!" Christian shouted. His men raised their weapons, but terror gripped them. Harrow fell to his knees, and goggled in horror at the oncoming immortals.

Jeanette laughed. "Can you destroy a thousand of us, mortal?"

With a scream, Mariko leapt and attacked Karl. As they fought across the platform, Jeanette and Lacey rushed at the humans. The guards opened fire, shooting into the mass of vampires indiscriminately. Several immortals were hit, and burst into flame, shrieking and stumbling against their comrades, who also turned into blazing torches.

Jeanette struck down one of the guards, but as she turned to attack another, a naphtha pellet hit her, and with a shriek, she too blazed fiercely, and was burned to ashes.

Lacey ripped the throat out of one of the guards, grasped another and threw him half-way down the hall, where the unfortunate mortal disappeared beneath a ravening crowd of vampires with a scream.

Lacey turned, and a naphtha pellet struck him. He went up in flames.

Karl and Mariko fought savagely, fangs and claws slashing and tearing each other. They were evenly matched; even though the German was a much older and stronger vampire, Mariko had been the wife of a Samurai, and she had been trained in all the forms of combat that that warrior race had been well steeped in. Time and time again, when Karl thought that he had the upper hand, she would turn his attack, and thwart his desire to destroy her.

Down on the floor, the circle of the remaining humans drew tighter and tighter, as the vampires hungrily closed in for the kill. Harrow closed his eyes, and waited for the end. Only three guards were left, and they stared at the immortals that lusted for their blood, their rifles empty.

Christian however, took off his jacket, dropped it on the floor, and rolled up his sleeve. He exposed his wrist, and held up his arm. Upon his wrist was a control unit, an identical one to that which the professor had worn. He showed it to the oncoming vampires. He activated it, and input a code into it using the keypad. A red light flashed upon the unit.

"Get back!" He cried, "or I'll destroy you all!"

The vampires ignored him, and prepared to rush in and drain the humans dry.

Christian pressed another button on the controller, and the light turned to a solid green. The effect was immediate. All of the immortals on the floor of the chamber instantly exploded into flame. They burned furiously, their shrieks deafening the mortals who watched, stupefied. Flames filled the chamber, and as the vampires burned to ashes, the air was filled with a thick black smoke that rolled upwards to the roof. In moments, not one of the thousand immortals that had threatened Christian and his companions were left. All of them had been incinerated. Flecks of ash floated in the air; the only remains to show that they had ever existed.

The scientist pressed another button on his controller, and it was deactivated. He rolled his sleeve down, and picked up his jacket. He shook the ashes from it fastidiously, and then tossed it over his shoulder nonchalantly.

"My god!" Harrow exclaimed. He and the guards stared at the ash covered floor in amazement.

Christian turned to him. "Always good to have a little insurance on your side, eh, Harrow?" He smiled.

The scientist nodded dumbly, still stunned over the vampire's destruction.

"You fitted them with your explosive devices?" Came a voice from the platform.

They all turned their attention to the speaker.

The German smiled wryly.

"Yes," Christian replied.

"So this is how much you trust us?"

"I trust no-one," Christian replied. His gaze swept the platform, and noted the ashes that lay there. "Where is Mariko? Did you kill her?"

"No. When you used your little toy, she threw me down, and escaped."

Christian's gaze went to the restraint upon which Romana had been shackled. It was empty. He leapt up onto the platform.

"She's gone!" he cried. He turned to Karl. "Did Mariko take her?"

"I don't know. Maybe she escaped in the confusion by herself."

"We have to find her," Christian said. He turned to the guards. "Get the others! Search her out!"

"Yes, sir!" Chorused the guards, and hurried away from the scene of devastation, relieved to be getting out of the chamber with their lives.

As they went to do his bidding, Karl said: "No need to look for her; she will come to us." He smiled knowingly.

"She'll come to us?" Christian echoed. His face was puzzled.

Karl nodded.

"The children!" Harrow cried exultantly. He clapped his hands.

"Yes," Karl said. "She will not leave them. All we need to do is set a trap for her. Romana is weak; we should be able to capture her with ease."

Harrow stared up at the broken chains that hung limply from the frame, mute evidence of great power. "Weak?" he said apprehensively.

Romana hurried through the corridors. She had no idea where she was, she only knew that this place that they had taken her to was remote and well hidden. The girl had found that out when she had listened to Harrow and Christian when they had been speaking. Where were her children? Romana was horrified that Harrow had taken them from her; she ached, and not only in a physical way from the after effects of the surgery, there was a gaping void inside her. She must not allow them to remain in the hands of such creatures.

Romana came to several doors that opened off the corridor. She halted. Should she try and find her children by checking them, or should she escape, and get to Erik and his friends, who were surely searching for her? They could then return and look for them. Romana stared at the doors. They were heavy, and were locked by some electronic device that was set into the rock wall beside them. There was no way for her to stumble upon the combination of numbers that unlocked them, and it would take far too long for her to break them all down and look inside, even with her strength. But she was exhausted. The effort of breaking her chains, and the aftermath of the surgery had both taken their toll. What should she do? She stood there uncertainly, her mind in a whirl. Torn between the desire to escape, and the need to find the children, the girl was lost in indecision.

It was a fatal error. A heavy body rushed out of the corridor from the direction she had come, and slammed into her. She fell sprawling. As the girl looked up, she met Mariko's reddened gaze.

"Foolish girl. You will come with me," the Japanese snarled. She stood baring her fangs in a display of power.

Romana rose to her feet, and took up a defensive stance.

"No," she said flatly. Her own eyes filled with blood, as she spread her arms wide. Her hands opened into deadly claws, and she crouched down, making ready to spring.

Mariko hissed. She mirrored the girl's posture, and they both began to advance.

"Can we play too?"

The pair whirled at the sound of the voice. Standing in the corridor were Null and Gyorgi. They were both dressed as Romana had seen them last, but one look at the pallor of their skin, and the glassy gaze that lay in their eyes told both her and Mariko that they were vampires like them.

"This is not your affair," Mariko warned. She edged away from the newcomers.

"Oh, but I think it is," Gyorgi said suavely. He smiled, showing his own fangs. "Romana is a friend of mine." He cocked his head to the left. "Besides, I don't think she wants to go with you. I think she'd rather come with us. Isn't that right, Romana?"

The girl regarded him doubtfully. She knew he had once been Sergei's friend. Could she trust him?

"Of course you can, my dear," he said, reading her thoughts.

"No," Mariko said. "She comes with me. Get back or I will destroy you."

"Fuck off, bitch," Null sneered. He folded his arms. "Think you can take us both? Bring it." A slow smile appeared on his face.

The Japanese fixed them with an icy stare. She knew that she must hurry; Karl and those mortal fools would soon be upon them. She had to take Romana now, but these meddlers stood in her way. Surely they were no match for her?

"Come on and try, my dear," Gyorgi said. His eyes filled with blood.

At his side, Null snickered. "Yeah, come on. Let's do it." His eyes reddened, and he unfolded his arms. With his right hand, he made a beckoning gesture.

As the four of them stood there, ready to spring into action, the sound of many feet came to them from down the corridor. Mariko's eyes flashed, and she glanced once at Romana, and then returned her attention to Gyorgi and Null.

"Sounds like we're gonna have company," the youth said. He smiled at the Japanese wickedly. "Are they your friends?"

"No," Romana said. "She escaped from the same chamber I was held in. She and her friends attempted to take me away from Karl. Several of them were destroyed by the naphtha rifles that Christian's men had." She glared at Mariko. "She has no friends here."

"Maybe we should just wait and see who it is?" The Georgian said reasonably.

"*Fool!*" Mariko hissed. "No matter who it is, they will kill us all!" She began to back away.

"Don't you wanna play?" Null said.

With an incoherent snarl, Mariko pushed past Romana, and hurtled down the corridor, away from the oncoming footfalls. Gyorgi rushed up to Romana, took her arm, and dragged her towards one of the doors.

"Quick! In here!" He turned and opened the door. Null leapt in behind him, and closed the door. An instant later, the hurrying feet clattered to a halt, and paused outside the door.

"Leave it, it's locked," came a voice.

"Ahead of us! Someone's running!"

"Go!" Came Karl's voice. "After them!"

The footfalls came again, and in moments, had faded and disappeared down the corridor.

Romana turned to Gyorgi. "How did you know it was unlocked?"

Null stepped forward. He reached into a bag that was hung from his shoulder, and took out a small contraption that was covered with keys, and had wires trailing from it that ended in different sized plugs.

"Just 'cause I'm a vampire now, don't mean that I've forgot all my tricks," he said with a smile. He returned the device to the bag.

"Thank you," Romana said. She turned to Gyorgi. "Thank you both. I do not think I could have defeated Mariko."

The Georgian regarded her. Now that the threat of combat with Mariko had gone, he could see how exhausted and gaunt she looked. "They took your babies?" He came and put his hand on her cheek. "I'm sorry."

"Those bastards!" Null snarled. "Let's kill 'em all!"

"No," the girl said. "We have to get out of here. We will return with Erik and the others and find the children." She walked over to the door, and turned when she sensed that Gyorgi and the boy were not following her. "What is it?"

They both stood there, unmoving.

Romana looked into their minds. They had no thought of taking her to Erik. They didn't even know where he was. They had their own agenda.

"You want my blood for yourselves," she said bitterly.

The Georgian spread his hands apologetically. "Please understand, my dear. It's nothing personal. We only want the power that you have."

Null spoke: "We won't take it all, Romana; just enough to give us the strength that you've got." A sly look appeared on his face. "If you give it to us, we'll help you take Karl and all his crew down. Whaddaya say?"

She regarded them with loathing and contempt. "So, you pretend to be my friends, but really just desire what everyone else wants. You are pitiful."

"Do you think that any vampire can ignore the pull of your blood?" The Georgian said. "It calls to us; its power is like a siren's call. We must have it; even your friends; Duvall, Gerald and Valeria would take it from you."

"You lie. They are true friends. They have never tried, nor would they." She watched them both, ready to defend herself.

"What about Erik?" Null said. "Don't he want to be like us?"

"No," the girl said. "He does not. He is just my companion."

The Georgian took a cautious step forward. He knew how strong Romana was. He had to get close enough to take her blood, but he couldn't alarm her. If they fought, he was sure to be the loser.

"What about when he ages, Romana?" He said logically. "He will age and die, like all mortals. Can you stand by and watch that? Surely you would be better to have another immortal by your side, through all eternity."

"An immortal like you?" She said sarcastically.

He smiled and bowed. "If you think you'd like that, yes."

"I would not." She looked from one to the other. "I am leaving. Do not try to stop me."

"We can't let you go, Romana," Null said, advancing. "We need your blood. Give it to us."

"And then you will let me go?"

The boy grinned, his fangs showing. "Yeah. Of course we will. C'mon, it won't take long."

Gyorgi took another step forward. "Please, Romana, don't make us force you. If you will only co-operate, it will be over in a moment."

Romana took up a defensive stance. "If you try, I will destroy you."

The Georgian's eyes filled with blood. "Are you strong enough to defend yourself?"

At his side, Null's eyes became blood red also. Both of them advanced a step towards her.

"I think you're still weak after your little operation," he said. "Don't you think so, Gyorgi?" He smiled wickedly.

"I think you're right, Null. Don't resist, Romana."

"I will destroy you both."

Suddenly, they heard voices in the corridor. They listened intently with their enhanced hearing.

"Should we check these doors?" It was the drummer.

"No. The laboratory is down that way." That was Octavius.

Romana had her gaze fixed upon Gyorgi and Null. She called out: "Erik! I am in here!"

Null and Gyorgi rushed her. The girl slammed her palm into the Georgian's chest, and he flew across the room, hitting the wall. Null leapt in, and she caught the boy by the neck, and held him fast.

"Romana!" The drummer cried out. "Are you all right?"

Gyorgi was getting to his feet. There was murder in his eyes.

"Quickly!" The girl shouted. "Get me out!"

The sound of keys being punched on the lock outside came to them. It was followed by a blow.

"Null." Romana hissed in his ear. "Use your device and open the door."

"No," he choked out.

She increased her grip. "I will break your neck. Do it."

The Georgian was advancing upon them. In a moment, he would spring.

"Do it," Romana repeated. "I *will* kill you."

Another heavy blow followed the first. The door shuddered, but held.

"Romana!" Erik cried out. "What's goin' on in there?"

"Gyorgi and Null are with me! They want to take my blood!"

"Get back!" Phillipe's voice roared. A thunderous impact shook the door. Two more followed, in quick succession. A forth, and the door was smashed in, and thrown across the room.

Phillipe stood in the doorway, glaring at Romana's attackers.

The girl hurled Null at Gyorgi, and the two of them went down in a heap. In a sudden rush, Sergei, Valeria, Octavius, and Phillipe were standing above them.

"What's this, my friend?" The Bear said. He stared at Gyorgi angrily. "You would hurt the lovely Romana?"

The Georgian regarded him. "If you were one of us you would feel the pull of her blood? Wouldn't you want it for yourself?"

"Niet. I cannot feel it. But even if I did, I would not take it from her."

Erik and Romana were standing by the door. He put his arms around her.

"They took our children?" He said. He stroked her hair, and then pulled back to look into her face.

"Yes," she said. "But now you are here, we will find them and take them back."

"Who did this?" Phillipe demanded.

"Harrow."

"Harrow," he echoed. "I should have known. Is Christian with him?"

"Yes. They are going to take the babies and experiment on them."

"Over my fuckin' dead body," the drummer said icily. "Let's go and find 'em."

"What about them?" Valeria said, indicating the pair on the floor. "We should destroy them."

"No," Romana said. "They cannot help themselves. They are only fledglings; the pull of my blood is overpowering to them. Leave them."

"Are you sure?" Erik said. "Just a minute ago, they were going to kill you."

"Nah," Null said, "We wouldn'ta done that, man. We only wanted a little."

"Silence," Sergei said.

The boy shut up.

"Are you sure of this, Romana?" The drummer said. "Should we let them go?"

She walked over, and looked down upon them.

"No," she said. "We should not let them go. We should do as Valeria says."

Null stared at her in horror.

"B-but - " He stammered.

"We're not your enemy," The Georgian said. He looked at the faces of the vampires surrounding them. One word from Romana, and they would fall upon them and feast on their blood.

"Can I believe you?" She said. "Can you promise me that you will not interfere with me again?"

"Yeah, yeah," Null said, nodding emphatically. "If you let us go, you'll never see us again."

"What about you, Gyorgi?"

"I agree. Let us go."

The girl held their gaze for a moment. They seemed to be telling the truth. She need only tell her friends to kill them, and they would drink them dry. She looked at the boy. He was obviously terrified. Even with his vampire strength, he was still just a boy. Romana knew how powerful the call of her blood was to them. She couldn't blame them for trying to take it. Christian and Karl, on the other hand...

"Get up," she said. "Leave this place, and never let me see you again."

The pair rose to their feet. They looked at her in amazement. Clearly, they had expected to be destroyed.

"Go!" Phillipe said. He took them both by the shoulders, and shoved them at the doorway. They stared, amazed that they had actually been released. Clearly they had both expected to die. For a moment more, they stood in the doorway. Finally, Gyorgi bowed to them, and then he and Null fled.

"You are too generous," Valeria said. "I would have killed them."

The girl turned to her. "There has been too much killing amongst us."

"No," Octavius said, "I fear that the killing has just begun. Now that the Clans have been dissolved, it is every immortal for themselves."

"Let's find our children, and get out of here," Erik said.

"Take us to the laboratory, Octavius," Romana said.

"This way," the Roman said, and they followed him out of the door and down the corridor.

25

The Rescue

Romana and her companions hurried along the corridor. She knew they had to risk running into Christian and his naphtha rifles. The children's safety was the only thing on her mind. Erik was at her side, and from time to time, he would glance at her. Romana knew of his scrutiny, and also knew that he had been very concerned for her wellbeing, and that of their children.

"They'll be okay, Romana," he said. He reached out and took her cold hand.

"I hope you are right," she replied.

They came to the end of the corridor, and the room where she had been operated on. *No,* she thought furiously, *it was here that they* violated *my body.*

The girl came to a halt. The group stopped, and they listened; the vampire's acute hearing brought small sounds to them from inside.

Romana made to enter the room, but the drummer grabbed her arm.

He leaned close, and whispered in her ear: *"Careful. It could be Christian in there, and he's got the guns."*

The girl cocked her head to the side and listened.

"No," she said. "It is Harrow, and two of his men. Christian is elsewhere, hunting Mariko with Karl."

She slipped from his grasp, and kicked the door in. It tumbled across the floor, and smashed into the opposite wall. With lightning speed, the vampires entered, and spread out, blocking the doorway.

Harrow and two technicians stood there in shock, staring dumbly at the newcomers. They had been gathering up what equipment had been undamaged in the fight. One of them went to grab a rifle that was lying on a table.

In a flash, Romana was on him. She grabbed him, and bent him backwards. As the man lay helpless in her powerful arms, she fixed her blood red eyes upon Harrow. The girl stared at the scientist for a long moment, and then she sank her teeth into the technician's throat, all the while keeping her gaze upon the terrified Harrow. He watched in horror as she drained the man dry. She dropped the corpse on the floor, and advanced upon the scientist, who shrank back, petrified.

"I - I was only f - following Christian's orders," he stammered. He backed away, trembling and sweating. He goggled at the oncoming vampire in terror.

"Oh yes," Romana said icily. "I understand. You did not wish to do the awful things that you did. Christian *made* you do them."

The scientist backed up against the wall. He had nowhere to go.

Harrow licked his lips nervously. "Yes! Yes!" He said, nodding fervently. "That's right, Christian made me do it. You must believe me."

"I do believe you," Romana said.

"You do?" Harrow said weakly.

"Of course. But I am still going to kill you." She stepped closer.

"*Wait!*" Harrow cried. "If you kill me, you won't know where your children have been taken to."

Romana came and stood inches away from Harrow's face. As she bared her fangs, he turned his head away, and closed his eyes. The girl reached out, took him by the chin, and turned his face towards her. She put her hands on either side of his head, forced open his eyes, and made him look at her.

"If you tell me where they have gone, I will not kill you," she said.

Harrow stared at her, in the grip of terror. He tried to shake his head, but Romana's grip prevented him.

"You're lying!" He cried. "If I tell you, you'll kill me!" Tears ran down his face.

The girl relaxed her grip, and took her hands away.

"I will not. Tell me where they have gone."

The scientist stared at her. "You won't kill me?"

"No."

Harrow giggled inanely. He was on the brink of madness. A sly look came to his face.

"You have to promise me you won't kill me. I know how much you vampires value honour. Do you promise not to kill me?"

"Yes, I promise."

"Christian has sent them to Paris." He smiled.

Romana's arm flashed out, she grabbed Harrow by the collar, and then she threw him across the floor. He looked up at the ring of vampires who stood over him like avenging angels.

"Feast, my friends," Romana said.

They fell upon the unfortunate scientist, their fangs tearing into him. Harrow vanished beneath them. He screamed once, and then moments later he was dead, empty of blood. His face was as white as the lab coat that he wore. His eyes were wide and staring, and his face wore an expression of extreme terror. The vampires rose to their feet, and eyed the remaining technician hungrily. The man stood there staring at them in horror, knowing that they would kill him next.

Erik had stood in the doorway, watching the little drama play out. He came into the room, and regarded Romana with shock.

"You said - " he began.

"*I* did not kill him," she said reasonably. "I told him the truth."

The drummer looked down at the perforated body. He felt the gulf that was between mortals and vampires. He looked up, and met her gaze.

"Guess it doesn't matter to him now, anyway."

"He deserved to die, Erik," she said fiercely. "How many of us has he experimented on? A hundred? A thousand?" She came over to him. "I looked into his mind, Erik. He *enjoyed* what he did. He was more a monster than we are."

Erik held her gaze for a moment, and then turned and indicated the remaining technician.

"What about this guy? Are you going to slaughter him too?"

Romana looked over at the terrified man.

"No. What is your name?"

The technician stared at her. He was paralysed with fright. His companion's death, and Harrow's horrific slaughter had struck him dumb.

Erik walked slowly over to him, holding his hands up to show he meant no harm.

"It's okay, man," he said softly. "What's your name?"

The man gaped at him. *"Murphy,"* he whispered.

"Well, Murphy, it's your lucky day. They're going to let you go." Erik turned to Romana. "That's right, isn't it?"

"Yes," the girl said. "Go and tell Christian we are coming to take our children back. We will kill anyone who gets our way."

Murphy stood amazed, unable to believe that he was to be set free.

"Go!" Romana cried, pointing at the doorway imperiously.

The technician jumped in shock, and slowly walked towards the doorway. The vampires opened the way for him. He ran out into the corridor, and fled. As the echoes of his footsteps died away, Romana moved towards the door.

"We are finished here, my friends. Thank you for coming for me. Let us go."

"No thanks are necessary, Romana," Octavius said.

"Da," the Bear added. "For you, we do anything."

The girl smiled. She stepped up to Erik, and put her cold arms around him.

"Thank you, my love."

"I'm glad you're okay. But can we leave without our children? Maybe they're still here." He indicated Harrow's corpse. "He could have lied to you."

Romana shook her head. "No, Erik. He spoke the truth. Christian has taken them to Paris. We gain nothing by searching this place. They are gone."

"I suggest we leave also," Phillipe said. "There are still armed guards out there. We don't want to run into them."

"Does this place have a bomb like your island did?" The drummer said. "I'd love to blow it up."

"No," the ex-scientist said. "Harrow brought all of his own portable equipment. This is one of Karl's strongholds."

"That is correct," The Roman said. "These caves have been here for centuries, and have been used by the Clans many times."

"Let us just go," Romana said. "I want to get out of here."

The drummer looked into her eyes. "Okay. I guess we need to figure out how we can get the children back. Let's go."

The group went into the corridor, and made their way back to the helicopters, warily keeping on the alert. Luckily, they didn't encounter anyone; mortal or otherwise. They got on board, the chopper's engines started up, and the Hinds leapt into the sky, and headed East.

Null and Gyorgi were moving through the trees. They were arguing.

"We should'a taken her," Null said.

"Idiot!" The Georgian replied. "There was no way we could have fought all of her friends."

"Now we've lost our chance. It's all *your* fault." The boy's face was sour.

"My fault?" Gyorgi echoed. "What do you mean? Why didn't you do something?"

"She had me by the throat," Null said. "I couldn't get free."

"You didn't even try," Gyorgi said accusingly.

Null stopped in his tracks. He glared at Gyorgi.

"What the fuck did you just say?" He said venomously.

The Georgian halted and regarded him with fury.

"You could have broken free, and we could have taken her blood there and then."

Null spat on the ground.

They squared off against each other.

The sound of hands clapping came from the depths of the forest. They both turned about, trying to locate where it was coming from. It seemed to move; one moment it was here, the next, there. It was followed by malicious laughter.

"Who's that?" Gyorgi demanded. "Come out!"

He and Null were crouched down in defensive postures.

The trees ahead of them parted, and Mariko stepped forward. She advanced towards them, smiling sarcastically as she slowly clapped her hands.

"You are both fools. You make enough noise that even the deafest mortal could find you." The Japanese stood before them, staring at them in unhidden contempt. "You are not worthy to be vampires. You could not survive a day, let alone for eternity."

"Fuck you," Null said acidly.

She fixed him with a freezing gaze. The boy shrank back.

"You think that you are so powerful now," she said icily. "A little vampire blood courses through your veins, and you think that you can do anything. You regard yourselves as gods, because you have killed a few pitiful mortals. You are pathetic. I will not waste my time killing you."

"Come on, you old bitch," Null said, "we can take you." His voice trembled.

"Is that right?" Mariko said softly.

With a lightning move, she was upon him, and took him by the throat. She lifted him from the ground, and held him at arm's length. The boy kicked and struggled, and tried to prise her hands away, but she was far more powerful than he was.

Gyorgi stared, awed at the display of power.

"I could snap your pretty little neck," Mariko said. "Do you want to die?"

"N - No," Null managed to say, choking.

The Japanese laughed again.

"Beg for your life, then." She regarded him coldly.

"I - I beg you - not to kill me," the boy said. Tears of blood started in his eyes. He shook with fear.

She held him for a moment longer, and then tossed him contemptuously to the ground at Gyorgi's feet. The Georgian helped him up. Null rubbed his aching throat and stared at her with new respect. He hadn't thought that she could be so strong. He wiped the tears from his face.

"I should leave you to Karl and his traitors." Mariko indicated with a nod of her head the forest that lay back the way they had come. They listened, and the sounds of someone moving through the undergrowth came to them.

"Come with me, and serve me, or stay and die," she said with finality.

Gyorgi and Null exchanged a glance. The boy nodded.

"Okay," Gyorgi said. "We accept."

"Come," Mariko said, and took to the air. The pair followed her. In moments, they had disappeared into the clouds above.

The trees parted a second time, and Karl stepped into the open, followed by two of Christian's men, who were armed with naphtha rifles. He looked up, and smiled.

I'll see you again, he thought. "They've gone," he said to the guards. "Let's go back."

The three of them vanished back into the trees.

Romana stared at the floor beneath her feet. She was tired. It was a strange feeling. For centuries, she had felt full of unnatural vigour; her vampire blood gave her strength and energy that was unmatched by any other vampire. But now she felt fatigue. Was it because her children had been taken from her? Or was it that Harrow had shot her so full of the anaesthetic that she still felt the effects?

"You think too much."

The girl turned and met Erik's gaze. She smiled wanly.

"Now it is my turn to be the daydreamer."

He put his arm around her shoulder and hugged her hard body to him.

"We'll get them back," he said. "I promise you we will."

She returned his embrace.

"I know we will." Tears of blood welled up in her eyes, and then spilled over and ran down her cheeks. She snuggled into him. Erik patted her reassuringly.

"Perhaps we should go to Paris?" Gerald said. He gazed at Romana with pity.

"Niet," Sergei said. "A plan is needed."

"Sergei is right," Phillipe said. "We cannot just rush into any action. Christian would expect that, and we would be slaughtered."

"What would you suggest?" Octavius asked.

Phillipe thought for a moment.

"We must find some way to break into the laboratory at the institute.

It's clear that is where Christian will take the babies." He shook his head. "It will be difficult. The security is foolproof."

"I know a guy," The drummer said. "I mean, I *knew* a guy."

"Da," The Bear added. "Is easy job for Null."

"But he is with them now," Valeria said. "How will you get him to help us?"

Romana turned her gaze on them. They could see the conviction in her eyes.

"I will convince him that it is the right thing for him to do."

"Do you think he and Gyorgi are with Karl?" Erik asked.

She paused, sending out her awareness.

"No. They have gone with Mariko."

"That crazy Jap? Hell. I wouldn't trust her."

"I think they had no choice in the matter," Gerald said.

"Yes," Octavius added. "That is what I feel also. She gave them an ultimatum."

"Join me or die, eh?" Erik said. "Mad bitch."

"So we must go to Japan, and convince Null to come with us," Phillipe said.

"Not straight away," Gerald said. "First we must work out a plan."

"Yes," Octavius said. "That is correct."

Romana addressed them all.

"I do not ask you to do this, my friends. You have done enough. I will do this myself."

There was a chorus of disagreement at her words.

"There's no way you're leavin' me at home," Erik said. "I'm stayin' with you until the end. They're my kids too."

"Da," Sergei added. "Valeria and I come too." The redhead hugged him.

"I also would like to help," Gerald said. "Perhaps it will make up for all of the times I have hunted you."

"I'd like to see you get your babies back, Romana," Phillipe said. "Plus, I would like to see Christian get his comeuppance."

"Count me in," Octavius said. "Is that not what you moderns say? I would be happy to assist."

Romana regarded them all. Her tears came again, but this time, they were of joy, not sadness.

"Thank you, my friends," she said. "For so long, I was alone. Now I have your friendship and support. It means so much to me." She beamed at them.

The helicopters rushed through the sky.

Erik walked into the lounge room. Everyone was sitting there, going over the plans. They'd landed and made their way to his loft. It was the best place for them to meet, as they had all been there, and because it was in a light industrial estate, people didn't go there during the night. The group had sat and discussed the way they were going to carry out the plan. The idea was sound; some of them would go to Japan, locate Null, and bring him to Paris. The others were to go there, and maintain a watch on the facility. Any unusual visitors would be noted, especially if there were identified as vampires. Would Karl show himself there? It wasn't certain.

The drummer had a drink in either hand. As he came up to them, Sergei rose to his feet and accepted one of the glasses from him. They both drank, and Sergei sighed with pleasure.

"Ah. Is good, Erik. This planning, is thirsty work, eh?"

"It pales in comparison to the feeling and taste that blood gives you," Gerald said.

"That's right, isn't it, Valeria?" Phillipe added.

She nodded.

"Yes. But if Sergei does not wish to join us, we must respect his choice."

Gerald looked at her in surprise.

"You do not want him to be with you?"

"Of course I do. But it is his decision to make. I will not force him to do it if he does not want to."

"He does not want to be immortal?" Gerald said. "How can that be? Mankind has always chased immortality."

"That is true," Octavius said. "But we all know that some of us cannot face eternity. An endless existence is not for all. To be an alien among strange times and peoples that one cannot relate to is a hard thing to face. Many of us decide to destroy ourselves. I have seen it many times."

The Bear sat down, and Valeria put her arm around him.

"Whatever you decide to do, I will respect your decision, my love."

Sergei was embarrassed.

"Please, I think more on this."

"Come on, guys," Erik said. "Don't pressure him. What's happening with the plan?"

The vampires regarded him. They broke out into smiles. He knew they were sharing their thoughts.

"What? What did I say? Is somethin' funny?"

"You are," Romana said. She grinned.

"I can remember a time not so long ago when you hated me, Erik," Gerald said. "You would have loved to destroy me."

The drummer shrugged.

"Yeah, well. We're all friends now, aren't we?"

"Of course we are," Phillipe said.

"As for the plan, Erik, we have worked out what we will do," The Roman said.

Erik fell into one of the lounge chairs. He crossed his legs, and took another pull at his drink.

"Do tell."

"Romana, Sergei, and Valeria will go to Japan. As Sergei was a good friend to Null, we feel he would be the best person to convince him to join us."

"Cool. Sounds good. What else?"

"Gerald, Phillipe and I will go to the Duvall facility in Paris and keep a close watch. We will report any and all movements that occur."

Erik finished his drink. He put the empty glass on the floor at the side of his chair.

"What about me? Don't I come too?"

"No. It will be better if you remain here."

The drummer's gaze swept the group. Romana refused to meet his eyes, and Sergei looked away too.

"What? How come?"

Octavius glanced at the others sidelong. For a moment, the vampires communed.

"Hey!" Erik said.

He jumped to his feet.

"None of that shit. Just tell me to my face why you think I shouldn't go."

They all regarded him.

"Well, is someone gonna tell me?"

"We are afraid you would be a liability," Gerald said.

"What? What do you mean?"

"You do not have combat training, Erik," Phillipe said. "It will be very dangerous where we are going."

Erik folded his arms.

"Oh, and you don't have time to nursemaid me, eh?" His face flushed with anger.

"They not mean that," The Russian said. "You are not soldier, Erik. We not want to lose you."

"Ha! Not a soldier, eh? Do you forget who came and saved your asses?" He stabbed a finger at Sergei. "Especially you. That vampire was going to kill you, but I saved you."

"Is right, Erik, but –"

"– no buts! I did my fair share. I can look after myself."

"We know you can, my love," Romana said. "We just think you should stay behind. Please."

He glowered at them.

"These are my kids." He poked himself in the chest. *My kids.* I'm not gonna sit here while you guys go off and save the day. I've got more right than any of you to go."

Romana stood up, and went to him.

"I know you do. But I cannot lose you. Please, Erik. Please stay here."

"Is better if you do, Erik," The Bear added.

The drummer looked him in the eye. Sergei lowered his gaze, abashed. Erik regarded them all in turn.

"My friends. My fuckin' friends." He glared at them in exasperation.

He stared at Romana.

"I'm going. You can decide who I go with. That's final."

He stormed off, taking long strides across the floor. He reached the bedroom, and slammed the door behind him. No-one spoke. Romana made to go to him.

"Niet, Romana," Sergei said. "Leave him be. I see him like this before."

"But I only want to talk to him."

"He not listen. Please, leave him be."

The girl stared at the bedroom door. She wished that Erik would re-appear, and apologise for his outburst, and then agree to stay. But she knew that was a forlorn hope. Romana knew that Erik was stubborn. *Once he has made up his mind,* she thought.

"There is no changing it?" Gerald said.

"Yes. I am afraid so," she said. Romana sighed. "We must take him with us."

"I do not like that," Phillipe said.

"Nor do I, Phillipe," she said, "But he is obstinate, and will not stay here. In fact, I think if we left him here, he would follow us regardless."

"Da," Sergei agreed. "He do that, for sure."

"Then we must make sure he remains safe," Octavius said.

"Which group should he go with?" Gerald asked.

"Whichever group faces the least danger," Phillipe said.

"That would be your group," Romana said.

"True," Octavius said. "We are only watchdogs, whereas you go to find Null. Do not forget Mariko. She is deadly. She was the wife of a Samurai hundreds of years ago. Mariko has been trained in their arts, and is a powerful vampire as well."

"Then it is settled, then," Gerald said. "Erik can come with us, and be a watchdog."

The bedroom door opened. They all turned to see Erik walking towards them. He was smiling. He held up a passport.

"Found it. Haven't used this for a while. Japan, here we come."

"Or," Valeria said, "He can come with us, and face the danger."

Romana made to speak, but Erik held up his hand to forestall her.

"I've made up my mind. You can't say anything to change it. Whether you like it or not, I'm going. I owe it to our kids to do everything in my power to save them."

He came up and put his hands on her shoulders.

"They're *our* kids, Romana. I can't stay here and do nothin'. I have to go. Please don't argue."

Romana looked deeply into his eyes, and could read determination there. There was no way that Erik was going to be left behind. She felt the love that he was filled with for their children. She smiled.

"I was not going to argue," she said. "I know how strongly you feel about this. You can come to Japan with me." She hugged him to her hard body.

"It'll be great to go back. I haven't been there for a couple of years. I love the place." As Romana released him, he addressed Sergei.

"It'll be like old times, eh, Bear? Remember the clubs in Tokyo? Awesome."

"Da, I remember. Was good times."

"This will not be a sightseeing trip," Romana said.

"I know. We have an important job to do. I can help with Null. He's a big fan of mine."

"We do not know how he has changed," Gerald said. "When you become a vampire, everything changes."

The drummer smiled.

"Well, he came here and still liked 'Kult's music. That's good, isn't it?"

"It is," The Roman said. "However, we know that he and Gyorgi went with Mariko, and she will make them her slaves. To her, anyone without Samurai or pure vampire blood is inferior."

"You will have to be very careful," Phillipe added.

"We will be," Erik replied.

He put his arm around Romana.

"We have the most powerful vampire on earth to look out for us. What could go wrong?" He grinned. He released her and went and retrieved his glass. "Another drink, Sergei?"

"Please," Sergei replied.

The drummer took his glass and went into the kitchen.

Gerald shook his head.

"What is it?" Romana asked.

"He is a surprise, this one."

"You have said that before. Why do you think this?"

He turned to her.

"For someone who did not want to have children, he is very driven to make sure that they are safe."

"Why should that not be the case?" Phillipe said. "They *are* his children."

"It is just strange that something so simple could change a person's viewpoint completely."

"Children change everything, Gerald," Octavius said.

Erik came out of the kitchen, bearing two glasses. He went up to The Bear and gave him one. He regarded the group, and said: "Here's to a successful mission." He held up his glass and then drained it on one gulp. "Everything will work out fine."

Romana looked at him as though she were seeing him for the last time. A sense of foreboding sat upon her. She felt there was something wrong, but couldn't put her finger on it. As she watched Erik talking to the others, a terrible sense of dread filled her. She shook it off, and joined the others.

But still, deep inside of her, there was the feeling of uneasiness.

26

The Cost

Sergei woke up. He slowly sat up on the couch. He and Valeria had stayed with Erik and Romana. The others had gone, to arrange transportation to Paris. He and the drummer had had quite a few drinks. His head was hazy. Sergei stretched out his arms and yawned cavernously. He threw off the blanket that covered him. Where was Valeria? They had both snuggled up on Erik's couch. He swung his feet to the floor.

Sounds of cooking came from the kitchen. Was that Valeria cooking? The smell of bacon and eggs wafted through the lounge room. The Bear inhaled deeply.

"Ah. So good."

He rose to his feet and picked up his jeans. He pulled them on and put on his shirt. He then put on his socks and boots. His coat was draped over a chair. Sergei put it on and wandered into the kitchen, where Valeria was standing by the stove. She was indeed cooking food. She was wearing one of Erik's robes. It was huge on her, and made her look like a child. He walked over to her, put his arms around her, and kissed the back of her neck.

"Mmmm. I like that," she said. "Good evening."

"I sleep so long? Good evening. You cook for me?"

"Yes. I know you like your food."

"Thank you. You are perfect woman."

Valeria laughed. She turned in his arms and gazed lovingly at him.

"Do you think so?"

"Da. Of all women I know, you are finest."

"You will make me blush. Kiss me."

She put her arms around him, and they kissed.

"Don't you make a lovely couple?"

Romana stood in the doorway. She was dressed in another robe that belonged to Erik. It was too large for her as well. She came over to them.

"You both look like little girl in those robes," Sergei said, grinning.

"Naughty girls?" Romana offered.

"Sometimes." He laughed.

"You wouldn't have us any other way," the redhead said, and returned her attention to the stove.

"Where is Erik?"

"He is having a shower. He said to tell you that he will take you to your place so you can get your 'stuff.'"

"Ah. He is good boy."

Valeria had served up Sergei's meal up on a plate.

"Will you eat it in here?" she asked.

"Da. I break Erik's table. Kitchen table will do."

Valeria nodded, and took the plate to the table and set it down. The Bear walked over, and sat down. He began eating hungrily. The two vampires watched him with smiles on their faces.

"Would you like coffee?" Romana asked.

"Please."

She went over and filled the jug with water, plugged it in, and turned it on. Then she got two cups out of the cupboard, and put coffee in them from a small tin. While they waited for the water to boil, Erik came in.

He was dressed in black jeans, and wore a black leather jacket over a KMFDM t-shirt. His feet were shod in a pair of black industrial boots.

"Hey, man. How are you?"

"Better now I eat something."

Erik came and sat down. The jug boiled, and Romana made their coffee. She brought the cups to them and set them down on the table. She and Valeria joined them.

"How's your head?" Erik asked.

"Is bit fuzzy," Sergei said. "I am not eighteen any more."

Erik laughed. He took a sip of coffee.

"Me either. Oh well, have to carry on."

The Bear picked up his cup and drank.

"Ahhh. Very good. Good coffee, Romana. I thank you."

"You are welcome."

"Are you coming with us?" Erik asked. "I know Valeria wanted to see Sergei's place."

"No. We are off for a drink."

"Ah. Okay."

"Yes," Valeria said. "You have both been fed. Now it is our turn."

"We will meet you back here," Romana said.

"Okay. In an hour?"

"Yes. That will do."

The Bear finished his meal. He put the cup and the cutlery on the plate, and carried it all over to the sink.

"Don't worry about washin' it," Erik said. He drained his cup and put it on the table. "I'll do it when we get back. Let's go." He stood, kissed Romana, and went to the door.

Sergei kissed Valeria, and followed him.

They went down the stairs into the garage. Erik walked up to his Porsche, which had been repaired. He got in, and Sergei followed suit. The Bear ran his eyes over the paintwork.

"Is good job, Erik."

"Yep. Just like new. Romana paid for it. Twenty grand."

The Bear whistled in appreciation.

"Lot of money."

"Yeah, but I love this car. It took me ages to save up to buy it."

Erik put the key in the ignition and turned it. The car started immediately. He listened to it idling.

"Carlo does a great job too. Listen to her purr."

"Is very nice."

Erik opened the glove box and took out a remote. He pressed the button, and the garage door began to rise. He put the remote back where it came from. When the door was fully open, he put the Porsche in gear, and they rolled out of the garage. When they were in the open, he gunned the engine, and they sped away as the roller door closed.

Minutes later they were speeding down the freeway. The lights whipped past above them as they went along. They both grinned as the wind blew their hair back. The exhilaration that comes with the sensation of speed enveloped them both.

"Is not bike, but is good ride!" Sergei shouted.

Erik laughed.

"This is better than a bike, man!" He replied.

They looked at each other. Manic grins were pasted on their faces.

Erik returned his attention to the road. Suddenly, a figure appeared from nowhere directly in front of them.

"Look out!" Sergei shouted.

"Fuck!" Erik cried, and stomped on the brakes. Nothing happened. They hurtled towards the shape in their path. Erik ripped on the handbrake, but it accomplished nothing as well. They sped towards the figure. With a curse, the drummer spun the wheel, and they rushed past the form, and skidded towards the barrier at the side of the road. They smashed into it, and the car broke apart under the impact. Bonnet, doors, and tyres flew in all directions as the disintegrating car tumbled end over end.

Sergei was thrown from the vehicle. He hit the road, and bounced around like a rag doll. He finally came to a rest not far from the Porsche's scattered remains. For a few moments, the only sound was the hissing of the destroyed radiator as its heated water sprayed everywhere, and then Sergei groaned.

"So you're alive. You're pretty tough."

The Bear's eyes slowly opened. A deep gash on his forehead was bleeding. He put his hand up and touched it gingerly. He became aware of the speaker's presence.

"Who –" he began. He peered at the figure that stood over him.

"Don't you recognise your old friend?" Gyorgi said. He knelt down and inspected Sergei's wound. "That looks nasty."

Sergei sat up. He stared at Gyorgi.

"What are you doing here?"

"Just visiting. What happened to your brakes?"

Sergei wiped some blood out of his eyes.

"They fail."

"That's unfortunate. The handbrake failed as well? What a terrible coincidence."

The Russian heard the sarcasm in his voice. Gyorgi was smiling at him.

"The brakes?" he said. "You do something to them?"

Gyorgi's smile became wider.

"That's right. It was easy. You were all talking and planning together. Null and I broke in, fixed the brakes so they would fail, and then waited for you and Erik to go to your place. You didn't even know we had been there."

"But why?" Sergei asked. "We are no threat to you."

"Of course you are. Every mortal is a threat now."

There was a blur of motion, and Null stood by Gyorgi's side. He was carrying Erik as though he weighed nothing. He gently put him down on the road. The Russian gasped, and tried to go to him, but a sharp pain told him that he had broken something, and could not move. He gritted his teeth against the agony and lay back.

"He's still alive," Null said.

"Not for long," Gyorgi said. He rose to his feet, and went over to Erik.

Null blocked his way in an instant.

"No. Don't kill him."

The Georgian regarded him with distaste.

"Get out of the way. This is what we came here to do."

Null shook his head.

"No, man. Erik is my friend."

"*Ha!*" Gyorgi laughed, a short bark of derision. "No mortal is your friend now."

"Do not listen," Sergei said. He lay there, praying that Null wouldn't allow Gyorgi to hurt Erik.

The sound of an ambulance siren came to them. Someone must have heard the crash and called it in. Sergei knew he had to stall for time.

"Null, Erik is your friend. *I* am your friend." Sergei coughed. He felt pain in his chest. *Have I punctured lung?* He thought. He tasted blood in his mouth.

"He's right, Gyorgi," the boy said. "Erik and The Bear are the only ones who ever cared about me. You can't kill him."

Gyorgi turned blood red eyes upon him.

"Would you rather suffer the consequences of not doing what we were told to do?" He sneered. "You know she hates failure."

Null stood his ground.

"I don't give a fuck what she hates. I won't let you kill them."

The Georgian's eyes slitted.

"Will you explain to her why you didn't want to kill them?"

The boy nodded.

"You're a fool."

"You can think that if you like. I don't care."

The Russian was watching and listening to this exchange. He heard the ambulance coming closer. The two vampires glanced down the road. He knew that they wouldn't want to be discovered by anyone.

Gyorgi read his thoughts.

"That's right." He came over and knelt down at Sergei's side. "We aren't allowed to show ourselves. But I can kill you both and be gone long before they get here."

"No, Gyorgi," Null said. "Let's go."

The Georgian regarded him.

"Coward."

Null took up a defensive posture. His eyes filled with blood.

"Come on, then. Let's do it. I'm fuckin' tired of your shit. You're not my boss." He displayed his fangs.

They faced each other, ready to attack. The Russian stared at them as the sound of the ambulance came closer and closer. He desperately hoped it would arrive and drive them away.

Gyorgi turned to him and smiled.

"You'd like that, wouldn't you?"

The ambulance's lights swept the scene as it approached. Gyorgi and Null exchanged a glance and they both nodded.

"You're lucky this time, Sergei," Gyorgi said. "But if you come to Japan..." He showed his fangs.

Null appeared at his side. He gave The Bear a smile. Then they were both gone.

The ambulance pulled up with a screech of brakes. The siren stopped. The ambulance crew leaped out and ran towards him. Sergei heard a stretcher clattering across the road. In a moment, one of them was by his side.

"Sir? Can you hear me?"

"Da. I hear you."

The ambulance man quickly asserted Sergei's wounds. He put his case down, opened it, and pulled out a hypodermic. He rolled The Bear on his side, and eased his right arm out of his coat sleeve.

"For the pain," he said, and expertly injected the hypo. "I think you've punctured a lung, sir."

"Da. Is my thought also."

"We need to get you to hospital right away."

"My friend, you take him first."

The man looked over at his partner. He'd put Erik on a stretcher, and was wheeling him towards the ambulance. He gave his companion a thumbs-up.

"Sir, it's okay. We've got you both. Everything will be all right."

He eased the Russian onto a stretcher. His companion came back, and they raised the stretcher so they could take Sergei to the ambulance.

Sergei lay back and descended into darkness.

The Castle of Blood stood at the edge of the forest. It was far from any populated area. Only a small village lay ten miles away. Its inhabitants had passed down knowledge of the castle's reputation for centuries. Simple folk, they grew rice, even in this modern era. Not all people of Japan were industrialists, or businessmen. They still followed the ways of their ancestors; farmers that had worked the area for generations. If not for the occasional jet that flew over, or the highway twenty miles away that had bypassed the village, it could have been a scene from the sixteenth century, when the samurai and warlords had ruled supreme.

In fact, Tokugawa Ieyasu had sent an army to conquer and deliver the castle into his hands. They had been well armed, and were a force that was composed of his finest samurai. None had returned. They had vanished as though they had been swallowed up by the dark forest. Not even a helmet or pennant remained of them.

Looking out of the main tower's window was a lone figure. It stood gazing upon the forest, remembering the centuries that had flown by since that day. Mariko thought back, back to the day that the army had come to destroy and confiscate the castle.

Fools, she thought. *Mortals are such fools. They think they can overpower anything.*

She smiled, remembering how the vampires that inhabited Chi No Shiro had made short work of the vaunted samurai. For all of their prowess, they were helpless in the face of such unnatural power that the vampires possessed. They had been slaughtered to a man. In the end, many had panicked, and had run. They had been slain with the rest.

Sato had ensured that not one of them had remained alive.

Ah, Sato, she mused. *You were the most powerful of vampires.*

She recalled how he had been; short and stocky, but with such strength! Even as a man, he had been an impressive specimen. As a vampire, he was without peer.

Or, should it be said; he had *been* without peer. For Mariko had destroyed him herself. Not at first, though. In the beginning she had only been one of a group of travelling players that had roamed from town to town. The money that they had made during their progress through the islands was barely enough to keep them alive. Her beauty was well known, though, and so they had many people who would flock to their performances. Even so, life had been hard.

And then, Sato came.

She remembered that night. They had stopped at a small inn that lay in the mountains. She was tired; they had been travelling all day. The troupe was booked to perform in two days time, and the boss was driving them hard to reach their destination to ensure that everything would be set up and run properly. She wanted to sleep. Mariko was sorting costumes in one of the rooms when she heard the screams.

Running outside, she saw a horrific sight. Men were attacking the troupe and the other customers. She saw one of them grab one of the porters, and rip out his throat. She screamed. All around her were scenes of carnage. Mariko gasped at the horror that surrounded her. The girl wanted to run, but was transfixed by the death in front of her.

And then, Sato stood before her. She gaped at him. He was dressed in an archaic kimono, and his face and hands were covered in blood. His hair was long and wild. His eyes were crimson orbs that devoured her. She knew that look. He was going to rape her. Shocked out of her stupor, she turned to run, but before she could even take a step, he was there, and his arms were wrapped around her in a vicelike embrace. She saw his terrible fangs, and knew this was the end. Mariko fainted.

But it wasn't the end, was it? She mused. *No, because you desired me as your companion, didn't you, Sato?*

Her attention was suddenly drawn to two shapes that were flying towards the castle. She turned away from the window, and walked over to the seat that stood on a raised platform. The castle had been kept as it had been over three hundred years ago. Armour and weapons sat there on display as they had done for centuries. At either side of the throne were two guards, clad not in samurai armour, but modern suits. Mariko sat down on the lord's seat. She was the master here now.

Null and Gyorgi flew in through the window. They came up to her.

She regarded them imperiously.

They bowed, as if they had just remembered to do so.

"Well," She demanded, "is it done?"

"We did as you asked us," the Georgian said.

"So Erik is dead?"

Gyorgi shook his head.

"No."

Her eyes blazed.

"Why not?" Her nostrils flared. "I gave you specific instructions. My orders were to be followed to the letter."

"It's my fault," Null offered.

Mariko's eyes filled with blood.

"And why is it your fault, little boy?" She sneered.

Null looked as though he were indeed a little boy. One who had been caught with his hand in the cookie jar. He lowered his head.

"I couldn't kill them," he said softly.

"I beg your pardon," she said. "I cannot hear you. Speak up."

The boy raised his head, and stared into her angry face.

"I couldn't kill them. They're my friends. They were the only ones who ever did anything for me."

Mariko's eyes narrowed. At her side was a small ornate table. Upon it was a golden bell. She picked up the bell and rang it twice, and then put it back on the table. She rose to her feet as four more guards entered and stood behind Gyorgi and Null.

"I see," Mariko said. "You cannot do as you are told. What use are you to me if you cannot do as ordered?"

Gyorgi took a step forward.

"It's not my fault. He wouldn't let me kill them."

Mariko regarded him with scorn.

"And you would not fight him to do my bidding? You would rather come here and tell me you failed?"

"No," Null said. "I take the blame for it all. Gyorgi wanted to kill them."

"But –" Gyorgi began.

"*Silence!*" She hissed.

The Georgian's mouth snapped shut like a trap. Mariko stalked towards them.

"I give you an order, and you fail. Why should I keep you alive?"

She walked behind them.

"My men obey me immediately without question. This is loyalty. This is duty. You cannot do this. Tell me why I should keep you alive?"

They made no reply.

"Well?"

"Erik is badly injured," Gyorgi offered.

"Yes?" she said, prompting him to continue.

"He was badly hurt in the smash," Null said. "He's no threat to you now." He looked forlorn. "He might even die."

Mariko came close and spoke into his ear.

"That was the point."

Null jumped.

Mariko signalled one of the guards on the platform. She pointed to one of the swords that stood there in a stand. The guard went to it, picked it up, and brought it to her. He knelt and offered it to Mariko as a samurai would offer his sword to his liege lord. She took hold of the handle, and slowly drew the blade from its sheath. It whispered from the scabbard. The steely sound made the only noise in the room as the sword was revealed.

The guard rose to his feet as she faced the two that had failed her. She raised the katana, and laid it upon Null's shoulder. The boy shivered as the razor sharp steel touched his neck.

"Why should I not kill you now?" she purred.

Null gulped.

"We-we did as you wanted –"

She shook her head. The boy ceased to speak.

"No," she said reasonably. "You did not. I ordered you to *kill* Erik. You did not do it."

Mustering his courage, Null spoke.

"We did better than that,' he said.

"What do you mean?" she asked.

"His injury will make Romana angry. And Sergei saw us; he knew what had happened was no accident."

"Yes," the Georgian added, "surely Sergei will tell Romana, and she will come to have revenge."

"Of course she will," Mariko said. "But his death would have served the same purpose."

"She'll be so furious that she'll be off her guard," Null said.

"That is true," Mariko agreed. She lifted the sword away from his throat.

Null licked his lips. He sighed in relief.

Mariko lowered the katana to where it was before.

"But it does not alter the fact that you defied me," she said. "I expect total obedience. Will you give it to me?"

"Yes," they chorused.

She regarded them both in turn.

"Good." She said.

Without warning, she lifted the katana, spun about, and slashed the head from the guard. The corpse immediately turned to dust. The scabbard fell to the floor with a clatter. Mariko turned and addressed them both.

"Remember this."

The pair nodded shakily, appalled by the guard's death.

Mariko gestured and two of the guards who had entered the room came and took Null in their grasp.

"Take him below and seal him in a coffin. Leave him there for three days. That will teach him respect."

The guards nodded, and began to drag Null away. A smile played on Gyorgi's lips.

"It's what he deserves. He defied you," he said.

"Yes," she agreed.

She turned and regarded him.

"But you did nothing about it." She gestured again, and the other two guards came and grabbed Gyorgi.

"I shouldn't be punished –" he protested.

In a flash, the sword was at his throat.

"You allowed him to disobey me. That is almost as bad as his disobedience. You can share his punishment. Take them away."

As the guards took them away Mariko said: "Do not worry. Three days without blood will not kill you. But you will suffer the pangs of the Dark Thirst. Do not fail me again."

They were dragged from the room. Mariko picked up the scabbard, and sheathed the sword. She replaced it in the stand, and went to the throne and sat down. In moments, she was lost in her memories of the past.

Romana stared at the machines in the hospital room. She knew that they were keeping Erik alive. Displays glowed in the dim light, showing his vital signs. None of it made any sense to her, but she knew that his life hung on a thread. The car crash had put him into a coma. The doctors had told her that he may never awaken from it.

Her gaze went to him. His face was peaceful. It seemed like he only slept. She moved closer soundlessly, and touched his hand. It was almost as cold as her own. She listened closely, and could make out the sound of his blood as it flowed in his veins. Sluggish, that flow was; not full and lively as it usually was. His breathing was shallow too.

How could she lose him now, after finding him? She had been alone for so long. He *must* not die, now that she had discovered in him the perfect companion. Romana had had many companions over the centuries, but none other had felt so close to her as Erik did.

The girl stared at his face, and tears of blood welled up in her eyes. She stroked his face gently. The tears spilled over and ran down her cold cheek unheeded. She ran her fingers through his hair.

"*Do not die, my love,*" she whispered. "*I am waiting for you. Come back to me.*"

She straightened up and wiped the blood from her face as a sound from the corridor came to her. The door opened slowly. Valeria appeared in the opening. She came in, and Sergei followed.

The Russian was dressed in a hospital gown, and he was dragging a stand on wheels that had a drip feed hung upon it. This went into his arm. He was pale, and walked slowly and unsurely. Valeria was holding his arm and helping him along. He shuffled across the room and stood at the foot of the bed.

"Sergei," Romana said, "you should be resting."

He waved away her protest with an impatient hand.

"I come to see Erik. Is there any change?"

She shook her head.

The Bear looked mournful.

"Is my fault, all this." He hung his head in shame.

The redhead left his side, and brought a chair over to him. She eased him into it.

"No, Sergei," Romana said. "It is not your fault."

"Da. It is. If Erik had not taken car to go with me..."

"No," Romana repeated. "It is not your fault."

"Gyorgi is to blame," Valeria said. "He and Null did this."

"I will kill them both," the girl said.

"Niet, Romana. Mariko make them do this. Null, he save me and Erik."

"So you told me," she said coldly.

"That changes nothing," Valeria said. "They should die."

"I will go to Japan and deal with them myself. Mariko too." Romana's face was grim.

"But they know you will come," Sergei said. "Is trap for you." He stared at her imploringly.

Romana came and put her hand on his shoulder.

"I can look after myself," she said. "I will be very careful."

"Take Valeria with you," Sergei said. "Please."

"No. She is to remain here to keep an eye on Erik. Mariko could send another assassin; one who has no feelings for him, and he would die."

She gave him a wan smile.

"Besides, she is to look after you as well."

"If he were one of us, he would have healed instantly," Valeria added.

"You have not made your decision regarding that?" the girl asked.

"He has not," the redhead said peevishly.

"Sergei," Romana said, "if you join us, injuries like this will not affect you at all. Instead of taking weeks or months to heal, it would take moments. Do you love Valeria?"

"Da," he said. "I love her truly. She is most wonderful woman."

"Then why do you hold back?" Valeria asked. "If you become one of us, we will be together forever." She stopped talking, and walked over to look out of the window. She was clearly upset, and Romana knew that she and Sergei had been arguing about the subject almost as much as she and Erik had.

Sergei was about to say something, when there came a light tap at the door. It opened, and Elektra, Peach, and Suzi came in. The keyboardist came straight over to Romana, and hugged her.

"Oh, Ro. I'm so sorry. Are you okay? What a terrible thing to happen."

"Thank you, Suzi," the girl said. "I am as well as could be expected."

"Are you all right, Bear?" Peach asked.

"Da."

"The car was a complete wreck, man." Peach shook his head. "Absolutely trashed."

"What happened, Sergei?" Elektra asked.

The Bear glanced at Romana. He knew that he couldn't say anything about the attack.

He shrugged.

"The brakes. They fail. We hit the wall."

"That's it?" Suzi said.

"Is all I can remember."

Valeria turned away from the window. She came over to them.

"This is all trivial. It means nothing."

The newcomers stared at her in surprise.

Romana went up and took her arm.

"Why don't you take Sergei back to his room? He must be tired. Are you tired, Sergei?"

"Da. Is good idea. Come, my love, help me."

Valeria and Romana stared at each other for a long moment. The Russian knew they were sharing thoughts. The others looked at them, wondering what the hell was going on. Finally, Valeria came and helped him to his feet.

"I see you later." Sergei said.

"No worries, man."

"Okay."

"Take it easy. Go and rest up."

Valeria said nothing as she led him out the door. It closed behind them.

"What was that all about?" Elektra asked.

"Valeria's parents were killed in a car accident," Romana lied. "She got very emotional when she saw Erik and Sergei like this."

"Ah," Elektra said. "I see."

"She's hot," Peach said. "But a bit weird."

"She's upset, Peach," Suzi said. "Cut her some slack."

He raised his hands.

"She ain't mine. I don't care."

"That's enough," Elektra said. "Do you need anything, Romana?"

"No, thank you."

"What did the doctor say about Erik?" Suzi said.

"His vital signs are stable, but there is no way of knowing when or even if he will awaken from the coma."

"Oh. That's awful. Can we do anything?"

"If you would visit him from time to time, that would be appreciated. I must go away for a while. I have business to attend to. Valeria will stay here to watch over Erik and Sergei."

Elektra regarded her. How could she leave Erik at a time like this? What kind of business could make such a demand upon her that she couldn't leave it to be with him?

"I know you must be wondering how I could do this while Erik needs me. I must assure you that the business I speak of is of the utmost importance, and must be dealt with. There is nothing else on earth that could drag me away from him at this time."

They looked at her strangely. She knew that they were all thinking how unusual it was for her to abandon Erik in the state he was in.

Suzi stepped forward.

"It's okay, Ro. We'll call in every day to see how he's doing. You go and do what you have to do." She came closer and hugged the girl again.

Romana smiled.

"Thank you. That means a great deal to me."

"If you need anything, anything at all, don't hesitate to contact me," Elektra said.

"Thank you very much. I will do so if it is necessary."

"Same goes for me," Peach added. "Do ya have Erik's phone?"

"Yes," she replied.

"Our numbers are in it," the singer said. "Take it with you."

"I will do that. Thank you again."

"Well, we'd best be going," Elektra said. "You'll want to be alone with Erik for a few minutes. Come on, guys." She turned to go.

Suzi gave Romana a smile, and Peach nodded to her.

"See ya," the roadie said.

"Thank you for your visit."

They went out. Romana turned to the bed, and gazed down at Erik's peaceful face.

"I will not be gone long, my love. I will deal with Gyorgi and Null. They will be sorry that they did this to you."

She leaned down and kissed him. He was cold. The machines whirred on. She straightened up.

"I will deal with Mariko too. She had no right to send them against you." She thought for a moment. "After that, we will see how we can get our children back from Christian." Her lips turned downward. "If he thinks he has seen how much damage a vampire can do before, he will find himself sadly mistaken. I will destroy his little empire before I kill him. Very slowly."

The girl stroked Erik's cheek.

"And then I will come back to you, my love, with our children beside me. Then we will live in peace." She turned and walked to the door.

"I must go. I will return soon."

Romana opened the door. She stood there staring at him lying there for what seemed a long time. Then, she went out into the corridor. The door whispered shut. The machines hummed on. The small sounds that filled hospitals the world over came dimly from outside. Women walked past; their high heels clicking on the floor. A doctor was summoned to an emergency ward. Several gurneys rattled past the room. People went to and fro, their conversations muffled by the corridor walls.

There was a groan.

"Romana?"